Zombie Fallout 2 A Plague Upon Your Family

Mark Tufo

DevilDog Press

D1518172

Copyright 2010 Mark Tufo
(rev. 3 - 2.17.13)

Electronic Edition, License Notes
This ebook is licensed for your personal enjoyment only.
This ebook may not be re-sold or given away to other people.
If you would like to share this book with another person,
please purchase an additional copy for each recipient. If
you're reading this book and did not purchase it, or it was not
purchased for your use only, then please purchase your own
copy. Thank you for respecting the hard work of the author.

Discover other titles by Mark Tufo at amazon.com
Visit us at marktufo.com
And http://zombiefallout.blogspot.com/
And find me on FACEBOOK

I swear I did not write this review myself but I definitely approve of the message!!!

Zombie Fallout 2 "A Plague Upon Your Family" not only picks up where the first book left off, it pretty much picks up the whole zombie fiction genre then drops it on its collective ass. I don't know which has more twists, the storyline or Mike Talbot's psyche. I read this book in one day, not because I had nothing better to do, but because once I started reading it, I felt like I was betraying every character in the book if I didn't stick it out with them for the duration. Mark Tufo's raw and real writing style makes you feel less like a reader of a story and more a participant who is being brought up to speed as to what they missed while out looking for Pop-Tarts. The strangest things creep into your mind during stressful times and Mark's exploration of these seemingly absurd things make me chuckle with "Okay, maybe I'm not the only guy that thinks about sex, sex, food, sex and sex" running through my frontal lobe. A damn good story from the most natural storyteller I have ever read.
Rich Baker – Zombie Fan Extraordinaire

DEDICATION(S)

First off I would like to dedicate this book to my wife and not merely because that seems the most prudent thing to do. She has spent countless hours listening to me ramble on about this story line or that character and how maybe I should have this happen instead of that. Her constant belief that I would stay sane long enough to pen this novel was of great inspiration for me. Thank you, my love.

Second, my brother Ron who devoted an endless amount of time reading and rereading this book in an attempt to make it as sound as possible, both story wise and grammatically. THANK YOU! He has also told me numerous times of how proud of me he is, and coming from a big brother that means a lot.

Third, is the Tufo clan, for truly, how far can an errant nut fall from the tree. If not for their constant influence I might have written a love story.

Fifth, is to the brave men and women of the armed services. Thank you for all you do.

Sixth, (but by no means lastly) are you my fans. I still cannot for the life of me get over the fact that I have fans. I so want to individually name every one of you but I am so fearful that I will leave someone out. But you know who you are, we have had dialog, we are friends on Facebook, you have been so kind as to share your thoughts and opinions and countless ways in which I could improve this second book. THANK YOU, you are the driving force that keeps me typing. Henry's tail wags in your general direction!

STOP!

This is Michael Talbot's second journal. If you have not already read his first journal

Zombie Fallout

You can pick it up at amazon.com!

It started with a flu shot, there is no end in sight. At least not one that ends well.

Eliza's Origin – Prologue One

The earth was dank, dark, deep, and sweet. Its embrace was as comforting as a small child's blanket. Eliza was hungry – so, so hungry. But something was not quite right. She had fed deeply less than twenty-four hours ago. She should be sated for at least another three days. Still, the need within her grew by the moment. The huntress arose out of her earthen bed, grateful to leave behind the past she had been dwelling on.

Eliza grew up in a time when being a child was not a protected status. Children were more of a disposable asset to be used and abused as their masters saw fit. As a child of a dirt farmer, she was the lowest of the low in early 1550s Germany. As the winds of war tore across the ravaged countryside she was swept along like so much chaff. She was no more than a slave to one master after another. It was in this harsh reality that her steel temperament was honed.

On her nineteenth birthday, she was finally able to remove the shackles that had her bound for the better part of ten years. It was a dark stranger that approached her and offered her the opportunity of freedom. She had not blanched in the least as he laid out what the future would hold for her. Her black mind was completely clouded with the thoughts of reeking revenge on all of those that had wronged her. The list was long and she knew exactly where she was going to start.

The pain was sharp as the stranger dragged his teeth across her dirty neck. She could not help but smell the scent of the man as he bit deeply into her carotid artery. The odor was all too familiar. Death clung to him like a newborn to its mother, waiting for his next offering. The man was a harvester of misery and despair.

What he saw in Eliza, she wasn't sure. Maybe he realized that death to her would be a release, a freedom from the horrors of a war torn world. But she was wrong. He didn't want to do her any favors. He wanted to drag her along into this new and unchartered realm of purgatory. She had survived the worst of what the world could offer. To turn her was to unleash a new hell upon the land.

For forty years she suffered under the severe tutelage of her new master. His cruelty, degenerative behavior, and propensity for violence had far surpassed even the worst of her previous masters. So when she finally severed his corrupted head from his depraved body it was more of a new beginning than an end. She was truly FREE. She was powerful and she was pissed off.

Although most of those who had wronged her were dead and buried, no one was safe. She slid along the countryside, always in the shadows, always in the peripheral. Death didn't just cling to her. It hung around expectantly. Why go out and reap the dying when it had a diligent purveyor that handed it out indiscriminately? Tremors of fear washed across those she passed by. Feelings of dread were quickly replaced by euphoria when a potential victim felt the talons of a gruesome demise pass on to another.

For close to five hundred years she had gone on like this, occasionally turning a companion to share in her vengeance. But she remembered all too well the elation when she had liberated herself and would never let any of her fledgling offspring live more than a decade or two. The frozen grimace of betrayal etched on their faces as she killed them never ceased to amaze or humor her.

Eliza, like many great predators, was nomadic. She moved to where the prey was. As whispers of demons and monsters passed throughout the villages and towns she preyed upon, food became scarce. Townsfolk were less and less likely to go out into the hidden evils of the night. She did not fear retribution. She only feared the gnawing hunger that tore at her soul, the hunger to rip, rend, to destroy and to tear asunder all that the world had taken from her. So when she finally made it to the 'New World' in the early 18th century, Eliza knew that she had found home. The wide open, sparsely populated country helped foster her legend. The Native Americans mistakenly labeled her as the Wendigo; mountain men and some of the smaller towns were quick to dismiss the Indians' accounts of a dark stranger that bled the soul dry. As more of their own began to disappear, it seemed more than just mere happenstance. Her legend grew, and to Eliza's surprise, so did her ego. Before that, she couldn't even begin to remember the last time that she had anything akin to a human emotion.

Love was not an emotion she had ever harbored – even as a child. Love was extravagant, a waste of time. Survival, now *there* was something you could hang on to. Eliza did not feel pity or remorse; she did not possess the capacity for mercy. She had needs. She had hunger. Everything she did in her life was to try to sate those two insatiable attributes.

When she awoke on that cold day in late fall in the year 2010, she had no reason to believe that this day would not be like the myriad of others she had endured over the centuries of her existence. She was hungry. It was feeding time. Time to thin the human herd. Eliza stayed away from the old. Their blood had become insipid. It had turned to an inedible watery stew of prescription drugs and cheap TV dinners. Healthy adults were a satisfactory meal, but unless she planned on draining them dry, she shied away so as not to leave any witnesses. She also didn't like teens, as more times than not their blood would be proliferated with drugs and alcohol. No, Eliza's meal of choice was infants. The new rich scent of them stirred something deep within her instinctually. Was it the lost legacy of motherhood that stimulated her senses, or was it the closeness to creation that babies' blood brought to her? These were questions she asked herself on occasion, but dwelling on her own idiosyncrasies was not one of Eliza's personality behaviors. Action best fit her persona.

All legends tend to have a kernel of truth to them no matter how much Hollywood tries to distort them. As for the old wives' tale that a vampire cannot come into your house until it is invited, this has very strong ties to reality. It's just that this is only half the story. Vampires can go into anyone's home unless they are expressly forbidden to do so. In this day and age when magic is more of the playing card variety, what is the incentive to bless one's abode against vampires (and witches by the way)? It is an ancient custom that the druids knew how to perform and passed down to countless European cultures. Unfortunately, though, this knowledge never crossed the ocean. Once an entrance-blocking ritual was performed, the vanquished vampire could then only enter when invited to do so. Why, at that point, one would invite the vampire inside is open to debate.

Vampires do have the ability for mind control, but it is generally within a limited distance, and eye contact must be maintained. As for vampires being invisible in mirrors, this also is a half-truth. While it is true they cannot be seen in a mirror, it is not due to their soullessness. It has to do with their innate ability to bend light. This is not something they do consciously, but it can be controlled. It is their predatory version of camouflage, like the lion's color which matches the Savannah grass or the tiger's stripes which break up its profile in the jungles of India. This refraction makes it very difficult for humans to 'see' a vampire. Usually a vampire is only seen in the peripheral as a black shadow passing by. If a vampire was spotted, it was because they wanted to be, quite probably to instill fear in their victims. It is said that the adrenaline that pours through a human during times of fear is like ambrosia that makes the blood all that much sweeter.

There were times when Eliza thrilled in the hunt, the taste of the max-stressed blood, the scent of terror as it trailed behind her intended victim. The panic, the horror, she craved these feelings from her stock. Those emotions out of her chattel proved her superiority, her place of dominion in this world of *man*.

The derisiveness of the word 'man' was used as both the hatred for mankind as a whole and especially for the lesser of the two sexes. She would feed on whatever was available if need be, but she took a cruel sort of satisfaction in feeding a little deeper in the arteries of a man, tearing the walls of the blood vessel more savagely than necessary. Of another important note, vampires do not leave puncture wounds (unless they want to). Unless a vampire is trying to make a point (usually 'Don't fuck with me!'), they will scarcely leave a mark. Most times, a vampire bite will be attributed to bug bites. These also have the added benefits of healing fast and diminishing to a red spot no bigger than the tip of a pencil lead. This aids in the hunter's ability to stay hidden, to make her prey less wary. An unsuspecting victim is an easy fruit to pick.

Eliza Present Day – Prologue Two

It was 6:30 in the morning when Eric Hoto traveled down the length of his extensive driveway wrapped only in an ill-fitting jacket, pajama bottoms, and snow boots, to grab the morning paper.

"How many times have I told that kid to bring the paper up to the house?" Mr. Hoto said aloud, mainly to keep his teeth from chattering together in the frigid arctic-blasted air.

As he stood, a sense of immense apprehension tugged at his essence. The paper and the paperboy nearly forgotten, he redoubled his efforts to close the jacket against the preternaturally chilly air that surrounded him. The sense of something dancing in and out of his vision made him nearly run. Vertigo threatened to drop him where he stood. As suddenly as it started, it stopped. The air around him warmed considerably, even though it was only ten degrees out. His thrashing heart beat a little easier against his near battered rib cage. His breath came a little more evenly. His shaking legs almost stilled.

I feel like a rabbit looking down the snout of a fox. Eric could not even fathom how absolutely close to reality those feelings were. But, like most humans, he was quick to ignore his baser instincts and use higher reasoning to completely gloss over the unthinkable. "I think I need a vacation. If I wasn't thirty-four, I would think that I had just suffered a stroke. That's it! That boy either brings the paper up to the door or I'm switching to *USA Today*."

Eric's steps faltered again halfway up the steep grade to his front door. His storm door opened slowly, as he watched, without the benefit of any apparent human locomotion. That unpleasant sensation of being stalked greasily crept across his scalp and was whipped away with a stiff breeze. He was left feeling oddly unclean, unhealthy.

"Wind must be stronger than I thought," Eric said, now not so willing to get out of the elements and into the 'safety' of his home. His eyebrows drew closer as he questioned his new unwillingness to enter the 'lion's den.' "Now why did I think that? And why do I keep talking to my damn self?"

The monologue continued.

"Because it's what you do when you're mad…or scared."

"Something's in your house!"

"You're an engineer, Eric. Think rationally. The wind opened that door. That's all."

"Then why aren't you hurrying up to get out of this cold weather?"

"I'm going."

"What about your wife and baby?"

"It's too late," he moaned.

The sound of heartless laughter would be the last thing Eric heard. It would be two more days before his frozen body was found, but by then there were much bigger happenings going on.

Eliza's Transformation – Prologue Three

Eliza hadn't intended on killing the mother and her child, but the impudent animal had somehow sensed the invasion and gone to do what any good mother would – protect her offspring.

Eliza was reveling in the freshness, the newness of the baby's blood, its closeness to the source of life, when the woman had come in. Eliza stood there in all her startling cruelty. She was surprised when the woman, instead of cowering and shrieking and running away, stood her ground. Not only stood her ground, but against all of her instincts, advanced on the predator. This was the same as the gazelle turning on the lion and charging, the lion might be momentarily stunned, more from the shock of something so unusual happening than from any perceived threat. But still, the impertinent bitch, who did she think she was? With one lightning fast movement, Eliza wrapped her ungodly strong hand around the slender woman's throat. Instead of immediately crushing the worthless life out of her, Eliza held her at bay as she drank the baby's essence into the netherworlds.

The mother watched wide-eyed with anguish as her child was taken from her. By the time Eliza was finished with the baby, crushing the wind out of the mother was almost unnecessary. Practically all signs of life had been extinguished from her when her baby passed. Eliza laughed as her fingers punched through the soft skin surrounding the woman's throat. Unlike the previous encounter, there was no more fight in this creature. Blood shot out at all angles as if happy to be free of its veiny trappings. Giant swaths of the nectar bathed Eliza's face and she greedily licked up the offerings even as she watched the light of life dim and then fade away.

Unbeknownst to Eliza, she may have done the Hoto family a favor, although none of the Hotos were around to appreciate that fact. Eileen Hoto R.N. had secretly stolen three of the very difficult-to-find H1N1 vaccinations. As a caregiver, she would be given preferential treatment, as would her baby. But her husband, who constantly got sick due to the stresses he placed on himself, would most likely never be in a position to get the sought after shot. So, in her head, she was only stealing one shot, and she rationalized it by telling herself that her husband, a well-respected engineer and an involved member of the community, was more deserving than some crack baby down at the clinic where she worked.

An hour before her husband made his death march to get the newspaper, she had administered the shots to all three of them. She did it early in the morning in the hopes that their baby might not even realize what was happening. True to her cherubic nature, Gilly Hoto never once protested as her mother gave her the vaccination.

The tainted inoculation had already begun to overcome what little resistance the beleaguered white blood cells could muster when Eliza had drunk her fill.

Prologue Four
Mike's Journal

Hello, my name is Michael Talbot and this is my journal. If you have found this, then most likely I am dead. I swore that after I left my first journal behind at my homestead in Little Turtle, I would not let the same fate befall this one. I have no way of knowing what the world has turned out like. While I was alive we were at war, a war where eighty-five percent of the combatants didn't know that fact. They simply felt a need to eat and we simply felt a need not to be eaten. The story of me, my family and my friends are in these pages. It is as true an account of what happened to the Talbots as can be written by one that has lived through it. Is some of it biased? Probably. Is some of it subjective? Definitely. In a perfect world, I'm hoping that I left this book behind in some haste to evacuate an area. But more than likely I have fallen. I have been so tired, maybe now I can finally rest.

CHAPTER 1

Zombie bodies exploded under the crushing weight of the tractor trailer. Splintered bones rained down all around us. The occasional eyeball struck the side of the trailer with a hollow thudding. The noise was sickening from atop. I could only imagine what it sounded like inside. Noxious gases issued forth from burst beings; some unlucky few that got stuck in the plow works were slowly eroded away like the world's largest eraser on the biggest mistake in mankind – which wasn't far from the truth.

The truck was an island that floated along a sea of death and decay. I had never felt more afraid for my family since this whole thing started. The constant jostling as we hit, and subsequently ran over, zombies made holding on for dear life take on a whole new meaning.

For some friggin' reason, I had not had the foresight to rope my English Bulldog Henry to the truck; I now had one arm wrapped around Henry like he was an expensive Saks Fifth Avenue package and I was in Central Park at night. My other hand was gripped onto a handle secured to the top of the truck with two entirely way too small screws.

Again, if you read my first journal, you'll know I would no sooner let go of Henry than I would one of my natural born. For those of you that say he's only a dog...you must be cat lovers and just don't know any better. I won't hold it against you. Luckily, Henry wasn't squirming or this would be a short novella punctuated by my untimely demise.

The screws were puckering up the top of the truck. I knew without a shadow of a doubt that they were going to give under the strain I was placing on them. My last few moments on earth were going to be the loud audible pop as the screws tore loose and then my ungraceful swan dive off the top of this trailer and into the waiting arms of an adoring crowd of brain and flesh eaters. Thankfully, Alex was a much better craftsman than I gave him credit for, because I'm still alive to write this journal.

Alex is a man that I've only known a few weeks, but I consider him a true friend, especially since he saved my family's collective ass today – Christmas Day.

Alex was one of the newest residents of Little Turtle after the deaders came. He set up or engineered most of the defenses we used in our now shattered community. If not for the stalwart supports he had added to our walls, I would have never made it out of my cell and to my house in time that last fateful day.

With that thought I had a pang of remorse as I remembered Jed. At one time, and in a much simpler world, we had been bitter enemies, when what time you put your trash out actually carried meaning. I hadn't seen Jed since the day the walls came down, literally. He had let me out of my cell as I was awaiting my trial for murder. Sure, I had killed a perverted piece of shit and the world was a better place for it, but it was still murder. Why I had killed him is not something I am going to revisit, especially on this the most sacred of days. If you really want to know, you're going to have to go back to Little Turtle on the Denver/Aurora line in Colorado. I left my journal in my old office before we made our narrow escape to the attic. I'm sure the zombies will be gone in a few days; there'll be nothing left there to eat.

The jostling of the truck slowly decreased as we moved

further and further away from the kill zone. I could almost hear the collective sighs of relief, but more likely it was the great intake of air as everyone felt it was finally safe to breathe deeply; not because of our temporary reprieve from fear, but because of the improvement of the air quality. The dead have no clue about personal hygiene. Saying zombies smelled 'bad' was akin to saying lepers had a mild case of acne.

Exactly one-point-one miles from my previous home, the truck pulled to a halt. I let go of Henry with my left arm. I was going to need that hand to pry my right fingers from the handle. It seems I had frozen it in place. Again, I didn't think to grab cold weather gear as zombies were pouring into my bedroom. Yeah, you sit there in your bomb shelter and judge me all you want for not being properly prepared, but I've got a leg up on at least ninety percent of the rest of the world. I'm still alive – or at least not one of the living dead – and that's pretty damn good in my book.

There were no zombies in sight, but I knew that could change at any moment as I helped my wife Tracy down from the top. She seemed a little perturbed that I had gotten Henry safely to turf before turning my attention to her. You know how it is, man's best friend and all. That, and I think he had to take a piss. I'd known him long enough to know he'd go anywhere and on anyone once the need was there.

Brendon, my daughter's fiancé, helped Nicole down. They were still in that 'new love' phase when chivalry ruled. That would die when he ripped his first big fart in front of her, but for now it was all still tea and roses. My best friend Paul had alit from the far side of the truck. I could hear his wife Erin grousing about trying to rub the circulation back into her arms. My son Travis had scrambled off the truck and was patrolling our perimeter, bless his heart. My other son Justin, who was still suffering the ill effects from his zombie scratch, was helped down by Tommy into Paul's waiting arms. Justin was both relieved and embarrassed; relieved that he had made it off the truck in one piece and embarrassed that he needed the help in the first place.

The biggest enigma – both literally and figuratively – Tommy, was the last person off the roof. I used to think I had saved the kid's ass back at Walmart so seemingly long ago, but now I think *he* was meant to save *us*. In his previous life he had been a Walmart greeter, all stickers and smiles. What his so called 'normal mind' lacked was more than made up for by the infectious grin and overwhelming heart that the kid possessed. But that was not everything about Tommy, not by a long shot.

Don't get me wrong, I loved the kid for those reasons. But there was something way above my pay grade going on with this kid. For starters, he has a spirit guide that (by Tommy's accounts) sounds and looks like Ryan Seacrest. There's that, and then there's things he knows that he just can't know about…and then there's this fuckin' truck. Don't get me wrong, I'm thrilled Alex showed up when he did, but it wasn't by coincidence.

Alex's wife Marta is related to Tommy on his mother's side. Somehow he was able to hone in on that connection and summon them for help. I usually had to shake my head at the dichotomy that was Tommy. I laughed as I saw the savior of the human race jump down from the small ladder and land with a thud on the ground. He looked at me, smiling, with a huge glob of peanut butter on the tip of his nose. This did not go unnoticed by Travis as he rounded the corner of the truck on his circuitous patrol route.

Travis stopped his motion, now staring straight at the offending heap of gooey goodness on Tommy's nose.

"What?" Tommy asked, clearly wondering why he was now the center of Travis' attention. Travis kept staring. Finally Tommy's eyes tracked down to the tip of his nose. All he could do was sheepishly smile and shrug his shoulders.

"What was it?" Travis asked, a small measure of

wonderment and envy in his tone.

Tommy looked like he was having an inner debate with himself whether to come clean or just deny the whole thing. Of course his good side won out. "Snickers," he said hesitantly.

"We have Peanut Butter Snickers? They don't even make those anymore!" Travis said pleadingly, looking to me.

I just shrugged my shoulders in reply to Travis' imploring look. At this point I wouldn't doubt that Tommy went to an alternate universe where they still make Peanut Butter Snickers and just snagged himself a few. Okay…well…actually I *don't* believe that, because knowing Tommy he would have paid for them.

"Weef did," Tommy said as he wiped the peanut butter off his nose with the tip of one sticky finger and popped the near dime-sized morsel lovingly into his mouth.

Any doubt to the authenticity of Tommy's food choice was immediately set asunder as I pulled a slightly worse for wear Peanut Butter Snickers wrapper out of Henry's mouth. I was heavily tempted to see where that candy bar had been made, but if I turned the wrapper over and it said something to the effect of 'proudly produced in the United States of Columbia' I would be wasting more precious minutes than I had trying to puzzle this piece out. The world had gone to hell and there was no hand basket, but I still couldn't find it in myself to litter. I put the Henry-slimed wrapper in my pocket. The germaphobe in me shuddered as I pulled my goo-covered hand out of my jeans pocket.

"Fuckin' gross," I said to no one in particular.

My diatribe was cut short as I looked over lovingly at my Jeep. A week or so previously, Brendon and I had stowed our cars about a mile outside the gates of Little Turtle. His was a huge Ford Explorer and mine was a Jeep Wrangler. They were both loaded with camping gear, ammo, food, and water; so much so, that fitting us all in was going to look like a Ringling Brothers event.

Alex was going to wait until both SUVs started before he placed the big rig in gear. Some of the passengers in the back of the truck were loudly protesting that they had stopped so close to the now-defunct Little Turtle housing community. I didn't begrudge them that. I was still amazed that they had let the truck turn around at all.

I watched as Tommy disengaged himself from his aunt's arms.

"Are you sure, Tommy?" Marta looked up at him questioningly.

I hadn't heard the entire conversation, but I got the general gist. Marta wanted her nephew to go in the truck with them. Marta had finally pulled herself out of the shell-shocked near catatonic state the zombies had placed her in. She did not want to jeopardize the progress she had fought for, and losing any more family would be unacceptable. I completely understood her distress when Tommy answered her.

"No, Auntie, I can't," Tommy said sadly.

"But why, Tommy, you're all that's left of my family," she pleaded.

I knew this struck a truly tender chord with the kid, and I was more than half tempted to tell her to leave him alone when I realized how in the wrong I would be. They were family after all. I was the outsider in all this. Hell, I'd only known the kid for a relatively short while.

CHAPTER 2

Mike's Journal Entry Two

I would later ask Alex how he hadn't recognized Tommy as his nephew when he was part of his work crew, and he answered me, "Never met him, Mike." It seemed for a few moments that he was going to be content with that answer. As God is my witness, I wanted to pry so badly, but discretion got the better of me; I was going to leave it at that. Alex, it seems, had delayed his answer for fear of how I might react.

"I did some time when I was eighteen," Alex said with his face angled down, embarrassment strangling his words. My mouth may have dropped a little, but he couldn't see it from his vantage point. "Marta's family hated me and disowned her because she married a convict." He looked up at me, a nervous smile playing across his lips. He continued, "Her parents are...or were," he corrected himself, "strict Catholics. Which makes no sense, because, of all religions, don't they preach forgiveness?" He looked like he was getting ready to blow a gasket. This was apparently a sore spot for him.

"Uh, Alex," I said as I put my hand on his shoulder. I wanted to tell him we had bigger fish to fry at this point, but he quickly realized that small little tidbit himself.

"I know, Mike, I know. Her parents and the majority of

her family are probably gone, but they caused my Marta so much pain. Her parents never EVER came to see our kids. For Christ sake, Mike, twelve years ago I did time for boosting some cars."

Whew, I was so happy he didn't say rape or child molestation or something heinous like that, because no matter how much I liked him now, I would never have been able to look at him the same way. There are some transgressions in life you just don't get over, and that was in the top five.

"It didn't matter to them that while I was in jail I got my degree, and then when I got out I worked my ass off as a carpenter's apprentice to pay for my Engineering Masters. None of that mattered to them. I was always going to be that convict that corrupted their daughter. Hell, I hadn't even met her when I got in trouble. To hear them talk, you would have thought I had her out there watching for cops while I was popping ignitions.

"I had just started at an engineering firm after getting my degree. She was the HR Generalist. We dated, we fell in love. At my first dinner meeting her folks, I told them about my past just to make sure everything was out in the open so that there would be no surprises down the road. Her father flipped out. He kicked me out of the house and forbade his daughter to ever see me again.

"So the first thing we did was elope. At that point, her parents disowned her. She was upset, but she didn't truly think it would be a lifelong ban. Surely after our baby was born they would come around. The uptight bastards never even called to congratulate her on the birth of our first child. A little piece of my Marta died the day she realized her parents were fully done with her.

"After Vera, our second, was born…she slipped even deeper into her self-imposed, depot of despair. When the zombies came clawing at our house, she went over the edge. At first I thought she had become one of them." I shuddered.

Alex continued, "She was slowly pulling herself back out of her depression, but when Tommy did whatever he did, sending a signal, lighting a beacon? Whatever...that was the first time in the seven years I've known her that she has been completely free and clear of the shackles that her parents put on her."

"Yeah, I know. Tommy can have that effect on people," I said without really thinking.

Alex just looked at me like I was loco. I didn't clarify my words, thus leaving him thoroughly confused.

"So when she told me to turn the truck around, I didn't hesitate. I would have driven to Hell on two flats to see that spark of life back in her eyes."

"Shit, Alex, you kind of did," I said. He nodded in agreement.

"So back to your original question. She had told me all about her family, her sisters and brothers and nieces and nephews, but she didn't have any pictures of them. The day we eloped, her parents threw everything in her room out. She was forbidden from going and getting any of her belongings, and her siblings were told if they so much as mentioned her name the same fate would befall them. So, for all intents and purposes, she was an orphan. You know, now that I think about it, I caught Tommy looking at me a lot while we were working. Do you think he knew who I was? Maybe he had a picture or something."

"Oh, I'm sure he knew who you were. And no, nothing quite as mundane as a picture," I answered. Again Alex looked at me, hoping that I would elaborate. "Ever been on *Idol*?" I asked casually.

"Mike, what did I tell you about drinking tequila?"

"Can't stand the stuff, wish I had some. Good night, Alex."

"One more thing, Mike?" Alex asked. I turned to face him. "How did he tell Marta? To come back?"

"Aw shit, Alex, you might as well ask me how the

universe was created, or which came first, the chicken or the egg, or even better…what is a woman thinking at any given moment. Those I could give you some sort of informed bullshit answer. I don't have a foggy clue in Hades what is going on with Tommy. All I know is that whatever it is, it's powerful and it has a purpose. Beyond that…" I shrugged my shoulders.

CHAPTER 3

Mike's Journal Entry Three

Tommy's next words jolted me to a stop as effective as a two-inch thick chain around my neck. "I have to stay with Mr. T, Auntie, he's going to need me to save him. Eliza wants him dead and I have to make sure that doesn't happen."

I had an inkling who Eliza might be. I hoped I was wrong. The mere vocalization of her name sent worms of fear crawling across my spine, which is not a sensation I would wish on anyone. I know it is naïve of me, but I had hoped that by leaving Little Turtle behind we were leaving the worst of this new world behind, too. Apparently that wasn't to be the case. Sweat had broken out across my brow, and I wasn't attempting anything more difficult than standing erect. A cold breeze turned the moisture on my forehead into tiny daggers that laced across my head like an angry bee's nest to a honey bear's sensitive nose.

Marta tsk-tsked Tommy. "Tommy, how could you possibly know who needs help? And who's Eliza? Tommy, I'm your aunt, I've known you seemingly forever. Your mom would want me to watch out for you."

That was kind of funny her saying that. Here's this little waif of a woman saying she's going to look out for this two hundred and fifty pound hulking bear of a kid. But Tommy brought that out in you. It was almost instinctual that you wanted to go out of your way to make sure he was happy and safe. Was it because he was supposedly 'slow?' I doubt it. The kid definitely had some vulnerability, but on the flip side of that...his powers might be limitless.

Tommy blushed as his aunt spoke about his past. "That was a long time ago, Auntie. I'm all grown up now."

I snorted a laugh and did my best to stifle it. Marta glared over at me. Dammit, like I needed another woman mad at me. I quickly replaced my mirth with a 'fortress of solitude' face. What is that exactly? Tough to say. Kind of stoic, definitely not a shit-eating grin type of thing. It doesn't often work, but it's better than my normal cheesy smile that tends to get me in trouble.

"It's alright, Auntie, we'll be in the Jeep right behind you," Tommy continued.

I hadn't really thought about it, but I guess, yeah we would be; there was no need or sense to split up, at least not yet. I had grand illusions of making it back East at some point to try to ascertain the status of my family; and as long as Alex was headed in that general direction, then I was all for safety in numbers.

This seemed to placate Marta somewhat, but her glare beamed back over in my general direction as if this was all my fault. I did what any hapless man would do under the circumstances: I shrugged my shoulders and walked away. Marta may have continued her relentless objections on Tommy, but just at that opportune moment, her baby squealed in consternation. Tommy looked relieved and pleased with himself. I think he gave baby Vera a psychic tickle, the better to help him out of his predicament. Marta said the standard "Fine" and stomped away. Well, stomping may be a little over the top, more like padded away heavily. Tommy caught me looking at him and quickly let the look of satisfaction run away from his features.

"Your secret's safe with me, kid. Come on," I told him.

26

As he caught up, I put my arm around his shoulder.

After a brief conversation with Paul, we (and by 'we' I mean 'he') determined it would be best if he and his wife rode in the truck for a while. Yeah, big sacrifice. Heated trailer loaded with sleeping bags and plenty of leg room. I was a little pissed to say the least, maybe more envious, too. I wanted to stretch out and get some sleep. After the frigid conditions of the past few nights, it was going to take a lot of warmth and rest to take out the chill that had settled deep in my bones. Little did I know at the time that the chill I felt had less to do with the weather and more to do with my condition. Well time, as they say, is the great narrator. All things are laid out before her whether you want them to be or not.

CHAPTER 4

Mike's Journal Entry Four

With no general plan in my mind except to put as much distance between us and our previous home as possible, we headed north on Interstate 25 and then east on Interstate 70. We'd be relatively safe for a while, east of Denver would bring us into the plains of Colorado and then into Kansas. During the heyday of humanity this was not a densely populated area, so the corollary (see I did learn something in the sixth grade that I could use later in life) was that the likelihood of coming across a great brood of zombies would be slight. That was the thought anyway.

Getting out of Denver proper was a nightmare. It looked like any natural (or unnatural) disaster movie you've ever seen in your life. Cars and trucks, motorcycles and scooters – hell I'd seen a rickshaw a few miles back – were abandoned everywhere. It looked more like the world's largest used car lot than a highway of any sort, that is of course if you took away the bullet casings that littered the ground like so many metallic insects, or the blood-splattered remains of the zombies that were merely trying to garner a meal; or hey, even the thousands of humans that had become, for lack of a better word, Spam. (Do you get the reference? Meat in a can?) I know it's gross, but that was the only way I could think of it (of them) without blowing chunks. It looked like an all-you-can-eat buffet had opened up right next to a Fat Camp with a damaged fence; everything and everyone had been torn apart.

The battle had been savage and quick, with non-infected people clearly on the losing side. This I garnered by the sheer number of cars stuck on the roadway. If the people had won, they would not have hung around.

At some points I would drive ahead of the truck, scouting out potential routes, and other times Alex would need to lead just to push some slag out of the way. For eight excruciating hours we navigated through the worst rush hour traffic known to man. By the time we reached a small town called Bennett, about thirty miles east of Denver, I was wiped.

Tracy had volunteered on more than one occasion to take over the driving, but I couldn't get over the sneaking suspicion that she had an ulterior motive. I could see her sideswiping a sign just for a small measure of payback for what I had done to her car. Most likely it was my deep-seated paranoia rearing its ugly head, but then again…maybe not, I was paranoid, how the hell would I know.

Not once on our eight-hour trek did we spot a living person. Zombies? That was a different story. There weren't many of them that we saw, but every one turned and walked towards us as if drawn like a fine metal filament to a powerful magnet.

We stopped at Bennett to stretch our legs, top off our tanks, and possibly try to choke down a power bar or two. My brain was completely against the idea of eating anything after witnessing the destruction a few miles back, but my stomach wasn't listening.

Travis, Tommy, and Henry for that matter, had been sleeping for most of the morning. I was thankful for that small favor, although what I was shielding them from, I don't know. They had already seen everything we had passed in spades and then some. Bennett looked surprisingly untouched, as if the tidal wave of shit that had hit the rest of

---

the state had completely missed this small oasis. At least that was how it *looked*. How it felt was a completely different story.

Alex hopped off the big rig, rubbing his arms for warmth, but more likely to ward off the evil that emanated from every corner of this burg. "This place doesn't feel right, Mike."

I wanted to agree with him and tell him this felt like we had just stepped into the door of the biggest surprise party ever given and we were still waiting for the shout of 'SURPRISE' to come. An expectation hung in the air; it was palpable, it was overbearing, it was just plain creepy. But even after all those emotions were churning in my head, there was only one thing I wanted to know. "When the hell did you learn how to drive that truck?"

Alex stared long and hard at me like I'd lost my marbles, and now he was wondering why he had decided to hitch his cart to mine.

"Listen, I know this place feels like a tomb, Alex. My nerves are taut, and I can feel my spinal fluid quivering. I want to get some gas and get the hell out of here. I was just curious."

"You're nuts, Mike, I'll give you that. I feel like I can barely breathe because of the weight of this place, and you want to talk banalities."

"Hey, I take offense to that, at least, I didn't bring up the weather."

"You would have, given enough time."

"Yeah, you're probably right," I sighed. "That still doesn't change the fact that when I met you, you didn't know how to drive the damn thing."

"Fine, you crazy gringo, I'll stand in this damn ghost town just a little longer so that I can explain to you that I had Carl give me a few lessons while I was securing the plow. I had him do that because I was afraid the wall was going to give exactly like it happened, all of a sudden and without warning, and I was afraid that Carl would be nowhere in sight and we would be stuck on this giant paperweight with nobody to drive it."

"Now was that so hard?" I asked as I ripped the wrapper off of a granola bar. "Alex," I started, and from my tone he knew I was going in a more serious direction. "Where are you planning on going?" Alex wasn't dumb. He caught my meaning of using 'you' and not 'we'. He looked deep in thought; there was a conflict roiling within him. Sure, we were fast friends, but Alex had stronger bonds elsewhere, as did I.

"I'm thinking Florida," he answered almost apologetically, as if I held any sway over his decision-making. "I might still have family there. Any chance you'd be going that way?"

I shook my head slowly. "Even if I did, I wouldn't go. Florida, the Sunburn State."

He smiled at my crappy joke. I loved him even more. "I have to go home (meaning the Northeast), if..." I swallowed hard. "If my family is still alive, I want to be with them."

Alex nodded solemnly. "I agree," he said softly.

"And on top of that, Tracy wants to go and get her mom."

"Her mom? Where is she?"

"Yeah, her seventy-nine-year-old, widowed mother that lives on an old farm by herself in North Dakota."

"Mike, come on, man, why are you going to go on a fool's errand? We both know what you're likely to find."

"You tell her that, Alex, and I'll give you fifty bucks and a case of beef jerky."

"Write to me and let me know how the weather is," Alex said as he walked away to see if he could find a switch to power on the pumps, or a hose of some sort to get gas out of the ground tanks.

"Yeah, real nice!" I shouted to him. I was halfway through my power bar when the back of the tractor-trailer hatch opened. I almost choked on the piece in my mouth when I saw who was getting out of the back.

"How long are we staying in this little shithole?" the voice bellowed from the second largest man I had ever seen in my life. (Next to that crazy bastard Durgan, who was now so much Zombie Chow.) Something Tynes, aka Big Tiny, aka BT.

We had picked up the guy while we were making a food run to the local Safeway store. He'd been trying to get into a pissing contest with me ever since. He was looking right at me while he asked the question.

He continued in a menacing tone, "You gonna answer or what?"

I did the only prudent thing I could think of, I turned and walked away.

"I'm talking to you, Talbot!" he yelled.

"Yeah, I figured as much," I said over my shoulder. "I just don't feel like listening." I'm not thinking that was the right answer. I heard – or more like felt – the ground shake as he hopped off the back of the trailer. The train was coming; I had about ten seconds until contact. Luckily I was saved...sort of.

"Dad!" Travis yelled, and this wasn't a warning about BT coming up behind me. Travis was on my right side behind the gas pumps. From his vantage point he couldn't see the little melodrama that was playing out.

When I turned to go and see what was causing that distressed tone in my son's voice, BT sheared off as well, whether to intercept my current course or to sate his own curiosity I wasn't sure. I trotted up to Trav's side a couple of seconds before BT. The big man gave me the once over before following Travis' pointing finger. About two hundred yards away was a man...and he was coming at full sprint.

"You think it's a survivor?" BT asked.

I could tell there was a little more than a tremor of fear in his voice. Well, it was good to know the guy was afraid of something. A hundred and fifty yards and the runner's pace hadn't slowed down. What was more worrisome was that he didn't wave or try to gain our attention in any sort of fashion. The skeevies I was feeling were felt by all of us; something wasn't quite right, but I couldn't put my finger on it.

"Man, his clothes look like shit," BT said in a hushed tone. I nodded in agreement. But that wasn't enough to convince me something was amiss. Washing clothes was on the low end of the survival spectrum. BT continued his muttered comments to me. "That ain't no zombie is it, Talbot? It's running way too fast."

A hundred yards away and it was clearly fixed on us, still no friendly wave, no gesture of peace, nothing but determination etched in his/its ashen features. My mind was made up.

"BT, tell everyone to get back to the truck and ready to leave." He didn't move so I stomped on his foot. I thought he was going to punch me on the top of the head. "BT!" I yelled. "Get everyone back in the truck." I could tell he was still debating about the punch.

"NOW, FUCKER!" I gave it my best Marine bellow.

He jumped. I was most likely going to pay for this later, but it still felt like the right thing to do. BT kept looking over his shoulder as he ran back towards the tractor-trailer. Most of the survivors were outside the truck lounging, smoking cigarettes, getting some fresh air, eating, and even some of the baser necessities – pissing and crapping in the nearest bushes. But when a giant black man is screaming at the top of his lungs in a post-apocalyptic world that you need to get your skinny asses back on the truck to save yourselves, you tend to listen.

Twenty-five feet away...I waited until I was one hundred percent sure and still I wasn't. It didn't seem like a zombie, but if he was human once, he no longer suffered from that affliction, not anymore.

"Now, Dad?" Travis asked with a note of trepidation in his voice.

"Aw shit!" I just wasn't convinced.

I couldn't even begin to wrap my mind around this new development. The guy was within spitting distance, sure Olympic-class spitting distance, but you get the point, when it became clear that Travis had made up his mind. The Mossberg bellowed a triumphant roar. The 12-gauge slug caught the man square in the chest. The effect was devastating. I watched in fascinated slow motion as his chest cavity became fully exposed and blood flowed rampant as his full speed sprint was halted in mid stride; the 1500-feet-per-second slug struck with enough force to blow the man back four feet. I hoped for both mine and Travis' sanity that when we checked the body there would be some telltale sign of humanity lost.

The smoke from the shotgun barrel had barely begun to dissipate when we obtained our definitive answer. Mr. Speedy Sneakers (the name seemed appropriate at the time) started to rise without so much as a grunt or a groan or a 'Dude, why the hell did you shoot me?' At this point you really didn't need to be a rocket scientist to figure out that the rules to our deadly game had just been altered drastically and we hadn't received the revisions.

Travis looked over at me, apprehension contorting his features. I understood his fear, this guy just looked too normal. Sure his clothes looked like shit, but we don't go around shooting people because they wear crappy clothes. If that was the case, we would have eradicated bums and high fashion models years ago. His countenance was pale, but more in a sickly way than a deathly one. Hell, Justin, who was still suffering the ill effects of his zombie scratch, had worse color than this guy.

As I was lost in thought, my enigma sat up. Ignoring the silver dollar-sized hole in his chest, he was trying in vain to get his feet up under him. The brain is a powerful tool, but apparently it has its limitations, this poor bastard's spinal column was shattered into at least a half dozen pieces. No amount of function rerouting was going to get him back up

—

on his feet. Travis and I watched in horror as our mystery guest rolled himself over and began to military crawl his way over towards us. A few more seconds of our indecision and Speedy Sneakers was going to make it to his final destination, our tasty flesh.

Travis flinched as I put my hand out to his shoulder. "Go back to the Jeep," I said to him.

He didn't need any persuading. Travis had no sooner turned the corner, when I put a well-aimed shot through Speedy's forehead. He slumped over to the left in an assemblage of monster parts that uncannily resembled a human. I walked slowly back to the big rig doing my best to reincorporate the bile that was threatening to make its grand exit. I fully expected to see nobody – by that I meant nobody outside the truck. However, Alex was by the back door of the truck looking around.

"What are you doing, man?" I asked, maybe with a little more harshness than I meant, but I hadn't fully recovered from my zombie/human hybrid encounter yet.

"We're light four," he answered gruffly. He hadn't even witnessed the event, and he was in more of a mood to leave than I was. I looked longingly over towards the Jeep and the Explorer where Travis was getting a much needed hug from his mother. Paul and Brendon were securing some stuff on top of the Ford, and Erin was getting some water for Justin who was shakily smoking a cigarette. Tommy was not visible, at least not at first, and then I saw him in the back seat of the Jeep. Even from this distance I could tell he was in a rush to get going. He didn't say anything. Words would have been superfluous.

"Shit," I answered as I turned back towards Alex. "Who's missing?"

CHAPTER 5

As April and Cash walked into the abandoned house, the smell of dust and Old Spice filled the air. The only sound to break the silence was the squeaking of the not so oiled hinges and the hitched breathing of Cash. Cash was asthmatic, and high stress environments like the one he found himself in now tended to exacerbate the problem.

"Come on, April, we should get back to the truck," Cash semi-begged, trying his best not to sound desperate.

"What's your rush, Cash, can't wait to huddle up with BT?" she retorted snidely.

Cash's cheeks burned from the jibe. He couldn't understand why he had left the relative safety of the truck. It was when he looked back towards the curvaceous brunette two years his senior that he divined the answer. "Traitorous penis," he muttered.

"What did you say?" April asked as she entered the defunct kitchen. At twenty-one, April knew enough to know that she affected men and could generally get what she wanted just by batting her lashes or using her patented pouty lips. Normally she went for guys that could help her actualize her higher standard of living. Cash, however, was dirt poor, acne riddled and wheezed entirely too much. In short, he was someone she wouldn't date if he was the last man on earth. But since that was rapidly becoming the case, she thought she might have to rethink her strategy, she had physical needs too.

When the door had finally rolled up on that stuffy trailer, she made up some lame excuse to go and stretch her legs. With just two words, 'Come on,' she had gotten Cash to follow her. She loved the power her looks granted her.

Loud crashes emanated from the kitchen as April ransacked the place looking for something good to eat. Cabinets clattered, bottles smashed, each loud jolt made Cash's heart skip a beat.

"May...maybe you shouldn't be so loud, April," Cash said cautiously, not sure whether he was more afraid of zombies hearing them or pissing April off. After all, they hadn't seen any zombies yet, and he had a feeling he was this close to getting laid.

"God! All these people have is Cheerios and popcorn!" April shouted. "You should find me something I CAN eat!"

Cash looked longingly back at the front door before he turned and went into the kitchen. In a week, a family of rabid raccoons couldn't have done the damage April had accomplished in five minutes. Cash numbly stared at the destruction of the small kitchen. April, catching his gaping stare, responded in her usual vulgar style. She was so self-assured of her beauty that she knew it didn't matter how she acted.

"What? It's not like the people that used to live here are going to give a shit." She laughed as she smashed a pickle jar against the far side wall. The sour smell of vinegar permeated everything. April's laugh became a little shriller. Cash was petrified. Cash was mesmerized. Cash was standing at attention...or at least part of him was.

April focused her eyes on Cash. "Do me!" she said hungrily. Cash's jaw dropped. April laughed at his reaction. "What are you a virgin or something?" Cash's face reddened. "Oh my God?! You are!" She laughed again. Cash's face burned from the chafing she was giving him. He turned dejectedly back towards the front door. "Well, let's take care of that, lover," she continued greedily.

Cash was not a Mensa member, but you didn't need a high IQ to figure this puzzle out. He fumbled with his belt, his fingers suddenly losing all dexterity. Just as he got the clasp undone, he heard the shotgun roar in the distance. "We...we...we should go," he said hastily.

"*Oui, oui, oui*, what are you, French now?" Her eyes never left his.

"But the gun..."

"Probably just target practice," she answered.

Cash knew better. Target practice meant using something that was in diminishing supply, while also alerting anything nearby to your presence. He strained his ears to listen for any signs of trouble.

"I'm getting booorrreddd..." April drawled as she sat on the table.

Her skirt hiked up, and Cash could see that she wasn't wearing any panties. As the blood rushed out of Cash's brain and towards his groin, his higher reasoning flew out the window. He unzipped his pants and in one deft movement pushed his pants and underwear down. It was at this point that he realized his mistake. At ten feet away from his conquest, he would have to duck walk over to her, which was obviously not the sexiest move ever. As he began his waddling approach, a lone shot from the AR-15 rang out. It was too late. Cash's lower brain was committed and its quarry was within striking distance. Cash finished his awkward shuffle over to the table, and like a heat seeking missile to a raging volcano he struck home.

"Oh my God!!!" April screamed. Cash was inwardly pleased with himself that he was eliciting this reaction from such a beautiful woman. "Get off me!" she screamed as she pounded on his chest. He was dejected, confused and hurt. "Get the fuck off me!" As she placed her foot on his chest and pushed him back, he fell into something, or more correctly, someone. He turned, simultaneously trying to say his apologies while pulling up his pants.

"Sir, I'm so, so sorry," he stammered. "We...we thought this place was abandoned. We didn't mean any harm, we were just looking for some food." Although even a blind man would have known that wasn't the case. "We'll clean up the place... right, April?"

Cash looked back towards April. She had climbed off the table and was slowly working her way towards the back door. "April... wait." But April was having none of it.

Her full attention was on this new man's face and she was clearly terror stricken. Cash had finally gotten his pants up into a serviceable fashion when he was able to look up at the homeowner's face. Two horrifying facts struck him at once. The stench was hideous, even the intense smell of the vinegar could not hide it. It wasn't quite the unmistakable stench of death, but it was damn close and making a case of its own for top dog. The face of the farmer for the most part looked hale, there was a slight pallor, but nothing a day or two in the sun wouldn't cure. The sun, however, would not be able to fix those two flat black orbs; a shark showed more humanity in its eyes.

April reached behind her, feeling for the door handle, all the while never taking her eyes off the man.

Everything happened in an instant. Cold air blew in from the back door, April lunged out, running at a full tilt by the time she got down the three back stairs. Her screaming seemed to enrage the occupant of the house. The man reached out and grabbed a hold of Cash's jacket. Cash didn't think twice as he shucked his coat off and headed for the same egress April had used a moment before.

Cash was down the stairs and barely away from the house when the first asthmatic asphyxiation struck. Calm down, Cash, he thought. *Just breathe, you got away, he can't catch you. Breathe.* Cash was halfway through his calming technique when the zombie appeared at the top of the small porch. Okay, that was a little fast, Cash thought, *but I've been here for a few seconds trying to catch my breath.* The zombie leaped over the three stairs, landed on the ground, and stopped, looking intently at Cash. He was now no more than twenty feet away.

"Oh no!" Cash wheezed.

CHAPTER 6

Mike's Journal Entry Five

It was impossible not to hear the girl's screams. Her shrieks pierced the air like a chorus of harpies. "I take it she's one of the missing people?" I asked Alex.

He nodded, stress imprinted on his face. "Yeah, April was with that pimply kid. What the hell was his name? Moola? Dinero? Cash? Yeah, that's it."

"Not sure that matters right now, buddy," I said as I peered through my sights looking for what was causing that much distress in the girl.

April was no more than twenty-five yards away, and still I saw no sign of trouble. Was it just some contrived drama for our viewing pleasure? Possible, but I hadn't seen acting that good since my daughter was caught sneaking out of the house and she tried to blame it on sleep walking. If I hadn't been watching her the whole time and caught pieces of her conversation over her cell phone I almost would have given her the benefit of the doubt. Well...not really, I might be a guy, but I'm not *that* stupid. Anyway, suffice to say it was an Oscar-worthy performance nonetheless.

April never stopped shrieking as she hurdled up into the back of the truck.

"One down, three to go, Alex," I said. "I guess I'm going to have to go see what's going on."

"Why?" he asked. "You have your family to look out for, Mike."

"I know," I said earnestly. "It just seems like the right thing to do."

By now, a small crowd was at the back of the truck looking expectantly in the direction from whence April had come.

"I'll go with you, Talbot," BT said. His deep bass voice startled me out of my thoughts. Any animosity between us seemed to have been swept completely away with that small gesture. Well, I guess it wasn't that small of a gesture; he was putting his life on the line.

"I appreciate that, BT. I really do, but I think our second wayward chickadee is returning to the roost...look," I said, pointing.

Cash swung around the corner of a row of houses at full speed, even from this distance I could tell his pants were doing their damnedest to fall. Cash was struggling with one hand to hold his pants up, and with the other he was doing a motion that only someone with experience might be able to pick up on. He was taking mighty puffs from an inhaler.

I turned to Alex and BT. "I think this is more a case of a date gone bad." I breathed a sigh of relief. Don't get me wrong, I understood the severity of the potential crime and Cash would be dealt with accordingly, but it still beat the hell out of the alternative.

"I don't think so, Mike," BT said, a tremor of warning in his voice as he pointed.

For the life of me, I did not want to follow the direction that offending digit indicated. Into the cold gates of hell it led. Not ten feet away from Cash was one of the new breed, fast and hungry. The kid was easily a couple of hundred feet away from us, and he was directly in my line of sight to the zombie. Between holding his pants up and the constant hits on his inhaler, he was losing more ground than the French in WWII.

42

Like Icarus to the sun I flew. The outcome was a foregone conclusion and still I ran towards him, motioning him to drop down so I could take a shot. He was too panicked to understand my gestures. By the time the kid's pants fell and brought him down in a gangly mash of elbows and knees, the zombie had pounced on him. It was all over except for the screaming.

As the zombie took its first rending bite of meat, what was once that young man's pride and joy hung in bloody shreds from its mouth. The high-pitched keening that issued from Cash was heart tearing. Every guy that witnessed the event winced in sympathy and subconsciously placed their hands over their own privates just to make sure their own house was in order.

The first bullet should have been for Cash – just to put him out of his misery. Five shots later, my trembling hands were able to put a kill shot into the zombie's head. I started to run over to the kid; what I was going to be able to do for him was beyond me. His all-out wails had become more of a struggling wheeze. Blood vacated his body in gushes. I got down on my haunches by the kid's head. I couldn't look at the damage done, the chord it struck was entirely too fundamental to my existence. Cash's hand grabbed mine, his fevered, pain-addled eyes looked up at me beseechingly.

"Don't let me die," he begged.

I wanted to answer him and tell him everything was going to be okay, but I wasn't the actor my daughter was. My voice would betray me, my posture would belie me, my cadence would divulge the truth.

I barely registered the staccato burst of firearms, but the angry hiss of displaced air as bullets passed dangerously close to my head got my attention. I looked back to BT who was firing what looked like a bazooka from this angle. I guess our earlier spat wasn't completed yet, but this seemed a little extreme even for him. Then I looked past him and saw that Alex was gesticulating crazily. Everyone else seemed to be yelling incoherent strings of words and pointing towards me, but occasionally I picked up the word "Run!" I looked behind me.

Before my heart began to start the trip hammer routine, I thought for one short millisecond my heart might just stop from the shock. Twenty, maybe thirty zombies were running full bore towards me. I was seconds away from sharing the same fate as Cash; hopefully not in the same manner, though. I grabbed the kid's shoulder, meaning to put him in a fireman's carry, but the opaque glaze of his eyes let me know the futility of the maneuver.

"Run, you stupid shit!" I heard BT yell over the roar of his rifle.

A zombie dropped no more than ten feet from me. More rifles took up the covering of my hasty retreat. Within three strides I was at full speed and still some of the zombies kept pace.

I made it back to the firing line without any undue incidents. The tattered remnants of the ones that were still pursuing me were quickly dispatched.

"Well that sucked!" I said as I stood up and surveyed the scene laid out before us. "Thanks, BT, I owe you one."

"What is going on, Talbot?" BT asked. He looked more shaken than I did, and I was the one that had been chased.

"No time, BT!" I pointed. A larger contingent of speeders were heading our way. I'd already had enough excitement for the day. "Let's go!"

"Mike, we can take them," Brendon said. "There's still two more of our own out there. We have to go get them."

I understood the hero mentality, I truly did. But they were a lost cause, if they weren't already dead they soon would be. "To what end, Brendon? We risk ourselves, our loved ones, and we waste bullets. There is no honor in casually throwing away one's life in a hollow attempt at bravery. They're gone." I was all for the eradication of this plague, but this was akin to trying to put out a seven-alarm blaze with a

Super Soaker.

"Mike, what if it was one of your kids?" Brendon asked brazenly.

"Don't you fuckin' dare, Brendon!" I screamed. He backed up. He was bigger than me, but I was definitely crazier, and in case you didn't know, crazy out-trumps size every time. "I have done everything I possibly can to keep everyone around me safe! If you're so fucking ready to die, go find them yourself. I'll wait, but only for as long as I can still make a safe retreat!"

Brendon's shoulders sagged as he looked back at Nicole who was witnessing the entire event. There was a look of unbridled shock on her face. I watched as the inner demons in Brendon wrestled for control. On one side was the overwhelming necessity to protect Nicole, and on the other was the desire to help someone in need.

"Not so easy now, huh?" I taunted.

"Fuck you, Mike," he answered dejectedly.

I swung the Jeep past Alex's big rig. Brendon was following closely. I was watching in my rear view mirror as some of the faster zombies – who looked mostly like high school kids – smashed headlong into the truck.

I had no desire to see how many hits my Jeep could take. I flooded the engine with high-octane gas and I was rewarded with the desired result. I was putting this particular circle of hell behind us. Alex was finally getting the tractor-trailer up to a speed where even the track team couldn't keep up. I had to look over my shoulder to get the full brunt of what my rear view mirror was trying to convey. I should have left it alone. Half the population of what had once been Bennett, Colorado was, in one form or another, in pursuit of our small caravan. Speeders bowled over their slower cousins, the deaders. So it looked like manners hadn't made the cross over into death.

"I don't think we should go back there, Mr. T," Tommy said. "Is Cash going to be alright?"

I couldn't fathom how to even begin to answer that

question. First off, Cash was dead. He had bled out after having his genitals savagely ripped from his body. Was he going to turn into a zombie? Odds were against it; when I'd last seen Cash I had seen a small dog pile of the living dead making short work of his remains. Would he get to pass through St. Peter's gate? If I were so inclined to believe in that path, I'd probably say yes, but then what God would allow this situation to be unfolding on its present course? Oh yeah, God can't have direct involvement, how heretical of me. Wouldn't want some omnipotent being that basically can control ALL of creation to lend a helping hand. God helps those who help themselves, you know. Okay, enough deity bashing, I had been under the false impression that once we got out of Denver we would have put the worst of it behind us. Silly me, the fun was just beginning.

CHAPTER 7

Justin slept on in the back seat of Brendon's truck, barely acknowledging the quick, jerky maneuvering as Brendon evaded first one and then another speeder that had raced out from a gas station at the outskirts of town. His dark dreams were bothered only by the incessant buzzing that pervaded every aspect of the tortured vista his fevered mind had drummed up.

A brigade of zombies had stormed mankind's last holdout. As they overwhelmed the humans' piss poor defenses, the zombies planted a flag that consisted of an unnaturally large femur for a pole and a flag which, when unfurled, looked entirely too much like a weathered flap of human skin. Justin smiled in his sleep, the final victory of zombie-kind resonating strongly in the deep recesses of his mind.

Justin... Justin jolted awake at the sound of his name being spoken out loud.

"What?" Justin answered groggily.

Nicole looked back, her features looking paler than should be right, even in the dead of winter. "Huh?" she answered back.

"What do you want?" Justin said, annoyed. "I was sleeping."

"Nobody said anything," Brendon chimed in before his fiancée and his friend got into it.

He'd known them long enough to realize it didn't take much more than a cross-eyed look to get them at each other's throat, and right now he just couldn't take it. This new development of fast zombies was fucking with his head, and there was no room, at least not right now, for any more bullshit.

Tommy stared through the back window of the speeding Jeep and directly into the windshield of Brendon's trailing Ford. "Oh no," he muttered solemnly.

He turned back around, his hands visibly twitching. The tic went completely unnoticed by the rest of the occupants in the car. The horror of Bennett was still fresh and everybody was doing their best to assimilate the new information in the best manner available to them.

"Fine," Justin said as he laid his head back down.

Justin.

Again with his name being called out. Even though the voice was loud this time, somehow Justin knew enough not to wake up. A warm breeze flitted through his hair; the sun, as large as a ripe cantaloupe, blazed high overhead. Justin spun in a slow circle, surrounded by chest-high golden wheat which swayed all around in a gentle current of air. Curiously, the growth flowed in a different direction from the prevailing breeze. Even Justin's shadow stretched in the same direction as the wheat though the sun was at high noon.

Something inside him knew enough that to stay here was dangerous but leaving might be worse. In the hazy mist of distance, he saw something coming. It shimmered in the sun much like a mirage. Even as he watched it, no, *her*, come closer, the wind at his back picked up in a vain attempt to try to slow her progress. The wheat arched further back in a futile attempt to get away; if the stalks could have miraculously grown legs it would have been the biggest crop exodus since the great Dust Bowl of the 20s. Justin had legs and his shadow was showing him the way he should be going; his higher psyche just couldn't get the transmission in gear despite all the revving the engine was doing.

Justin looked down at his feet, wondering why they were betraying him so. When he looked up, death was inches from his face. That feeling was quickly replaced by euphoric feelings of love and devotion. The girl, no, the woman that stood before him was the epitome of beauty, grace, black bottomless cruelty, and grandeur.

Wait, go back one, Justin thought. But as soon as the doubt crept into his mind it was washed away in the glory that was Eliza. *Eliza! Eliza!* his mind screamed in triumphant joy.

"Where are you going, my love?" Eliza asked without moving her mouth. Her soft angelic hand caressed his cheek.

"How are you talking in my head?" Justin answered.

The sound of the loud crack was quickly followed by the sensation of pain in his cheek. She had moved so fast he hadn't even seen her hand strike. Justin's heart seized for the briefest of seconds as Eliza let her true visage show. Soft smooth skin faded into sallow pale cheeks, her sky blue eyes transformed into twin black pools of death and destruction. Her soft hand that a moment before had stroked his cheek was now a gnarled, calcified hideous claw of bone. In an instant, she again became the object of cold ethereal beauty. Justin couldn't hope to keep up with the transformations. His mind could not make sense of the events as they unfolded before him.

"I asked you a question, Justin." Eliza smiled. Justin could tell it was not a gesture that came easily or willingly. A cobra would have had an easier time pulling that off.

Justin was scared…and with good reason. "I don't know," he stammered.

The smile never left her as she struck again. The blow burned on the side of his face. "I think you're lying to me, Justin. But we'll talk more." Justin shivered. Eliza looked over her right shoulder and then was gone.

"Justin! Justin! Wake up." Tommy shook his friend a

little harder than he meant to. Justin's head bounced off of the car window.

"What the fu—? Oh…hey, Tommy. What's going on? Did we stop?"

"What happened to your face, Justin?" Tommy asked.

Justin sat up and looked at his right cheek in the rear view mirror. Angry red welts the size and shape of a slender woman's fingers were clearly outlined.

"Shit, hell if I know," Justin said as he gingerly pressed along the edges of the contusion. Justin had never been so scared about a nightmare in his life.

"I think you're lying to me, Justin," Tommy said with a sad disappointment in his eyes. Tommy stepped out of the car and headed back to the Jeep.

"I've heard that before," Justin said as he wrapped the blanket tighter around himself.

CHAPTER 8

Mike's Journal Entry Six

We had traveled fifty miles east of Bennett. I thought my bladder was going to burst. I was looking for any excuse to pull over and relieve myself. So when Tommy said he needed to talk to Justin, I was all for it. I flashed my high beams until Alex acknowledged me with a quick toot of his horn. The big rig stopped in the middle of the road. There really was no reason to pull over onto the shoulder. The beauty of being this far east of Denver is that the landscape is much like Kansas: flat and unremarkable. We'd be able to see zombies for miles, unless of course they were hiding in snowdrifts or scrub brush.

Great, I thought, *I'm not even going to be able to enjoy this piss, I'll be so busy looking for the damn things I'll probably end up going on myself.* That was Number thirty-three on my list of hang-ups, but who's counting. *Obviously I am*, I answered myself.

Alex looked around nervously as he stepped down off the truck. "What's up, Mike?"

"Dude, I just need to take a quick leak!" (and rip some major ass, I didn't tell him that part) I yelled back.

After the events of the last few weeks, I did not want to stray too far from the relative safety of the cars, but I was still holding on to the vestiges of decency. That, and I wanted everyone to be far enough away from my back blast. Twenty something years of married life and I had never (willingly) ripped a fart in front of Tracy. Sure, I've let go of my share in my sleep. I've even woken myself up with a few that were air-splittingly loud. Whether or not I woke Tracy as well I don't know and she never let on.

I found the best middle ground available. I walked over to a small cattle fence ten feet from the edge of the road. I could tell by the way the gas was heating the rear of my pants this one was going to be a stinker. I just hoped it wouldn't leave a vapor trail in the frigid air. I was thankful to all the gods that still walked across the land that this wasn't a call to nature that involved the other end. There wasn't so much as a stop sign to hide that action. At least I could use my body to shield the majority of this most basic of necessities.

"Wonderful," I heard from the back of the truck as the door rolled up. "I'm stuck in that truck for God knows how long and that's what I have to witness when I finally get out."

"Oh no." My head exploded. Civilization, and possibly humanity itself is hanging on by a thread and *that's* what survives?

Mrs. Deneaux was gently lowered from the rear of the truck by BT and her nephew, Thad (the manager from Safeway). I almost lost the grip on my manhood as it tried in vain to pull up into my body, the better to protect itself from the soul-sucking bitch that was walking on the snow swept roadway. I finished, yanking my zipper up and nearly severed what my priest had circumcised forty something years ago.

Alright, enough with the surprises, I thought as I walked back towards the rear of the truck to see who else would be popping out of the back like a rabbit from a magician's hat. My purpose was mostly to gauge our strength, but partly to see what other malcontents might make themselves known.

I looked into the murky interior, hoping that Jed had somehow managed to get aboard. Unless he was cowering behind the nearly catatonic April, this wasn't going to be the case. In this new reality I would more likely expect to see Fritzy (the cat-suit wearing zombie rapist I had killed) than my unexpected ally Jed. Close to April, pushed against the back of the truck was Little Turtle's guest greeter, Joann, she was clutching on to a small group of children – three, I thought, but wasn't completely sure. I wasn't even sure if they were hers, not that it mattered, it seemed like a pretty symbiotic relationship. They clutched each other so tightly I thought it might take acetone to release them. Bad analogy, I know, I was going with the whole super glue thing. Anyway, there would be no immediate help from that small scrum. Next was Igor, the Russian gate guard. He was sleeping comfortably against the left side of the truck with what appeared to be a bottle of vodka held firmly in his left hand. That was a welcome surprise. He was a little older and a little overweight, but I thought I'd be able to trust him in a fight. Provided, of course, that he stayed awake. And then my eyes widened.

"Hi, neighbor, happy to see me?" Jen asked.

Are you fucking kidding me?

Besides Alex and his recovering wife, we had five small kids, a waifish woman that was holding on to two of the kids not in Joann's clutches, one über-bitch, über-bitch's nephew that looked like he would be more comfortable counting zombies than killing them, Joann and April that had checked out and most likely needed an intravenous dose of Xanax, a giant black man that I was more than convinced wanted to break me in half, a drunk Russian, and then the kicker...my lesbian neighbor Jen. Don't get me wrong, it's not that I don't like lesbians, hell, I want to *be* one. It's just that Jen had pretty much told me that she no longer had the will to live, and to top it off proved she was useless in a fight having cowered in the truck on the day we had made a stop at the local National Guard armory.

Paul pressed on my shoulder as he jumped from the back.

53

"Thanks, man," he said.

"Yeah, any time I can be of help," I answered, never taking my eyes off Jen.

"Well, are you going to help a lady down, or are you just going to keep staring at me?" Jen asked as she held her hand out to me.

"Why are *you* in the truck?" I asked. It came out before I could stop it. It sure as hell wasn't the politically correct thing to say but, man, I really wanted to know.

She pulled her hand back as if it had been stung. "Listen, Mike, I know how you feel about me—" she started.

Jen, if you had any idea of how I felt about you, you'd be over there huddling with the others. I wanted to say it out loud, my inner demons screamed to say it, my immature side cried to say it, my socially conscious, higher civility reasoning, stupid jerk other side had a different thought on the matter, and forced me to keep my mouth shut.

She continued, "I want revenge, Mike."

"Jen, we've had this conversation before."

Her eyes teared up a bit, friggin women, they always know which damn buttons of mine to push. Maybe I should stop wearing mine on my sleeve. If I put them under my jacket, they'd be a little tougher to get to. I pursed my lips and shook my head. She seemed to take that as an acknowledgement that it was okay to continue uninterrupted.

"When we got back that day, I sat in my and Jo's bedroom. Most of the time it was with a .32 caliber pushed to my temple." I involuntarily blew out air. Jen choked up for a moment and then went on. "I just wanted it to be over, the pain, the hopelessness, everything. I mean what was the point, right?" I found myself nodding with her. "I awoke the next morning with the gun still pressed against my head."

"Holy crap, you were a muscle spasm away from…well, you know," I said in disbelief.

She smiled wanly. "I dreamt about Jo that night." Her eyes got that faraway look. "I dreamt about her love of life.

No matter how shitty things got for her, she appreciated and looked forward to the small things in life, a cup of hot cocoa, a trip to IKEA, a new bottle of patchouli, a game of softball. Oh, God, I miss her," she sobbed. I looked away for a few seconds, letting her collect herself. She seemed grateful for the gesture. "Whew, sorry, I had to get that out. Jo would have wanted me to live, to love, to embrace everything. Not wallow in despair. If she knew that I had wanted to kill myself, she would have kicked my ass."

By the way, I would have paid to see that. Sorry, just a side note.

"When I finally realized why my skull ached that morning, I pulled the gun away from my head and tossed it across the room. When it knocked over the hat I had put over the picture of me and her on our union day I knew then and there that Jo was still with me and I wouldn't let her, or for that matter *you*, down again."

That remains to be seen. I didn't say it. I'm an immature dick, not a monster. I helped Jen down and handed her a power bar. I turned as I heard Brendon's truck door open. Justin stepped out into the severely lit day, embracing his blanket like only Linus could.

"God, he looks so pale," Jen said. "Almost like he's...sorry." She looked over to me. We were both thinking it though. Justin's head swiveled to the left and then up and over to his right and down again, almost like he was watching a monster serve that became an ace in a tennis match.

"What's he doing?" Jen asked.

I watched as a fly circled around and around Justin's head. Terror mounted. Well, my Marine Corps buddies were going to love this, big bad ass, afraid of a fly. What was going to be next? Was I going to be scared of the French? I watched as the fly did two more circuitous routes around his head and then landed on the very tip of his nose. Justin only stared down at it, never once unwrapping his hands from under the blanket to brush the thing away. My skin crawled with unseen, many legged bugs of varying size and color.

"Okay, everyone, I think it's about time to go," I shouted, never taking my eyes off the offending fly.

"Oh don't be a bother, Talbot, we just stopped," Mrs. Deneaux said as she puffed on a cigarette. "These idiots," she said as she swept her hand to encompass pretty much everyone, "won't let me smoke in the back of the truck, some gibberish about second hand smoke."

"Fuck, stay, I don't give a shit! Finish your cigarette. Finish a carton. Hell, go pull some grass, dry it out and smoke it. I'm leaving," I answered in a yell.

Mrs. Deneaux looked like she wanted to add fuel to the fire, but this wasn't a scene at Walmart where she could bitch someone out and basically get whatever her cold shriveled little heart wanted. Something in the look of my eyes must have told her that I truly would leave her there without a second thought. She ground out the remainder of her smoke under her shoe.

BT came up to the rear of the truck. "Who made *you* boss?" his voice boomed.

"You know what, BT?" I said as I tried to make myself as tall and intimidating as possible. Not an easy trick to pull off when I was pretty much looking him in the sternum.

"No, what?" he asked.

"Rhetorical, BT, rhetorical. *Nobody* made me boss. In fact, I don't want to be boss at all. That would make this entire fuck fest a lot easier if I didn't have to worry about any of my decisions getting people killed. I would like nothing more than to lie in the back of that truck and help Igor polish off whatever liquor he has stowed away. So, my giant friend, feel free to take the reins of this carnival ride and do with it what you may. I'm just too tired to deal with it."

"Aw, I'm just busting your balls, Talbot," he said as he basically just stepped up into the back of the truck. "You're just crazy enough to get us out of this." And then he laughed.

I didn't know whether to be relieved or petrified.

Alex had just finished up with his wife Marta, changing the baby's diaper. "Hey, Mike, what's up? Not to be a pain in the ass, but driving this truck is a bitch. I wouldn't mind taking a few minutes for the blood in my kidneys to start circulating again."

I didn't even need to turn around when I pointed behind me. Alex's face fell. "What is it, Alex?" I asked.

He tore his gaze from over my left shoulder and back to me. "What do you mean, Mike? You just pointed it out to me."

"Is it bad?"

"Are you messing with me, Mike?" Alex said with a frown.

I shook my head negatively.

"It's a speeder."

"How far away?" I asked, although I could almost approximate its distance as the minute tickle in my brain began to expand.

Alex looked back over my shoulder. "Maybe a quarter of a mile. What's going on, *cuate*? How could that thing possibly know that we're here? We're in the middle of nowhere."

"I'm not sure, Alex, but look at Justin."

Alex slowly pivoted his head, reluctant to look. The day was almost already a total disaster and it wasn't half completed. "He's just standing there. He looks pale, but no worse than he was earlier."

"Look closer, Alex."

"What's he looking at? Is that a fly on his nose? So?"

"What's a fly doing out here, Alex? In the dead of winter."

"It could have been in the truck, Mike," he said, but I could tell that the words didn't even ring true in his own head. Alex made the sign of the Holy Trinity on his chest. "Marta, finish up, we're leaving."

The zombie crossing the snow-covered field wasn't going to get to us any time soon, but it was disconcerting to be the prey as a predator closed in. I'm sure there isn't a gazelle in the world that feels comfortable with a lion in the general vicinity. The fly finally alit from Justin's face as he turned to look at our approaching company. Color rose in his cheeks, but because he was scared or enraptured was difficult to say.

Tracy helped Justin back in to Brendon's car and then looked over to me. She was worried, as was I, but for differing reasons. She was concerned with his physical well-being. I was more concerned with what was going on inside his head. I was beginning to wonder if Justin was a zombie GPS. Our own portable 'Harmin' (you know rhymes with Garmin) or better yet how about a Zom-Zom. Wonderful, death all around and I'm making plays on product names.

By the time we pulled away I was able to make out facial features on our would-be assailant. He looked none too pleased to see that we were making a hasty retreat. In the distance I could see more of his kind begin the fruitless journey across the frozen tundra in search of a meal. For one minute second I thought, *If Justin were to stay here, would they stop pursuing?* I said I *thought* about it, this isn't the Bible, I can't get in trouble for contemplating. Eventually we were going to have to stop and fight, but the middle of a highway didn't seem like the wisest place to make our last stand.

CHAPTER 9

Mike's Journal Entry Seven

The next two hours of driving did little to abate my feelings of dread. In fact, it did more to intensify it. I was trying to go over the events of the day to find some sort of alternate explanation for what was going on.

First off, sprinting zombies were not on my agenda. Our survivability odds had just been greatly reduced. Any mode of transportation that didn't include wheels was tantamount to suicide. These new zombies could run full tilt probably forever. In my heyday I could sprint for a max of maybe a quarter mile, now, hell, maybe a hundred yards before some significant body part failed. I shivered thinking back to our escape from Walmart. If we had encountered speeders then…well, I guess it would have been all over by now and I wouldn't have to be fixating on the damn issue at hand.

The main problem right now was the sun. Well, the sun and its gradual decline. We were going to have to stop, sooner rather than later, and with our own shining lighthouse transmitting our whereabouts, I couldn't fathom where we would find sanctuary. I'm not above sleeping in a car, but with three other people, it was not going to be a comfortable affair. We could all sleep in the truck bed, but if something happened we would have to abandon the Jeep and the Explorer, which was not an option. We could find a defensible house, but images of the old *Night of the Living Dead* movie flickered through my brain plate, hands coming through windows and all that stuff. Come to think of it, that didn't turn out to be such a good idea either.

This was not looking good for the home team. Let's see: we were outnumbered probably thousands to one; they don't need sleep; and they have just harnessed a second gear. Yep, not good at all. I was thinking about the myriad ways of our demise when I nearly finished the job myself. Alex had been slowing down for near on a half mile trying to gain my attention to pull alongside. My thoughts were elsewhere when I almost slammed into his tailgate, his brake lights as large as saucers in my field of vision.

"Two other cars on the road and you almost crash into one of them," my wife stated. "I knew I shouldn't have let you drive my Jeep."

I was pissed and had to bite back a sardonic reply, mostly because she was right. Not about smashing up her Jeep, but the part about almost making us road kill. I had read once in one of those bathroom readers… Okay, don't go getting all highbrow on me. One of my past life's small pleasures was to sit on the throne and, while passing time (and other things), gain some useless knowledge. And one of those little nuggets (get the pun?) was the fact that back in Oklahoma in 1899, there were two cars in the whole state and they had an accident with each other. They say history repeats itself; well…there's proof positive, almost.

"Talbot!" my wife said with some force. "Alex wants something."

I pulled my hand across my face hoping to pull off the growing fog in my head. It didn't work. I pulled up alongside the semi, a low throbbing apprehension coursing through my body.

"What's up, Alex?" I yelled over the sound of our engines.

"I'm getting tired, Mike," Alex yelled back. The words

were superfluous, he looked exhausted and he had two small kids up in the cab with him. Young children could make you tired if you were just lying in bed, and this was far from that peaceful scenario.

"Getting?" I asked sarcastically.

Something got lost in translation or he was just too tired to grab onto the barb. He just shrugged.

"Any ideas?" he asked.

"I've been thinking the same thing, Alex." Alex had been expecting me to elaborate with my plan. Unfortunately, I didn't have one. When I didn't answer right away Alex took that as a cue.

"There's a small town up ahead called Vona," he offered.

Now it was my turn to shrug. "So what." Vona, Detroit, fuckin' Paris. Where could we go without a flesh eater joining us for company?

"They have a sheriff's office," he concluded.

Light and hope began to not so much blaze...but at least glimmer. A sheriff's office should have holding cells and a bit more fortification than the average house. "Lead on, Tonto!" I yelled.

"Who the hell is Tonto?" he retorted.

"Never mind, how much further?"

"Ten minutes at the most."

"Alright, we'll scout ahead." I accelerated past him. It would be safer to have my Jeep go in first. It was much more maneuverable and would be easier to vacate a hostile area if the need arose.

Five minutes later, I was taking the off ramp down into Vona. Alex stayed at the top of the ramp with the engine idling. If I wasn't back in twenty minutes the plan was for him to leave. I knew he wouldn't, but that was the plan.

My guts felt like I had swallowed a salamander. As calm and collected as I could – which wasn't working very well by the way – I turned to see if I could garner any information from my early warning detection system: Tommy. I was neither alarmed nor relieved.

"Hey, buddy, got any feelings?" I asked as nonchalantly as possible.

"I got a bunch, Mr. T," he said with a small smile on his face.

I waited for a second, hoping for some sort of revelation. Then it dawned on me that Tommy's 'feelings' probably had more to do with how much he liked Pop-Tarts than with the outcome of our lives as we entered into Vona.

"Hey, Mr. T?"

"Yeah, Tommy," I answered as I slowed the Jeep down to around fifteen mph; slow enough to look for trouble and quick enough to get away from it.

"What's it mean when you put your hand over your mouth?" he asked.

I was about to answer that it generally means to be quiet, but the universal sign for that usually only entails using your pointer finger. "I'm not sure, Tommy, why?"

"Well, Ryan has one hand over his mouth and the other hand is pointing to his throat and he's shaking his head from side to side."

My foot involuntarily slipped off the gas and onto the brake; I stalled the car.

"What's the matter, Mike?" Tracy asked. "The last time you stalled your car we had almost hit a moose while four-wheeling."

"This is worse. Something or someone is blocking Tommy's abilities."

As if on command, we all stared out the windows, convinced that whatever was causing this was within range. But Vona in death was a lot like Vona in life, dead. Why they had a sheriff's office was beyond me; maybe if they had a rash of cow tippings, they could lock the hooligans up. Or maybe if things got real bad and mailboxes started to get smashed they would have somewhere to put the bad guys. Hell, we were three-quarters of the way through town and I hadn't seen a bar or a liquor store; so no real need to even lock up the town drunk. Ah, wasteful government spending at its best.

"Tommy, can Ryan write?" I asked, hoping beyond hope. It seemed like a far-fetched idea, but I was open to suggestions. "Maybe a small note to kind of let us know what's going on?"

"Oh, God!" Tommy moaned.

I ground the starter a little bit in response to his alarm, looking around wildly for what had caused the distress in his voice. I was still on edge, but when nothing visible showed itself, I relaxed a bit. Just a bit, this was still Tommy we were talking about.

"What's the matter, Tommy?" Travis asked. Even Henry, shifted uneasily, he could feel the change in atmospheric pressure in the car as we waited for Tommy to elaborate.

"All of Ryan's fingers are all crunched up and broken looking," Tommy murmured almost silently, a small sob escaping him.

"Oh fuck, oh fuck," I said nervously.

"What's that mean, Mike?" Tracy asked me, panic beginning to well in her chest to match mine and Tommy's. Only Travis seemed the least affected, but I noticed his knuckles turning a brighter shade of white as they gripped his shotgun.

"We're being hunted, I think," I answered.

Tracy's tension eased a bit. "Well, duh. Zombies have been after us for weeks now! What's so new about that?"

"No...this is different. This isn't just about some zombies stumbling across us and trying to eat us. We're being singled out...purposefully tracked."

"How? That's not even possible," she yelled back, more in defense of her sanity than in any answer to transgression on my part.

"Possible? You're pulling the possible card out?" I asked.

"Okay, sorry. But how?" she said in a more subdued

63

voice. "And I guess, why? And who?"

"Maybe we taste better," I said. Tracy glared at me. "Sorry." I held my hands up to ward off any attempted blows. "Poor choice of words."

"You think?"

I was scared shitless, but I was trying my best to put on a brave face for Travis, Tommy, and Tracy and, well, if I'm being honest, even for myself. "I'm pretty sure about the 'Who,' somewhat sure about the 'Why' and not a fucking clue as to 'How.'"

I laid out my concerns about Justin and how he could potentially be guiding every nearby zombie to our location. Tracy wasn't buying it. I'm sure the majority of her reasoning had to do with plausible deniability. What mother ever wants to think her child could bring harm unto others. Tracy looked over at me like I had just spit into her Cheerios.

"It's a theory, I didn't say it was fact."

"Come up with something else, college boy," she said as she crossed her arms over her chest and turned to stare out of the windshield.

Lesson learned. Fact number one – never throw one of your children under the bus in front of your wife.

We started slowly back on our silent trek through Vona. We were almost out of the center of town when we came upon the nondescript sheriff's office. I passed by slowly, looking for any sign of problems. I was really getting sick of the 'calm before the storm' crap. It was quiet, eerily so. The place wasn't much bigger than your average Laundromat and about as appealing, but it would fit all of us easily enough. The two windows in the front were barred, thankfully, and the door looked heavily fortified enough. Why I kept remembering the motto for the roach motel, I don't know. My brain put its usual sick spin on it. *Humans go in, but they don't come out.*

"Man, I just don't like the looks of this," I said out loud to no one in particular.

Tracy mirrored my unease. "Then let's just go."

"Yeah, but I like the idea of sleeping in the Jeep on the road even less. So it's really the lesser of two crappy situations that I'm contemplating. Vona it is then."

"You sure?" my wife asked, looking around the cabin of the Jeep like all of a sudden it went from matchbox size to palatialness.

As if in answer I yawned. My non-response was the worst decision I had made thus far. I turned my blinker on to go into the parking lot, so as to warn the multitude of drivers behind me.

"What are you doing?" she asked.

"Cooking an omelet," I shot back. One of these days my brain-to-mouth filter will work, but for now I'll have to just go back to what I do best, back-peddle. "Aw hell, I'm sorry, Tracy, I'm just beat."

Did that get me off the hook? I looked over cautiously. When confronted with a wild animal (in this case a female human), it is best to avoid direct eye contact and make no fast or sudden movements. I could tell by the way her hands were folded in her lap that I was in little danger of being struck, but as I slowly raised my gaze, the look of fire in her eyes confirmed my suspicions: I was still in the doghouse.

"Talbot, are you going to check to see if the door is open?"

The question was reasonable. My reaction was not. All of a sudden the thought of vacating the relative safety of our rolling arsenal seemed like the worst idea ever presented. Damn her logic! I was going to suggest that I'd pull up to the front door and she could give it a quick yank, but we all know how well that would have gone over. I even began to form the arguments in my head like 'I'll stay behind the wheel and you can hop in so we can get away fast.' Or 'Have you ever seen how bad you drive a stick?' or even better 'You're smaller, so they won't want to eat you as bad.' Dammit.

65

"Sounds great, can't wait," I forced through a Cheshire cat smile.

I pulled onto the gravel parking lot. The crunch of small stones under my tires set a flock of ravens into flight. *Oh pissa*, my brain slipping back into my comfortable old Boston idioms. (Otherwise known as "Cool.") *That doesn't seem too ominous*, I thought sarcastically.

"Trav, can you hand me the .357?" I asked.

He checked to make sure the cylinder was loaded. "You want me to come with you, Dad?"

The answer was obviously yes, but I had already had this battle once with Tracy and she was not about to go 0 and 2. "No," I gulped out. I could feel some of the tension in Tracy drain out. "Grab the AR and cover my retreat if needed."

I didn't want him using the shotgun; the last thing I wanted to do was pull buckshot out of my ass. I looked over to Tommy again, hoping for some divine intervention, but there was nothing, no last minute stay of execution from the governor. He shrugged in response.

I took a deep breath as I stepped out of the Jeep, the cold wind whipping across my face. I sucked in a shock of super frigid breath, my exhalation leaving a long plume. It was five purposeful strides to the front door of the sheriff's office. I did it in fifteen small cautious ones. *Be locked, be locked, be locked!* The handle turned quietly, the door silently slid open. The pea soup murkiness inside the jail was broken only by ribbons of light that streamed in through the dusty windows. Dust lazily swirled about in those rays of sun. The smell was intense. I staggered back. Tracy had climbed into the driver's seat and Travis stepped out to get a clearer shot.

I jumped when she yelled, "What is it?"

Well, if they didn't know we were here, they did now. I did not turn my head away from the door to respond. "It smells like Henry after a bean burrito." It was kind of funny I think. Tracy actually turned green with the olfactory thought of that. We had only been removed from the stench for less

—

than a day and this was not something you quickly forgot. "Death."

"Get in, let's go," she said nervously.

I loved the suggestion, but when I wasn't immediately attacked I let curiosity get the better of me. Plus, being the gun nut that I am, I figured we could get all sorts of new armaments from here. "Hey, pull up here and turn the lights on."

"Are you serious? I think we should just go," she replied.

"You're probably right, but come over here anyway."

Travis walked alongside the Jeep constantly scanning for problems. Tommy nervously stared through the window, but not the front. He was looking back the way we had come. Whether he sensed something coming, or wished we were heading back, he didn't say. Tracy pulled up closer, the headlights perfectly straddling the sides of the office door, lighting up the outside wall perfectly, and the inside, well not so much. "Um, could you maybe back up and get one of the headlights to shine into the doorway?" I asked as nicely as possible.

"You didn't say that's what you wanted," she shot back.

If I ever wanted to have relations with my wife again it was abundantly clear to me that I was going to have to not say what had bubbled to the top of my brain plate. "Yep you're right," I struggled to get out in a civil tone. When did 'common sense' not become a common virtue? I hope to God she never reads these journals.

She backed up with a jerk, the Jeep stalling. Okay, this is about the time in any classic horror movie where the monster makes itself known. I jumped a measure or two when she turned the ignition over, the reverberation of the catching engine off the wall drowning out all other sound. This should be it. I tensed. A hand, a mouth, a bite, something should be happening soon.

"Oops," Tracy said out the window.

That was pretty much the sentiment I had when I thought

I had messed my underwear. Again, these aren't proud moments. I'm not some action movie star with stand-in stunt doubles, or a character in an Xbox360 game. I don't get multiple retakes or extra lives. This life is a one shot deal; something goes wrong and I can't hit 'reset.'

Tracy repositioned the Jeep, the one headlight cutting through the dark. The small office was mostly lit up, but I still imagined the worst lurking in the musty corners. To the right was a desk with a small wilted plant on top. Most likely the chair once seated a cheery older heavyset woman. The receptionist would have known everyone and their mother in this one-car town. Beyond her desk was the door to the town sheriff's office. How did I know this? Well, the door said 'Sheriff' making that fairly self-explanatory. For the life of me, I could not get the image of 'Andy' from Mayberry out of my head. As long as Barney Fife didn't show up, everything should be fine.

A half-empty gun rack stood against the left side. It looked like the sheriff hadn't been caught completely off guard. I imagined him dying in the line of duty to protect those he served. I didn't know him and never would, but he was a hero as far as I was concerned.

My attention was brought back to the rear of the office. Back there were the holding cells. I could see the heavy metal bars, but nothing more. The light from the Jeep penetrated only that far, as if what lay beyond had decided it did not yet want to yield its hidden prize. Whatever the secret was, it was definitely the source of the stink.

What kind of survivalist was I? I didn't even have a flashlight with me. Shouldn't be too big of a problem, though. I walked over to where the gun case was and grabbed one of the two remaining utility belts. The heavy weight of the club-like flashlight felt comforting in my hand. I hoped that the 4 D-cell batteries that powered the potential bludgeon still held juice. Like any smart person in my predicament, I made sure the light was pointing right in my eyes when I turned it on. Nothing like a case of temporary blindness to get your adrenaline running. I immediately pulled the light away and swung it from side to side praying that I was in time to stop whatever was hurtling my way. The smash as glass struck the floor brought Travis running through the door. The loss of light as he stepped in front of the headlight pitched the room back into darkness. Unless our would-be assailant was a desk lamp or hiding on the ceiling (where the flashlight was pointed) we were going to make it through the next couple of minutes. I wonder if John Wayne ever had these moments.

"You alright, Dad? What's going on?" Travis asked, stepping completely into the room as he realized that he was blocking the light source.

I was alright, that much was true. But how to answer the second part? That was a little trickier. Did I lie and tell him that I was fending off legions of the living dead? I still carried some semblance of pride in me. I would lose any salvageability of that woeful human trait if I told him that I had inadvertently blinded myself and then damn near shit myself as I knocked over a lamp in my haste to thwart an as yet unseen enemy. Nope, lying seemed the best course of action. Pride would stay intact. Integrity would have to take one for the team.

"Saw a bat."

Travis looked up. Completely unconvinced, he looked back over at me.

Damn, he must have got that scrutinous eye from his mother. I pointed the flashlight towards the holding cells, mostly to take the attention off of me. The sight was disturbing to say the least, but not as bad as it could have been. Locked in the cell furthest from us was a man. He looked on the younger side. The blue tinge of death-by-frostbite, however, made age recognition a complicated task. He was curled up on the small cot in a fetal position, most likely trying in vain to preserve his body heat with the small airline-style blanket.

"Poor bastard. Probably got locked up the day this whole thing went down."

"Are we going to be able to get him out of there?" Travis asked.

"What's taking so long?" Tracy yelled from the Jeep.

"Just doing some housekeeping." I went back to where I had got the flashlight and grabbed the oversized key ring. I really thought they only used those in movies. I hesitated for a moment as I placed the key into the lock. What if it was a zombie playing possum?

"Dad?" Travis asked. The implied question went unasked. I had done my job well. My paranoia had been genetically passed on.

Dammit, I wasn't going to go in there and be in the middle of moving him when the damn thing decided to sit up and gnaw on my femur. "Go tell Mom to be ready. God forgive me for what I am about to do." The Catholic in me would have a very difficult time letting go of the guilt I was about to heap on myself, but the survivalist part of me would get over it. Frozen brain matter sprayed against the far wall as I carefully placed a well-aimed shot through the man's head.

A soft crackling noise replaced the roar of the weapon in the confined space. It was long moments before I realized it was frozen blood dropping to the floor. Add that to my list of growing nightmare fodder.

I dragged the body across the floor of the office, thankful that frozen congealed blood didn't leave a telltale sign of my sin. I uneremoniously dumped the nearly decapitated body on the far side of the building. Little did I realize then my mistake, but I might as well have been chumming for sharks. I had just laid out the number one food group for our enemy.

I left the front door open with the expectation that the majority of the stink would be gone by the time we got back. We headed back up the off ramp – which I have to admit made me somewhat nervous. For so long, the laws of the road had been ingrained in me; to just drive as I pleased hadn't quite settled with me yet. Alex was anxiously standing by the truck when we pulled up.

"How's it looking, Mike?"

I wanted to pull out the standard answer of 'that town is dead,' but the joke was getting tired.

"Well, crap, Alex, my gut doesn't like it. We didn't *see* anything, no people, no deaders and no speeders. The jail only has one way in. On a good note, the windows are barred and the door looks pretty sturdy. I say we go in and park the semi pretty much right up against the front door, that way if some friends come calling for dinner we can get into the cab."

"What good is that going to do, Mike? We can't all fit in the cab," Alex said exasperatedly.

"You must be tired, my friend," I said as I clapped him on the shoulder. He didn't appreciate the gesture. "Fine." I took my hand off of him.

"Sorry, Mike, I'm wiped."

Yeah! Well fucking me too! Whoa, that was an overreaction. I yelled so loud in my head, I figured he had to have picked it up. "No sweat, you just need to get in the cab and then back the truck up to the doors."

He nodded in understanding. God, he was a good friend, I hoped I didn't screw it up. My tendency towards hotheadedness had lost me more than one potential ally in this world, and right now I could ill afford that.

"What about your cars?"

"It'll suck to lose them, but it'd be even worse to die." I said it so casually Alex actually snorted a small laugh. "Okay, the sheriff's office is almost all the way through town on the right hand side, I'll lead."

Alex climbed into his truck without another word. In just the ten minutes it took to get Alex and come back, the sunlight had faded to a mere shadow of itself. The door still stood ajar. It waited expectantly for our return, like a hungry grizzly for a salmon.

Imagination while in survival mode is a curse. Events were already unfolding in a fantastical manner, and to make them even more so really seemed like overkill. Yet my mind plunged on. I was wholly convinced that No-Head Fred had self-resurrected himself and was now waiting patiently for us inside. Maybe I should send Deneaux in first. That seemed the wisest thing, kind of like an offering, the whole sacrificial thing and all. Nobody was going to miss her. What? Like you weren't thinking that too!

CHAPTER 10

Mike's Journal Entry Eight

Within twenty minutes, we had all entered the office. A couple of large flashlights set up like candles illuminated most of the office except for the farthest cell, where of course my gaze kept wandering to. Jen managed to find some fuel for a small pot belly stove in the far corner. I had missed it on my first foray, but I wasn't going to hold that against myself. The stink of death had mostly been replaced by the smell of the living. On a bad day (which was most days lately) we can certainly rival our stiffer relatives in the odoriferous department. I had, on more than one occasion, received a dirty look from a fellow survivor as Henry let loose with some flatulence.

Another ten minutes later, we had done what humans always tend to do. We had marked out our territory. The Talbots were taking up residency in the first cell furthest away from 'Fred's' previous abode. We were on the complete opposite side of the stove, but because of that we were also furthest away from the door and the windows. I just couldn't shake the feeling of '*something wicked this way comes.*' Even with the bars and the storm shutters closed, the windows were still the most vulnerable part of this building. It would take a while for the heat of the stove to travel this far if at all, but with all the bodies stuffed in this small office that shouldn't present a problem.

As the heat in the building increased, conversation conversely decreased. Exhausted refugees began to drift off to hopefully better places. (Even though it would be tough to come up with a nightmare worse than the one we were already living.)

"Merry Christmas," I said to everyone. I got a few mumbled 'Merry Christmases' in return, but for the most part, the sentiment went largely unnoticed.

I was asleep in minutes, even with the hushed conversations, coughing, and the flashlights burning bright. This was a feat for me. I used to be kind of a *prima donna* when it came to sleeping. I needed a white noise sound machine playing 'Summer Crickets' before I could even begin to think of sleeping, and even then, if a mouse farted too loudly I would wake up.

"Talbot!"

I sat straight up. "What?" I asked…no one.

It was impossible to tell how long I had been asleep, but it was still night time. Everyone was asleep except for one guard placed at the windows (Igor), and he wasn't even looking at me. *Who the hell said my name?* I thought sleepily. I was more than half convinced that someone had said it in their sleep, probably shouting my name while they were wringing my neck for some past transgression. I was on a lot of people's shit list, hell it could have been Tracy. *No, that didn't feel right, the tone of the disembodied voice felt male.* Screw it, BT can yell at me tomorrow. I scooted back down onto my chair cushion/pillow.

"TALBOT!" It came more forcefully.

I sat bolt upright, still the guard didn't turn my way. There was no way he hadn't heard that. Come to think of it, that shout should have awoken half of the people here. *WTF.* I actually thought the letters WTF instead of What The F…well you get the picture, damn text age. Great, I was hearing voices in my head and it wasn't Tommy. I looked over to the big kid. He had a worried expression on his face, but he was most assuredly asleep.

"TALBOT!" it screamed.

I jumped up. "Dammit, what?!" Now Igor turned, luckily I wasn't loud enough to wake anyone. "Nothing...nothing," I said to Igor. Apparently I seemed convincing enough or he just didn't care, he mumbled something in Russian and turned back to the window. I said "What?" again but in a barely audible range. It was still louder than it had to be, the voice was in my head. That CAT scan seemed like a better idea with every waking moment.

"I'm coming!" the voice said again, and like a television set being turned off, the signal was gone.

Cold dread swept over me. I had recognized the voice. Could it be possible? How? My first instinct was to go over to the windows and see if anything was going on.

I was almost out the cell door when Henry looked up at me with imploring eyes. I knew that look. He had to go. "Come on, boy." His stumpy tail wagged in enthusiasm. It was no easy journey getting across the room navigating through the strewn bodies, especially with Henry in tow.

"Vere you going?" Igor asked as I approached the door.

"The dog's got to go."

"I vealize that, I have been smelling him all night."

"Sorry," I said bowing my head. Exposing someone unwillingly to Henry's toxic fumes will not generally win you any friends. I began to turn the handle.

"I vouldn't do that." His tone was casual...his stance was not. I was completely convinced that he would use that gun he was holding if I turned the knob any further. "This is not Vendy's, vee are not Open Late." He was so amused with himself that he couldn't help but flash his gap toothed smile.

I had no clue what he was talking about. I figured he must still be taking pulls off his stock of booze. "Igor, if you think Henry's farts can peel paint, wait until he drops a steaming hot mess for you. When everyone wakes up

---

because of the stench, I'll tell them it's because you wouldn't let him out." The idle threat did little to yield his previous stance. Then the lights in the dimmed Talbot belfry began to illuminate. I understood the Wendy's reference now. 'Oh shit.'

"How many?" I asked "And when?"

"Da, so now you know." He smiled again. Although WTF was so funny I don't know. (This time I actually thought the words out.) "Only a couple and it looks like the sheriff and his deputy have come back to vork. Been here vor about fifteen minutes."

"You haven't told anybody?" I asked incredulously.

"Vy, vhat good vould it do? Dey are out there, vee are in here."

I wanted to yell at him, but he was right. We were human and we needed rest. But this place could easily become a lobster trap. Options became extremely limited when you only had one way of egress.

"Vee can take care of them in the morning ven everyone is awake."

Again with the sound logic, when did he become Socrates? "Has either one of them said anything?" I asked. Igor looked at me like I had found and drank his private stash. "I'll take that as a no?" Henry whined.

"You had better take him into the bathroom."

I began to walk Henry over to the facilities. "Igor, you'll let me know if more of them come." It wasn't so much a question as a statement.

"Da, da," he said absently as he waved his hand at me dismissively and turned back towards the window.

When I got back from taking care of Henry's needs, I noticed that Justin was awake.

"You should get some sleep, bud. Tomorrow's going to be another long day," I said. I meant it in terms of driving, but my thoughts kept drifting back to our guests outside. I don't think any of us were quite ready for another battle for survival.

"I slept all day. I'll go to sleep if I need to," Justin answered on the snappish side.

Normally this kind of insolence, especially from my kids, would send me through the roof. But he looked like crap and I felt like crap, so we basically cancelled each other out.

"We should kill him. He's always telling us what to do."

"He is, isn't he? I could teach him a thing or two!"

"That's it, one quick shot to the heart and all your troubles would be over."

"Wait wouldn't it be all of OUR troubles?"

"Kill him."

"Who are you? I can't kill him, he's my father." Justin shivered involuntarily

Henry fell back asleep in seconds flat, not so tough when you have as much practice as he does. I, unfortunately, wasn't so lucky. I was having a difficult time getting any sort of comfortable. When I rolled over for the third effen time I saw Justin looking at me. The gaze was not a comforting one. I got the distinct impression he wanted to do me bodily harm. When he realized I was looking at him the hostility fell off his features. For a second he looked confused, and then he rolled over as if he was embarrassed because he got caught doing something he shouldn't have.

The next morning couldn't come quick enough. This night would have a hard time getting any stranger. With the sunlight came the thumping; my dream of hooking up with Wonder Woman was getting frustrating. Every time we moved, the headboard slammed up against the wall, the noise was so loud it eventually woke me up. Not only did I realize I wasn't banging Wonder Woman, I also had the uncomfortable task of readjusting my manhood, so to speak. Then, to top off this glorious day, I realized the banging wasn't so much due to some heavy amorous lovemaking, but rather some unwanted breakfast guests. And they weren't delivering, they were picking up.

I sat up quickly. Igor was still at his post...but he was fast asleep. A couple of other folks started to stir, but nobody yet realized the danger we were in. I got up quickly, not thrilled with the fact that my still-erect penis scraping against my zipper had caused an unpleasant sensation. I bent over at the waist to give more room for adjustment and to attempt to minimize the imminent immense pain that was coming. Fuck the zombies. This was going to take priority. After several deep breaths, and a conscious effort not to puke, I realized the worst of my endeavor had passed. If this was the worst that the day had to offer it might not be so bad. (Later edit...yeah that wasn't the case, the day started off bad and got progressively worse.) I began my unfolding at the waist when I was rudely interrupted by another thump at the door. Shards of brilliant sunlight shot in along the edges as the door rattled on its frame, but it didn't seem like it was going to give anytime soon.

I crossed over to the windows, receiving loud protests as I pulled back the storm shutters. Sunlight flooded into all the dark crevices within our makeshift motel room. The remonstrations were nothing compared with the shattering of glass as a hand shot through the barred glass and sought purchase on my T-shirt. I jumped back with an agility I hadn't attained since my high school football days. I felt a fingernail pull against my skin, I only hoped it wasn't deep enough to mar the flesh. The scar I could live with, the effects of the infection were quite another.

Igor awoke in a flash. The air-rending explosion of his rifle had everyone on their feet. The zombie that had made its presence known howled in frustration as I danced out of its grasp. The rifle shot to its shoulder seemed to do little to distract it from its primary target. I watched as fresh blood poured from its wound. I wasn't sure what had me more intrigued, the fact that the blood wasn't some congealed, blood-red bacon-fat looking substance, or the constant mewling of the zombie as it keened in disappointment.

Without meaning to, I found myself continually backing away as the zombie tried its best to fit itself through the six-inch space between the bars to get at me. Igor was saying something loudly in Russian; from his tone and volume I assumed it was swearing (but who can tell, a love song spoken in Russian sounds like taunts in a bar fight) as he tried to un-pry a jammed bullet in his HK-47. (*Russian piece of shit weapon.* No, I'm not kidding, that went through my head as I kept backing up, while looking at the zombie and checking my stomach for any telltale signs of red, welt-ish weeping wounds.)

The zombie was shoulder deep through the bars and trying in vain to fit its oversize melon through when Jen came up and finished off what Igor had started.

"Thank you," I stammered as I sent a silent prayer to the patron saint of Intact Flesh. I pulled my shirt up, thankful to realize that whatever saint I had prayed to had come through.

Jen looked a bit shaken – but, pardon the pun – not stirred. She had a determination to her now; something she had not possessed at the armory. She wasn't there yet, but she was looking increasingly like someone I would want on my team should the need arise.

"What was it doing?" she asked, a worried look on her face. I couldn't blame her, killing a speeder seemed more like taking down one of our own. "Was I imagining it or was that thing showing anger?"

"Anger, frustration, hunger? Hell I don't know, welcome to Zombies, Version 2.0, the new and improved model," I answered sarcastically.

"The better to kill YOU," Justin said as he came up to witness the butchery.

I couldn't help but focus on the word 'You' and how Justin made sure he was making eye contact with me when he said it. My concentration was broken, however, as the sheriff and his deputy finally made their way over to the window.

The slower older Zombie Version 1.0s were savagely cut down as Igor finally righted his rifle and made short work of them. I guess we were actually the rude guests, after all this was their place of work. We came in uninvited, locked them out, and then killed them when they tried to gain entry. Oh well, manners were low on my list of priorities.

"Igor, do you see any more of them?" I asked tentatively.

I wanted out. The more I looked at this situation, the stronger I felt the urge to leave. The constricted confines of the jail, pressed in from all sides. I fucking started to swoon as I felt my equilibrium spin on its axis. And as suddenly as the static in my mind attacked, it abated, and the room returned to its original dimensions. It had happened so suddenly that no one even noticed my distress...except for one. Justin was looking directly at me, a small sneer spread across his thin lips.

Fuck, what is going on! I never took my eyes off him as Igor finally answered my question.

"Da, five or six, maybe more, can't see past the truck, and the windows are only in the front."

I understood the implied meaning, and obviously my over active, scary movie-fed imagination, pictured a thousand or more zombies to the rear of the building just waiting patiently for the front door to open so that they could make a human meat and cheese McMuffin for breakfast. That sounded good, my stomach grumbled; mind you not the 'human meat' part, the McMuffin part. Remember where I said the zombie HADN'T broken skin when he scratched me?

—

April ran into the center of the room, her finger wildly gesturing back to where she had come from, her fragmented thoughts trying desperately for cohesion as her mouth soundlessly opened and closed.

"Spit it out," Mrs. Deneaux said. "You look like a fish out of water with your mouth flapping like that. It's not an attractive appearance on you."

Well, it was good to see that Mrs. Deneaux hadn't placed that thought filter on her mouth yet. I didn't like Deneaux, but I was in agreement with her on this one.

"A noise…a noise," April stated, and then as her brain caught up she elaborated. "I heard some scraping on the wall by where I was sleeping."

"It was probably just a mouse," Mrs. Deneaux said caustically.

I was tempted to agree with her again. In fact I wanted to, as opposed to accepting the alternative. The noise that we were now all hearing was suspiciously close to where I had deposited our dead jail bird.

"Stupid," I whispered as I inwardly slapped my hand up against my forehead. *May as well have hung up a Denny's sign: Come get your country-folk buffet.* I was frozen in indecision, damned if you do, damned if you don't. We couldn't stay here, that much was certain, but going outside meant uncertainty. BT came to my rescue. Not purposefully, but still, I'll take it.

"Talbot," his voice boomed in the restricted room. "Let's get our gear and get the hell out of here."

My engine was racing. Finally, with the nudge from BT, my transmission kicked into gear. Indecision was now in my rear view mirror and fading fast.

"Alright, Alex, you get ready. I'm going to get a five-man fire team ready. We're going to blow a hole into any opposition, and then you go right up into the cab. Don't go until I tell you, though. If something happens to you, I'll have to drive that effen truck and we all know how well that will go over."

"Yeah, I have a weak stomach," BT said smiling.

"BT, I can't imagine anything weak on you," I said, looking up at the big man.

"Why tempt fate, Talbot?" he said as he clapped my shoulder.

I nearly fell over from the force. I don't know if he does it purposefully, or if he just doesn't know his own strength. Okay, I'm not that naïve. He's definitely doing it on purpose. Fine, as long as he was tentatively on my side, then I could deal with it.

Igor and I stood shoulder-to-shoulder by the doorway. BT and Brendon stood immediately behind us and Travis took up the rear, with the shotgun. It would have been wisest to put the scattergun up front, but I'd be damned if I was going to go into battle BEHIND one of my own.

Jen was at the door ready to pull it open at my command, at which point Igor and I would go out with guns blazing *a la* Paul Newman and Robert Redford in *Butch Cassidy and the Sundance Kid*. As we exited the building and became able to fan out more, BT and Brendon would join in the fray. By that time my hope was that the battle would be over and Travis and Alex could saunter out.

Jen nodded once to me. "You ready?" she asked.

No, I thought, then took a deep breath and nodded my head in return. The door flew open and she jumped back. Immediately I realized my mistake, I had fucked up. The morning sun blazed into my eyes, I couldn't see shit! I was more likely to shoot Igor than a zombie.

Igor's rifle fired in rapid succession. I couldn't tell if he was suffering the same affliction as me and was being proactive by sending a hail of bullets down range, or if we were truly under attack. Something batted my rifle. I involuntarily pulled the trigger. The sound of shattering bone cracked over the din. I pressed outward. My only hope at this point was help from the rear. Whatever or whoever had been in front of me was now a few ounces heavier with lead poisoning. To my right, Igor's gun silenced as I sensed him go down. *Oh, this isn't good!* A rifle shot above my ear told me that BT had joined the skirmish.

"Can you see anything, BT?" I screamed over the blasts.

"I can see enough!" he yelled. "Get your white ass back into the jail." He didn't wait for a response as he literally lifted me up by my collar. My feet weren't even touching the ground as he pulled me back in. Jen and Brendon slammed the door shut, Travis placing the cross bar into place as the door was assaulted from the outside. I heard kids screaming, and some sobbing, but could still see nothing. I was snow blind.

"Fuck man! Fuck!" BT shouted. "There were dozens of them. When the door opened they came. They were waiting, Talbot! Waiting! Fuck!"

"What about Igor?" I asked. The silence in the room spoke volumes.

The short, intense battle had cost us dearly. And with nothing gained, the loss was felt throughout the room. April openly wept, the kids mostly hid under blankets, but these monsters were real, blankets weren't going to save them. My sight was coming back, but I didn't like what I was seeing. The zombies knew we had only one way out and had lain in wait. It was a textbook ambush. If they had waited a few seconds more until we were all outside they could have completely taken us. As my sight finally adjusted to the abysmal interior, they settled on Justin. He seemed the most apathetic of us all.

"What do you know?!" I screamed at him. Tracy ran up to shield Justin from me.

"What are you doing, Mike?" she yelled back.

"He knows something!" I shouted "And I want to know what it is." The rest of the occupants looked at me like I had finally lost my marbles. I attempted to push past Tracy to get to Justin. BT was having none of it.

"Have you lost your damn mind?" BT asked as he grabbed my arm.

I would have shrugged him off but I would have had an easier time taking a tire lug nut off with my fingers. You get the point, right?

"Fuck!" I shouted as I turned away. BT let go as he realized that my offensive had petered out.

"You done lost your mind, Talbot. The fight's outside," BT reiterated.

As if in response to BT's words, it became obvious that the zombies were realizing their opportunity at an ambush had come to an end. They were now launching an all-out offensive on the small sheriff's office. Shards of glass splashed inside as cut and bleeding arms shot through broken windows attempting to ensnare anything that might venture close enough to them. No matter how close or far we were to the windows we all backed up a step.

It was clear the zombies couldn't get in. It was also clear we couldn't get out. But just because they couldn't get in, didn't mean we could stay. We had left the majority of our supplies, including food, in the trucks...and they were outside. The thought had been that if we had to evacuate in a hurry we wouldn't be hampered with the added weight. Add in the fact that we now had central air conditioning installed via the broken windows, and we had a multitude of ways in which we could face our demise, none of which seemed that appealing. Let's see, we could start with starvation, but that could take up to ten days. There was always exposure, that would be quicker. Probably take approximately three days. Or the least savory of the trio, death by consumption, and not the kind that killed good Ol' Doc Holliday.

I went back to my cell. Calling it that seemed more apt at the moment. Paul came over to see how I was doing.

"You alright, bud? You seemed to have flipped there for a minute," he said.

If I had installed laser beams in my eyes he would have

been severed in two. The damn zombies had upgraded, why couldn't I?

"You know we're screwed right?" I asked him. He nodded in agreement.

"Mike, I never thought it would end like this," Paul said solemnly.

I let my sarcastic side out. "Like what, Paul? In a jail cell, in a fly speck of a town surrounded by zombies?" His head bowed even lower. Now I felt like a shit. "I'm sorry, man, it just came out."

He looked up at me. "Dude...no...you're right. Even with all that's been going on, I still haven't completely wrapped my head around the idea that what is happening is 'real.' Do you know what I mean?"

I nodded, because I did know what he meant. In horror book after horror book they talk about how it just seemed like a nightmare and eventually you will wake up and that werewolf chewing your leg off isn't real. The boogeyman that comes out of your closet in the middle of the night to steal your soul is merely fiction. We're just innately not built with the capacity to wrap our heads around things with this much magnitude. We push it aside or underneath; or we choose to completely ignore rather than accept what is directly in our face.

I knew this guy in high school, Jeff, he was a senior when I was a junior. He was going out with this girl Hillary who was arguably the hottest chick in the school. But that's neither here nor there. They were the epitome of the traditional high school sweethearts. They had known each other in grade school and as they matured, their relationship developed. They dated the entire four years of their high school experience. Upon graduating they went off to the same college so they could stay together, and during their sophomore year at college they decided to tie the knot. They wanted it to be a large, elaborate traditional wedding. They came back home during the Thanksgiving break to tell

—

everyone of their momentous decision, although it would have been to no one's amazement. But this isn't Oz, some douche bag decided to wash his car during a cold spell in the Northeast, the runoff from rinsing his car froze out on the street that night. Jeff lost control of his car and hit a UPS truck head on. When they finally extracted his 302 hp engine from Hillary's lap, her inner light had long expired. For the two weeks Jeff spent in the hospital he had to be constantly sedated because he would wander from room to room looking for her. I even heard that years later he would periodically call Hillary's parents and ask if she was home. How would any of us react to that set of circumstances?

The zombies were like that for us. It was a difficult concept to accept as reality. I even found myself sometimes wondering when I could go home and play with the Wii again, or mow the lawn, or just sit and watch a baseball game. But that was all over, whether I wanted to believe it or not. Our new reality involved monsters of mythical proportions. Every day was a struggle to survive. That was truth. Living was now a burden to be hefted onto one's shoulders until the accumulated weight of despair broke our backs.

Paul leaned in for a man hug. As I did my best to console him, my gaze was driven skyward because of his head.

"Holy shit!" I exclaimed as I nearly kneed Paul in the nose when I jumped up. I ran up to the cell bars trying my best to suppress my enthusiasm until I could make sure that the idea forming in my head could hold any water whatsoever.

"What is it, Mike?" Paul asked, doing his best to wipe away the tears that had built up under his eyes before I could notice. MAN CODE ALERT: Dudes don't cry in front of other dudes. They just merely 'Sit on their keys,' bringing a tear to one's eye.

Alex and BT had come over to watch and try to figure out why I was so interested in the bars.

"What's up, Talbot? You already going stir crazy?" BT asked. He laughed as he said it, probably thinking it was exactly what was happening.

Alex, however, was taking more notice of what I was doing. "Hex heads, Mike?"

I nodded. "All the way around, Alex," I answered enthusiastically.

"Who's a hex head?" BT said angrily, thinking that he might be the butt of a joke he didn't understand. Personally, that was like poking a bear holding a beehive. Why would you even want to go there?

"No, BT," Alex said, diffusing BT's ire. "The bars are mounted into the ceiling and walls with hex head screws."

"Who gives a shit?" BT asked "Hex heads, screws, nails, magnets, fucking bubble gum, what's the difference?"

"This means we can take them down," I answered with excitement in my voice. More people were taking notice, but I think only to witness the completion of my mental breakdown. "We're going to need tools, Alex."

"I'll look, Mike, but I'm still not sure what taking those down is going to accomplish," Alex said.

"Alex, how far away do you think the cab of the truck is?"

"Maybe five, six feet, seven at the most. Why?"

"How long across do you think these bars are?" I asked him.

"Eight...oh I see where you're going," Alex answered, happiness and hope spreading across his face.

"What?" BT asked. "I don't get it."

"Don't worry, big man. You're going to play an integral part in all this, that is, if we can find some tools," I told him.

BT didn't ask any more questions, but he did have a concerned look. Alex came back a few minutes later. "Man, all I could find was a pair of channel locks under the sink."

"Shit, not exactly what I was looking for, but it'll have to do. You sure there wasn't a ratchet set there, too?" I asked, only half kidding.

"Yeah, Mike, I'm holding out on you."

"See, you'll get this sarcasm thing down eventually."

"Let's hope."

That dampened the mood a bit, but it didn't extinguish the flame completely. It was slow, finger-cramping work, but an hour and a half later we had removed two cell bar assemblies. Of course it was the very last screw that threatened to sideline the whole plan. Repeated attempts at trying to remove the stubborn nut had turned the hex head into a near cylindrical fastener; only BT's unbelievably strong viselike grip was able to find purchase on the head. He didn't unscrew the nut, he sheered it off. Didn't matter to me how it came off, as long as it did.

CHAPTER 11

Mike's Journal Entry Nine

"Alright I'm going to need some help standing these things up," I told everybody. BT grabbed one set by himself. Travis, Brendon, and Alex grabbed the other. "BT, you want some help with that one? I need it over here, I want to lean the two sections together so they form an 'A.'"

BT strained, the cords in his neck stuck out like thick ropes as he manhandled the five hundred pound bars into place. "Holy shit, BT, what do you bench? Chevies?" The floor shook as he dropped the bars into place. I grabbed two sets of handcuffs and pulled a desk over to the bars so that I could reach the top. I fastened the bars together with the cuffs about a foot in on each side. On the bottom of the bars I had attached the two utility belts so that the bottom didn't flare out like a cheerleader doing the splits. It was Alex who came up with the idea to duct tape the police batons to the bottom. In theory, this would keep the assembly from collapsing under the impending assault.

"What are you planning on doing with this thing, Talbot?" BT asked. He knew the answer. I just think he wanted it spoken out loud.

"Have you ever been to the aquarium?" I asked him.

"Do I look like I've been to the aquarium?"

I didn't know how to answer the question, I wasn't sure

what the right answer was, and I had seen his Kung-Fu grip in action and didn't want any of it near my neck. I did what any good self-preservationist would do…I ignored it. "Okay, at some of the bigger aquariums they have underwater walkways so that people can view the fish and sharks in their own habitat. So basically we're making a zombie walkway."

"Is there a gift shop?" Brendon asked. After a few seconds of some good humored laughter from the group, I resumed.

"That was a good one, Brendon," I said wiping a tear away from my eye. MAN CODE note, it is acceptable to shed a tear in front of others if it is due to excessive laughter or if one's sporting team wins a major event, i.e. the Red Sox in the 2004 World Series.

"Dad," Travis said pointing to the windows. "Do you think they know what's going on?"

The zombies were not completely standing idle, their arms still futilely waved about trying to grasp anything that might be foolish enough to wander close, and there was still that soft, high-pitched mewling that would probably make me insane long before I ever froze to death. But the arms weren't waving around quite as frantically and the mewling had softened noticeably. And the look in some of their eyes was almost questioning, like they were trying to puzzle out this new factor.

"Let's thin this herd a little bit, give them something else to think about," I answered. If this failed, there was no contingency plan.

"We don't have a shit load of ammo in here, Mike," Brendon said. Needlessly I might add. I had struggled with this decision last night with how much ammo to bring in, and I had come up wanting.

"I don't want a sustained fire fight. I just want them to remember that we're still in charge. And watch out for the bars, I don't want any ricochets," I explained.

Travis, BT and Brendon lined up for the firing squad.

Everyone else had pretty much gone as far back to the rear as was physically possible.

"Hey, Trav, you should probably get back there, too. That buckshot will bounce right off the bars."

That, in part, was why I wanted him off the line. The other more significant issue was that he looked entirely too eager to be a part of the killing. I was afraid for him. Bloodlust can overwhelm even the strongest of men, and my son had just barely joined the rank of manhood. I had seen it enough in Iraq, once the sickness got in you, it was damn near impossible to eradicate it. Squads would go into remote villages in the mountains and just slaughter everything: men, women, children, goats, it made no difference. If it spilled blood and could die, it was fair game. The higher echelons usually covered these transgressions, usually with a rocket attack to wipe out any evidence.

"No sweat, Dad, I switched over to slugs," Travis answered with a smile.

"Fuck," I muttered.

What good was surviving if we had to drag our souls through the mud? I might not be a holy man, but I was still afraid of what God would think when I showed up at the pearly gates dragging the dilapidated leftovers of my shredded soul.

"So, Michael Talbot, what have you done in your life that warrants your entrance into this the most Holy of Sanctuaries?" God, Saint Peter, or Buddha, might ask.

"I survived," would be my meek reply. Might as well have said "Blue! No, No, Yellow!!" Right before I was launched into the abyss. (You would have to be a fan of *Monty Python and the Search for the Holy Grail* to catch the reference. If you have by some chance gone this far in your life and have not witnessed one of the greatest comedies created then odds are you're not going to find a DVD player that works now, sorry.)

My meager portion of breakfast was not sitting well and I

---

did not want to sour it any further. I went back to the cell where Nicole and Tracy were sitting. Justin was facing away from the windows, presumably sleeping, but I don't know how with all the noise we had been making. Tommy was sitting in the corner, holding an unopened bag of Pop-Tarts. That more than the expression of woe on his face told me that he was extremely upset. I was about to ask him what was the matter when the first volley of shots exploded within the confined area. I covered my ears, as did almost everyone else. Within a minute the shooting had stopped. It would be another fifteen before the choking smoke cleared.

I walked over to Tommy and put my hand on his shoulder. "You all right, Tommy?"

Tommy looked up. "He's close, Mr. T," he stammered out.

"Is Ryan back?" I asked. That would be the best thing I had heard today.

"No, it's someone else," he answered somberly.

My ass clamped tight. I don't know why, it was an involuntary reaction to Tommy's words. Apparently my body thought it was the right thing to do, who's to say. I turned back to face the windows and it was a sight to behold – not a zombie in view.

With renewed hope and an unclenching sphincter I asked, "Did you get them all?"

"Naw, Mike, they left," Brendon answered.

"Son of a bitch, that's something new. They usually hang around for their punishment." We had all witnessed hundreds of zombies walking into sheets of lead without so much as a pause while their 'comrades-in-mouths' fell. That these zombies were smart enough to realize the pointlessness of staying at the windows was foreboding.

"We killed a good ten or fifteen of them, Dad," Travis said beaming.

BT cautiously walked up to the window to better survey the damage done and to try to assess our odds of success.

"What's going on, BT? Can you see anything?" Alex asked.

"Yeah, damnedest thing. They pulled back about hundred feet or so and they are just standing there looking at me."

"How many?" I asked. *Please say, two maybe three PLEASE!*

"Two maybe three...hundred."

Well, that's what you get for wishing, how many times my mother told me to be more specific when I asked for something, I thought in disgust.

"They're just kind of standing out there in a loose semicircle. Guys, I wouldn't want to bet my life on it, but they look like they're waiting for something."

"Or somebody," I finished.

"Mike, what if the zombies at the window were just a distraction?" Alex asked me. A new thought furrowing his brow.

It took me a quick second to get over the initial shock of how many zombies we were contending with. "How so, Alex?"

"I mean we knew they couldn't get to us...and I think they knew they couldn't get to us. But they sure did keep us away from the windows," Alex stated. "That would keep us in the dark to how many of them were out there."

"Or they were just stalling us," I said. These new developments were coming faster than I could recognize them.

"What's going on, Mike? You seem to know more than you're letting on," Alex asked.

"Not really, Alex. It's just a feeling I'm getting. I don't have any *knowledge*, but all the same, I think the quicker we get out of here the better off we're going to be."

Alex kept looking at my face hard, trying to glean some inkling to what I was feeling. There was nothing there to give him.

"Brendon, can you hit the zombies from here?"

"Shit yeah, Mike. It's a hundred feet. I used to shoot gophers at a hundred yards back in Missouri."

"Take a shot every few seconds so that they don't get any crazy ideas about coming back. Apparently the thought of dying again doesn't sit well with them. Jen, you ready for round two with the door?"

She stomped out her cigarette and nodded grimly.

"BT, how much help will you need pushing our causeway through the door?" I asked.

"Seriously, Talbot?" BT answered, looking at me like I had asked him if he could cut up his steak by himself.

"Fine, BT, but we're not going to have a lot of time for you to build up a head of steam and get that thing going. The fucker's got to weigh half a ton."

"You worry about protecting my ass. I'll get this to the truck."

"Alex, I want you to put on as much clothing as you can and still be able to move, including gloves."

"Why don't I just make a run for it? They're a hundred feet away, I only have to go six. I'm not Speedy Gonzalez, but shit, a tortoise would like those odds."

"I've got a feeling, Alex, that as soon as we open that door they've got a surprise waiting for us."

"Yeah this plan just gets better and better," Alex answered grimly as he grabbed a pair of sweat pants that he had been using as a pillow.

"See, hang around with me for a few more weeks and you'll be able to pass as a New Englander, no problem."

Alex grumbled something in Spanish; it had to be swear words...and a colorful variety, too, because his wife was trying to shield her kids' ears.

Alex looked like a sumo by the time he was finished, I thought it might be better to roll him to his destination. The killjoy didn't see the humor in my revelation and he let me know in no uncertain terms. We positioned the bars by the door. BT rolled his neck in a large circle in preparation. Jen had her hand on the handle. Alex was dripping sweat as he waited tensely for the shortest sprint in human history. Brendon kept the zombie crowd at bay. Travis and I positioned ourselves on either side of the door to lay covering fire when and if needed. The plan was ready, and it looked pretty damn good on paper if I do say so myself. Too bad the paper wasn't of the toilet variety, because the plan went to shit in a hurry.

"Ready?" Jen asked everyone.

No, I thought, but I nodded.

The door swung open and hell came through. (Actually, all hell broke loose, but poetically the original sentence sounds way better. I might be fighting for my life, but it doesn't mean I can't go for the dramatic overtones.) My hunch proved to be true, much to my chagrin. Why do my hunches always involve the negative? Couldn't I have ever had a hunch about the winning lottery numbers? I could have been waiting out the apocalypse in my gun turreted castle somewhere in the mountains of Vail.

When Jen stepped clear of the door, the first of the zombies tried to gain entry. I can only figure that they were hiding against the exterior wall in the event that we would open the door. There could be no other explanation. Travis' shotgun roared; I immediately found myself covered in a visceral mixture of bone and brain. The salty, metal taste of blood drained down my throat. I would have puked if I had had enough time to really comprehend what was happening. The zombies Brendon was 'holding' at bay broke for the opening in our defenses as soon as the first of their brethren hit the ground.

The bars started their slow arduous journey forward. A couple of things stuck out immediately. The first was the disgusting taste of raw innards as they made their way down my gullet. The second was that the bars weren't moving nearly fast enough to beat our adoring fans to the truck. The third and possibly the most important was the quarter-inch high threshold that was about to become a major roadblock. BT had managed to get the bars to within a foot of the doors and he was gaining momentum. Through it all Travis' gun roared as he kept our attackers away.

As soon as BT hit that threshold, those bars would stop and then we'd be sunk, the door to the building wouldn't be able to close and we would have built an awning for our guests to arrive through before they dined. All we needed was a red carpet. We were all about ambiance at Club Chez, home of the delectable jellied brain.

"PULL IT BACK!" I screamed.

"I can do it, Talbot," BT grunted.

"Dad, I'm out!" Travis yelled. "Look out!"

I had turned to yell at BT, but when I looked back over towards Travis, the terror in his eyes told me all that I needed to know. My time on earth was measured in seconds. Jen's pistol destroyed what little hearing remained in my right ear. If she had fired her shot any closer, she could have made a lead earring for me. The world around me was reduced to the bitter smell of smoke and the incessant ringing in my ears. Travis seemed to be yelling something. I couldn't hear it. BT had completely ignored my plea. Jen, I think, was still shooting her pistol; but by now, all I could hear was a distant crack, like maybe somebody was slapping a baby's ass two rooms away.

I had a second or two to decide what to do, although there was no real choice, so it was basically like when my wife would ask me to do something. She would ASK because it was the civilized thing to do, but I didn't really have the choice of NOT doing it.

Before BT completely sealed off the door, I stepped outside and through the outer edge of our makeshift 'A' frame. BT looked at me like I had gone insane, I gave credit to him though, he didn't stop pushing. The leading edge was, at the most, three inches from the threshold by the time I got a good handhold on the bars.

It was at this point I was probably the most thankful that I suffered from the affliction known as 'survivalism' because I was almost completely sure that the world was going to end badly, one way or the other. I had stayed in relatively decent shape over the years. I had done miles and miles of cardio and tons and tons of weight lifting (obviously I'm talking cumulatively). I wouldn't be able to beat BT in an arm wrestling competition even if I used both arms and a leg, but there was an underlying strength there that might not be obvious at first notice. I bent slightly at the knees and thrust up like I was Superman trying to leap a tall building. The resulting effect wasn't nearly as cool as seeing the Man of Steel jump. Something felt like it splintered in my back. Red pain flared out, wrapping around the base of my skull. The pain was all-consuming. All my other senses were lost. The world turned scarlet as I fought against the laws of gravity. My heart pumped in overdrive. Adrenaline flooded every fiber of my being. The curtain of ruby parted slightly as I strained upward. The bars moved a fraction of an inch or my ankles collapsed, either way something was giving.

The bars had cleared the threshold! I might never walk erect again, but perpetually going through life dragging my knuckles like our predecessors (if you believe in that kind of thing) seemed a small price to pay. My celebration was short lived. BT had the bars moving at a good clip, but he was still a good two feet away from the truck when the first of our party crashers made their presence known.

Through all the gun smoke I could tell that BT wasn't alone in his efforts to move the behemoth, but it wasn't going to be enough. The zombies were going to come through the opening and the first thing they were going to encounter was me. Well, no one said you had to stand up straight to fire a gun.

There was a moment's hesitation from the lead zombies as they banged up against the bars in frustration, but these weren't your daddy's zombies. These had the ability to learn and adapt. Through the opening they flooded. I was alone and trapped in a tunnel with the enemy. My AR was firing almost on its own. Zombies fell. Bone was devastated, blood spilled, innards became disemboweled. Sure, my sight was still recovering from the blistering pain, and my hearing was nearly nonexistent, but SMELL, lovely SMELL was 100% intact. What a cruel, cruel world we lived in now.

The smell more than anything nearly sapped my will to live. I dropped to one knee as the olfactory invasion hit me with its full force. Intestines slithered toward me with a mind of their own as the red ribbons spilled forth their contents. I retched. The sight of a small child's fingers, one still wearing what looked like a Barbie ring came to a rest mere inches from where my face would hit the ground when I passed out.

I felt the low thrum of vibration as the bars completed their journey, smacking into the side of the truck. Before I had the opportunity to fall forward, someone grabbed me from behind and dragged me back through into the office. The smell of shit that was probably forever burned into my nose decreased, but conversely, whatever had popped in my back and ankle renewed their fervor of agony. Scarlet again threatened to overwhelm my senses, and all I could think about was that I now had an excuse to not go dancing when my wife asked me to. (Go back to the part about ASKING.)

I was dragged unceremoniously a few feet further into the office. It was no big deal. The pain at this point couldn't get any worse. It was many long minutes that I took to recover from the worst of it. It receded slowly, like high tide. It kept coming in to shore but each progressive wave just a wee bit shorter than the previous. Five, six days max I might feel decent again.

"Mike! Mike!" someone said urgently as they shook my shoulder. High tide surged in with the force of a full moon.

"Fuck, stop," I said weakly, holding up my hand.

"Sorry, Mike," Alex said.

I wanted to say it was nothing, but the energy exerted to

tell the lie didn't seem worth the effort.

"Mike, what do we do once I get to the truck and pull away?"

I wanted to tell him to go to a pharmacy first and get me some Percocet. Then find a little Asian masseuse (I wouldn't even care if she was cute or not) to do some deep tissue massage on every part of my aching body. But again, that would call for a lot of effort on my flagging reserves and with no real promise of a pay out on my requests. What was the point?

"Mike?!" He nearly shook me again, but I think the look of wretchedness in my eyes kept him at bay. "As soon as I pull away, you'll have an opening back into the office."

"The best laid plans," I said. I had never thought that far. I figured that once we had access to the truck everything else would fall into place. Yeah, not so much. Once the truck was gone, we would effectively open up our restaurant for business. Brainer King's, McFleshald's, take your pick. The devil is in the details.

"A few might follow the truck, but once the rest see that hole, they'll come flooding in here," Alex reiterated.

BT thumped down next to me. Even in my distress I could tell he was exhausted, sweat droplets the size of nickels dotted his forehead. His shirt was soaked. He hung his head down, taking deep breaths. "You did all right, Talbot," he said with his chin touching his chest.

"You too, BT," I said between clenched teeth.

"You look like you broke your nuts."

"I might have, BT," came my glum reply. "But I'm married, so I don't really need them."

Even in his wiped out state I still was able to receive a healthy laugh from him.

"Mike," Alex beseeched.

"Right, I almost forgot." Well, maybe not so much *not* remembering as it was wishful deniability.

"What's up?" BT asked as he raised his head off his

chest.

"Once the truck leaves, we'll have an open door policy."

BT looked at me for a second, digesting the new information.

"I guess you didn't think this out too well?" BT stated flatly. And then he did something completely unexpected. He busted out laughing. It was infectious. In between moans I was laughing, too, tears streaming out of my eyes. I won't lie, some were from the pain, but most were from the sheer mad hatter laugh.

"What the fuck, Mike?" Alex said so seriously, I burst out with a whole new round of gut-splitting (bad example in light of recent events) laughter.

"Sorry, sorry," I said, grabbing on to my stomach to ease the muscle spasms. "Okay, I'm fine, sorry." Alex's look of consternation set me off again. BT was literally prostrate on the floor slapping his hand down on the ground because he was laughing so hard. "Okay, I'm better now," I said through a huge grin that threatened to split my face in two, though some might consider that an improvement.

BT sat back up, wiping his broad forehead with his hand. "Whew. I think I'm done." He looked over to me, and I'm pretty sure the pathetic look on my face is what set him off again. Riotous laughter exploded from BT; even the zombies stopped moaning for a second.

After several long moments, BT was able to finally string a question together. "Did you swallow some?" BT asked.

"Swallow what?" I asked innocently as the bile in my stomach churned.

"Talbot, you have a piece of what looks like a liver on your chin."

I absently wiped the incriminating evidence away, while also shuddering in revulsion.

"What happens if he eats a zombie? Does he become one?" Eddy, one of the previously silent children, asked.

Ah, precocious kids, don't you just want to throw them

up against a wall and see if they stick?

BT looked at me like I had the answer to Eddy's query.

"How the fuck would I know?" I answered his unasked question.

"You'd probably have to have an ulcer or something so that the infection could get into your blood stream." Joann stepped up and gave her educated guess.

"Well, what of it, Talbot, you got any ulcers?" BT asked with not a hint of his earlier merriment.

"Shit, BT, even if I did, do you think now would be the time for me to disclose that?"

BT didn't know whether to shoot me or laugh his ass off again.

Tracy saved the day. "BT, he doesn't give a shit enough about anything besides himself to develop an ulcer."

That was all it took. BT's threatening stance instantly turned back to laughter. I hoped Tracy and Joann were right and Eddy could go fuck himself. My stomach lurched under the strain of digesting the zombie's unmentionables.

I was SO ready to let go again and join BT, although this trip down the rabbit hole might lead me to a rubber room. But let's reason this out, if you are out-of-your mind insane in a sane world, then it is like algebra, you have a negative times a positive, so that makes it a negative. So far so good. Now if you are an off-your-rocker lunatic in a demented, deranged world, then you have a negative times a negative, which is a positive. I think I was on to something. It was like the old adage, if you can't beat them, become as crazy as a fucking loon and enjoy the ride, or something along those lines.

BT had finished up his latest laugh-spell and was looking over to me while I was pondering the benefits of psychosis. "So what's the plan, Talbot?"

"Huh? Oh, what the hell makes you think I've got a plan?"

"I've known you long enough, Talbot. I haven't seen you

yet *not* have a plan, whether they are good or not doesn't matter, you still always have one."

"Fine, but you're not going to like it."

"Does it involve me getting eaten by those ugly freaks?" he asked, motioning with his head over to the door.

I spent the next minute laying out what I wanted to get done (it wasn't much of a plan, so it didn't require much narration).

"Yeah you're right, I don't like it," BT moaned. He stood up, preparing his body for the task at hand.

I looked up with an imploring expression.

"Really?" BT asked. I just kept staring at him with what I hope were puppy dog eyes. "Fine," he said, shaking his head.

BT got behind me and put his forearms under my armpits. He hefted me up no harder than if I was a ten pound bag of dog shit (which I felt like). My knees cracked like rifle shots as they flexed open. I took three or four shaky steps before my lower back finally decided to disengage its fusion from my ass.

"You're a sight, Mike," Alex said.

"That's what my wife says," I answered as I placed my fist into my lower back, hoping in vain to unloosen the sailor knot that most likely was going to be a perpetual fixture in my ever widening list of painful areas.

"Don't flatter yourself," Tracy threw in for good measure. She rubbed the sore spot as best she could, but this was going to take a team of Svens (Swedish masseuses) working around the clock a couple of years to fix.

"Dad, you alright?" Nicole asked, coming up to my side and hugging me, although I think she was trying to make sure I didn't fall over. To confirm my suspicion, she whispered into my ear, "You can lean on me."

"It's tolerable," I lied. She knew. Funny how parents want to protect their kids even when the truth is right there in front of God and everyone.

"Talbot, come on, man. I want to get this over with," BT

said grudgingly from across the room. Alex nodded in agreement.

"Dad?" Coley asked. The concern was etched deeply in her small features.

"I'm fine," I answered, doing the best I could to make my shuffling walk look like a cockney strut. And trying to make my scowl of pain look like the traditional happy-go-lucky smile I generally walked around with. If the entire world's a stage, and we are merely players, I would never earn an Emmy for my performance that day.

"Alex, you ready?" A superfluous question, but one that needed asking anyway.

The poor guy was sweating profusely from the mountain of clothing that he was wearing. Well, that and the fact that he was about to make a dash through a throng of hungry meat-eaters. He looked at me like I was fucking nuts. *Ah, so my plan was working already. Lithium here I come!*

"In or out?" BT asked.

Sarcasm is going to get me killed sooner rather than later. "What's that, your sex-ed book?"

BT wasn't nearly as close to his slap happy mood as he had been a few minutes previous.

"The bars, Talbot, what do you want me to do with them?"

"In," I said solemnly.

"I knew it, two feet to get it out the door, six feet to get it back in."

"I'm just trying to ascertain that you are truly involved with the synergy of this colossal undertaking. It's going to be a team effort, something in which we are all going to have to pull together and think outside of…"

"Fuckin' stop, Talbot," BT pleaded. "I was a project manager for a while before I decided to de-stress my life. Zombies I can handle. Corporate-speak bullshit…well that's a different matter. I swore that if I ever had to listen to one more suit-and-tie or dog-and-pony conference call, I was going to go postal."

"Did you know that's a misnomer? For the amount of the workforce, the percentage of violence in the post office is below that of the national average for workplace violence."

"What's the percentage in sheriff's offices?"

I got the point and shut up.

A few moments later, I stood at the door, plumes of human exhaust issuing from my mouth. I watched as zombies pressed into our makeshift walkway from both sides. Their arms nearly met in the middle, it was not going to be a fun walk for Alex. I shivered at the thought of all those germ-infested hands reaching out and touching someone, hopefully not me.

"We're going to have to push the bars outside, BT," I told him.

"I wish you'd make up your mind," he grumbled.

"We'll never be able to pull it in with all those zombies pressing in on it."

Alex was standing next to me looking like a bowling ball with a sweater on. More sweat popped on his brow as he looked down the expanse of the gate; all that could be seen was a sea of arms and fingernails. As if on cue we turned to look at the huddled form of Justin in the far corner. One didn't have to be bitten to suffer some effects from the zombies.

"Mike, I'm losing my taste for this quest," Alex said.

"If you stay low, Alex, there is a clear pathway," I said it, but I didn't believe it. It was clear now, when the zombies saw him they would adjust to get closer.

Brendon had been behind us the whole time, just waiting for some sort of instructions or plan. "This sucks," he said more to himself than anyone else. The sentiment was appreciated by us all.

"I hear that freezing to death isn't so bad," I said with a touch of resignation.

BT looked pissed. He burned some frustration by

shooting a few rounds into the growing mass of zombies. As one zombie fell, two moved in to take its place. We'd never be able to fire enough rounds to clear a wide enough hole for Alex. First off would be the fear of hitting him inadvertently; the other was that we just didn't have enough rounds to keep up a continuous barrage of bullets. The roach motel moniker looked like it was going to stick.

"FUCK!" I shouted. A baby let loose a long throated wail as if in response. "Sorry," I muttered earnestly.

The office had become as quiet as a church. "Mommy, I found some sleds," one of the little kids said eagerly.

"Hush now, Eddy," his mother answered him.

I turned to look, if only to be distracted from what lay outside. I walked over to little Eddy, who looked suspiciously like a little old man. His mother pulled Eddy close to herself and shied away from my advancing form.

"He didn't mean anything, Mr. Talbot, he was just exploring...you...you know like little kids do," she said nervously. "I...I promise he'll be good and quiet."

"It's fine, Miss...?"

"Jodi, Jodi Ybarra."

"Jodi, everything's fine. Do you mind if I talk to Eddy?"

"Sure...sure," she said nervously. This lady looked like a cat that had had her tail stepped on one too many times. She was ready to jump at the smallest infraction.

I sat down on my haunches, instantly regretting my decision to get down to Eddy's level. My knees felt like they were going to shoot straight out of my jeans like Roman candles on the Fourth of July. Well, I was here now, might as well get down to business.

"Whatcha you got there, Eddy?" I asked with my nicest voice, but that was in direct contradiction to the distorted sneer I wore on my face from the blistering pain that was emanating from my knees and back.

Eddy looked at me nervously, trying to ascertain my true intent. But like any six-year-old, exuberance won out. "I found a sled!"

"Do you mind if I take a look at it?"

Eddy eyed me suspiciously like I was going to take his prized possession. I felt for him, I truly did, he had already lost almost everything he had owned. But the riot shield he was holding might be the solution to all our problems.

"Sure, mister, there was a whole closet of them."

"Awesome, do you think you could help me back up?"

Eddy looked at me like I was crazy. "Adults are funny," he answered.

I have to admit, the little bugger was a lot stronger than he looked. He didn't buckle once as I placed almost all my weight on his shoulder in a concerted effort to arise like Lazarus. Lazarus was more successful.

"Can you show me where the sleds are Eddy?" He stepped back as my right knee popped like a firecracker.

"Wow, that was cool! Can you do it again?"

"I'd rather bite the head off a bat."

I could tell Eddy was wondering if I was serious or not, and also when I might get around to doing just that, because that would also be awesome.

A minute later, Brendon, Travis, Alex, BT, and I were standing behind a beaming Eddy who seemed very pleased with himself that he was the one who found something that we were all so excited to see.

I pulled out a large dusty box from the back of the sheriff's coat closet. The box had suspiciously been ripped open from the bottom. Eddy flushed as the damaged box came into full view.

I tousled his hair. "You did good, kid." He stood up straighter, pride swelling his small chest.

BT finished what Eddy had started. Three more 'sleds' spilled on to the floor along with at least ten gun shaped Tasers, boxes of shotgun bean bag rounds, and canisters of tear gas, along with five gas masks.

"Why in the hell does a sheriff's office in the friggin

middle of nowhere have all this gear?" Brendon asked.

I shook my head.

BT spoke up. "Back after 9/11, when the feds thought that a terrorist plot was being hatched everywhere, they sent these riot control packages to just about every police force in the country."

"Ah, our federal tax dollars at work," Alex said sarcastically.

"Yeah this shit just might save our lives, though," I answered. Alex nodded in agreement.

Travis was busy grabbing the bean bag rounds, they might not be fatal; but up close they could still do some real damage.

CHAPTER 12

Mike's Journal Entry Ten

"Ready?"

"Why do you keep asking me that, Mike?" Alex fumed, his body heat creating a sauna in his makeshift armor. "I just want to get this over with so I can get out of all these clothes."

"Brendon, you all set?" I asked. His stance said he was all set, but his eyes belied him.

BT must have picked up on Brendon's hesitancy because for the fourth time he offered to do what Brendon was about to.

I looked at BT with my best expression of exasperation. "BT, we've been through this."

"But he's just a kid, Talbot."

"Dad?" Nicole asked, her eyes expressing volumes. Her unspoken words were "why was I putting her fiancé in danger?"

I had fully intended on playing the role Brendon was about to embark on, but my ankles, knees, and back made a stand-in necessary.

"Who else, Nicole?" I begged for her forgiveness.

The hurt of being let down shone through clearly in her eyes. The pain of my injuries paled in comparison.

"Talbot, there has got to be a better way," Tracy chimed

in.

"*Et tu, Brutus?*" I said in desperation.

"Mike, let's do this," Brendon said, saving me from the accusations as he hefted up two riot shields. Covering most of his front and all of his sides he looked like the world's largest beetle. I prayed that it would be enough.

"Just hit the hole hard and always keep your legs moving," Travis the football player threw in for good measure.

"Alex, you stay close in behind him. But if he gets stuck you have to come back," I said, the implied meaning obvious to everyone. If Brendon couldn't break a hole through the zombies he would be at their mercy, and that was not an attribute they possessed.

"Mike, for God's sake, I can't leave him behind!" Alex beseeched.

"There is no God," I said flatly.

Marta hastily did the sign of the trinity on her chest in preparation to ward off the Almighty's smiting of my heresy.

"Alex, the train is leaving, you coming?" Brendon asked. He turned to give my weeping daughter a long soulful kiss.

I turned away, embarrassed, and yes…I have to admit, a little pissed. She would always be my little girl, if only in my memories, but that illusion was threatened every time I had to witness these intrusions into my fantasy world. It was much easier in my own world not having to think of my little princess doing adult things…much, much easier.

Nicole's disappointment in me was clear as her gaze slid across my face before she turned to go further back into the jailhouse, hesitant to witness firsthand the events that were about to occur. No matter how this turned out, Nicole and I had just come to a turning point in our relationship. No longer would she look to me as the man that could solve all of her problems, another tiny death suffered. Each one amounted to a paper cut on my soul; as they stood singly, not enough to kill me, but cumulatively they would fray the vestiges of my humanity.

"Stay low," I offered.

Brendon snorted twice, he was psyching himself up. The zombies pressed in on the bars, their arms swinging wildly back and forth like speed metal concert-goers on crack. Brendon backed up ten feet to get as much speed going as was possible. Alex had a tough time keeping up being encumbered in his extra clothing. The plan almost came to a screeching, devastating halt as Brendon failed to heed my last words to him. The top right edge of his shield clipped the bars as he entered into the opening. His forward momentum spun him to the right. He nearly toppled over and into the arms of the zombies. God, divine intervention, sheer blind luck, who fuckin' knows, but something kept him from going over. Alex had just reached the opening as Brendon's shield made first contact.

Ulnas, radii and humorous bones first bent unnaturally, twisted perversely, and then snapped normally. Brendon's propulsion, even with the stumbling, easily took him halfway to his destination. I tried my best to equate the snapping of bones to that of wood being chopped. It didn't work so well, more than one person in our group became sick from the explosion of noise. The forest of arms persisted though, and I could see that Brendon's initial thrust was slowing. The danger was that once the injured zombies retreated and their healthier brethren filled in the void, any chance of escape would be cut off. We didn't have the ammo or safe enough shooting angles to extract them. He would literally be four feet away, but it might as well be four thousand.

Alex, sensing that they weren't moving forward fast enough, plowed into Brendon's back willing him forward through sheer sense of desperation and instinct. Miraculously or not, some of the last zombies on the line pulled their arms out, most likely to try to prevent any unnecessary injuries. What would a good zombie doctor charge for a house call out in the country? A chicken brain at the least? A cow brain max.

Brendon stepped onto the truck's running board, placing his shield between the truck and the cage. It was a tight fit, but Alex was able to get between Brendon and the bars to heft himself into the cab. Brendon quickly followed, dropping the shields down into the prying arms of the resurging enemy.

"Hope he's got the keys," BT said as he stepped up alongside me.

"Not fucking funny, BT. Not fucking funny at all." I knew it was a joke, but the relief that flooded through me when I heard the truck engine turn over was palpable – if only to myself.

Brendon gave me the thumbs up sign. Now I knew it was our turn. Once that truck pulled away we would have seconds to clear the cage from the door, and judging by the added weight of all the zombies that were still tangled up in it this was not going to be easy. But *"Is anything worthwhile in life ever easy?"* as my dad would say. I guess life is worthwhile, ergo it made sense that we should try as hard as we could to make this happen.

"Wouldn't it just be easier if they tied the gate to the truck and just pulled it away?" Joann asked, having come up to get a closer look.

Without turning to face her I answered. "Easier if it worked, disastrous if it didn't." I didn't wait for her to ask the inevitable 'How so?' I kept rambling on. "If the gate doesn't come straight out, there's a good chance he'd rip the door frame right out of this building. No sense in having a door if we don't have anything to close it on. Second, the gate could get hung up under the truck, and if that truck gets stopped…"

"I get the picture," Joann answered.

I could feel her shudder, the tiny fluctuations of displaced air rippled up my arms. I had sympathy shudders with her, that or someone had walked over my grave, which I hoped wasn't in the nearby vicinity. Somewhere in Quebec would be cool. Hell, Switzerland would be even better. I figured my odds of actually getting across the sea were slim, so if my grave was there...you see where I'm going with this, right? Yeah, me neither.

Brendon was still holding his thumb up waiting for my reply. I was not in such a rush to mess with the status quo. This status quo had us alive, and who knows what was in store once we switched over.

"BT, Trav, and anyone else that thinks they can get a hand in here, let's go," I said as I placed my hands onto the gate. BT and Travis were immediately to my left and right sides. There were no other takers.

I nodded once to Brendon and turned to BT. "You remember we're pushing, right?"

He grimaced in response. I wasn't happy. I'm into clear and concise, not vague and gray-like. The truck pulled away, and for a fleeting moment, I thought that was the end of us. The weight of the zombies pushing on the bars made it nearly impossible to move. I was resigned to becoming zombie chow. Maybe if I was lucky some zombie chef would make a nice *pâté* out of my liver. My knee literally screamed in protest. NO, I mean I really heard it. Sure, it was in my head, but it was saying 'DUDE WHAT ARE YOU DOING! THIS REALLY, REALLY HURTSSSSSSS!' or something to that effect.

Whatever ligaments were still precariously attached to my patella did everything in their power to stay attached and give me some forward thrust. But if not for the super human strength of BT, we would have been sunk. Hell, I probably could have been pulling against the bars and he still would have forced them through the doors.

The truck was no more than twenty feet away from the gate when some of the zombies that had graduated from Brain Rending And Intestine Nibbling (B.R.A.I.N.) University discovered there was a way in. The bars were moving...but by fractions of inches (or millimeters for you more European thinking folks). Point was that time was not on our side. I couldn't decide if I should abandon my post and go on the defensive or keep pushing. BT was unaware of how close we were to our demise. His eyes were closed with the intense effort he was expending to move the behemoth gate. Zombies were in the gate, and the lead one was eyeing me like I was the last McRib sandwich for the season. Eight feet equated to about a second and a half of sweet life remaining.

Explosions ripped from below my waist, for one horrifying moment I really thought that the stress I was putting on my body had made me cut a hellacious fart. *Just fucking great, my last moments on Earth were going to be punctuated with a great gas blast. And then again maybe that wasn't such a bad thing.* Another Monty Python reference. Me being the French and the Zombies being King Arthur. "I fart in your general direction!" (You should really try to find a backup generator so you can watch this movie in whatever shelter you have deemed safe enough to wait out Armageddon. But can you really wait out Armageddon? I mean just by its implied meaning, it IS the end of the world.) YES, in the millisecond it took for the explosion to register in my ears and then for me to realize that it was not the largest release of natural gas through my ass, all the above went through my head. Curse or blessing, or a more strange mixture of both, my mind is always approaching the speed of light. I'll let you know when I can find the on/off switch.

Another explosion shattered my thoughts, or more likely coalesced the more important ones. I hastened a quick look down below me and saw something that was INFINITELY more scary than anything that was coming at me. A gun toting, man-hating lesbian carrying a huge pistol was situated in the one-kneed position between my spread legs firing off high caliber, high speed, genital-crushing rounds. I willed the bars forward. I wanted out of this predicament as fast as was humanly possible.

"MOVE!" Joann shouted from off to our right.

I for one did not need to be told even once. I pulled Travis out of the way of the crashing door. The office shook as the door slammed home. My knees were shaking, mostly from the pain, but some…some of it was from Jen's shooting.

"Looks like Mike just put a cork on a wine bottle," Mrs. Deneaux said from off to the side of the room.

"Excuse me?" my wife asked her in as nice a tone as she could contrive. But seething beneath the surface was a fury looking for a place to be unleashed. I didn't say a word, lest that luminous ire shine my way.

Mrs. Deneaux took many moments to answer Tracy. She took two full inhales from her cigarette and answered on her second exhale, the smoke somehow punctuating her words. "I said, it looks like Mike just put a cork on a wine bottle."

"I know what you said, you old bat!" Tracy burned. (I was doing an imaginary fist bump with her, 'You go, girl!')

Mrs. Deneaux was made of stauncher stuff than I had given her credit for, though. No one in their right mind would ever call Tracy anything but a petite woman, but with anger issuing forth from every pore in her body, she looked like she could pull the sagging gray-green skin right off of Mrs. Deneaux's old bones. But yet the 'old bat' as Tracy so eloquently put it, didn't bat an eyelash at Tracy's harsh words.

"Oh, honey," Mrs. Deneaux rasped through her smoke tortured throat. "I didn't mean anything by it."

"The FUCK you didn't!" Tracy screamed, her finger stopping just short of puncturing Deneaux's larynx. This time Deneaux did step back. "All the good people that died, and you survived! That above every other fucked up thing that has happened proves to me there is no GOD!"

The entire room held its collective breath – even the babies. How the hell they knew what was going on, I don't know. I went over to Tracy and grabbed her by the waist, pulling her close to me; she sobbed softly on my shoulder.

"Really, I didn't mean anything by it," Mrs. Deneaux said to a room full of deaf ears.

The truck came back a few minutes later, but it felt like hours. Time stretched worse than in a *Twilight Zone* episode. Mrs. Deneaux finally shuffled off to be with her nephew. Even he seemed reluctant to acknowledge her. Family duty, though, bound him to the task. He shrugged his shoulders at me, whether to let me know 'What can you do? She's an old cantankerous bitch.' or 'Don't lump me in with this old cantankerous bitch.' I wasn't sure. We all turned as the familiar telltale sounds of a truck backing up impeded our individual conversations.

"What's he doing?" I said, more to say something than to gain a response.

"Backing up I would imagine," Joann said seriously. She seemed to be holding onto this small piece of hope with both hands.

"We can't go through the gate, Talbot," BT said matter-of-factly.

"Why?" Joann asked. It was hard to watch the hope sail out of her like a popped balloon.

"Umm well let's see—" I started.

Thankfully (because I didn't have to do it) or not (because he was a prick about it) Justin had the ill-temper to quash out whatever remnants of promise Joann hung onto as he answered in my stead. "Because the inside of the gate is full of dead zombies and the outside is full of live ones." He laughed, dark circles under his eyes lending menace to his words.

"That's all I meant," Mrs. Deneaux said. Her nephew did his best to quiet her.

But yet the back-up beeping persisted. "Come on," I said desperately. "Alex has to be thinking the same thing we are."

"Brendon!" my daughter screamed, not from terror but from concern. "What are you doing?" Almost like a well-trained platoon, all the occupants of the room took up strategic placement with Nicole by the windows. Brendon was on the top of the truck with a rope and some sort of makeshift grappling hook. It looked like a crow bar, but it was tough to tell from all the rope that was tied around it.

I saw immediately what Alex and Brendon had planned. "That's not going to work," I said to myself.

"What's not going to work?" BT asked.

"Watch," I answered. BT didn't seem all too pleased with my response. I don't think he was big on surprises either. Really, I hoped that what they had planned would work, but physics wasn't on their side.

Brendon lowered the 'grappling hook' down to the cage assembly. After a couple of tries and some errant zombies getting in the way, Brendon was able to snag the cage.

"Alright! Got it, Alex...go slow!" he shouted over his shoulder. As Alex placed the truck in gear there was one long second where we all held our breaths as Brendon nearly took a header. Nicole nearly fainted. Brendon quickly righted himself and gave us all a weak smile to let us know he was okay. Alex pulled ahead slowly as Brendon let slack out of the rope. Finally, the truck had gone far enough that the true test of this experiment would come to its unfulfilling conclusion. The end of the rope was tied off to the truck's rear bumper; I didn't gauge that as being the problem area, that or the rope itself looked heavy enough to leash a T-Rex. No, the problem lay in the grappling hook assembly, without a hole to thread the rope through, no knot was going to be able to stand up to the forces applied to it.

The loud 'twang' was immediately followed by a string of curses as Brendon nearly sacrificed his ear in a valiant-but-doomed attempt to free us. The rope had snapped back dangerously close to Brendon's head as it slipped freely from the pry bar. The cage had rocked slightly and tried in vain to prove me wrong.

"Plan B, Alex!" Brendon yelled. "Give me a sec!" He

leaned down and removed a small piece of rope that had been tied around the tubes that are used to keep the trailer's doors in place. Then he swung them completely open.

We had no idea what 'Plan B' was, but those were usually a last ditch effort, and they were never thought out well. Ever heard of a Plan C? No, you haven't, because nobody ever survives Plan B.

"You guys are going to want to get away from the door!" Brendon yelled to us.

Nearly everyone looked at him like a deer in the headlights, some backed up. I could only muster an "Oh fuck" as Tracy dragged me away from the window.

Alex ground the truck into reverse. When he hit the cage at five miles per hour, it sounded like Thor had taken his hammer to a mountaintop. Wood splintered and shattered as the bars were forced back through the office. Babies wailed, women cried. I might have pissed myself; I wasn't stopping to check. The truck came to a sudden stop as the rear end ran into the stout walls of the sheriff's office. The bars traveled mercifully another two feet before they came crashing into a desk, stopping all momentum. Dust and debris were settling all around us when a small round of cheers erupted and abruptly stopped with Brendon's shouts of warning.

"Get the fuck in the truck. They're going underneath!"

Who 'they' were was implicitly known. Why they were going under the truck also didn't need any further explanation. Marta and her two kids, along with Jodi and Eddy, plus Joann and the two kids she was helping to take care of were thrust to the forefront.

I had watched *Titanic*. It's always women and children first, but apparently Thad hadn't learned the chivalry lesson. He cut off the women and the children and headed for the rear of the tractor trailer where the open doors led into a black hole of relative safety. Thad had one foot on the bumper and one on the ground. I wanted to run up and grab the prick and beat some gallantry into him when somebody (thing) beat me to it. Thad's eyes grew wide in horror as a hand shot out from under the truck and grabbed his ankle. I watched in (satisfactory) horror as he was pulled over. His head violently slammed into the ground as he lost balance. Could we have helped him? Maybe, but his selfish act turned into our salvation. Thad's body became a wedge between us and them. We could hear his muffled screams. Thankfully it wasn't too loud. I was certain that either the third or fourth bite had ripped out his Adam's apple. Marta and Joann stood transfixed, but now was not the time for delay.

I ran ahead and made sure to get both feet on the rear bumper. "Come on!" I shouted. You don't survive this long in a zombie apocalypse without having some quick-witted decision-making. For their part, I was proud of Marta and Joann. Even as the strum of sinew snapping and splintering sounds of bone chewing issued forth from beneath the truck, they moved forward and thrust their children up into my waiting arms. Within a minute almost all the refugees were on aboard, save one: Mrs. Deneaux.

"Mrs. Deneaux, we're leaving," I said as I extended my hand out to her. She looked for a moment where her nephew had disappeared and where now heads and extended hands of zombies began to appear. "Now or never."

She stepped on one of the zombies' hands as she took my proffered hand. "Twit," she said. Whether to me or to her newly dearly departed nephew I wasn't sure.

I watched in dismay as the town of Vona and my beloved Jeep faded into the distance. Alex waited until we had outpaced even the most determined zombies before he pulled over. The relief in his face as he hugged his wife and kids was immeasurable. No matter how hard I tried, though, I couldn't shake the feelings of foreboding. We had escaped this latest disaster, but at a significant loss of lives and materials, and both were in very short supply.

CHAPTER 13

Mike's Journal Entry Eleven

"My Jeep," I mumbled as I hung my head low.

Joann came up to put an arm around me. "Thad sacrificed himself for us," she said, not realizing the true reasons for my demeanor.

I looked up, my eyes red rimmed. I swear I almost said, 'Huh?' She took my silence as agreement to her sentiment. Fuck him. He got what he deserved. If she needed to assimilate what she saw in a different light to suit her needs, what right did I have to rain on her parade.

"Hey, Mr. T, Ryan's back," Tommy said delightedly as he licked blueberry off his lips.

I almost didn't hear him through my thoughts. I was in mourning for my Jeep, replaying some of the highlights I had shared with her. There were the hundreds of off-road excursions, some nearly ending in both of our demises. There were the Saturday road trips with the top off, and the time I got caught in a torrential downpour. It was miserable back then; but still, it yielded me a bittersweet smile now.

"Mike, it's only a car," Tracy said, placing her hand on my cheek ever so slightly placing pressure on it to turn my gaze away from the direction we had left behind. She knew...she knew me probably too well.

"Is this how you felt, when I...I ruined your car?" I asked

hopefully, looking for an ally in my misery.

"Uh, no, Mike. It was a car, not a kid. Get a grip," she answered.

Ah, my Tracy, she knew how to knock some much needed sense into me. I'll miss that car till they lay me down to rest but at least I now know enough not to show it.

"Wait. What?" I said. turning towards Tommy, his words finally registering in my brain.

"I said..." Tommy answered, looking slightly exasperated which I knew was all show.

Was that strawberry jam on his chin?

"Ryan's back!" he finished gleefully. I thought he was going to break out into a happy dance. His influence was contagious. Thoughts of my Jeep plunged to the rear of my desolated thoughts.

"What's he saying, Tommy?" I asked guardedly.

Ryan was a valuable asset to our existence but the majority of his 'messages' were of the dire warning type. Not usually something you liked to listen to on an empty stomach. Speaking of which, I was starving. I couldn't even remember the last time I had eaten something that did not come out of a stupid foil pack. I momentarily shifted my gaze to the long gone boxes of MREs stored in the back of my Jeep. *Oh my poor Jeep.* I shook my head; I wasn't going down that road again, not just yet. It was exceedingly difficult to not think of food as Tommy's cinnamon and syrup laced breath washed over my olfactory receptors.

"Wait...did you just have some French toast?" I asked in disbelief. He looked like he was going to give me an answer I would have a difficult time swallowing. "Never mind," I said holding up my hand. "I don't want to know."

"He says we should get far away from Vona."

More than some part of that message seemed to be coming directly from the messenger and not the spirit guide but I was going to let it slide, if only this one time.

Tommy's visage changed considerably as he passed on

the next bit of Ryan's message. "He also says that what we gain next is going to be greatly overshadowed by what we lose."

"Any chance he could be a little more cryptic?" I asked sardonically.

Tommy just tilted his head at me. I was pondering those ominous words as I watched my bully, Henry, go from person to person to receive a much needed scratch behind the ears or belly rub. My little socialite seemed to be spreading as much love as he received. People that I hadn't seen smile in days were openly grinning as they petted and praised the brown butt-wiggling butterball. Henry made sure that everyone got a chance to sample his wares, with the very noticeable exception of two. The first was Mrs. Deneaux, that wasn't so much a surprise as she just exuded bitchiness. The second however rocked me to my core. Henry wanted nothing to do with Justin. The dog made a wide skirt around him. I watched as Justin seemed to casually dismiss the slight. But I caught a look on Justin's face of pure murderous intent as the dog walked on by. He slowly let his countenance fade as he realized I was looking at him. I shivered. He smiled coldly.

Riding in the rear of the tractor-trailer was not all it was cracked up to be. I couldn't believe that I had bitched when Paul had decided to ride in the truck instead of in the Jeep. That had been more of a self-imposed punishment for him than anything else. What little we had for padding did nothing to prevent teeth rattling contact with the floor and walls whenever the truck hit anything larger than a penny or deeper than a dinner plate on the roadway. After three weeks (okay, melodramatic, it was actually only eight hours), of kidney crushing, liver lacerating, pancreas punching, heart hammering, esophagus eschewing (should I keep going on?) brain busting, ass aching, riding, Alex brought the truck to a much needed stop.

Tracy openly laughed at me as I grabbed onto the small

railing halfway up the trailer walls. My slow ascent was punctuated by the pops and protestations of my aching body.

Tommy sheepishly grinned. "Want some help, old man?" he said, and then as he watched my astonished expression he threw Tracy under the bus. "Mrs. T told me to say that!" he fairly wailed.

Even Travis had to smile as he placed a shoulder under my arm to help me up. All of this was pretty funny and I was happy for the relief if only in brevity, but the hampering of my destroyed knee had brought the odds of my family's survivability down a few notches. I did not want to have to survive being dependent on others to get me through this plight. My eyes slid across the back of Mrs. Deneaux as she was helped off the back of the truck. That bitch was going to be the one that danced across my grave. I could almost feel it in my bones.

Alex came around the rear of the truck to see how his 'charges' were doing. He smiled as he watched me finally gain my full longitudinal ability.

"Blow me," I told him as I hobbled towards the exit.

"What?" he asked innocently. "I didn't say anything."

I braced myself on his shoulder as I gingerly stepped down off the truck. Alex thankfully waited until the pain that clouded my higher reasoning ability tailed off before he began to speak. "Mike, we're about an hour or so out of Kansas City, Missouri." I looked at him questioningly. "That's where I'm going to start my southerly route." My face must have visibly fallen because he hastened on. "You should be able to get some transportation in the city, and then you can catch Route 29 all the way into Fargo."

My heart suddenly felt heavy. This parting was going to have all the finality of death. We would go on and give each other addresses where the other was going to be just in case we were in the neighborhood, but even in the old realm of machinations, this was an empty promise. One made only as a courtesy.

There could be no secrets across a group this small, mainly because everyone had learned to not be more than a few feet away from everybody else. So when BT came storming up it wasn't a surprise. "Whaddaya mean we're splitting up?" he demanded.

Alex took the reins. "Mike has family he wants to try to find, as do I."

BT's expression turned stormy. "Whoa, listen, both of you. We all have family, and we'd love to find out what happened to them. But now *we* are all family," he punctuated this by thumping his chest and spreading his arms to include all of us. "This isn't about individual quests, this is about mutual survival. We are ALL we have left!" his voice thundered. His words hit hard. I hoped he was wrong.

"BT, this is something I have to do," I said gravely.

"Talbot, how far you going to make it on that knee?" he shouted; my hair blew back from the force of it.

"BT," Alex said, stepping between the angry giant and myself, risking amputation by placing his hand on BT's chest. BT swatted it away.

"You just going to let him go, Alex?" BT seemed to deflate a little within his own skin. "Look at him, Alex. If his hand wasn't on your shoulder, he'd fall over from the pain. He's nearly crippled."

The words stung, but I'd be damned if I'd take my hand from Alex and prove him right.

"What do you want me to do, BT? He's a grown man, he can make his own decisions."

"Yeah, but his decisions affect us all now," BT said, several degrees of volume lower than when he had started. The wind truly did seem to be out of his sails now. But I was leery. Gusts and gales could pop up unexpectedly.

"Still here," I said.

"Besides, how's he getting to where he's going? His Jeep is gone," BT continued.

"We're going to get him a new car in Kansas City."

"Guys, what is this, the Ghost of Christmas past? I'm still here," I said.

"Oh, just perfect, shouldn't be any zombies in a major city. We can just stop off at the local Chevy dealer and go pick up a Geo or something," BT scowled.

"I was really hoping for a GMC or something along those lines," I intoned. I hadn't been this ignored since Tracy thought I was cheating on her. All those declarations had fallen to the ground like leaves on a crisp fall day. "It would be great if it had an extended cab, too. Maybe a roof rack, oh shit and a gun rack. It would be great if it also had different climate controls. That way when Tracy is cold and she wants to turn the heat on to the 'melt' setting, I won't need to take my clothes off."

Alex turned around. "Mike, what the fuck are you talking about?"

BT was looking at me like I had lost my fuckin' mind. BT's next words threw me for a loop. "I'm going with you, Mike."

Alex turned back around. "BT, what the fuck are *you* talking about?"

Now it was my and Alex's turn to look at BT like he had lost his damn mind.

Paul decided that it was in this maelstrom that he should throw his penny and a half in. "Mike, I've been meaning to talk to you…"

Then it dawned on me. Paul and Erin's families were both in North Carolina right along the path Alex would need to take to get to Florida. I don't know why I was having such a difficult time digesting this information. Was I such a selfish person that I felt that everybody should be wrapped up in the same things I was? Shit, I hadn't spent more than two seconds thinking about what anybody else would want to do. I just ass-umed my mission was theirs.

"I'm going with Mike!" Jen thrust forward, like we were back in gym class and she didn't want to wait to get picked last and possibly placed on a team she didn't like.

"Wait, this isn't about choosing sides," I started.

"I'm going with Alex," April whispered. "I don't want to be near him anymore." She pointed towards Justin. "He gives me the creeps."

"Stop," I said without much force. "This isn't about choosing sides. We're all individuals, just because we've been thrust into this nightmare together doesn't mean we have to stay that way."

"Ever seen *Friday the 13th*?" Tommy asked enigmatically.

Nobody paid much heed to his words except for me. The meaning was exceptionally strong. It was always the individuals that went off alone to check the circuit breakers in the basements that quickly found themselves suspended above the floor pierced in some ungodly manner in a particularly vulnerable area.

I would not let BT, Paul, Alex, or even Ryan deter me from my desired goal. I knew Tracy silently prayed that I would not stray from the predetermined course. Sure, she could make my life an even more special living hell if I were to not attempt to rescue her mom, but in the end she would have to go as I did. I don't know who was kidding whom though. She'd had my balls wrapped up in wax paper since the day we got married. On occasion she would bring them out and let me stare longingly at them; but as for who wore the pants in the family? Let's just say, I was President Bush to her Dick Cheney.

The ride into Kansas City was a somber one. It seemed that everyone was lost in his or her own thoughts of these new developments. Even the outgoing Tommy was silent. His Aunt Marta had made it clear in no uncertain terms that he was supposed to go with her. There was no doubt after that conversation who had emerged the victor. Tommy sat up in the cab with Alex and me to avoid the brow beating being administered by the defeated Marta – so much for losing graciously.

But let's be fair, this wasn't about an MLB game, even if it might be the Red Sox against the Yankees. The stakes were as high as they could get, life or death. Some might argue that there were higher stakes, possibly your eternal soul if you were so inclined, but really? I had a sneaky suspicion we had already failed God's ultimate test and were already experiencing his wrath.

Tommy hadn't eaten a Pop-Tart in nearly an hour. I knew he was upset. I was about to start a conversation with him when he beat me to the punch.

"Hey, Mr. T, I don't think going to get Mrs. T's mom is such a good idea."

It felt like ice cubes were being dragged down my spine. Alex looked over to gauge my response, a small surge of hope flaring in his eyes.

"Mike, dude, just come with us, you know the odds of one old woman surviving."

The remnants of the chill still dripped down my back. I struck back with a punch I knew would close the door on this conversation. "What if it was Marta asking you to get her mother?" Yeah, I knew it was a low blow, but if he harangued me for much longer I would have caved. Tommy's one-liners were more than enough ammunition to realize the folly of what I was attempting.

"Not cool, Mike," Alex finished with a hurt look on his face.

I nodded in assent. "Sorry."

"I understand."

"Hey, Uncle Alex, do you want to get off at the next exit?" Tommy asked.

The phrase was asked as a question, but the intent was not. Alex got off at the next exit. Within a half mile of our exit, my horror mounted to near epic proportions. Tommy was smiling ear to ear as Alex pulled into a used minivan car lot.

"No!" I cried. "There has got to be something else."

Alex was nearly full on laughing. "Oh, *bendejo*, you have a growing family now. You're going to need something big enough to accommodate them all."

"Oh this sucks!" I yelled. My worst nightmare in life was coming to fruition. "You did this shit on purpose," I said, pointing to Tommy. He paid me little heed as he unwrapped a S'mores Pop-Tart.

Tracy was first out of the truck at the sounds of my dismay. Her concern quickly melted away to merriment as she looked around at her surroundings. "Ah, so the beast has finally been tamed."

I would have dropped to my knees and cried to the heavens if I thought I could get back up. Within twenty minutes we had two minivans loaded with our meager supplies and passengers. Mine was a brilliant teal color with faux wood paneling; the mere sight of which brought the scant contents of my stomach churning up into my throat.

Brendon didn't seem nearly as distressed as he got behind the wheel of his gray-greenish piece of…minivan. Is there anything more emasculating than driving a minivan? Maybe riding bitch on a Harley while your wife drives, but that's really about it. I had thought that BT would have wanted to drive one of the vans, but he mumbled something about having lost his license. I really couldn't see him being all that concerned about getting a ticket for that infraction. No, I got the distinct impression from the way he reacted when I asked him if he wanted to drive, that he didn't know how to. I could potentially see why, probably wasn't a car made that would accommodate his frame between the seat and the steering wheel.

Saying our goodbyes had me rethinking my strategy all over.

Marta solemnly walked over to Tommy and reached up to cup his face in her hands. I could see her lips moving, but couldn't hear what was said. Tommy enveloped her in a gentle bear hug, then released her and stepped away. Marta turned back toward the truck, moving stiffly like an old woman.

I turned to my friend, my *compadre*. "Goodbye, Alex," I said, holding on to a stiff upper lip.

Alex had no such compunction as he openly wept and moved in for a giant hug. This is fully appropriate behavior according to the Man Code. (I looked it up.) "Good luck, Mike," he said as he sniffed his nose, wiped his eyes and quickly climbed into the cab of the truck.

It was all I could do to get out "You too," before he shut the door.

Erin was next, she was crying more than Alex, but she wasn't under the constraints of the Man Code. "Mike, thank you for everything. Without you and your family we would have never made it." I wanted to answer with 'It was nothing.' But my boys *had* risked everything to save them, and I was unsure still if Justin was ever truly coming back. She openly wept as Paul came up to me.

He gave me the 'secret' handshake we had developed long ago in our days at college, the classic handshake followed by the forearm grasp and then the finger curl clasp immediately culminating in a hug. "It was a great ride, Mike."

Tears welled up in my eyes. "The best, Paul."

And that was it, I was unsure if I would find out what happened to any of them as I watched them depart. I wanted to always hold fast in my heart that they safely made it to their respective destinations and lived out the rest of their days in as much happiness as could be afforded them.

Tommy cried as the big rig pulled away. His look was one of regret. I couldn't tell if it was because he was staying with me or because of what would befall the departing group. I would never ask for an answer. I didn't want to know, any answer he gave me would be nothing I wanted to hear. We all stayed an extra minute longer, way past when the last remnants of the truck vanished over a small rise. Maybe we expected they would have a change of heart and come with us. It didn't happen.

CHAPTER 14

Mike's Journal Entry Twelve

"Alright," I said, looking at a little map I had gotten off the salesman's desk, "I don't want to go into the city itself, but according to the Yellow Pages there's a sporting goods store a few miles up the road. I want to try to bolster up our arsenal, get some rounds, and hopefully some dehydrated food stores or whatever we can muster."

Brendon was getting antsy. Being around this many buildings with so many hiding spots had us all a little on edge. Without the comfort of the rolling tank, that unease was even more magnified. "Do you think they're going to have anything left? I mean, everyone must have had the same idea."

"How much of a chance did *we* have to get to the store?" I asked.

"I see your point."

The plague had hit so hard and so fast, most were caught ill-prepared to deal with it. Only the truly paranoid had received even the slightest chance of survival. I laughed a little internally, even if we as a species somehow eked out a niche of survival, we would be hard pressed to flourish, so mistrustful would be the survivors that we would never go out and seek others. In the end we would all still die…suspicious and alone.

Tracy, Tommy, Henry, Travis, Jen, and I climbed into my Terrible Teal Machine. Brendon, Nicole, Justin, and BT hopped into the second.

It was approaching dusk as we rolled up into the sporting goods store parking lot. No one had left a light on for us. The black was as pitch as it could get. As human beings we are inherently built to fear the dark. That is why our ancestors harnessed the use of fire…to chase away 'the demons.' The night was scary enough when we just *thought* that there were monsters roaming around. Now that the abnormal was the normal, well you can imagine that our imaginations were in overdrive. But really, how vivid did one's visualization need to be, every magnificent horror was now a reality. There was nothing left to the imagination. All of this ran through my mind as I tried in utter vain to peer into the near inky obsidian that was the interior of the store.

"I'm going to get out and see if I can scope out the inside of the store," I said, hoping that someone would say we should wait until the morning.

Nobody fucking did. Fuckers. I opened the door to the minivan, still pissed that this was my new ride. I would have slammed the door closed in frustration but I didn't want to give anything nearby an excuse to come investigate. Well, mostly that, but partly I thought the piece of shit door might fall off, too. I'd be damned if I drove around in a zombie infested world without a door. That would be like peeling back the lid on a can of spam in Hawaii.

Except for the silent purring engines on two minivans (sarcasm – it sounded more like some cats and a large bag of batteries had been placed in a dryer) the night was still. Deathly still. (Well you knew that was coming). I got as far away from the vans as I felt was prudently wise, straining my ears to hear any errant sound. But that really is a misnomer though, how the hell does one 'strain' their ears? It's not like you can flex them, you can't 'listen' any harder. I guess what I was doing was concentrating harder on listening. My wife would have been so proud.

Nothing. I heard nothing. Yet I wasn't relieved. The quiet was somehow more disturbing. With sound, there would be something to focus on. Without the benefit of a séance I was wildly free to speculate on any number of things. I placed my face up against the cool plate glass window, cupping my hands on the side of my eyes and straining my best to see something. (See previous section on 'straining'.) I had about the same results. Nothing. So this is where, in a low budget movie, something slams into the glass on the other side, startling the shit out of the hero/heroine and the audience. Don't be fooled, being there in real life, I FULLY expected that to be the case. I was pleasantly surprised to not have to suffer that little truism.

BT and Travis had both exited their respective rides. I jumped a little when they opened their doors. I hoped that it wasn't too obvious that I might have released my bladder at that moment. I tried to hang on to my dignity.

"Anything?" BT shouted. His booming voice reverberated off the glass.

"Well, there wasn't, but there might be now," I answered peevishly.

"What!" he yelled back.

"Grab the tire iron!" I yelled back.

Travis was coming towards me as BT was rummaging in the back of the van looking for the tire iron.

"Got it!" BT yelled back triumphantly.

"Dude, stop yelling!" I screeched. *Lead by example, breathe.*

"Oh right!" he yelled as he came towards me. The giant man silhouetted in the headlights, approaching me with a pistol in one hand and a tire iron in the other, was the stuff of most horror novels. I lamented that this most pedestrian theme was NOT the cause of all our desolation.

"What are you planning on doing with this?" BT asked as he handed me the tool.

I tapped the glass, in response.

"Oh," BT said as he backed away a pace or two.

I was lining up my shot, doing my best to shield my eyes from flying glass, and my ears from the fulminating noise. But again, you can't really do much there. God didn't deign that we should have earlids, although how cool would that be. However, the boon might also be a curse. Can you imagine that? As guys, we could ACTUALLY turn off our significant others' diatribes? The problem though, would be not only would they suspect that we weren't listening, but with our ear flaps closed, they would also have visual proof. Okay not one of my better ideas.

"Dad," Travis said matter-of-factly. I stopped in mid-swing. Although if this was baseball, my check swing would have been called a strike as my forward momentum brought the tire iron to a gentle tapping on the window. "Door's open."

"Yup, I knew that," I said, handing the tire iron back to BT. "Tracy!" I yelled over my shoulder.

"Yeah, yeah, I know the drill," she said as she slid out of her bucket seat and into mine. After a few seconds of adjusting the seat and the steering wheel to her liking she gave me the universal sign for A-OK – two thumbs up.

"Aren't you going to adjust the mirrors?" I asked her. She gave me another universal sign, this one not quite so pleasant.

I took a deep breath. I was pulling on all of my reserves of intestinal fortitude to go through that door. BT was behind me and Travis was bringing up the rear. I took one more long pull of the piercing air. Tommy brushed past me and in.

"Where the hell did he come from?" BT asked incredulously.

"I guess it's safe," I said as I followed him into the black midst.

I stopped less than two steps in from the doorway, not for fear or some innate prescience. I just couldn't see a damn thing. I had no desire to be skewered by a ski pole, or walk nuts first into a dumbbell display. I could hear Tommy walking around like he had a floor plan. I was tempted to follow in his assured sounding footfalls.

BT nearly sent me sprawling as he walked into my back. "Sorry, my man. Where's the kid?"

"Shit, BT, I'd be lucky if I could tell where my hand is."

Both BT and I turned to look at the same instance. Whether we thought the same thing I'm not sure, but BT's expression of awe left little doubt. Tommy was lit up like the Archangel Michael come to seek vengeance on a wicked world. As our eyes adjusted to the radiance it became clear that Tommy was merely holding a battery powered Coleman lantern. I shook my head in consternation, I will swear to my dying days that for the briefest of seconds there was more to it than that. I wanted to ask BT but I think he'd deny it, hell I'm not even sure what I saw and I was there.

"Found some coconut roasted marshmallows!" Tommy said as he stuffed another handful into his mouth.

"Did you hear him open a bag?" BT asked.

"I'm really trying to stop wondering what the kid does, BT, it gives me a headache."

"Yeah, I hear that."

Within twenty minutes, everyone was in the store in the far left corner. We had a bunch of lanterns lit. We even had a couple of tents pitched. Tommy thought that was the coolest thing since the marshmallows. We propped (well BT did) a half-ton of weights by the front door so it couldn't open. But the Vona sheriff's office was still fresh in everyone's mind. I parked one van by the front door and the second by the emergency exit in the rear. Worst case scenario we would have to cram into one van for a while. If there was a just God in the universe, we would get to leave the Terrible Teal Machine behind.

Thankfully we were in Missouri and not some neo-fascist state like New York. We had more guns and ammo to choose from than we would ever be able to carry. If not for the huge plate glass windows in front I would have put my two cents in on why we should hunker down here until the spring.

Food, while not of the high cuisine type, was plentiful. There was an unbelievable assortment of dried meats, including ostrich. Which, as funny as it sounds, did not taste like chicken, it was friggin horrible. There were dried food packets of every conceivable concoction including Thanksgiving Dinner readily available. We busted a bunch of those open and had a small feast so to speak. It wasn't quite the Indians and the Pilgrims, but we were thankful to be alive and with each other. Unfortunately there were no dried beer packets or an NFL game on to accompany our meal. The boys grabbed some bows and arrows and some of the clothing dummies and had a blast shooting at something that didn't necessarily want to eat you. Even Justin perked up more than I had seen out of him in a few days. It was a welcome respite.

It was getting late and we were all tired. Tracy watched with curiosity as I prepared another tent a few yards away from the rest. I then made an exaggerated stretch and let everyone know I was heading off to bed. I had other things on my mind, but it didn't stop me from almost immediately falling asleep.

Colors flooded my senses, I felt like I was in Candy Land, I'm not making this stuff up. There was a river of chocolate lazily flowing through a rolling landscape of what looked like whipped cream. There were cliché candy cane trees, and what appeared to be giant broccoli sprouts which seemed wholly out of place, but stranger still were the variety of Pop-Tart fruit, still in their leafy foil packets that hung bountifully down from their boughs. Tommy was paddling from the distant shore towards me on the world's largest Snicker's bar; he would occasionally pause from his paddling duties and take a generous bite.

"Hey, Mr. T!" Tommy shouted. Smatterings of chocolate

nearly covered him from head to toe.

Henry came bounding up, a huge white chocolate bone in his mouth. "You know that chocolate's not really good for dogs, Tommy."

"It's not real chocolate!" he yelled in his best stage whisper. "It's cacao, dogs can eat that!" Tommy had stepped off his makeshift boat and approached me, all smiles and happiness. "Didn't think I could do it, Mr. T, but I did," he said proudly.

"Do what, Tommy?" I asked. I figured he was referring to getting his chocolate bar across the river. "And what's with the broccoli?"

"Get you here," he answered. "And Mom always said I should eat more greens."

"Get me here? This is a dream, Tommy. What's going on?"

"Just testing a little, you'd better go, Mrs. T is coming."

"Wait, what?"

I snapped awake as Tracy came through the front flap of the tent.

"Nice place you got here."

"Hi, hon," I said groggily and somewhat disoriented. Something incredible had just happened, but it would be days later before I could put it to page. Tracy proceeded to get into the sleeping bag I had set up. Within seconds, my earlier 'dream' forgotten, I pounced on her with all the grace of a jungle cat on Valium.

"What the hell are you doing?" she asked with a trace of bewilderment.

"You know," I said softly.

"No I don't," she answered.

"Come on...*you* know," I said, trying to lead her on.

"No I do not...wait...are you trying to fool around?" she asked incredulously. "Are you effen crazy?!" she barked. Her voice was rising exponentially. "You've got a better chance of shitting gold coins!"

I didn't think that was feasible, so apparently getting laid was out of the question. My humiliation was compounded by the riotous laughing of BT from his sleeping area a few feet away. I'm a guy, no matter how dire the situation, if we're not quite dead yet, we're thinking about sex. My face flamed as I fell asleep. No wonder I dreamt about a tanning bed.

'Why do they put nipples on modeling dummies?' I pondered the next morning as I arose out of the tent, shifting around what the good God gave me. Fuckin' BT, always Johnny on the spot, was there to witness my indignation.

"Got any change for a twenty dollar Gold Eagle? I see you didn't get that taken care of last night?" he laughed.

I was about to verbally whiplash him, when the next word out of his mouth saved the day.

"Coffee?"

I started walking over to him.

"Don't get too close, we hardly know one another." He laughed again.

"Fuckin' funny," I said as I grabbed a mug of the steaming goodness. Dunkies it wasn't, but it was still incredible in its own right. I sat down next to him just to fuck with him. I attempted to put my arm around him.

BT shot up like a bottle rocket. "Dude?!" BT said disbelievingly.

I feigned innocence.

BT moved his smallish camping chair to the far side of our impromptu campfire. Sometime during the night someone had found and placed a Styrofoam prop fire resplendent with rocks and logs into the middle of our clearing.

As BT settled his not insignificant weight into the chair I had to ask. "How the hell is that thing supporting your weight?"

"Play nice, boys," Jen said as she came from the direction of the restrooms. She handed BT a canteen heavy with water. BT drank greedily, easily consuming half of the contents.

"Want some?" BT asked as he held the canteen out towards me.

"No, I'm good. I'll go get my own," I answered.

"Mike, just take this one, man," he said, thrusting the canteen a little closer to my face.

"Don't sweat it, man. I'll go get my own."

"There's some right here. Don't be difficult," BT said, his dander starting to get a little riled.

"BT, I don't want it. I'll get my own," I said a little more sternly.

"It's because I'm black, isn't it!" he yelled.

Jen had stopped what she was doing to see how this potentially volatile situation panned out. Oh, I knew how it would end up; my teeth in BT's knuckles seemed the most likely scenario.

"BT, come on, you know me better than that."

"I don't know shit," he hissed, his bulk seemingly swelled in proportion to his anger. He was a second and a half from coming out of his chair.

All the boys were now a few feet away, Brendon was coming to the forefront, trying his best to throw a wedge between me and BT. I didn't think he would even qualify as a speed bump if BT got going.

Tracy had taken this, the most blessed of opportunities to emerge from our tent.

"BT," she said with no small amount of force.

"My beef's not with you, Tracy," BT said, never taking his eyes off of me. "Is this how you want it, Mike? Your woman doing your battles for you?"

"BT!" my wife yelled.

"What, WOMAN!" he shouted back.

"He wouldn't take that canteen if *I* handed it to him," Tracy said.

"Huh?" BT asked, confusion creasing his brow.

"BT, Mike is a germaphobe. I swear to you as I stand here, he would not take that canteen from me if I had just taken a drink from it."

"Really?" BT asked incredulously. He then turned back to me. "I guess I owe you an apology," he said as he laughed. "Wait then, how do you two kiss? Forget it, I don't want to know." And then apparently this was the funniest thing in the world. In between swigs of the canteen BT would break out into spontaneous laughter. "Can't...kiss." He laughed. "You could get cooties." If the guy wasn't such a solid block of granite he probably would have split his sides he ended up laughing so hard.

"No shit, Mike? You can't drink off someone else's beverage?" Jen asked. "That's funny."

I forced an anemic smile. Neurosis number twenty-two had reared its ugly head.

"How'd you have kids? Artificial insemination?" BT said roaring with laughter. "Immaculate conception? Wait...wait...I know...stunt double!"

I got up and left BT to his own devices. At this pace it would be hours before he realized I was gone.

"Holy shit, Mike. That was close," Brendon said as we put a few feet between us and the tittering titan.

"Yeah about that, Brendon, I appreciate the sentiment. But you've seen the propensity I have for getting into trouble."

"In a hurry," he added.

"In a hurry," I conceded. "The point is, Brendon, I don't want to drag anyone else down with me." He looked crestfallen. "Like I said, Brendon, I do appreciate the help, I just couldn't live with the guilt if anything happened to any one of you...especially if it was to save my ass." He looked like he was about to say something. I didn't want to give him any room for maneuverability. "Besides, can you imagine how bad Nicole would make it for me?" I looked at him questioningly.

"I suppose you're right," Brendon acknowledged.

I arched an eyebrow at him.

"No, you're definitely right," he conceded.

BT had for the most part calmed down. Tracy, I guess, wasn't ready to let me off the hook quite yet. "Yeah, you should see what he has to do before he gets on a toilet."

"Tracy!" I shouted, more than a smidgeon mortified.

"Oh, that's not even the worst of it, at…"

"Oh for the love of God."

Justin, Travis, and Tommy had resumed their dummy target practice. Now seemed as good a time as any to see how it was going. Two rows of seven dummies were lined up like advancing zombies. Errant arrows were strewn everywhere – including the ceiling, but more than a proportionate amount had struck their targets with withering precision. As we came up to the 'range' Tommy was drawing the bow back, he let loose an arrow that created sparks as it plunged well short of its intended target by several feet.

"Good one, Tommy," Travis said. "That's your closest one yet."

Tommy was beaming. "You fink?" he asked as he handed the strawberry jelly-coated bow to Justin.

"Uck," Justin said as he pulled out a small box of wipes just for this occasion.

Brendon and I both looked quizzically at each other. Brendon broke the silence first.

"Mike this is about a third of the distance when he shot that guy from Durgan's assault."

I nodded; what words were there?

"And now he has a professional bow, not that piece of crap kid's toy."

I nodded again. It was nice to know that someone else was seeing what I'd been seeing for a while.

"What's up, hon?" Nicole said as she wrapped her arms around Brendon. "You look a little out of sorts."

"Nothing, babe," Brendon said as he leaned down to kiss her.

I turned away slightly. I didn't want to make anybody

else uneasy. It was just that, well dammit, I could not get the image of my daughter being anything other than that precious, seven-year-old daddy's little girl out of my head. I know she's an adult and she has her own life now. It's just that, in my reality, she has chosen the realm of celibacy. It's small measures like this that allow me to sleep at night. One of these days I know, sooner rather than later, my brain is just going to freeze up. It will be the human equivalent of the blue screen of death. Unfortunately, I have yet to discover my reboot button.

Justin let loose his shot. Everyone laughed and cringed in equal measures as the arrow struck the dummy's stones. I swear he looked right at me for half a heartbeat before he joined in the celebration with everyone else.

Just then a loud 'thud' up by the front of the store cut the revelry short. I should have immediately taken charge and started delegating. Getting out of the store alive should have been my main objective. But I'll admit, curiosity got the better of me, so I started towards the front door. For one fleeting night since this whole shit storm started I had felt good – safe even. But it was all an illusion as I was about to painfully learn.

Travis was first to the front. "No biggie, Dad, there's only one."

He didn't have to add…zombie.

"Uh…Dad…there's more," Travis said hesitantly.

"Well shit, there's always more. They're like fucking wolves, pack animals," I said testily. I was more than a little pissed that my home away from home was no longer the safe haven I had deemed it to be.

Brendon and Nicole had reached the front and were standing next to Travis. Suddenly Nicole turned and ran back to our 'campsite'. She said nothing as she brushed past, but I saw tears on her face.

"What's the matter with her?" I asked. I was really hoping it was the overly dramatic part of Nicole coming out.

It wasn't.

"Mike, you're going to want to see this." Brendon swallowed hard.

"Am I?" I asked. I was liking this less and less. And then someone punched the shit out of me. Figuratively, although literally would have been better. My old world nemesis stood less than three feet away from me separated only by a flimsy pane of glass no thicker than a Coke bottle.

"Oh, Jed. What did they do to you?"

I wanted to cry. I fell to my knees, hampered somewhat by the new sports brace I had acquired. But still, to the ground I went. I buried my face in my hands, tears of true sorrow leaking through my clenched fingers. My body tensed each time Jed's head butted the glass, his mouth snapping wildly at the air, drool running viscously down the front of his tattered shirt. A broken tooth protruded at a slight angle from his top lip. Dirty hands with torn fingernails scratched at the glass. Cataract-clouded eyes stared pitilessly at me. It wasn't until I let my gaze travel lower that my resolve got steeled, or more likely my innards got liquefied.

"Brendon, take Justin and Travis and let's start the evacuation process like we talked about last night."

Brendon had learned quickly enough to not question orders. For that I was thankful. "One car or two, Mike?" he shot back quickly.

"We'll do two, but let's make it really quick."

Curiosity was killing him, I could almost sense it. "There's only a couple, Mike. I know it's Jed and all, but still…"

I pointed to a small nametag festooned to Jed's breast pocket.

"Oh fuck." Brendon turned on a dime, Travis and Justin on his heels.

I stared long and hard into Jed's eyes trying with every particle of my being to discern some small part of him that may have retained anything remotely resembling humanity.

There was nothing there. He would eat me as quickly as the next without the smallest bit of remorse for what he did. I slowly removed the weights that BT had placed the night before. Each one seemed to be attached to my heart, miring it down into the depths of despair. BT came up just as I had finished pulling the last fifty pounder out of the way.

"Oh, I knew if I waited long enough I wouldn't have to move those things again," BT said in way too jovial a mood for my liking. He saw that I was not enjoying his conviviality. "What's up, Mike? I mean, Nicole came back crying...and then the boys said that we had to get stuff ready to go, but they said there were only a few zombies."

I just pointed out through the glass door. Jed had followed me and was watching me hungrily as I cleared the doorway.

"It's just a...Jed? Is that Jed? What the fuck is Jed doing here?"

"Look at his name tag."

"What the fuck is a zombie doing with a name tag?" BT asked. His features turned ashen as he focused in on the little white card.

I hated nametags, and this one wasn't going to do anything to change that. Anyplace you ever had to go where people needed a nametag was not a place that I wanted to frequent. I don't give a shit if you're Cindy from Spokane, I didn't know you before tonight and I have no desire to know you after. Do they use them at high school reunions so that you recognize then laugh at the football jock who is now fifty pounds overweight and balding? Or maybe for the prom queen who pumped out five kids, smokes like a chimney and now scratches her ass in public? I mean, if that's the case then I guess they're alright; but Jed's nametag didn't give a name, only a message. "Found You."

Those two ominous words were a personal affront. Don't get me wrong, I understood that this world was now all about survival of the fittest. It was a depraved, cruel world and getting harsher by the moment. Zombies were everywhere and would attempt to eat us with wild abandonment. Renegade bands of thieves, muggers, pillagers, and general degenerates were also out there and given the opportunity would take everything they could from us. But this was different. We were being hunted – purposefully sought out for extermination. My fears for my family plummeted to new depths of wretchedness. Like life wasn't already hard enough. I had come to love Jed, but I thought no more for the bullet I put through his head than he would have had he got a hold of my flesh.

"FUCK YOU!" I screamed into the day, hopeful that my words would find the ears of those that had come after us.

And they did, but not with the desired effect. The car that had delivered Jed sat idling in the shadows of an alleyway across from the sporting goods store.

Cigarette smoke poured out through the slightly open window, a mirthless laugh escaped the driver's dry and cracked lips "Soon, Talbot, so very, very soon." The car pulled out and away on the deserted roadway as Jed's body twitched one final time on the frozen pavement.

CHAPTER 15

Mike's Journal Entry Thirteen

Within ten minutes we were loaded up and on the road. My mood couldn't have been any more sour if I had just come home to realize my wife had run off with my best friend and taken the dog. (Wait, scratch that, if she had taken Henry that would have been worse.) A small grim grin bubbled to the surface with that new thought.

"Mike," Tracy said, her face a lighter shade of white. "Mike," she said again when I didn't immediately respond. "Brendon's having a tough time keeping up."

"Huh," I said, breaking free from my black thoughts.

"Brendon…the other minivan, they can't keep up," she said, her knuckles white on the dashboard.

The tachometer was buried deep in the red as the Terrible Teal Machine was topping out at somewhere near 120 miles per hour. I couldn't be sure because the numbers only went to 110, but the needle was pressed firmly against the upraised stop pin. Brendon's van was a distant memory in the rearview mirror.

Tracy placed her hand on my shoulder. "Mike," she said pleadingly.

BT sat quietly in the back. A few more shades lighter and he would be able to get into some of the finer country clubs in the area. A tire blow out now would most likely send us into the *Guinness Book of Records* for most barrel rolls. Well, as a kid I had always wanted to get into that book of oddities. Probably for something more mundane like how many pieces of bubble gum I could chew; not necessarily for being the world's largest rolling meat grinder. My foot eased off the accelerator. I had placed so much force on my right leg trying to press the gas pedal into the floorboard that I was now in the unenviable process of trying to alleviate a charley horse while also keeping this missile on the straight and narrow.

Even with Brendon traveling at a steady seventy miles per hour, I was out of the van and massaging my offending calf before Brendon even came into sight on the horizon.

"Jesus, Mike, what the hell are you doing?" Jen asked as she came out of the van.

I looked over to Brendon; he looked strained. Pushing the non-aerodynamic brick down the highway at speeds he didn't feel comfortable with had made him break out in a sweat.

"Sorry, man," I said to him.

"It's nothing," he lied as he pulled his fingers off the steering wheel.

"Dad, you don't look good," Nicole said with concern.

Justin smiled from the rear seat in the van.

"It doesn't matter," I said bleakly.

"What doesn't matter, Mike?" Tracy asked as she came up beside me.

"All of this…none of this. No matter how hard we run, no matter where we go, they'll still come. There'll come a time, no matter what I do, I won't be able to stop them from taking you…any of you."

"Mike, it's not just you," BT said tenderly. (I wasn't going to add this part, but it's part of the story and it only scratches on the outer corners of breaking the Man Code.) He had come out and was actually giving me a hug. "We're in this together. We'll look out for each other. I would no sooner let anything happen to any of your kin than I would let something happen to myself."

He was big enough to be my dad when I was maybe five or six years old – the proportion was correct. I lived that lie for a few more seconds as I collected my despair, and didn't so much dispose of it as try to compartmentalize it. I could tell it was surging and would soon leak from under the door of my makeshift compartment and probably out through the keyhole, but for now I had gained a measure of composure and was again ready to face the world, for the most part.

"Tracy, you want to drive?" I asked her. It was then I think everyone must have thought I had finally given up. I looked around the somber group. "What? My knee is killing me."

"Uh huh," BT said as he got back into the van.

That was mostly true, but there was still a part of me that might have relished the thought of screaming off the road at a buck twenty and plowing into a utility pole. I would not give my pursuers that satisfaction. Someone was going to catch a lot of lead for pushing me this hard, and maybe an arrow or two for good measure.

Tracy drove well, which in itself was something of a feat. Normally the only way she got behind the wheel with me in the car was when I was entirely too inebriated or had suffered one of my many varied injuries. Under either circumstance I didn't give a rat's ass on how she got me to where we were going. I can't even begin to relate to you in this narrative how many times the kids had come home from somewhere where their mom had driven them and had horror stories about this and that person being cut off, semi's turning over and small planes bursting into flame. I think there was even something in there about a dam bursting, but that might possibly have been an over-exaggeration. I dozed in and out of a fitful sleep. My mood fluctuating between pissed off at my lot in life and happy that I wasn't being pissed on. Basically, varying degrees of suckydom.

Tracy kept to a geriatric pace of fifty-five-ish. It wasn't

that the conditions merited the reduction in speed, I'm just not so sure how willing she was to get to where we were going. It's all great in the abstract. 'I'm going to save my mom!' but when you get down to the nitty-gritty and you realize that you haven't heard anything in weeks from your seventy-nine-year-old mom who lives alone on a farm in North Dakota in one of the coldest winters in recorded history during an outbreak of zombieism, reality begins to make a weight of its own. Like a dying star, it creates its own mass and sucks everything, including your inner light, into it. The odds were about as great as winning the lottery that we would find Carol, hale of health.

"You want me to take over driving?" I asked her.

Tracy turned to me. Grim determination and concern mixed in with a heavy dose of anxiety spilled out of her features. "Do you mind? I don't feel right driving without you bleeding." We both laughed; the tiny release of endorphins was like a surge of adrenaline to my flagging spirits.

Ten minutes and a bunch of potty breaks later we were back on the road. The natural order of the universe was restored as I cruised down the highway at a more respectable seventy-five mph. Any faster than that, and the Terrible Teal Machine began to shudder in protest. How I had got this bucket to one-twenty was beyond my comprehension.

My stomach grumbled as we passed one of those blue highway information signs. You know, the kind that tell you gas, food and lodging are up ahead. This one had the big 'M' logo for McDonald's on it. A quarter pounder with cheese, large fries and a thirst-quenching Coke sounded like the best thing in the world.

"Oh, man, I could go for a juicy Quarter Pounder, aw, man with that dripping cheese and sesame seed bun. I'd put a layer of golden french fries on top of the cheese and I'd eat that thing in like a minute and a half." I know Henry understood what I was talking about because his head was tilted and he had a little drool coming out of his maw. I scratched his head. "You know what I'm talking about, don't you, my good boy." His small tail wagged vigorously, the better to disperse the deadly gas that exuded from his kiester. "Henry! You're ruining my fantasy," I said. The van swerved as I did my best to find the electric window control. I was frantic, the edges of my vision were beginning to blur, as I held on tight to the only good air within breathable proximity.

"Oh God, Talbot! Did you run over a zombie?" BT said, sitting bolt upright from his nap. Not a pleasant way to return to the world of the awoken. "I can't breathe," he hitched.

Tommy smiled as he stuffed two mini-marshmallows up his nose. "Iths noth so badth."

Tracy again saved the day as all the windows in the van simultaneously rolled down. Brendon's van swayed slightly as they passed through the toxic cloud that leaked out from our van. I'd freeze to death before I had to breathe in another piece of Henry's airified excrement. It was another two or three miles before the last remnants of Henry's oily feculence made rolling the windows up a doable possibility. It still smelled like dirty feet and burnt Fritos, but it was passable. All thoughts of food had been wiped cleanly from my mind.

But again back to the basics, I'm a guy. If not in survival mode (and then sometimes even then) my mind has about three factors that contend with each other. Hunker down ladies. If you're reading this with your man in some safe zone. I am about to give you all the knowledge you will ever need. If ten thoughts were to pass through your man's mind it would look like this: sex, sex, sex, food, sex, sex, football, sex, food, sleep, sex. (Did you count? I really put down eleven thoughts. Yup, that's how important sex is to us.) We'll only sleep if you're not offering sex or a sandwich. All that other bullshit we used to do in our 'regular' lives, like going to work, or painting the bathroom, or going to the fucking art museum, or seeing ANY chick flick, we did that so we could POSSIBLY get into your pants. Plain and simple. I don't at this point see any reason to mince words. We love sex in all its pure and depraved forms. Why this most basic of all animalistic rituals has thus far mostly eluded the feminine persuasion is beyond me. I would clean gutters in a hail storm in my underwear at midnight if it meant I MIGHT get to have sex. (I'd do all the above BUT in my regular clothes for an awesome Philly Cheese steak.) And that, my dear lady survivors, is ALL you will ever need to know about that big, dumb, hairy animal snoring next to you. Sorry guys, I didn't mean to let the cat out of the bag, but rapid procreation might be the only way we can stave off extinction.

"Don't you remember what happened the last time you went to McDonald's?" Tracy asked, circling back to my initial intercourse. (Doesn't seem like the right word to use here, but somehow it does.)

"What about…oh yeah," I answered.

CHAPTER 16 - THE CUT AWAY

It was a brutally hot day in July when I received my layoff notice. I had immediately called Tracy to let her know that she needed to stop the order we had put in for the hot tub in the backyard. I could 'feel' the tension and anger that she emitted right through the phone. "Fine," she had answered me in the curt tone that drove me friggin nuts. (In a bad way.)

"Everything alright?" I asked like an idiot.

"Everything's peachy," she had replied. (Just so you know, 'peachy' means 'anything but.') "The kids want McDonald's for dinner, and Nicole and Brendon are over."

Now was not the time, but I really wanted to tell her that maybe we should start to tighten the belt up a little. "The usual?" I asked abashed.

"What do you think?" she said, and then she hung up.

I would have smashed my phone against a wall if I had the income to replace it. I was screaming in my head. 'FUCK! Does she think I fired *myself*? Yeah, it must be all *my* FUCKIN' fault!' It was with this attitude that I rolled on up to the McDonald's drive thru. You kind of see where this is going?

Okay, just a little backfill so you can really get a grasp of where I'm coming from. During my Marine Corps days I worked on an airfield, and because of this I had lost no small measure of my hearing. Couple that with a cheap ass speaker system at any fast food drive thru and we were already in the midst of a communication barrier. Add to the fact that on that fateful night, Samir from the Great Republic of India had just gotten off a plane from his native country and had begun working the 'hole' as they call the place where your drive thru order is taken.

The dialog you are about to read is *after* I had put my order in for the third time and Samir had botched it for the third straight time.

"No, listen! I want a fucking Quarter Pounder with cheese AND FUCKING extra pickles!"

"You would like a cheeseburger with no cheese then, sir?"

"Are you fucking with me?" I was near screaming. "A fucking cheeseburger without cheese is a hamburger, where the fuck are you from?" Although it would have been impossible not to tell where he was from, unless of course you have not used ANY customer support line in the last five years.

"I am from Bangladesh, sir."

"You don't say?! Listen, I want a Quarter Pounder with cheese and extra pickles."

"Okay a large French fried with mustard then?"

"Do you smoke crack, Baba Ganoush?"

"Samir, sir."

"What?"

My name is Samir, sir. And no, I have never smoked anything, sir."

"Oh for the love of all that is holy."

"Would you like to pray, sir?"

I just wanted to back the car up and drive forward, running over the speaker. I couldn't stop looking at the box like it, and not money, was the root of all evil in the world.

"Sir, I have your order for four Mint McShakes, two small Dr. Pepper's, a cheeseburger with no cheese, two Quarter Pounders with cheese, one with extra onions and one without buns, a girl toy Chicken McNugget Happy Meal with apple slices, two Big McMacs and eighteen super-sized french fries with mustard."

Not one order, not one fucking order was right. I had nothing left, Samir had beaten me.

"Is that not correct, sir?" When I did not answer him, he finished. "That will be $52.75 sir."

I was numb as I pulled my car up to the first window, groping for my wallet. The next car in the growing line pulled up to the box, even from this distance, I could hear that I had in no way been singled out.

"NO! Not a McFlurrie with bacon!"

I pulled up to the first window, hoping beyond hope that I would find an ally to help me through these troubling times. Pimply faced 'Becka' was not going to be that person. She was busy talking to, I believe, 'Tonya' about what a jerk some guy named Spence was through her Bluetooth headset.

She didn't so much as look at me when she fairly demanded the money. "That's $52.75, oh my gawd he's the biggest jerk ever."

"Excuse me, miss?"

"So then he says to me, 'Did you see what Darla was wearing?' And I'm like why would I care what that beeyotch had on." She re-thrust her hand out seeking something I wasn't willing to entrust to her.

"Excuse me, miss?" I asked again, I would have had an easier time getting a response from Samir. I shuddered at that thought.

When Becka realized that I hadn't paid yet, she finally looked at me with that condescending teenager look that says 'I know everything and why are you still breathing? Don't you have a coffin to fill?' (I hate teenage girls, is there any species more foreign on this planet?)

"That's $52.75," she said again, this time with less veneer. Not that she was laying the 'nice' on too heavy to begin with.

"Miss, I had some problems with the drive thru."

Apparently Tonya came back with some profound insight, because Becka again completely forgot that I existed.

"I know, right?!" she replied excitedly, looking off into the distance.

How could Samir all of a sudden become the good employee in all of this? At least he paid me attention, even if he had no clue.

"Yeah, so then I sort of...oh wait, Tonya," she said, turning to me again. "This guy is at my window and won't leave. Yeah, I don't think he has any money. Oh gross, Tonya! No, he's not cute, he's like sixty-five or something."

Did she think I couldn't hear her end of the conversation? Did she care? Sixty-five? And I am kind of cute...aren't I? Why am I letting Becka make me doubt everything that I am? The human ego is very delicate; more like a thin-skinned tomato than the hardy coconut. It can be bruised easily with little more than some mishandling.

"Miss," I said. "My order isn't right."

"Hold on, Tonya. Didn't you just make it at the speaker? Gawd, Tonya, some of these people can be such dolts," she finished, looking straight at me.

Did she think she was texting? This couldn't be happening, could it? I was on *Punk'd* or something. Someone must be making a YouTube video. "Where's the camera?" I asked in the hopes that this was some masterful prank and not the true state of the world.

"No, he's still here. I think he may be a 'tard.'"

"Are you fucking kidding me? What is your problem?" Bruised ego or not, there was only so much I could take.

"Geez, there's no reason to get all hostile and stuff, it's not my fault you couldn't make your order right the first time."

I would have peeled away leaving a trail of rubber, but that's not really a specialty of Jeeps. I did drive away from the window and I did entertain the thought of just leaving and trying my luck at Burger King. Odds were today though, that I would encounter more of the same. Had I the clairvoyance to have checked my horoscope this morning I would have known how this day was going to turn out. It read just one word 'HIDE.'

If I went home now empty-handed, Tracy would make Becka's mishandling of my ego seem like a feather's caress. Nearly every fiber of my being revolted at the thought of going into the lion's den unarmed. I parked the car, stepped out and onto five or six ketchup packets that had been strategically placed for just this effect. Red sticky liquid nearly made it to the knee of my tan Dockers, my expensive Italian leather shoes looking like I had just followed OJ through a crime scene. Ronald McDonald mocked me with his feral grin, sitting on his bench all smug and self-centered.

Two of the largest women I had ever seen in my life nearly bowled me over as I tried to gain entrance into the inner sanctum of absurdity. Twins they were, but not of the 'Doublemint' variety. One was swathed in head-to-toe spandex. Anything resembling my appetite was lost. Her sister had on a skirt that struggled for all it was worth to stay attached at the seams. The skirt barely covered massive varicose-stained thighs. It looked like the world's most detailed map had been tattooed on her, but I really had my doubts that it led to anything resembling treasure.

"Oh, *he* looks good enough to eat," I heard one of the sisters murmur to the other.

The other sister placed her hand to her mouth and tittered. She looked about as dainty as a hippo.

Like I said, though, egos are fragile and tender. As easily as they can be broken they can be propped up. Now I wouldn't touch either one of these girls with a stick to see if they were alive, but still, at least one of them thought I was cute. Does 'good enough to eat' equal cute? It did in my world.

"Ladies," I said with my cheesiest grin as I held the door open. This time they both tittered. I felt magnanimous. I didn't have the slightest clue then that in just a few short months I was going to expend a magazine of high caliber rounds into each corpulent sibling.

It was with this much-improved demeanor that I walked into the restaurant and up to the counter. My mood was only slightly diminished as I felt the tackiness of my red sauce-covered shoe as it tried to adhere itself to the less than sanitary flooring. One young, harried mother was at the counter ordering, two of her children were running around like they had just sucked down a couple of Red Bulls. Her third child was busy picking up errant french fries that had ended up on the deck. I cringed as she placed these 'floor prizes' into her mouth.

"Lexus!" the mother screamed. "Stop that, I'm ordering your supper right now!"

Wait, so she wasn't upset that 'Lexus' was eating food off of a disgusting floor, but rather that she would ruin her appetite? Lexus didn't heed her mother's words as she placed another dirt encrusted something into her mouth. I don't think it was a french fry, but I tell myself that it was, so that I can make it through the day without dry-heaving. The germaphobe in me would have had to disown this kid if she was mine.

"Lexus, Mercedes, Fred, come on! I've got Happy Meals," the mother of the year yelled.

All three stopped, even Lexus with what appeared to be the midsection of a cockroach halfway to her mouth. The offending insect was discarded and rapidly forgotten as Lexus screamed merrily about getting a princess toy. My earlier jollity was completely destroyed as I stepped up to the counter. A sad faced man named Don (his name tag identified him as the shift supervisor) greeted me. I was to learn rather quickly that Don's day had pretty much paralleled my own (except for the part about losing his job, but that part would come later after I left).

"Sir, how may I help you?" Don asked, doing his best to hold on to what little remained of his dignity.

I'm not proud of some of the things I have done in my

life. You could count this as one of them. I am one of those people that is quick to anger and then let slide something that should have never left my brain to begin with. Quick to react, slow to think. Unfortunately, this was something my Nicole had picked up on early in life. She would scream bloody murder and I would come running. Justin usually became the hapless victim in this game as I would punish him before I even knew what was going on. If my daughter wrote that story she could probably call it, *The Manipulation of Michael Talbot*. And then the worst part of this whole affair would be the swallowing of my pride and admitting to my son that I was wrong. This was a shortcoming that had been a work in progress with me for years. That day I slid a long way back down the progress path.

Maybe it was the way he looked so pathetic, like he had already given up, that made me act the way I did. Maybe it was a baser evolutionary thing like the strong dominating the weak. I'm not saying I was right or trying to justify my actions, I'm just making an observation. You can be the judge if you want. But remember, I had just lost my job, my wife was pissed at me, it was 102 degrees out, Samir and his partner-in-crime Becka had conspired to make my trip to a fast food restaurant into an epic adventure worthy of any M. Night Shyamalan movie. I had ketchup half way up my pants. My expensive shoes were ruined. A giant fat lady wanted to eat me. I had just witnessed the singular most disgusting culinary experience in my life and now Don the Defeated was going to champion my cause? I think not.

All of this was going through my head as I formulated my reply to Don. "Fuck you!" Yep that's how I started off. Proud? Not a chance. Don's demeanor dipped even a little farther, but I thought I caught a glimpse of something else. I think my words sparked a flame of defiance in him.

"Sir?" he asked incredulously. Don's day had been shit thus far, but I was the first to cross the usually uncrossable unseen civilized barrier.

I knew in my heart of hearts that 'fuck you' was as inappropriate a response as I could go with, except maybe something about his mother. But again, my emotions were ruling my higher functioning. So when I told him to 'Go fuck yourself!' I had again taken a giant step against mankind. I'll give it to the guy, though, he wasn't quite ready to throw the towel in yet and step down into the primordial soup with me.

"Sir, if you could just please keep your voice down and keep the language more appropriate, I think we can resolve whatever problem you may be having."

At this point my loftier self was able to step away from the situation and take a more objective look at what was happening here from Don's point of view. Some ketchup-stained guy that appeared to have just smoked some bad crack comes into a family oriented restaurant throwing profanity around like a hooker throws pussy around at a dentist convention. That Don hadn't gone screaming into the rear of the store looking for a weapon was a testament to his inner strength, OR more likely I wasn't the first person that had come in after dealing with the dynamic duo of dipshits at the drive thru.

His words were having the desired effect. He had not escalated the confrontation. The more time he was giving me to reflect on my actions the better able I was to bridle my mental state – such as it was. I actually might have been able to salvage this encounter, if Becka's pimply-faced countenance hadn't taken this inopportune time to peek out from her workstation.

"Oh shit, Tonya. The half-wit came in the store! You should see his clothes, he looks like he's eaten, but couldn't tell exactly where his mouth was. I know, right?" She laughed. "He's got ketchup all down his legs! It's hilarious, Tonya. Hold on, I'm going to take a picture and send it to you."

Becka began to walk out from behind her work window, her phone lining up to take my most unflattering photograph since the DMV.

"Becka," Don began. "Don't you have some work you could be doing?"

'Oh please,' her expression dripped scorn. The sour look did little to dissuade Becka from her present course of action. I was too shocked to do anything as Becka took not one, but three pictures of me. I heard later that at least two of them ended up on the Internet.

Don and I both shared a moment of commiseration as we stared at the retreating form of the laughing Becka. "I'm sending it now, Tonya. Let me know when you get it! GET OUT!" she shrieked. "Bobby Ricci asked you out?!" The rest of the stimulating teenage-ese dialog was lost to us as Don and I again resumed our parley.

"You could start helping me...by firing her." I pointed vehemently to where the demon spawn had retreated.

"She's the best of the last seven people I've had working there," Don answered me back, his tone laced with dejection.

And just like that, the heat of my anger ebbed. Don was as much if not more of a victim in this whole affair as I was. He had been dealing with irate customers seemingly his entire professional life.

"Samir!" one of the fry cooks shouted from behind us. "What the hell is a fried salad wrap with M&M's?"

Don put his hands over his face. If he had access to anything sharper than a plastic butter knife, I think he would have taken the opportunity to perform hari-kari on himself.

I wanted this encounter to be over with and get out of here before it got any more bizarre. Sometimes I amaze myself with my flashes of prophecy. "Listen," I said hopefully. "I just want to get my order and get out of here." Don didn't respond, and I somehow took that as a good sign. "Okay," I said, nervously licking my lips. "I'd like to get two Quarter Pounders with cheese meals, a crispy chicken sandwich meal, two Big Mac meals, and the two cheeseburger meal with extra pickles. Oh yeah, and all of them with Coke is fine." Don still hadn't moved, not to even put my order into the not-so-idiot proof picture-laden register. At first I was sort of impressed that he would have the ability to memorize my whole order. Still nothing was happening. "Don?" I asked cautiously.

"YOU WANT! YOU WANT! What the fuck about what *I* want!" he screamed. The entire restaurant stopped and stared, even the nearly useless work staff. "You think I want to manage a bunch of zit pocked, hormone infused, spoiled brats that would rather be at home jerking off than making an honest living? And do you think I can get any of them to wash their hands after they're in the bathroom for half an hour doing God knows what?" I heard distant retching as one of the customers realized what they might be eating. One of the sandwich assemblers laughed out loud as he realized that he had just been called out. I noticed with disdain the nearly full box of sani-gloves next to his workstation that were going completely unused.

Customers began to leave in droves as if they could sense the oncoming explosion, why had my prophetic self chosen this time to desert. Of my entire order why he focused on this next part I'll never know.

"You want some extra fucking pickles?!" he yelled.

I nodded dumbly, eyes wide open along with my gaping mouth.

"I've got your fucking extra pickles right here!"

I can't express to you how relieved I was when he didn't pull his pants down and expose his 'male pickle' to me. My respite was short lived as he picked up a ten pound jar of pickle slices and began to hurl handfuls of the tangy sandwich slices at me. I stood dumbfounded as the rippled briny preserves slapped against my entire body. I guess I should be glad they were the sandwich slice variety as opposed to the spears. (Poor joke, I know, but how much further into ludicrousness could I travel.) I walked out of the store under a hail of fire, slices stuck to my face, neck and head. The sun began to instantly brown them as I strode to my car in a daze. I cannot recall the rest of the ride home. It wasn't until I walked in the back door and Tracy 'greeted' me, that the day began to come back into focus.

"Where's the food?" she shot out, her initial anger at my becoming unemployed still highly evident.

As she began to look closer at the near comatose expression on my face, the ketchup on my pants and shoes, and the pickle slices that dripped to the floor, her demeanor changed. "Oh, Talbot, how do you get into these messes?"

I would have aimlessly argued that I had nothing to do with it, but her ensuing laughter was like the siren call to sailors of lore. I joined in with her wholeheartedly. After heavy moments of out-of-control laughter we locked into a vinegar infused kiss that temporarily made all of our earthly concerns melt away. For twenty beats of my heart, the entire day had been worth the payout.

CHAPTER 17

Mike's Journal Entry Fourteen

"You're probably right," I said, answering her original question back in the here and now. But I still looked longingly at the rapidly departing, true King of Hamburgers. My heavy sigh went unnoticed or ignored, didn't really matter which, I wasn't getting any golden bronzed, dipped-in-sunlight french fries no matter how much I pouted.

We were still hours away from Carol's, and the weakened winter sunlight was doing its best to retreat into the west ahead of the frigid night. We had some choices, none of them particularly grand. We could push on through the night and get to Carol's in the blackest part of the evening. My feelings were that entering into that nightmare during the brightest part of the day might make it minutely more palatable. So we could cross off option number one. Number two consisted of pulling off to the shoulder of the road and sleeping in the car, but one look at the depleted gas tank gauge revealed that we would not be able to keep the car and subsequently the heater running for the entire night. Of the 'choices' we were contending with, we would have to pick the one that was the least unsavory. That doesn't mean it was a good choice, just better than the rest. It's like the choice to eat chocolate covered ants or caviar. They're both choices, but they both suck. Kind of like having to vote for either candidate in a presidential race – no matter which way you go, you're guaranteed taxes will increase and the winner will blame the losing parties' ineptitude for the necessity of the increase.

Option three involved pulling off the highway, getting some much needed gas, and finding some sort of safe haven to sleep the night away. Our luck at safe havens had been largely devoid these last few nights. I had my doubts that would turn around tonight. I pulled the van over and waited for Brendon to come up alongside. I laid out all my thoughts, hoping that someone might potentially have a better idea or possibly dissuade me from my present course of action. I'm a control freak in the strongest sense of the phrase but only insofar as a situation can be controlled. I've yet to come across a zombie that 'heeled' when I told it to.

"How long would it take to get to mom's?" Tracy asked with a strange mixture of hope and resignation.

"Shit…maybe four hours," I said, rubbing my eyes. "I'm exhausted though and we'll still need to pull over somewhere and get gas."

"What about finding a motel or something like that?" Brendon asked. "We could stay on the second floor, there's usually only one or two staircases that we would have to defend."

What he omitted, probably unintentionally, is that one or two staircases meant only one or two escape routes. Our lives depended on me always keeping vigilant. But it was still a decent idea. We had to stop; that was not the issue. We might as well be as comfortable as humanly possible, while we were still humans.

The stress I felt everyone exuding was tangible. It had a texture, a thickness to it. When we were moving we were safe. Every time we stopped the danger caught up to us. Only Justin and Tommy thought stopping was a good idea.

My hope was that Justin wanted to stop to give his low grade fever a chance to dissipate. I would not dwell any longer on any wild theories that I could not prove but could still feel in the depths of my soul. Damn it, the warring factions in me were mere children throwing stones compared to what was going on in his head. He might be the biggest threat to all of our survivals and he was my son. My soul wept, my essence raged, but nothing changed.

"Ryan says something about a lantern being on," Tommy said, his eyebrows pinched in a frown as he tried to make sense of his 'seer's' words.

You could hear a pin drop or Jen peeing a few feet away, you decide which descriptor fits. They were both accurate if not both politically correct. However, I don't think this was going to be on any ACLU docket in the foreseeable future.

"What'd I miss?" Jen asked as she came back, wiping her hands clean with some snow.

BT gave her the short version. "Brendon thinks we should stay at a motel and Tommy says there's a street light on somewhere."

She looked as confused as the rest of us, but she recovered a lot faster than any of us. She leaned her head into the minivan.

"Hi, Tommy," Jen said with a smile. Tommy blushed. "Whatcha got there?"

"Triple berry Pop-Tart with peanut butter frosting," he said proudly.

"Dad," Travis entreated. "You said we were out of Pop-Tarts."

I shrugged my shoulders. "Wait." Now I leaned my head into the minivan. "Did you say peanut butter frosting?"

"Uh huh," Tommy said, shifting uncomfortably as he noticed that everyone was looking at him.

"Did you spread peanut butter on your Pop-Tart, Tommy?" I asked.

He looked at me like I was crazy. His eyes rolled as he answered me. "We don't even have any peanut butter, Mr. T."

"But Pop-Tarts never made a peanut butter frosted

variety, Tommy," I stated.

"Oh forget the Pop-Tarts, Talbot," Jen hushed me.

(I let it go then, but I haven't forgotten about them yet, and I can guarantee when the savage vestiges of Alzheimer's are rendering my mind into brain flavored oat meal and I am slinging my own shit against the walls, I'll remember triple berry Pop-Tarts with peanut butter frosting. Oh you, dear reader, can be assured that after Jen got her answers I checked that Pop-Tart out and it was indeed the flavor he described. Not that the kid had ever lied, but maybe he got confused. He hadn't.)

"Okay, let me get this straight…Brendon says 'motel' and Tommy says 'street light is on,' right?" Jen asked.

Nicole clarified with "Lantern, he said a lantern was on, not a street light."

"Let's go, we've got a motel to find," Jen said with a huge smile on her face.

"Um, any chance you could let the rest of us know what mystery you figured out?" BT asked.

"Come on in, we'll leave the light on for you," Jen beamed.

"Huh?" BT asked.

Tommy, around mouthfuls of an impossibly flavored snack, nodded fervently in agreement.

"The old Motel 6 catch phrase," I wrapped up.

"Exactly," Jen said. "Let's go, I'm freezing."

Nobody needed any more persuading than that.

Within twenty minutes we came up on a viable choice for our overnight stay, even if there wasn't a Dunkin' Donuts. Beresford, South Dakota was about to become our home away from home – at least for the night. It was by far the prettiest place we had stopped thus far in our journey, with its tree-lined streets and the pond in the center of town. But 'pretty' doesn't equate to safe.

It was a given that zombies travel to where the food is. So, by pure theory alone, small towns should be the first places to become devoid of the offending vermin. Like flesh-eating locusts, they plunder and pillage the local resources and move on. They don't hunker down and make roots. Can't really cultivate a human farm, can you? I shuddered as I thought about *The Matrix*. Okay, but that was about machines harvesting humans for energy. If I come across penned up humans with zombie cowboys, my tentative grip on the fringes of sanity will be forever frayed. I shook my head, trying my best to dislodge the offending vision. Like this shit isn't bad enough…I've got to try to drum up even more exciting scenarios.

"Ah, what I'd do for a nuclear bomb."

"A nuclear what?" my wife asked. Her contortion of fear was clearly outlined.

"Did I say that out loud?" I asked, clearly confused.

When had I last let the inner thoughts of my unkempt mind out for all to see? My inner trappings were not a pretty place and I always made a careful case to make sure that my mind was shuttered against even the most curious onlookers. Tracy had long ago learned not to try and find out what I was thinking. My sometimes candid answers more often than not left her confused, concerned and just plain weirded out. Honest to God, I used to think that everybody thought the way I did, and were just as good at hiding it as I was. That, however, wasn't the case. My depths of paranoia, conspiracy and psychosis approached and most likely surpassed levels that should have been medicated away. But it was these same 'malfunctions' of my mind that had kept my family thus far safe and sound. If I had really been able to 'realize' my dream though, we would be riding this out in style in some giant underground shelter. I envy all of you that had the resources to pull that off.

"Look, the light is on!" Tommy said excitedly.

And it was. The chill of icy fingers that ran up my spine was back and it was corpse cold. I shuddered involuntarily. Nobody but Tommy saw good in the stupid little hundred-watt bulb shining bright through the twilight.

"How is that light still on, Talbot?" BT asked in hushed tones with a note of reverence in his voice.

"There's a machine with Kit-Kats in there, do you have any change, Mr. T?" Tommy asked hopefully.

It's amazing to me that all of us had known Tommy long enough that nobody even looked halfway cross-eyed at him at his pronouncement. If Tommy had said that a convention of clowns respite with balloon animals was in there singing Billy Joel songs, we would all have believed him. Of course I wouldn't have gone in, clowns are evil, but I still would have believed him.

I pulled into the parking lot. Brendon wisely remained on the street in the event that he needed to make a quick getaway. A few more years of exposure to me and he would be completely infected with my derangement. I was like a proud papa watching his baby take his first steps.

"What are you doing, Talbot?" BT leaned in to me and asked, still in that hushed tone.

I wanted to let him know that zombies were more olfactory stimulated than auditory, but then I remembered that there were other demons out there that still went bump in the night. Durgan invaded my thoughts for a moment. I snuffed the thought before it could grow.

My mind malignancy could not get past the thought that something was amiss here. Zombies are notorious dark dwellers, relying mostly on smell to track down their prey. Odds of zombies being around were about ten percent. Next on my list were bad guys, your average low life, *Mad Max* types – take whatever you will and destroy the rest. Again this is a relatively small percentage, maybe ten percent also. This type, while very dangerous, doesn't lie in wait. They go out and seek to take. Okay, next came just regular folks doing their best to survive. I hate to keep beating a dead horse, but this is also a small percentage, I'll stick with the ten percent.

I might not be the greatest role model for this example, but I can guarantee I wouldn't be hanging a 'We're Open' shingle out on my front door.

Next we have our garden variety bad guy, using a lure to bring in some unsuspecting slobs. This percentage was considerably higher than the others, maybe twenty percent. But unless you carried your own personal physician with you, inviting trouble was not always a viable advantage. It was still early enough in the apocalypse that supplies were fairly abundant. Food, clothes, and ammo were everywhere. Zombies had little use for them and by this time outnumbered humans thousands-to-one.

So what was in small supply and would become a high trade commodity? Women, goddammit, it always comes down to women. The bane of our existence, and our small party contained three of the golden ones. Okay, that twenty percent might go up.

Now this part is something I've let very few people know. That's a lie. I've let nobody know. This, I've come to learn is a huge character flaw in myself. I don't want to change it and I recognize it for what it is. It's the inability to reach out and help those in need. I don't feel the altruistic requirement to help people. Sure, I'll die for my family or my friends if the demands require it. I've risked my neck for the men I've fought next to and even for people that I've been tentatively tethered to (think Cash). But I will not go out of my way to help those in need. I'm blown away by the people that used to go to Africa and try to help populations dying from starvation. My first response was always, 'What is their ulterior motive?' Yeah, there's the cynic in me rearing its grotesque head. Doctors and nurses could only be in it for the money, rich people giving to charities was for tax purposes, actors donating time to build houses, free publicity. So the thought that some people were in that motel wanting to help others was by and far the largest percentage of probability and it was easily the most difficult for me to reconcile in my mind.

I looked over my right shoulder as I backed out of the parking lot. Tommy looked like I had just run over a family of rabbits with a lawnmower.

"Did I tell you about the Kit-Kats, Mr. T?" Tommy lamented.

"What are you doing, Talbot?" Tracy asked. She hated to see the distress in Tommy's face.

"Hedging my bets," was my terse reply.

"Against what?" Tracy asked. "What's going on?" She had inklings of how deep my disturbed waters ran, and for the most part made sure that she didn't wade too far from shore. But since this whole undertaking had begun she had started to indulge me more and more. I felt sadness that she would someday swim in the turmoil I was mired in daily, but that was beyond my control for now.

I parked next to Brendon on the road without telling anyone my plan. I grabbed my gun and got out. "Tra…" She was already moving into the driver's seat.

"Hold on, Talbot, I'm coming with you," BT said as he fumbled with his seat belt. The material looked stretched to its capacity around his immense bulk.

"Hold on, BT, *I* know that you're a big sweetheart." He grumbled at that. "But any poor folks in there are going to look at you and think you're a raging T-Rex." He took no umbrage to my words. A small smile may have passed his lips. It was difficult to tell in the light available to us.

Travis was halfway out the door. I stopped him. "Not this time, champ." I motioned for him to get back in the car.

"Talbot, let's just go," Tracy entreated.

"Go where? I haven't given up on this place, I'm just not a hundred percent convinced yet," I answered.

"How convinced are you?" Tracy asked. She had not been expecting an answer, so when I came back with "fifty-fifty," she understandably didn't know whether to be troubled or thankful.

I took that one calming breath that really doesn't do anything except focus you on the fact you are about to do something foolhardy or dangerous, or a combination of the two. All eyes watched me as I slowly approached the motel. Halfway across the parking lot my concern came to fruition in the form of a green laser dot painted plainly on my chest.

"Dad, why'd you stop?" Travis asked. His voice rang out too loudly in the unaccountable quiet. I hesitated to turn and tell him. I slowly raised my arms in the universal gesture of 'Don't put a cavernous hole in my body.'

"Oh fuck," I heard from a multitude of mouths behind me. I concurred with them completely. I heard multiple car doors open or slide, the cavalry was on the way.

"Make them stop or you'll be on the ground before you hear the shot," the disembodied voice said softly for my ears only. It seemed to be coming from above and to the left of me, but I wasn't willing to bet my life on that fact.

"STOP!" I said loudly. "He says that if you keep coming, he'll kill me." The sheer quantity of guns I heard being cocked behind me at least gave me the slight satisfaction in knowing that my death would be avenged tenfold.

"What's your business here?" the voice came again, and now I was willing to put some more stock in the premise of his location.

Odds were that he wasn't the only one on this field of play. No chance this was a laser device from a tape measure. Those were only of the red variety. Green lasers were much more powerful and generally included only on tactical weapons. Would I feel the splintering of my chest plate as it first contorted to accept the intruding projectile and then shattered around the bullet? Would my heart burst as the bullet tore through it like so many watermelons I had shot? And if I was somehow still alive after all that damage to myself, would I be able to register the paralysis my body suffered as my spinal column was severed in two? Would it be better to be shot with a full metal jacketed bullet that would strike small and leave a fist sized opening in my back? Or with a traditional lead round that would mushroom immediately upon impact thus allowing it to damage more vital organs as it crushed to a stop halfway through my being? Maybe a low velocity round that would hit somewhere center mass and tumble through my body only to find a hasty exit through my orbital socket? It was a gruesome picture I was painting. I truly wished I wasn't the model for it.

I answered my captor's question honestly. "My business is to not get shot." I wasn't expecting a laugh when I answered him but that's exactly what I received.

"I think that's all of our businesses." I could tell from his tone he enjoyed the response. But his prior wariness, if it had diminished at all, was only by a negligible amount. "I would feel more comfortable if you put that weapon on the ground," he said to me.

I wasn't really in a negotiable place, but what the hell. "And I'd feel more comfortable if I wasn't painted with a laser. It's a little unsettling."

"Well, that's the point isn't it?"

Great, I got to deal with a realist.

"Okay, you put that gun down, I'll take the laser off of you, but you do realize I'm not the only one that has a bead on you and your traveling party."

I had figured I was the target. Realizing my family was an errant mosquito bite away from coming under fire was almost more than I could bear. My body shook with rage, my soul quaked with fear. I gently placed my AR on the ground.

"Alright, I've held up my end of the agreement." The laser unwaveringly still dissected my body.

I could hear what sounded like a muffled high intensity argument. Seemed to me someone was very adamant about not having guests. That I was waiting patiently for someone else to decide my fate was not sitting well. I carefully eyed my rifle and got busy deciding how quick I could pick it up and at least go out in a blaze of glory.

"Don't even think about it," the same voice warned me.

"Too late," I said.

He laughed again. Fuckers have night vision goggles. I felt slightly envious and more than a little pissed at myself that I hadn't thought to pick some of those gems up. I'm sure Dick's Sporting Goods would have had some. Not of the military grade but something better than my impotent human vision. Odds were we would have picked this ambush up long before I stumbled my ass across the parking lot. More hushed skirmishing ensued. I had half a mind, the crazier half to be sure, to tell them to hurry up. Holding my arms over my head like this was killing my shoulders. No reason to poke a hornet's nest though, they don't even make honey.

After what seemed like indeterminable minutes the arguing stopped. Who won? The ones that wanted to kill us all outright, or the ones that wanted to kill just the men outright?

"Alright, I want you to tell all those people behind you to put their weapons down and come forward with their hands up," the voice said all business like.

I didn't need to ponder my response in the slightest. "No." I'd wished I had those goggles now just to see his expression.

"I don't think you understood me," he shot back...with words thankfully.

"Oh I understood you just fine. I'm just not doing what you asked." Impudence didn't seem like the right tact but there I was rattling off at the mouth again with reckless abandon.

"We can kill you where you stand. You get that, right?"

"I get that utterly and completely and that is why under no circumstances will I drag my family and friends into your killing zone."

More hushed arguing. "I'm putting my arms down. My shoulders are killing me!" I yelled.

"Slowly! And do not make a move for that gun!"

"Fine, fine!" I yelled back as I dropped my outstretched hands down and began to rub blood back into my numbed arms.

More hushed verbal brawling ensued. Obviously no succinct chain of command here, Democracies didn't generally fare so well in survivalist societies, but then I remembered I was the one in the less than desirable position.

A woman's voice shot out this time. I shouldn't have been surprised at all by her question but I was. "Do you have someone named Tommy with you?"

From behind her I heard another woman's voice say softly, "That was stupid, Maggie, you should have asked them their names."

I was reaching, but they had opened the door I might as well knock it off its hinges. "Do you have a Kit-Kat machine?" It would have been impossible to not hear their gasps of surprise. "I'll take that as a yes?"

"How could you know? It was delivered the day the zombies came. It never even made it out into the lobby," the same female voice asked disbelievingly.

"Maggie, why don't you just invite them in?" came the other feminine voice, it was worded as a sarcastic challenge and Maggie knew that, but she used the words for her own devices.

"Do you want to come in?" the one that must be Maggie asked.

Before I could even answer I heard Tommy shout from across the way. "Can we get some Kit-Kat bars!?"

"Tommy? Right?" Maggie asked me.

"One and the same," I answered. The potential for violence had passed like an ill wind, but I still wasn't taking any chances. "I'd like to grab my rifle and shoulder it."

"Oh yeah...sure, go ahead," came the male voice with not a hint of the earlier malice.

We had, in seconds, gone from Showdown at the OK

Corral to *Mr. Roger's Neighborhood* and again it was Tommy that saved the day. He was like a cat with the whole 'nine lives' thing going on. No, that wasn't quite right, because cats don't generally give their lives out for others. Whatever he was, he had at the very least saved my ass. I'd buy him that damned Kit-Kat machine.

The danger had passed. I can't tell you how exactly I'd known, but I did. I didn't consider it gambling our lives on a hunch either. I waved Tracy and Brendon into the parking lot. They must have felt the same way I did because neither of them hesitated, as it was Tracy almost clipped Brendon's front bumper in her haste to get in. Was Tommy broadcasting good cheer like a high wattage radio station? There was a good chance of it; and if Tommy wasn't concerned, then none of us should be.

The little motel wasn't much to look at. It was two stories tall and basically just a giant box. It was like any other motel you've seen 150,000 times before if you had ever traveled the highways of North America. That being said, it was in better shape than ninety-five percent of those other motels. I'd even wager that during the summer months the pool wasn't a shade of avocado green. As tired as I was, the Ritz Carlton would not have looked much better.

The man lowered a ladder down to us that I hadn't noticed before. Maybe because it was painted black, but more likely because I had a green laser dot on my chest. Those tend to transfix your attention to the detriment of all other things.

Tommy had come up beside me, eyeing the ladder warily.

I absently fingered the gun on my shoulder. Unease trickled in from a small black hole in the base of my skull. "What's the matter, Tommy?" I asked as innocently sounding as possible.

Tommy turned to look at me, his face a mask of seriousness. "The Kit-Kats aren't up there."

The unease evaporated under the light of a thousand suns. I laughed until tears streamed from my eyes and – I'm sorry to say – as snot sluiced from my nose. Tommy handed me a wrapper from his phantom Pop-Tarts. I started laughing harder at the prospect of wiping my nose with a piece of papery tinfoil. Catching my breath was becoming agonizingly difficult, in a good way.

Nicole had got out of the car to see what was so funny. When she saw the state that I was in she felt the need to comment. "Ew...gross, Dad, I'll get you a paper towel."

I started laughing harder, I guess it was the pent up endorphins. Under my tutelage, my daughter suffered to a degree of germaphobia. She doesn't have the advanced scope and breadth like I do, but she is working on her undergrad status. I laughed at how she cringed at my condition. Hell, if I wasn't laughing so hard I would have been grossed out, too. True to her word, within thirty-seconds or so she had brought me half a roll of paper towels. I was beginning to come down from my self-induced high. Shit I'm a cheap date. That almost got me going again, but streamers of snot nearly a foot long kept it at bay. Tommy was watching me fascinated. He kept absently wiping his nose, maybe in the hopes that I would follow his lead.

"Ew, Dad! Take these!" my daughter said, thrusting the paper towels into my hand.

"How's about a kiss for your dear old dad?" I made like I would go after her and she fled like I was the world's largest oozing sore.

I was moments away from bursting. My sinuses ached from the fluid I had pumped through them. I couldn't even begin to explain how happy I was when later Maggie would break out a first aid kit that contained Benadryl.

I assured Tommy that we would get some Kit-Kats before the night was through, but right now we should meet our hosts. That seemed to mollify him somewhat and at least his bottom lip stopped quivering. Tommy made sure he was first up the ladder. I think he did it just so that he could get the greeting part out of the way and the eating part underway. Again Tommy's action made me realize that this was a safe place but it still takes more than a minute or so to get the stain of a bullet beacon off of your mind.

While the event is taking place and adrenaline is surging through your veins, you have a difficult time assessing just how much danger you are in or how close you are to taking a dirt nap. It's after the fact, when you've burned through your go-go juice and the imminent danger has passed...that is when the mind fuck really starts to set in. You've never heard of Amid-Traumatic Stress Syndrome. There's no time to become a basket case in battle. My friends that didn't react back in Iraq, well, I buried them.

But now that this last crisis had passed, my knees were weak and my breath was ragged. I couldn't get the images out of my head of my inconsolable wife and daughter as they looked down on my lifeless body. I knew the boys would soldier on. I had prepared them well. Even Tommy would be alright. He had an uncanny ability to see the world in a better light, rather than the black one that covered us now. Could rose-colored glasses change the landscape that much? No, for the umpteenth time I knew in my depths it was something much grander than I was prepared to accept or acknowledge with him. I knew Henry would feel the loss, say what you will, but I know I'm more than just a food delivery system for him.

If you never had the grand opportunity to befriend (not own) a bully, then you have truly missed out on one of life's pleasures. I have never encountered a breed of dog that possessed more of the grander human traits, love and affection, without the less savory ones, hostility and aggression. Yes, Henry would feel the loss, of that I was sure. He would not have the capacity to understand where I had gone off to; hopefully he would think I went to live out the rest of my life on some huge hominid farm. Yes, these are all the thoughts that coursed through my head as I marshaled my reserves and ascended the ladder.

Tommy was already busy making new friends when I came over the railing. The man who had moments earlier been about to give me some internal air conditioning grabbed a handful of my jacket and helped me over. Under normal circumstances I might have been so inclined as to shrug his arm off of me but since I was pulling energy from my stashed resources, I accepted his offer. Brendon, BT, Travis, and Jen hung back by the cars in a loose semicircle, their placement making it very difficult to be taken out quickly in an ambush. Justin had never got out of the van and Tracy and Nicole both got into the driver's seat of their respective machines. All in all it was a very tactical maneuver, we were becoming good at the game of staying alive. We had to. The stakes were too large.

I had no sooner finished appraising our situation when the motel man spoke to me.

"Sorry about that," he said with a quick, mirthless smile. "Can't be too careful these days."

I nodded like a bobble head doll. I wanted to break his jaw.

When he saw I wasn't going to give him the standard 'It's okay. I understand that you had to point a gun at me and threaten to shred my innards into the contour of chipotle pulled pork. I get it, it's cool, let's be best friends. Do you mind if I break your jaw?' he continued. "Right. Well then, my name is Denmark and the lady over there giving the big fella a hug is my wife Maggie."

"Who's the one that wanted you to shoot me?"

He leaned in conspiratorially. "That's Maggie's sister, Greta. She's a mean bitch, that one."

"I gathered that."

He laughed. I wanted to, I just wasn't there yet.

Maggie disengaged from Tommy, her face beaming. Maggie asked Tommy one question before she came over to me. "Why the broccoli tree?"

"His mom says he should eat more greens," I answered for him.

Maggie came over to me with her hand outstretched. I took it only out of a courtesy I didn't feel. "Welcome, welcome!" she said, pumping my arm vigorously.

Her sour-faced sister looked over Maggie's shoulder. Greta's look still conveyed the feeling that Denmark should have taken the shot. One glance at Greta and I knew why she was such a 'mean bitch.' Maggie was slightly older than Greta, maybe late fifties to Greta's mid-fifties. But that was it for similarities. At one time it was easy to see that Maggie was quite the looker, even now she bore a stately beauty that belied her years. Greta must have pissed God off something fierce, because she had been whacked with the ugly stick a few dozen times. Where Maggie was tall and slender, Greta was short and rotund. Maggie's regal features were only more sharply pointed out by Greta's globbish ones. It must have been absolute hell growing up in that shadow.

I pulled Denmark close after Maggie's embracing welcome and Greta's dismissive nod. "They're sisters?"

Denmark nodded. "That goat's been a thorn in my side since I married her sister. But to have the one I had to accept the other. It's been a good deal, but there have been times I've thought of trying to fix Greta up with one of my friends. But not a one of my friends has ever crossed me enough to warrant that punishment 'Sides, I don't think she'd ever leave her sister and then I'd be stuck with her, her pissed off new husband, and a lost friend."

"I see your point." I liked Denmark. The previous incident, while not completely forgotten, was beginning to be covered over with better thoughts. Thank the stars for the copious amounts of weed I'd smoked as a kid. Having short-term memory loss could be a plus sometimes. "So what's your status here?" I asked.

Denmark hesitated, sure I had shook his hand and his

wife was completely enamored with Tommy, but we were still strangers. And as he gazed down at my traveling companions, he knew we were a small army unto ourselves. A sheer moment of trepidation crossed his face as he realized he may have just opened up his last holdout of safety to us.

I watched as his emotions ran the gambit from 'Thank God I have some help' to 'Oh, God, what have I done.' I could only take so much pleasure in the man's discomfort. Some small piece of me did like the fact that now he was the one to squirm, but I let the pettiness pass.

"You're fine, Denmark. We're somewhat good people just trying to make our way through."

He released the building tension within himself with a heavy sigh. "It's been a long time since I've been able to let my guard down." I put my hand on his shoulder. "It's just been me and the girls the last couple of weeks. We had a few guests at the time." He looked at me with doleful eyes. "Well, you know." I nodded in acknowledgement, I knew all too well. "They left to go back to wherever they had come from. I can't imagine they got to where they were going, though. It was a lot more chaotic back then. For the most part now, we only see the, the..." he groped for the right word.

How can anybody be alive in the twenty-first century and not know the name for the living dead? I was soon to learn that he was a fan of all novels...if they were of the Western variety. Not many zombies traversing down the Rio Grande back in those days.

"Zombies," I assisted him.

"Yeah right, those things. We had a hell of a time those first few days. Didn't sleep much, shot my way out of more jams than I care to remember." He shuddered as he thought back. "Maggie and Greta never so much as fired a gun. 'Sides, I didn't want her to be weighed down with those pictures in her head. Maggie that is, I thought Greta might be good at it, seeing as how mean she is. The only thing she was good at was pointing out what else needed to be shot, I suppose that had its own benefits."

"And minuses," I added.

"And minuses," he said, looking at me. "We tried to make a go of it from the lobby. Our place is downstairs and there's a full kitchen with food and amenities. But they kept breaking through whatever defenses we put up."

I sympathized. How many seemingly unbreakable defenses had they circumvented at Little Turtle? A pang of homesickness coursed through me like bad chili.

"After the fourth night of no sleep, we moved to the second floor. Seemed hardly worth it at the time, it just meant those things were going to be a little more tired before they ate us. Was Maggie had the idea to get rid of the steps. First we threw some dressers and beds, mattresses, whatever it took to keep them from getting up here. Then I grabbed a toolbox that I have in the utility room up here and smashed through the concrete step. The hardest part was sawing through the metal support each step had. Figured two steps would be enough, I did four on each stairwell."

"Great minds think alike." I recounted to him my whole stair removal and carnival ride installation. He got a good laugh when I told him how pissed off my wife had been.

"We lived on crappy candy bars, Mountain Dew, and old donuts for five days while those things hovered around looking for food. Then they just sort of up and left. I killed whatever stragglers came by, but the worst of it seemed over. I nearly broke my leg when I tried to jump over the missing steps. I went back to our apartment and grabbed boxes of food to bring back up, and then I realized I'd never be able to jump that gap going up. Not nearly as spry as I used to be, I used to play football when I was in high school, outside tackle."

He seemed to need to tell me all this; I didn't see any reason to stop him. Figuring I might be ensnared in his story for a bit, I took a moment as he sorted through his old memories to let everyone know below that it was A-OK up here and that they should park and bring ALL the ammo. If we were going to be in a firefight, I was going to make it as one sided as possible.

He continued as if I had never turned away. "But that was a long time ago and I would have played college ball 'cept for a knee injury my senior year. Last damn game of the season and we was winning forty-two to fourteen. I was laughing and joking and actually making eyes with this pretty little cheerleader."

"Maggie?"

"How'd you know?"

"Just a guess. You two look like you've been together for a long while."

"I'm really glad I didn't shoot you."

"You and me both, Denmark."

"So there I am making an ass out of myself and the play goes off and I'm not paying any attention. My own teammate blindsided me. Not his fault at all, I never moved. Saw nothing but red as I fell in pain. Maggie was the first one to me. Not sure if she felt guilty about the whole thing, but if it got her to say 'yes' when I asked her to marry me…then it all worked out for the best." His look was still of that far away, dreamy quality, in a much happier time and place. "Where was I?" He looked like a coma victim suddenly come back to awareness after a prolonged sleep.

"Mountain Dew and a bunch of food," I prodded.

"Oh that Mountain Dew, that's the devil's brew that is. Never so much as sniffed the stuff before they came. Now I'm addicted to it. Damn near cost me my life."

I laughed to myself. He talked about good old Mountain Dew like it was crack and you would have to go down to the seedier parts of towns and find a dealer. Did they pour it into little baggies? Would you buy it by the ounce? I let my inner thread stop as Denmark continued with his story.

"So first when'd…"

'When'd?' Is that a word? I'd have to ask Tracy later.

"...I realized I couldn't get back up the stairs I grabbed this here ladder."

Which was vibrating slightly from Brendon's third trip up with ammo. "You sure about all this ammo, Mike?" he asked pleadingly.

I nodded, not interrupting Denmark's story. I heard Brendon mumbling something about how 'just because you're my girlfriend's dad (mumble mumble) go fu...(grumble)...self.' The rest was lost as he moved further away and Jen came up with some food. I smiled. Sometimes command had its perks.

Denmark continued his narrative. "And that's how we've been getting stuff up here. That Mountain Dew though, I couldn't get enough. Emptied the soda machine up here within a couple of days and then the one downstairs a few days after that."

I thought that might be where his life had been endangered, but I was wrong.

"I went for about forty-eight hours without the stuff, I was sucking down Pepsis in hopes that they would ease the craving. It didn't work, I thought Sprite might do the trick, didn't even come close. Maggie thought I had lost my mind when I told her I had to go down to the Piggly Wiggly to get me some more. She told me I was going to do no such thing. Greta just gave me a list of things she wanted. Maggie got so upset I figured she was finally going to give her sister the old heave ho for that. Well, you can see that didn't happen."

I lamented with him at the appropriate time.

"So's I grabbed Ole Bessie here," he said, holding up his rifle.

It looked nothing like its namesake. It was a tricked out AK-47 with a sighting laser (obviously) and a 150 round ammunition drum attached. I had no idea where he would have come across such a monstrously wonderful weapon, but I was going to ask.

"And as I climbed down the ladder, the missus told me

that if I didn't come home safe and sound to not bother coming home at all. She was so upset I don't think she knew that she made absolutely no sense. I figured if I got in enough trouble that I couldn't get home, then I was pretty much dead."

I nodded with him in agreement.

"So then she tells me that if I'm going anyway I might as well get...well, you get the point, ended up she had a list, too. Felt like a damn fool heading to the Piggly Wiggly with a rifle strapped to my back. Drove my old pickup truck."

Which was actually a 2009 GMC Jimmy; the thing was pristine. I looked longingly at it and then back at the Terrible Teal Machine a few times during our stay there.

"Got to the mart and it was quiet, quiet like the world was holding its breath, wondering what was going to happen next. There was nothing on those two shopping lists I felt was worth my life, damn near turned around the second my boot crunched down on the pavement. I was gonna go back and tell Maggie my knee was acting up and I couldn't walk right, much less run iffen I had too. Maggie and Greta would have known I had chickened out, but Greta would have told me so to my face, that dour faced...is she around? No? Bitch. I had one foot on the ground and one still in the truck. That damn Dew made me do it. I had to have it. Seemed about the only thing in this world 'sides my Maggie worth living for."

I loved beer, and I couldn't even begin to explain how I longed to chug that nectar of the gods, but would I risk my life for it? I really, I mean really, pondered the question. Fuck, I think I would. Stupid, sure...but there's more than one person, starting with my wife, that'll tell you I'm not a rocket scientist.

"I used my tire iron to pry the doors open, no 'lectricity and all." He looked at me as he said this to see if I was judging him for his lapse in moral character.

It took me a second to understand what he was asking me. My understanding? My forgiveness? "We are all doing what we need to do, Denmark." Why he cared about my thoughts on the matter, I didn't know. I didn't then – and I don't now – have the power of absolution.

"Smell. The smell was what hit me first. I don't like to think of it much. I can still recall it. When I was fifteen had a Coon dog that got sprayed by a skunk, that was Chanel No. 5 in comparison."

Oh I knew that smell all too well, the zombies, not the Chanel No. 5. An SOS pad on a stick, shoved up my nose, and thoroughly whisked around would not eradicate the perpetual olfactory odor that had been burned into that unfortunate organ.

"Michael, I pretended it was the meat gone bad. I guess it kind of was." He laughed. "Just the wrong kind." His smile disappeared as rapidly as it had come on. "The regular lights were out. There were still a couple of red auxiliary lights hanging on to some small trickle of power. It did little to make the store seem more shoppable. If some little five-year-old had come from behind a register and said 'boogey-de-boo' I would have pissed myself."

I laughed. Denmark didn't share in my view. I get that a lot. Either my base of reference is highly skewed or everyone else's is. I figured it was everyone else, why shine that light on myself.

"I propped the door open to get some light and to let some breathable air in. It helped some, but only if I stayed within fifteen feet of the door. Figured my odds of everything on my lists being that close was slim to none." He laughed. I didn't. We'd synch up sooner or later.

"Good story, Mike?" Brendon said crabbily as he made his fourth? No, maybe seventh trip up the ladder.

I wanted to respond and tell him 'Yeah, not bad.' But I needed to remember that in the post-apocalyptical world virtually everyone was armed.

Denmark wiped his face with rough hands long exposed to the arduous life of hard work and cold weather. If he had cried, I pretended not to notice. "Then they started to come, Mike, those...those things. They were my friends and my neighbors. I blew the head off my kids' Sunday School teacher. Perts, the postman, nearly got me. I'd never seen him move so fast when he was delivering the mail."

I so wanted to laugh now; again...not appropriate.

"I put twenty rounds in him 'fore I had the good sense the Lord gave me to let go of the trigger."

I harkened back to my magazine emptying encounter with the double-fat twins. It felt like twenty years ago.

"And still they came, Mike, had to have been a couple dozen iffen there was one. My ammo drum came up empty as I killed the last one. If there had been just one more, I probably would have stood there while it did its thing. I think I was in shock."

"That's understandable, Denmark. Not many a man has had to go through what you've gone through." I almost thought of adding 'at least that's how it used to be, anybody alive now has had to.'

"I didn't even go back to the truck and get the extra ammo. I grabbed a cart and a sanitary wipe..."

A man after my own heart.

"...and shopped. I walked around the bodies like it was the most natural thing in the world. I did grab three of everything just because I never wanted to have to go back to that store again." He wiped his face again, attempting to remove the invisible stain that the encounter had placed on him.

I assured him that was the way of the world now. It wasn't a pleasant prospect, but he had done nothing shameful or worthy of his guilt. He appreciated the words but I don't know how effective they were.

CHAPTER 18

Mike's Journal Entry Fifteen

Within the hour we were all sitting in Unit 203. Denmark had salvaged an old potbelly stove that kept the room a balmy two degrees below the temperature on the surface of the sun. Occasionally I had to go outside to keep my lungs from cooking because of the super-heated air. If it bothered Denmark, Maggie or Greta in the least, they didn't let anyone know. The mood was convivial; even Greta smiled a few times, which I think really caught Denmark by surprise. I was fairly convinced he didn't think she had the muscle memory to do such an action.

Everyone had let their guard down somewhat. Maggie couldn't stop fussing over the boys. She said they reminded her of her own boys. They had not heard from Larry or Jim since the start of it all. For moments she would get lost in her thoughts and grief and then come back around full circle beginning with wiping Tommy's Kit-Kat-smeared face. Travis squirmed from her ministrations, torn between acting like the man he was rapidly and forcibly becoming and the boy who still looked to adults for all the answers and protection. Justin feigned sleep to be left alone. In my twisted brain I feared that it was the contact with goodness that so repelled him from her.

Denmark was a great storyteller and had the entire room

enthralled in some story involving a canoe, a tree that ate people, and a cat that saved the world. Between the length of the day, the heat from the stove, and a now sated belly, I found myself dozing off. I was startled awake to some raucous laughter, something about the cat falling out of the canoe and into the water. I stumbled out of the room. I had the uncomfortable feeling that my liver was beginning to cook from the inside out. This must be what that poodle felt like when its master tried to dry him off in the microwave. I opened the door and the bracing cold in my face as well as the fire behind was an invigorating sensation.

"What'd you grow up in…a barn?" came Denmark's voice.

I had heard the rebuke from my mother enough to know he wanted me to go in or out and shut the door in either case. My intention was to continue on out and pull in some cold fresh air into my lungs in hopes to store it against the stove's blistering heat.

"Michael?" Denmark asked when I didn't move.

Tracy turned to look due to Denmark's tone. I was a man frozen, but not by cold. "Talbot?" she queried. I could formulate no response.

Finally I turned. "Boys." And that was all it took.

Brendon and Travis grabbed their gear and followed me out onto the balcony. It was the smell that had clued me in. I couldn't see a damn thing below me. It was a new moon, and even if that wasn't the case, the thick cloud cover still would have blanketed any potential light. Between the smell and the shuffling, we again found ourselves in the midst of the enemy. It didn't quite smell or feel like the mother lode, but we wouldn't be able to tell until the morning.

"Sweet Jesus," Denmark said as he came to the railing.

"Den, don't you use that kind of language," Maggie shot from behind him.

"Haven't seen a one of them in nearly a week, I figured it was over," Denmark remarked.

I felt terrible. I knew without a shadow of a doubt we were the reason they were here. I don't know how I knew it, but I did. BT was busy moving some of the ammo cans into place. Jen was loading and then checking her loaded weapon over and over again like a looped tape.

Tommy stood next to me. I was going to have to ask him how he kept doing that. "He's coming, Mr. T."

He might as well have sliced through the thin skin up my spine, cutting through the small layer of connective tissues and nerves and then pulled the bloody pieces apart to drop ice into the wound. I managed to not convulse at his words, but not by much. Tommy hugged me tight although I didn't relish the attention. The last time Tommy hugged something this fiercely was when Bear had sacrificed himself for us. The ice on my spine turned to salt and my throat constricted.

"I'm sorry, Mr. T," Tommy wailed.

I wanted to assure him everything was going to be alright, but all that kept going through my head was, 'Oh fuck, oh fuck, oh fuck.' You get the point. I was collecting my thoughts when Jen asked me where she should set up.

"Uh…" My mind was addled. "Uh, maybe take Tommy back into the room and get some sleep. Tomorrow's going to be a long day and nothing's going to happen tonight." 'Unless I die,' I wanted to add.

"Tommy's still in the room," Jen answered.

"Wha—" I turned to look. Tommy was still seated in the far corner of the room. Maggie was busy wiping chocolate off his face.

He peered up and over her shoulder when he felt I was looking at him; his expression told me the encounter had been real. 'Oh fuck.'

I told myself over and over again that long night that I was still alive. But who was kidding whom. I was a dead man walking. Had Tommy cursed me with a self-fulfilling prophecy? Would I now seek out death? Or had he blessed me with the opportunity to tell the ones I loved how I felt?

Now remember, I am a former Marine raised by a former Marine, marching into death was my business. Telling people I loved how I felt about them scared the shit out of me.

"Jen, you've been doing a great job. That gun is loaded," I told her. Damn it, okay I'll get better with the next one.

I could feel her confusion at my words as she answered me. "Thanks, I think?"

"Hey, BT, how you doing, man?"

"What do you want, Talbot? Can't you see I'm busy?" BT was busy stacking ammo cans of varying calibers all around the top balcony of the motel. The Battle of Motel 6 might not become nearly as famous as the Alamo, but I would bet we would fire as many shots.

"I just wanted to tell you, BT, thank you for saving my life back there in Bennett."

Without looking back at me, he placed another fifty pound can down. "Didn't so much do it for you as I did it for myself." Now he stopped to look at me to find out my reaction. "I told you before, Talbot, you have this uncanny knack for getting out of jams and I want to be there when you do."

"Thanks...I think?" I answered him. "All the same, I wanted to make sure you knew I appreciated what you had done."

"You're welcome," he said as he lugged a few more ammo cans away.

I was walking around like a wraith, the hustle and bustle of the living barely disturbing me. "Brendon, you got a sec?"

"Mike, I got all the ammo, besides I wouldn't go down there now for a .50 cal machine gun."

"No, no, take a break for a sec and walk with me." We walked to the far end of the building. The air seemed marginally cleaner here. "Listen, if something were to happen to me, you need to remember who your first allegiance is to."

"Is this about Bennett, Mike? I got the message loud and

clear."

"Yes and no, Brendon. There is no one that is going to protect our backs but ourselves. Our first duty is to our family, I just need to know that you're willing to make that step no matter how much it pains you. That you will forego all others for the ultimate safety of Nicole and the rest of the family."

"Mike, you're talking crazy. I'll do whatever it takes to make sure Nicole is safe, and the rest of the family."

"That's all I needed to know. No matter what happens tomorrow, I just wanted to tell you that it has been an honor fighting next to you. I knew men with twice the training that only fought half as well as you." I couldn't be sure, but I just about felt his chest swelling with pride.

I was halfway back down the walkway when he said his "Thank You" followed by "That was weird."

I went back into Denmark's room. The only occupants were Justin and Henry. Justin was parked a mere foot and a half away from the stove. If I hadn't known better, I thought he might be trying to burn something out of himself. Shit, maybe he was. I could see him shivering as I approached.

"He's close, dad."

"Who's close, son?" I asked him

Justin looked up at me. His tortured eyes said it all. "Eliza said she has a surprise for you. She says that you left somebody behind at Little Turtle that she has found to be very, very useful."

My throat closed; not because of the forewarning omen, but because of the grip this evil, oily presence had on my son. I kept flashing back to him as a wide-eyed kid who loved to fish. He had even gone so far as to fill our bathtub up once and put all our expensive fish in it. Fury had pumped through my veins when I came across the small splashes of water that led to the bathroom. The accumulation of those fish had cost me over a thousand dollars. The door nearly came off its hinges when I barged through.

Justin smiled up at me, his two front teeth missing, and repeated the phrase I had taught him: "Catch and release, Dad. Catch and release." Like a Super Soaker to a match, the anger melted into laughter. I lost a few fish to the stress of the endeavor, but that seemed like a small price to pay for the parental wisdom I gained. We went camping the next weekend next to a stream. Didn't catch anything; best time ever.

"How you doing, son?" I asked. We both knew what I meant, wasn't really a secret between us.

"Slippin', Dad. When I think about it, I can hold it off, but when I'm tired or sleeping...or even in a bad mood, she starts to needle away in my head."

"You need to fight it with everything that you are, Justin. I wish I knew what you were fighting. It's a lot easier to take out an enemy that you can see. I need to know if you're a danger to them."

"Dad, we both know the answer to that. Sometimes I think it would be so much better if you just left me on the side of the road. But I'm so scared. She said she would exact her revenge personally if I left you."

"Can Tommy help?"

He shook his head negatively. "Tommy figured out some way to get around her influence, but he holds no sway over me. Every time I get within ten feet of him it's like someone is rabbit punching me in the kidneys. I think he feels the same way. I've seen him try to hide his grimaces."

I had no answer. Cialis couldn't cure this impotence. I couldn't track down a doctor in the world that would know what to do. Shaman maybe? I'm sure I could find a tribe of Black Feet around here somewhere.

"Dad, I'll do what's right if it comes to that."

I couldn't catch my breath. I wouldn't even acknowledge what he had implied. I told him I loved him as I stumbled out of the room. I nearly did a header over the railing before Tracy grabbed my arm. She had been watching my encounter with Justin. I knew that she had been keeping a close eye on us since my accusation.

"You alright, Talbot? You look like shit."

"Goes hand in hand with how I feel."

"What did you and Justin talk about?" she asked innocently enough.

I looked at her with as little facial expression as I could pull off. My muscles rippled underneath trying in vain to not display the stark terror that bristled through them.

"I was ah…asking him if he would be able to shoot tomorrow."

"It's a good thing you don't play poker, Talbot, you'd be living in a refrigerator box."

"Nothing wrong with that, it's easy to heat them." My piss poor attempt at humor didn't bring me far from the edge of my despair.

When Tracy felt I was no longer in danger of toppling over the railing, she headed into the room to see if I had upset Justin. Didn't that beat all? Travis was next on my list, only because he was closest.

"Hey, Trav," I started off innocently enough.

His eyes glistened in what murky light was available to us. Most would have thought it tears of fear. It wasn't. I'd seen it before in Iraq. It was bloodlust. We had hours to go before we started the dance of death and Travis was burning through adrenaline like a funny car through ethanol.

"What's up, Dad?" he asked, his stare never coming off the unseen enemy below us.

"You know I love you right?"

He nearly tore his gaze away to see what my major malfunction was, but even my seeming jaunt into femininity couldn't pull him away from the projected task at hand. "Dad," he fairly squirmed as he said it. It was good to see that under that steely eyed mask was still the kid who I had been tossing the football around with recently.

"I just want you to know son, no matter what happens,

it's... look at me." He turned. "It's important to remember it's not about the killing." By the stare in his eyes I could tell that he was not grasping the meaning of my words. "Trav, it's not about the killing, it's about the living. We kill so that we may live."

"Dad, that's what I'm doing," he said in that perfect teenage tone that implied he was master of all he surveyed. "That's what we're all doing."

"It's a fine line we walk, son. I take absolutely no joy in these kills." His gaze dipped. "As soon as we take enjoyment in the killing of others, no matter what the state of them, we have already lost."

"Lost what, Dad?"

"Our humanity. We fight and we kill to protect ourselves and those we love because there is no stronger bond than family. When all else goes to shit, we are all that we have to rely on."

"Like it has?"

"Like it has," I agreed. "We're it. We are our last line of defense. I would die a thousand deaths before I so much as thought one of you might get hurt. That is a heavy burden to carry. Someday when you have a family of your own it will be your burden to carry. We kill these monsters because we have to, not because we want to. It's a fine distinction, Travis, and I just don't want you to get lost along the way." I tousled his hair (which pissed him off), told him I loved him, and walked away before he saw the glistening in my eyes that had more to do with my inner feelings. Like any teenager, I figure he grasped about ten percent of what I was shooting for. It would be many long years (which I earnestly hoped he had) of deep reflection of this day before he would come to his own conclusion. I either made my point or I did not. With my death it would be something he would dwell on constantly. If my death kept him from losing himself in the battle then it would be worth it.

I had just finished masking the majority of my leaky duct

works when I came across Nicole. She was hovering close to Brendon without making it look too obvious that was what she was doing. "Hey, sweetie. How's my favorite daughter?" It was an old joke between us.

"Hey, Dad." Her smile put a glimmer of light in my blackened heart. Nicole was as intuitive as they come and saw no real reason to mince words. "Dad, I've seen you making your rounds, what gives?"

"Just giving the pre-battle pep talk," I lied badly. She didn't buy it.

"Dad?!" she fairly demanded. I thought she might even stomp her foot like she used to do when she was five and didn't get her way.

A parent's first instinct is to protect their children and that was my first inclination. I was going to blow off Nicole's concerns and gloss it over with frivolities. She would have seen through it for sure but it would have gotten me out from under her questioning stare. I decided to temper the truth. This time she let me get away with it. "I just don't have a good feeling about tomorrow, Coley." I hugged her fiercely.

"It'll be alright, Dad," she said, halfway between a statement and a question. I am supposed to be the rock upon which my kids can crash their concerns against. But this rock was feeling a little spongy at the moment.

Brendon saved the day. "Hey, Mike, we're all set, I'm gonna turn in before the fireworks begin. You coming, Coley?" he asked.

"Thanks Brendon." My dual recognition of his work and pulling Nicole away was not lost on him.

Nicole looked long and hard at me, trying her best to ascertain the underlying truth beneath my veiled words before she turned and followed her betrothed. "Good night, Dad," she called back. "I love you."

I croaked out an "I love you, too," thankful for the darkness in the night that hid the waterworks. I had thought I had completely escaped with my manhood unscathed, but I was wrong.

"Alright, Talbot, out with it." Tracy had come up behind me and had startled the hell out of me.

Nothing but the truth was going to appease her, and my mind was entirely too befuddled to come up with anything even fairly convincing. "Tommy hugged me," I told her. It sounded kind of pathetic when I put it that way.

"And?"

"And what?"

"What's the rest of it? Tommy gave you a hug, he does that all the time."

"He...he told me he was sorry."

"Sorry for what? Talbot, what aren't you telling me? One of the most lovable kids in the world gives you a hug and then apologizes. I don't see why that is making you walk around all long faced and telling everyone what a great job they're doing and that you love them." I watched as the light of recognition came on in Tracy's awareness and then she did something I never figured, she laughed. "Oh that's it! You think you're going to die tomorrow! That's hilarious!"

"But... but Tommy hugged me."

Her laugh stopped midstream. Her 'index finger of doom' lashed out. "Listen, Talbot!" I was all ears. "You are not dying tomorrow...or the next day for that matter or any time soon, I won't allow it! You cannot leave me alone in this nightmare!" Her index finger turned into a loose fist as she hollowly punched me in the chest, her forgotten laugh approaching a sob. "I won't allow it!" she screamed.

I was too stunned to even reply. Work that was nearly completed started again as people scrambled to look busy before Tracy could turn her angst on them. She spun on her heels and headed back to the room. The zombies waited patiently below, rocking slowly back and forth.

CHAPTER 19

Mike's Journal Entry Sixteen

The morning brought sunlight, and that was the end of the good news. Two hundred, maybe two hundred and fifty zombies stirred below and more were coming. We could see them approaching across frozen fields, from the highway and from God (if he cared) knows where. Let's see, I could use pert phrases like a moth to a flame, or maybe like a lawyer to a car accident, or maybe just the truth, like a zombie to a brain buffet. We could hear some of the zombies that had broken through into the rooms below and the lobby.

A large sheet of glass shattered as Tommy came up to the railing. "That's the Kit-Kat machine, Mr. T. Whew, pretty glad I got them all out last night." He was grinning as he hefted up a pillowcase stuffed to the brim with the delicacies.

Our encounter last night didn't seem to be on his radar at all. Was he purposefully suppressing it, or had I made too much out of it? Questions, questions and no fucking answers, isn't that the way of the world?

BT opened fire. The bloodbath had begun. Travis had waited as long as he could. The Mossberg thundered through the air followed shortly thereafter by the high concussion rounds of Denmark's AK-47. The smell of iron-rich blood as it poured down storm drains nearly masked the stench of the dead. Body parts littered the ground, blown clean off under the strain of trying to capture a high-speed lead projectile. Rotten half-digested stomach contents spilled out of lacerated intestines. Zombies were becoming mired in the detritus of body parts. More than one zombie fell over entangled in its own bowels. The smell of shit, believe it or not, was entirely more welcome than the gangrenous odor of the dead.

Denmark's rapid rate of fire and seemingly endless supply of ammunition had nearly halved the opposing force. Jen and Brendon had by now joined in to the chorus of destruction. Heads blew out their contents. Bone and brain pattered down like the world's most macabre hailstorm. The parking lot became bathed in hues of reds and browns. The light snow that fell did little to hide the destruction. It, more than anything else, highlighted the contrast between its purity and the stained contents of the zombies.

My grief was heavy as I shouldered my weapon and did my part to eradicate the world of what evolution had now deemed the dominant species. Three magazines of carefully aimed shots later I called for a cease fire. Three shouts later my command was heeded. Not much stood save a smallish boy, maybe ten years old. I turned my head away just as I saw a green laser dot clearly outlined on the boy's throat. I didn't know which hit the ground first, the boy's body or his decapitated head. Both rang hollowly in my ears.

"We showed them!" Denmark barked. His jubilation was joined by the others.

"Showed them what!" I bellowed in rage. "Do you think they give a shit? Do you think some other zombies are going to stumble across this and think 'Hmm, maybe we shouldn't fuck with those humans, they're bad ass. *They don't care.* They'll just keep coming, our former friends, our relatives, our postmen." I looked directly at Denmark and his gaze dropped. "They're not going to build a memorial for their fallen comrades. They're just going to keep coming until there's nothing left." Well, I guess I had finished what I had started. I had completely wiped out any satisfaction we may

197

have gained in our 'victory.' What a fuckin' killjoy I turned out to be.

"Way to mellow our high, Talbot," BT threw out there.

Not a sound was made, not even a stirring zombie. Nobody was sure in which direction I was going to go from BT's barb. The tension in the air was palpable. Finally I was able to spit out, "Fucker." And then I started laughing, joined in by the rest of the group. It seemed impossible that we would laugh amidst all the destruction below us but stress finds its own necessary release.

Stragglers, to prove my earlier point, kept coming in only to be met with unmitigated leaden justice. A more pressing concern lodged in my head as I watched the newest interloper go down in a cacophony of bullets (actually a couple of concerns). Our minivans were completely encased in the shards of zombie remains. This wasn't Alex's truck, we would never be able to just drive over them or push them out of the way. The Terrible Teal Machine would spin in place like a washing machine. Clearing out an exit for the cars wouldn't take an abnormally long amount of time but touching and dragging the bodies out of the way was not a palatable mission. Anything less than a Level 5 biohazard suit seemed to me to make the whole endeavor a nearly impossible assignment.

Second, and just as important, while we could clear a path and be on the road in the next half hour once our ammo and food were back in the cars, what kind of ungrateful bastard guests would we be if we had just made the world's worst mess and then abruptly left? The zombies had come for the Talbot party, table of eight. To leave this horrendous display of death for Denmark was incomprehensible to me. Moving the bloody, stinking mess of demolished bodies to a safe enough distance whilst also keeping a vigilant eye out for others of their kind was going to take hours.

I vomited four times that morning. The first was as my misplaced step off the ladder landed squarely on an eyeball.

The resounding pop and ooze of viscous liquid from beneath my boot propelled anything worth digesting out of my mouth and onto the rungs of the ladder.

"Oh, fucking Talbot!" BT lamented, as he was higher up the ladder and following me down.

"Sorry about that." I wiped my mouth; my agitated stomach letting me know just how much it was displeased with this course of events.

In such a confined area with that many bodies it was absolutely impossible to not keep stepping on THINGS. Yeah, hold onto that thought. They are NOT fingers and forearms and skull plates. They are THINGS. Oh, who am I kidding! This looked like the world's largest blender had been filled with humans and someone had held down the blend button for about a half second. Not nearly enough time to puree the contents, but merely chop down the bigger pieces. You thought liver smelled bad when your mom cooked it? Try stepping on one fresh out of a corpse. Vomit number two did nothing to mask the putrification around me. BT wasn't faring much better than I. If not for Jen's lead and our need to competitively 'keep up' with her, it might have been a job that didn't get done, no matter how much guilt I might feel for leaving Denmark in such a lurch. She set about the burden with a grim willpower.

Denmark and Travis stood watch over us as we dragged the human odds and ends out of the parking lot. If this were a real job that demanded compensation, I don't think there would be a sum worthy. But survival has its own price, one that we couldn't pay enough to satisfy. Occasionally a shot would ring out, hampering any more visitors from coming in for an afternoon meal.

As we stacked the bodies behind a close by Dairy Queen like cordwood, we took the time to watch each other's backs. We were not under the watchful eye of our lookouts from that vantage point. The distance, I hoped, would keep the majority of stench from wafting into the motel, but what is more important was the old adage, "out of sight, out of mind." Although anything less than Noah's Ark-type floodwaters was not going to wash away the gallons upon gallons of blood that had overrun everything.

My third mouth breaching came as I grabbed onto some kid's jacket. He was wedged under the body of a female that suspiciously bore a family resemblance. The family that eats together, stays together, you know. Whether in life, in walking death, or in absolute death, there was something about killing a family that tore something free from within me. I wanted to be out of this split femur soup. I reached down and grabbed the thing from underneath the armpits. I pulled with more exertion than the task demanded and was rewarded with a wet tearing sound as the boy's top half came loose from the disgorged innards that spilled like night crawlers from a broken bait box. I fell over, still holding tight to the top half of the boy's remains. Luckily, my fall was broken by the ample carcass of Frita, the IHOP waitress. Her nameplate was quickly lost under my voluminous cascade of bile. I stood up quickly, a dizzying spell nearly bringing me to my knees again. Flesh saturated with bodily fluids slapped against my blood soaked jeans. I dropped the boy to the ground. When I felt the worst of the attack had passed I reached down and grabbed the boy's hand, not in a gesture of good will, it was what allowed me the greatest grip. I did not turn around as I dragged the boy to his final resting spot.

Jen had somewhere acquired a snow shovel and cleaned up what had spilled out of the boy. My burden had been getting lighter as I walked, but I would not turn to detect the reason why. One more violent stomach outburst like the previous one and I would have left my spleen on that parking lot pavement. For the next hour I went through my duties like an automaton – bend, lift, drag, bend, lift, drag. I had become more like our enemy than I would have ever thought possible.

BT for all his bravado was two pukes ahead of me. Fine

by me he was welcome to that trophy. 'And winner of the 2010 Lord Upchucks Cup goes to Big Tiny! Huge applause!' I grinned madly. Nuggets of some distant forgotten meal bracketed my goatee. Pain wrenched my gut. My knee was on the verge of collapse, and my smile resembled something closer to a grimace. But still I soldiered on.

Tracy, Nicole, and Brendon spent the better part of the morning getting our belongings back into the minivans. They had just about finished by the time the death detail was down to single figure leftovers to remove. Just then, Denmark's warning came.

"Michael, you best come up here and take a look."

I hobbled over to the ladder. The blood of a hundred bodies was solidifying on every article of clothing I was wearing. Between my knee and the inflexibility of the frozen blood, my navigation of the ladder was haphazard at best. *If this is the way I die I am going to be seriously pissed off.*

"You say something?" Denmark asked as he reached out to help me up and over and then abruptly thought better of his gesture. He warred within himself; the disgust of possibly touching anything that was attached to me or the common courtesy of helping me up the ladder. Courtesy won out as he reached his hand out again.

"I've got it, don't worry, Denmark." I wanted to laugh as I watched the relief on his countenance.

"Dad, hurry!" Travis yelled.

Denmark went to clap me on the shoulder in an act of shared camaraderie and then pulled back as not even that innocuous part of me was free from debris. Within a few moments of caked blood cracking movement I was standing next to my son. I saw…nothing. Nicole and Tracy had packed the rest of the food into the back of the minivan. Brendon was finishing strapping something to the top of his minivan. BT and Jen were sharing a smoke that looked good, the savory tobacco smoke wisping up into the cold winter air. Even from this distance I could tell BT's hands were shaking.

Jen had to try to time her placement as she went to hand him the cigarette.

"What?" I asked perplexed.

Travis' pointing finger led my vision higher up the horizon. I saw a black smudge, a stain upon the skyline. I saw a plague upon my family. Hundreds, no thousands, tens of thousands of zombies blotted out the distant boundaries of my vision as they marched forward toward us.

"My God," Denmark noted in a hushed voice.

"Time to go, Mr. T," Tommy said as he reached to grab my hand.

I pulled away before he could make contact. "Oh, Tommy, I don't think I could stand it if I passed on what I've been touching." He understood, even if he wasn't a tenth as concerned about it as I was.

"We leaving now?" he begged.

The scene, while not nearly as heroic and without the accompanying foreboding music, reminded me of the movie *Lord of the Rings* when the orcs and cave trolls descended on Helm's Deep. I was transfixed. Stay and fight or just run. I looked to Denmark's fear-lined face and the consternation of his wife Maggie as she looked on, and even to a lesser extent the misery that was etched on Greta's face. My mind was made up. These people had opened their home and their hearts to us. What right did I have to bring this grisly end upon them?

"We're leaving, Tommy," I said. Tommy was relieved.

"Michael." Denmark peeled his eyes away from the abysmal vista and looked at me in rebuke. "I thought you were more of an admiral man than that."

"What? Did you mean admirable?" I asked. I didn't have the foggiest clue about what he was talking about.

"You are just going to leave me and Maggie and Greta like this?" he asked.

"Oh," I started. "Denmark, it's not like that at all." His arched eyebrow let me know exactly what he thought of that response. "First off, you're welcome to join us, although I don't see any benefits for you if you make that decision. Second, we're not leaving because we're afraid of a fight. We're leaving so that there won't *be* one."

"Huh?" Now it was his turn to question my words.

"Denmark, do you really think it was a coincidence that we had that assembly of zombies here this morning?" He was not following the general drift of the conversation. I was going to have to forcibly show him the way. "Denmark, we've been singled out. We're being hunted. Some lower power has decided that our time on this glorious planet must soon be concluded."

"Michael, I know this event has caused a lot of strain on folks, better men than you have folded under the pressure, but what makes *you* so special? Why would the zombies 'hunt' you?" Denmark begged.

I wanted to tell him that I was merely a byproduct of the hunt, maybe a six-point stag. The prize twelve-point trophy was Tommy. Eliza wanted Tommy. I didn't know if the kid knew it for sure or not, but I wasn't going to be the one to tell him. Denmark was about to pepper me with more accusations when Maggie interceded.

"It's true, Denny," she said, placing her hand on his taut shoulder.

"What are you talking about, Maggie? All I see here is a coward, a man that runs from his responsibilities. Oh, he's all bluster when he's sitting by a stove eating a home cooked meal. Put the iron in the fire, though, and you can test the true strength of the metal."

I knew his words were borne from fear and desperation. They didn't contain an iota of truth, but still they cut to the bone, if only because he believed what he said.

"Look at him, Maggie! He can't even defend himself now! How much do my words hurt, Michael? Will you be able to sleep tonight while my wife and I fight for our lives? Probably won't be a problem for the likes of you!"

"Dammit, Denny! Stop it!" Maggie grabbed him by the waist and turned him so that he could see the rage coursing through her body. "Justin! Justin told me everything!" she screamed.

"What are you talking about!?" The anger that mired his capacity to reason was blinding him.

"Since they left their home in Colorado they have been followed. The one who calls herself Eliza has some sort of hold on the zombies." Denmark was looking at his wife as if trying to figure out how hard it would be to get a hold of some anti-schizophrenic pills, iffen there was such a thing. "Justin knew they were coming, he just didn't know that they were this close." Maggie slowly closed her eyes and melted into her husband's comforting embrace.

Justin silently cried behind her. "I'm so sorry, Dad."

"This isn't your fault, Justin. You're caught up in it just like the rest of us," I told him. It was of small solace to him but he accepted it like a stranded wanderer in the desert accepts water, greedily.

"What is going on?" Denmark cried, the whites of his eyes threatening to become the dominant force on his strained features.

"I'm trying to tell you, Denmark. That if we leave, odds are that horde out there won't even stop here," I told him. He understood the words. He was just having a difficult time reconciling the validity of them. "Denmark, I swear to you, as much as you can trust a man in these dark days, trust me now. You are welcome to come with us. Hell, with the firepower you carry I'd be thrilled if you came with us. But that would be the worst decision of your life. I'm not going to guarantee to you that zombies aren't going to come your way eventually...but that legion out there..." We all turned to look. "That's especially for us."

Denmark looked to the gathering, then back to my face and back to the mob. He licked his lips and then the next words out of his mouth nearly crippled me.

"Any chance you could take Greta?"

Maggie slapped the shit out of his head.

"BT, Jen, come on!" I yelled down to them. "We've got to get going soon."

"Come on, Mike," Jen pleaded. "I'm covered in gore. I was hoping to boil some water and wash up, thoroughly."

"Sure you can, but come up the ladder a few rungs and then turn around." Even from this distance, I could see the confusion on her face. She did as I asked though.

It took her about half a second. "Right, I'll go grab my things," she said. I'll give her this, her face paled some, but she didn't go into panic mode.

Rabid pack of cannibalistic, disease infested man-eaters or not, there was no way I was leaving without scraping the heavy layers of dirt, sweat, blood, excrement and the multitude of body bits off of me. I grabbed my Ka-Bar knife and cut my clothes off of my body. The blood had congealed into body armor.

I stood naked in that dark motel room, looking in the full-length mirror. A month of zombies had done for me what no intense workout regimen could. Damn it, I looked good; I had the beginning signs of a six-pack on my stomach. My love handles were a thing of the past. My body looked lean and strong. Even the chunks of matter I could not identify stuck at odd angles and in strange places could not disguise how much my body had changed. I was close to the condition I had been over twenty years previously. Killing apparently had its perks. My brown eyes betrayed no mirth in that thought.

I turned the shower on, waiting a few seconds before sticking my hand under the sandblast force liquid. Waiting a few seconds for the water to heat up was a conditioned response, but I was not going to receive a favorable reply. I braced for the icy needles of pain that were about to lance my body. There isn't a one of you out there that doesn't know what I'm talking about. You can psyche yourself up all you want, maybe even slap yourself a few times in the face to try to forget the torture you are about to inflict on yourself. Doesn't matter. The moment that cold water hits anything above your knees the shock starts to set in. Catching a breath suddenly becomes the most difficult thing in the world. You breathe in these little ragged strips of air through clenched teeth. You cross your arms over your chest as if that is going to alleviate the immense discomfort bordering on psychotic pain that you are feeling. At this point you can't even begin to understand why you are subjugating yourself to this. A failed water heater should be the most perfect reason in the world to not go into work.

This time though was not normal. I was already numb. Numb to pain, and numb to the world. I placed my hands on the shower stall wall and bathed in the bitter water as it flayed my soul into the drain. Soap was an afterthought. I watched as the man that was/is Michael Talbot spread the tiny bar across his semi-exposed rib cage. Shampoo intermingled with viscera. The humanity stew clogged the drain. The Michael-man did not notice as he stepped out of the ice-sharded water. The part of me that was mostly me, but not all of me, took this opportune time to reunite with the more primitive side. I gently reminded that side that he should dry his freezing ass off before he caught pneumonia.

Tracy had come in with new clothes while I had been wringing out my soul. I stood again in front of the mirror shivering – partly from the cold, partly from the pain and mostly from the sense of loss. My body had adapted to the harsh conditions of this new life much quicker than my mind. Once that happened, though, would I still be the man I wanted to be…or just the man I needed to be?

Tracy's hand seared my flesh as she touched my side. The heat from her hand flooded my senses. That mere, sheer, sensuous touch reeled me back in. My body reacted in the way it had been meant to since the beginning of evolution (or the Garden of Eden, I don't want to deny anyone their due).

"You look tired, Talbot, but you look a lot like you did the day we got married."

I turned towards her. I was a Marine when we got married, so it only seemed right that I should be at the position of attention now. If you do not know what I am referring to, just take a moment to reread this part and then rethink it. I'll wait...got it?

Tracy laughed. "Yep, that looks a lot like it used to when we got married too, Mike."

"And?"

"Not a chance." She threw my clothes at me and laughed harder when my boxer briefs got hung up on their own personal hanger. "Get dressed, I want to get out of here before we bring any more trouble on these people."

"Are BT and Jen ready?" I asked as my 'hanger' drooped and dropped its 'load' so to speak.

"Mike, they've been ready for over half an hour. You were in the shower for forty-five minutes. How the hell you could stand it, I'm not sure."

"Forty-five minutes?" I could scarcely believe it myself.

"Maybe if you had gotten out sooner..." she said tauntingly.

"Oh that's fair!" I yelled. "Now you tell me!"

"Maybe next time," she said wistfully as she left the room to let me get dressed.

"I hope there is a next time," I said to the closed door.

Within five minutes I was dressed and back outside. The brisk January North Dakota winter had nothing on the cold I had just endured both physically and spiritually. It almost felt balmy in retrospect.

BT was at the railing smoking another cigarette.

"I didn't know you smoked," I commented as I put out my hand to take a drag.

"I don't," he replied as he handed it to me. "And you?"

"Me neither," I said as I took a big draft of the sweet leaf. I savored my long exhalation of the vapor. "You know, BT, you don't have to come with us."

"I know that, Talbot," he said as he took his cigarette back.

"You know that throng out there is coming for us, right?"

"I know that too, Talbot," he said as he handed the cigarette back to me.

"If we left here and you and Jen stayed behind... You'd be safe, you know that right?"

"That I don't know, Talbot. Stop bogarting and give me my cigarette back. What kind of man would I be if I left you now?"

"A live one," I answered honestly.

He laughed at that and tossed his used cigarette over the railing. The cherry fizzled and smoldered out in a puddle of blood. He didn't notice. I did.

"What do you expect me to do, Talbot?" He wasn't questioning me so much as he was asking my opinion.

I shrugged my shoulders. "There's a good chance that my road leads to a giant, fiery dead end."

"That seems better than whiling away my days with a lesbian and a shrew. I'm going to smoke another cigarette, Talbot, weigh the consequences of my actions, and then get in that fucking ugly ass minivan of yours." My cue given, I left, saddened in the fact that I wasn't going to get another drag of his cigarette.

I walked away just as Tracy was extracting herself from a hug with Maggie. "You're getting better, Talbot."

"Huh?"

"I saw you smoking that cigarette."

"Aw shit, didn't mean for you to see that."

"Relax, I wasn't talking about that. I meant that two months ago, hell two days ago you wouldn't have taken that cigarette from the Pope himself even if he had blessed it and dipped it in Holy Water first."

"Huh. I hadn't even thought about it."

She rose up on her tiptoes and kissed me. "You taste like

an ashtray." And with that she walked away to descend the ladder.

I gave Jen the same opportunity of Rights of Refusal to leave our merry band of misfits. Her answer, while different from BT's, was eerily similar.

"Would it be better if I spent the rest of my days with a muscle-headed man and a shrew?"

Tommy was crying as he disengaged from Maggie. "Are you sure, Miss Maggie, you won't take some of these?" Tommy asked as he shoved his pillow full of Kit-Kats at her.

"Oh no, dear, they just get stuck in my teeth and I never did have much of a sweet tooth."

Tommy cocked his head to the side like she had just uttered the craziest thing in the world. "Really?" His earlier distress somewhat relieved.

Tommy and I were the only ones of our gang left upstairs. I went over and gave Greta a perfunctory hug. I could feel her tense up as I moved in. I've gripped furniture that had more love in it. Maggie was the complete opposite. She apparently had enough love for both of them. Her tears nearly soaked through my jacket.

"Maggie, let him go," Denmark chided her softly. "You're gonna suffocate him."

"I'm not going to do any such thing," she told him, but the mild rebuke seemed to work as she let me go.

"Thank you, Denmark." I shook the older man's hand. "This has been a respite I will not soon forget."

"You had better not," he answered me. His lip quivered a bit, but the staunch old bastard didn't let any tears fall.

Once down in the car we all took our turns to wave. I beeped the horn as we headed north to our next destination.

Tommy turned around in his seat so that he could watch the motel fade from sight. It wasn't until it was completely out of view that he spoke. "They're not going to make it through the winter."

Brendon nearly slammed into my rear end as I screeched

to a stop.

"What if we stay, Tommy?" I asked of him.

He shook his head. "They'll die quicker."

"FUCK!" I yelled as I slammed my hands on the steering wheel. Brendon had a hard time keeping up as I slammed my gas pedal to the floor.

CHAPTER 20

Mike's Journal Entry Seventeen

We had been cruising down the highway for a couple of hours, distance doing little to help me forget about the Gustovs (Denmark's family name). How many times I wanted to turn back around, only to have Tommy's words bubble to the surface. I could only pray that our visit with them was not what hastened the Gustovs' demise.

The ride was passing in a moody silence. Nobody in the car was talking, and I don't think anyone would have listened even if they had. So when Tracy offered to drive because she knew the rest of the way, I relented. She'd be hard pressed to find anything worth hitting in this desolate white-blanketed landscape.

A few minutes later I found myself drifting in and out of sleep, only occasionally being awakened as Tracy jerked the wheel as if she had just remembered that she was driving and might want to keep the ton and a half van between the painted lines. Sleep grabbed hold and even Tracy's quick wheel movements could not shake the veil of it from me.

The one good thing about being alive during the age of the zombies was that nightmares no longer had any power. What's so scary about the boogeyman coming to get you and your legs feeling like lead? That sensation of not being able to run, the fear that pumped through your veins – the monster coming! And then blissful awareness, your mother scooping you up in her arms, kissing your sweat-dampened forehead. "It was all a dream, everything's fine," she would coo. Not *my* mother mind you, but someone's mother would. My mother was too narcissistic to care about my bad dreams other than to wonder why I had the nerve to wake her up in the middle of the night when I was a child.

No, these days I tended to dream in the idyllic, where a gentle breeze or a beautiful sunset would be punctuated by the appearance of a unicorn or maybe Bambi. From these I would awaken in a hell where monsters were real, and no matter how fast and how far I ran, they were always right behind me. That was far scarier than any nightmare my mind could have ever imagined. Come to think of it, no matter how many times my legs got mired in deep grass or heavy mud or ultra-shag carpeting, the boogeyman never caught me. Not once. Would I be that lucky in real life?

I was coming to alertness in degrees, between the incessant beeping of some asshole's horn and a not so gentle nudging. I was grudgingly letting go of my tentative grip on being figuratively dead to the world. Tracy's hand slipped off my shoulder and into my jaw. That shattered what little of my subconscious remained in dreamland.

"Mike." Tracy shook me again even though I was obviously awake. "Brendon is flashing his lights and beeping his horn."

"Got the horn part," I said as I gripped my jaw. "Maybe it's your driving."

"Ha, ha. No, I think he needs something."

"Then pull over." Well, that seemed simple enough, problem solved.

"No, I started slowing down and he started flashing his lights faster, I think Coley was pointing to something behind us."

I sat up fast. No way the zombies could be that close. I dreaded what I would see behind us. BT opened his eyes as soon as I turned around. He looked up at me, clearly seeing my anxiety.

"What is it, Talbot?" BT asked without turning to look himself.

"Don't know, don't see anything yet." We both let out a sigh of relief.

"Good grief. My two big bad asses," Tracy said.

I puffed out some indignation. Then I saw it. It was far away, but it was distinct. "It's a truck, no it's two of...wait, no, its three of them." A coldness swept across me. I don't know why, maybe some of Tommy's prescience had rubbed off on me, more than likely it was just my super-heightened sense of paranoia.

"Aw, Talbot, you got that look on you," BT deplored.

"What look, BT?" Tracy asked, looking in vain in the rear view mirror to see what had my panties all up in a bunch.

"Oh, that look that says trouble's coming."

"Yeah, and it's driving three white Ford pickup trucks, probably F-350s by the size of them. Travis?" I shook him awake. He came to full consciousness in under a handful of heartbeats.

"Yeah, Dad?"

"Start handing out guns," I told him without ever taking my eyes off the rapidly approaching trucks. He didn't question me. He didn't hesitate. Within thirty-seconds we were all outfitted with our favorite projectile lobbers. I motioned to Brendon through the rear windshield that he should do the same as I pointed vigorously to my rifle. He held his up in response. He was of the same ilk that I was.

"Do you want to drive, Mike?" Tracy asked.

There were pros and cons to that question. The pros being that I could have her hide under the dashboard in some semblance of safety. The cons were my shooting would be seriously hampered and we would have to pull over to make the change. Our pursuers, if that's what they were, would make up some valuable time.

"Mike?" she asked, looking for a response to her earlier query. I was still in the midst of weighing options. "Should I speed up?"

"God no!" BT shouted.

I inwardly laughed. Tracy's driving was suspect to begin with. Tracy driving with speed was tantamount to suicide by light pole.

Tracy turned all the way around to fix her steely eyed gaze full bore on BT.

"The road," he said meekly. "Eyes on the road." He pointed at his own as if to illustrate the point. "You gonna help me here, Talbot?"

"You're on your own, man."

After what seemed like an indeterminable amount of time she finally relented. Feeling that she had made her point, she turned back to the highway.

"Holy fuck," BT mumbled.

"You say something, BT?" Tracy asked angrily as she adjusted the rear view mirror to look at him. When only silence ensued from the backseat she smirked and said, "I didn't think so."

We waited, not as long as we wanted, but longer still than it seemed due to the tension. Tracy was traveling at a steady sixty-five, our chasers must have been doing a pavement chewing one hundred mph or so with the way they were gaining on us.

BT and I were now completely turned around, fixated on the chasers.

"Any chance they're military?" BT asked hopefully.

"Doubt it," I answered.

"Fellow survivors?" he asked.

"Well, they're survivors alright, but I don't think they are of the fellowship type." I knew BT was going to keep piece-mealing questions together until he got to the heart of my unease. I didn't give him the chance. "It's those damn white trucks, like they all had to get the same damn thing, like a gang. Normal folks just trying to get through the day wouldn't give a shit about what they were driving so long as they were driving away from a shit storm. And look at the way they're driving."

"Maybe they just need some help," Tracy interjected.

"Don't squash my neurotic obsessions, hon, they tend to keep us alive."

The lead truck had made its way to Brendon's wake. There was no waving, no horn beeping, no headlights flashing, no daisy throwing, no American flags.

"So much for needing help," I said sourly.

"It was just a suggestion," Tracy said peevishly, thinking that I was belittling her comment.

I was about to foolishly reply. It was my innate ability to get into trouble when no such thing existed, when I was saved by BT.

"Talbot," he said, getting my attention back.

The lead truck was pulling up alongside Brendon's minivan, the two trailing Fords filling in the vacant spaces, one on each side of the roadway. I saw a yellow, gap-toothed, mullet haired man, ironically wearing a Chevy cap, lean out of the passenger side door. He was looking straight down and into the smaller vehicle. His lascivious grin was evident even from this distance. I watched as he ducked back into the truck. He held up two fingers and laughed. I was sort of impressed that he had the ability to count.

"What's he doing?" Tracy asked nervously looking through her rear view mirrors.

"Counting," BT filled in.

"Counting what?" Tracy asked.

"Women," I said coldly.

"Dad!" Travis said, alarmed. "There are guys in the back of the truck."

I had been so fixated on the cab I hadn't looked. How the fuck I had missed them was beyond me. Three armed men were standing attached to some sort of harness device to a roll bar in the back.

"What the fuck are they doing?" BT asked.

"They're strapped in to the truck so they don't fall out when they try to take us over."

"Take us over? What are you talking about, Mike?" Tracy asked.

Her fear almost ended the confrontation right there and then. She had let her foot come off the accelerator and our minivan was slowing at an alarming rate while Brendon, who was intent on keeping an eye on the truck next to him, was inadvertently pressing down on the accelerator in a vain attempt to get out from the situation. He tapped our bumper before Tracy realized what was happening. Redneck number one thought it was the funniest thing he had ever seen. He motioned to the driver to speed up.

Within seconds, our newfound guests were alongside the Terrible Teal Machine. Redneck number one was even uglier up close; his pock marked face must have made him a true charmer in high school. If not for rape – farm animals or his sister – I was sure he would have never gotten laid. He leaned back in. My heart stilled as I watched him mouth the words 'Only one', and then he laughed. Before they sped up to get in front of us he leaned back out and made a 'V' sign with his fingers, his long tobacco stained tongue flicking back and forth in the base of the sign.

"Fuck you!" I yelled, leaning over Tracy's lap.

He laughed and spit out some chew, then motioned for the driver to pull ahead.

"Fuck. Tracy, you can't let him pull ahead of you."

"Why not, maybe they'll just keep going," she said hopefully.

"Remember that talk we had a few years back about the Easter Bunny and how he isn't real?"

"Fuck you, Talbot."

"That's the Tracy I'm looking for. Do not let him pull

ahead of us, once he does those three gunmen in the back have us."

Tracy's foot turned to molten lead. The Terrible Teal Machine, for all her ugliness, gave us all she had. Redneck number one was motioning for his driver to go faster, his expression, a cross between wonder and anger.

He was never going to hear me, but I said it anyway. It was more uplifting to us in the car anyway. "You picked the wrong caravan to waylay, dipshit. We're not your typical sheep."

He might not have heard me but I could tell my crazy grin had unsettled him some. He was yelling at the driver. The truck was inching forward, the cab of their truck was now even with our front grill.

"Tracy."

"I'm trying dammit!" she screamed. The minivan whined under the strain. Brendon and the two chaser trucks fell behind. The tachometer was buried in the red. I could hear the hamsters in the engine caterwauling for their lives. The Ford fell back a couple of inches or the minivan surged forward, tough to tell at a hundred and twenty mph. The three men in the back were even with us but seemed much more intent on holding on for dear life than firing off any rounds. We were creeping even again. Tracy was sweating bullets. Oh, nope that was me. I was dripping all over her while I leaned over to get a better vantage point.

"Talbot, get the fuck off my lap," she said in a strained voice.

"Oh right, sorry. It's going to get loud in here real soon. You ready?"

She spared a split second to look over at me. The strain of the event was beginning to wear on her. "They still haven't done anything, Mike."

"Yeah, and I'm not going to give them the chance."

Tommy picked this most inopportune time to talk. "I watched a special on the History Channel the night before the deaders came."

BT turned to look at him, even Tracy hazarded a glance in the rear view mirror. When Tommy spoke and it wasn't in regards to Pop-Tarts, you definitely wanted to listen.

"It was about Pearl Harbor and how the Japanese had struck before they had declared war. It was something that they still regret having done. It wasn't honorable."

FUCK Honor, this was our lives!!! My decision was now not sitting well with the rest of the occupants of the car. We were all ninety-nine percent sure of the intentions of the truck but there was still that one fucking percent chance they were just creeps, nothing worse. Tracy had managed to stay completely even with the lead truck. The engine was in danger of throwing a rod. Redneck number one opened up the back window to the truck bed. The ugly fuck erased all our doubts of their purpose. Even over the howling wind, it was impossible to not hear his words. I believe in my heart it was divine intervention we heard him at all. The physics of the speed we were traveling at and the whipping of the wind through the windows made hearing anything other than our engine's screaming protests a difficult prospect. But we all heard him as clear as if we were having tea in a library.

"Don't shoot the women, kill the rest."

I turned to Tommy, relatively sure he was the one that controlled the divine intervention. He nodded to me, an intense glare shone from his eyes. Pain, rage, and sorrow warred for his attention.

"They're readying their weapons, Talbot!" BT yelled, rivaling the explosions that were about to be issued forth.

"Tracy, this is gonna suck," I said as I half crawled over her, sticking the barrel of my AR out the window.

"Just get it done," she said through clenched teeth.

Travis hopped into the rear of the minivan. I jumped when he smashed out the large side glass window.

Our furtive movements did not go unnoticed. One of the gunmen got so nervous he dropped the magazine to his rifle.

Like two warships of old we broadsided each other.

"FIRE!" I yelled.

Bullets screamed! Lead struck. Metal, plastic, rubber and wood shattered under the assault. The noise was deafening and the clouds of smoke were blinding. Screams of savagery and pain were muffled by the explosions. The gunman closest to us was fatally struck. He leaned forward and pitched out of the truck bed. His crudely fashioned harness had not saved him from the disgrace of being unceremoniously dragged along the side of the truck. Redneck number one watched as his friend bounced and skipped along on the ground. A smear of blood and bone trailed for miles. Talk about chumming for zombies.

BT roared in pain as a bullet struck. I didn't have the time to look and see how bad it was. I was fumbling with a new magazine. My thinking was that if he had enough life in him to scream, then he was still breathing. Travis' shotgun ripped through the rear quarter panel of the truck; fuel was leaking from their truck like a sieve. Our front windshield exploded outwards, Tracy yelled and swerved and then she smashed sideways into the truck. The impact loosened the body of the hijacker. He tumbled backwards, seemingly gaining new heights as he bounced like a super ball. His springiness landed him onto the windshield of one of the trailing trucks. Our luck wasn't strong enough to hope he would take them out. They swerved sharply but recovered quickly.

We had all been watching the macabre accident. As I turned back around, I caught the gaze of Redneck number one. We locked onto each other for a heartbeat. I could feel his malice.

"Kill them all!" He screeched so loud, Tommy's special skills weren't needed.

A renewed vigor of bullets whined through our shell-pocked car. The cars were going so fast, the slightest imperfection in the roadway made anything less than a pure luck shot damn near impossible. But that didn't keep Travis from pumping round after round into the shredded gas tank. I kept waiting for the Hollywood explosion, but apparently they only know how to do that in Hollywood. It never happened.

Wisps of smoke emanated from the rear minivan. Brendon and Jen had joined into the fray. Sometime during our sea battle they had pulled in behind the leading Ford and were now adding their two cents of lead. The two gunmen in the rear swung their attention to the new threat.

"Wrong move, motherfuckers." I took a calming breath and unloaded a full magazine into them.

They danced like marionettes on springs as round after round of high-powered steel jacketed rounds burst through their bodies. Blood arced, teeth shattered. Their paid out bodies dropped faster than my spent bullet casings.

My reverie was short lived as Redneck number one had at some point pulled out a Desert Eagle 45 and was busy trying to place a hole in my forehead. The top of our steering wheel exploded into fragments of ragged materials. It was long moments after that thunderous concussion that I noticed there were no more shots being fired. The odds were beyond hope that the spectacular weapon had jammed or the idiot was too dim to keep it fully loaded. No, finally Travis's fuel tank shredding tactic had come to fruition. I watched as Redneck number one slammed his fists in frustration against his dashboard. I would have loved to hear his expletives. By the way he was going I was convinced I would learn some new and interesting words and colorful phrases.

"Talbot, I'm hit," BT said through a clamped mouth.

Fuckin' reality. "Shit…where, BT?"

He moved his hand slightly on his thigh, blood pulsed through his fingers.

"Is it bad?" he asked without looking down.

Fuck if I know? "Naw, it's only a flesh wound."

"Yeah, but it's my flesh," he said, trying to joke.

Tracy had completely turned around and over her

shoulder to look at the wound. Sure, we weren't going the earth shattering speed of a hundred and twenty, but at seventy we could still get into a lot of trouble real quickly. "Do you want me to stop?" she asked, her concern for BT apparent.

"Can't."

"What?" she asked incredulously.

"Do you think our friends back there are going to stop? They're just transferring their stuff over and will be following us in a minute or two."

Tracy looked over to BT. "He's right," BT answered.

Now I'm no doctor, and I didn't even play one on TV, but even if BT's wound wasn't fatal now, I could tell he would bleed out sooner rather than later.

"Fuck that," Tracy said quietly.

I was thrown against the passenger door violently as she did something physics-wise I didn't think was possible. She had U-turned a minivan at seventy miles per hour and we didn't violently flip down the roadway. Somehow Tommy had had the foresight to grip the roof-mounted handgrip and hadn't even lost a beat as he popped what appeared to be the remainder of a Kit-Kat bar into his mouth. It would have been humorous if I wasn't pinned nearly upside down by the g-forces being applied to my body. Brendon respected applied pressures (even if Tracy didn't) and slowed his car down to a saner but still scary forty-five miles per hour before he tried to do the same maneuver. Within a quarter mile he was alongside our right side.

He nearly shattered his voice to be heard above the whistling wind as it came in through our now defunct windshield. "What's going on, Mike?"

I wanted to give him the full story about BT's injury and the need to get him some attention and quickly. Being succinct seemed more prudent. "We're going to finish what they started."

He nodded gravely at my words. Jen had replaced Nicole

in the front seat and was busy loading her extra magazines. There was a barbarous set to her features. BT was breathing laboriously through the haze of pain as Travis and Tommy fashioned a crude tourniquet on his upper thigh.

"Dad, I think it broke his leg, but we got the blood stopped."

"Holy shit, BT, does it hurt?" I asked stupidly. It's common knowledge that there is no greater pain on the planet than a broken femur, yet he hadn't cried out since the initial shot that caused his injury.

"What do you think, Talbot?" BT winced as Tommy pulled the slipknot tighter on the tourniquet.

I winced in sympathy with him. Then, like an idiot, I let my thoughts wander and wonder. Is a broken leg worse pain than say, someone gripping one of your nuts in a pair of pliers and crushing it? Oh, God, I nearly vomited at my own speculation. Better not to go there at all.

Within thirty seconds of cresting a small rise in the road, our quarry was in sight. The hunters had become the hunted. Redneck number one might be an asshole, but he wasn't a dipshit. While his traveling companions were staring in awe at us as we bore down on them, he was punching and cajoling and kicking them into action. They were nearly done with the transfer of supplies and the unceremonious disposal of their brethren when we had come upon them. If they got behind the wheels of those trucks and got them moving this was going to become a very dangerous game of chicken.

I saw Tracy hesitate. She wasn't sure if she should keep going or turn around. The odds of making another seventy mile per hour U-turn unscathed weighed heavily against us. She pinned the gas pedal down. I tasted tooth fragments as my head slammed back into the headrest and my teeth snapped together. Tracy used the minivan like a guided missile as she smashed the living shit out of the nearest redneck that had not been thoroughly convinced to get his ass moving. His ass was moving now, at least what was left of it.

His broken body hurtled into the air like he carried his own jetpack. I prayed that I would not be able to hear the sound his body made when it crashed back to earth. What was not already broken would shatter like dry sticks under a hefty moose's hoof.

I barely had time to recover as Tracy peeled the car off to the left. I'd like to say she narrowly missed the parked truck, but that would be an outright lie. The shower of sparks and the squeal of metal on metal would have made me a liar. The caustic smell of burning paint assaulted my nostrils. Sparks showered my lap looking for fuel to grow into a larger version of itself. A loud telltale report let me know that someone's tire had burst. I could only hope it wasn't ours. I was thinking it was going to be a bitch to get Triple A out here on such short notice.

And then it was over. The metallic burnt smell whisked out of our car. The din of war was reduced to just wind coming through our various new ventilation systems. Brendon had come through the far side in much better shape than us. They had decided wisely to use more conventional weapons. They had struck at least two and possibly three men. What was left of our would-be hijackers would fit comfortably in a tollbooth. Tracy had tears streaming down her face as the stress finally wore her down. How the hell she could see through the stream of tears and the shear of wind through the dispersed windshield was again something that eluded me.

"Tracy," I said softly. She looked over. "We need to go back." She didn't question my sanity, she merely acknowledged my words. BT was near to passing out as his eyes were beginning to roll up into his head. "Do you want me to drive?"

She turned the car around and sped back to the trucks. That was sufficient answer for me. This time, however, there was no call to arms as Redneck number one and one of his militia sprinted out into the snow-covered field, throwing their weapons to the side as they did so.

"So much for comrades in arms," I said as I pointed to the lone injured gunmen that hobbled desperately to keep up with his fleeing leader.

By the time we were abreast of the trucks, the two lead runners were nearly out of sight and didn't look like they were going to stop any time soon. The injured one had fallen over maybe a hundred yards away and seemed to be rapidly succumbing to whatever injury had taken him down. "Stop," I told Tracy.

Now she did question my sanity in a rapid fire of neatly phrased expletives. I was duly impressed.

"Hon," I placed my hand on her shoulder. "We need to work on BT. Plus, how far do you think we can go in this cold weather without a windshield? I'm already freezing my ass off and I must have a couple of quarts of adrenaline running through me."

She didn't think I was any saner for my response, but she did as I asked. I knew appealing to a lack of warmth would get to her. I have the heating bills to prove it.

I shivered as I went through the contents of the trucks. Not because of the cold but because of what they contained. There were handcuffs, zip ties, duct tape, rope, a variety of knives and what could only be described as medieval torture tools. Everything the home rapist could wish for. Jen had been more and more disgusted as we moved from cargo hold to cargo hold. There was food and medical supplies and even some Oxycodone, which I knew BT would appreciate. But interlaced with this were the true purport of what these animals were up to – S&M magazines strewn about that would only arouse the sickest and twisted that society had to offer.

Polaroids of previous victims spilled out from the glove compartment as I searched through the truck. These pictures made the magazines seem tame in comparison. The reality of how close we were to disaster struck me physically. I could see the tortured faces of my wife and daughter in these pictures of misery. These women and girls screamed in agony as every inconceivable act of depravity was forced upon them. I had not noticed Jen as she peered over my shoulder. I bumped into her as I grabbed the pictures and headed for the nearest snow bank. No one else needed to see this.

She walked wordlessly away from me as I dug a hole in the snow and tossed the offending images in, covering them quickly. Fearful that the infused evil on them would seep through my gloves, I hastily wiped snow vigorously on them. Two pistol shots pulled me away from my infected finger wear. Jen was standing in the field over the prone body of our intended assailant. If he had had a flicker of life in him before, Jen had made sure to extinguish it. I felt no pity. I don't think that under his tutelage our demises would have been so 'clean' for lack of a better word.

Tracy hadn't flinched at Jen's actions. I rightly assumed she must have come across her own grotesque cache of monstrous mementos.

"I can't find an exit wound on BT. I'm pretty sure that bullet is lodged on his bone," she said.

I turned to her. My eyes just plain felt heavy. If there were such thing as a stressometer, mine was rapidly red lining. I was pretty good at field sutures and staunching blood flow, even setting the occasional bone, but this would require full on surgery. There was no way around it. I blanched at the prospect. Sewing torn skin was vastly different from intentionally cutting someone open and feeling around for a bullet. Rooting around in muscle and tissue, making sure to not nick any major arteries while also ensuring that I did not cut myself on any of his bone fragments was not something I was looking forward to. Pondering leads to hesitation, which leads to mistakes.

"Brendon! Hey, man, come over here. You've got to help me get BT into the truck bed."

"I'll help, Mr. T," Tommy said as he handed a bottle of whiskey to Tracy.

Tommy's helping turned into a one-man wonder show. If I hadn't been watching it with my own eyes, I would have cried 'bullshit' and still I almost did. Short of having an engine lift I don't know how Tommy could do it. It wasn't with the ease he had displayed during the Walmart encounter but still I watched in awe as Tommy hefted the burly giant out of the minivan. Twenty feet later he gently placed BT in the bed of the truck as Brendon and Travis hopped up on the back to help.

"Tracy, put a couple of those smaller knives to flame," I said as I grabbed the bottle of liquor from her.

"What do you need that for?" she asked.

"Disinfectant," I told her, right before I unscrewed the cap and took a long pull of the bitter, burnt gasoline derivative.

"Yeah, disinfectant," she said mockingly as she went to sterilize some knives.

Jen returned, seemingly no worse for the wear. She looked like she had just returned from taking out the garbage; and I guess in reality that was all she had really done. She grabbed the bottle from me. I felt a little ashamed as she made my rather significant drag from the bottle seem childlike in comparison. She wiped her sleeve over her mouth before she spoke. The tenor of her voice belied her true feelings to a point, but not completely.

"What are you doing, Talbot? Besides drinking this rot gut. Oh what I wouldn't do for a nice Pinot Noir." She took another long pull.

"Uh, could you save me some, I need it for BT."

She smiled abashedly. "Sorry," she said as she absently wiped her mouth again. "For what?"

"Huh?"

"Why do you need this?" she asked, as she shook the bottle in front of my face, not really handing it back.

"The bullet didn't come out. I've got to go in and get it."

"Have you ever done that?" she asked, quickly thrusting the bottle into my hands. I guess she thought whoever possessed the bottle had to perform the surgery.

"I filled in pot holes, Jen. Not much call for field surgery in that line of work."

"What about before that?" she grasped.

"Oh yeah sure, I left a lucrative and life-fulfilling job as a highly skilled surgeon to live the prosaic life of a road crew man. Filling holes seemed a much nobler profession."

"Don't go there, Talbot. Don't cover over your insecurities with sarcasm. You know what I mean."

I sighed. I knew what she meant. She was asking if I had ever had the need to put any of my friends back together after some raghead had done their best to make Humpty Dumpty fall. "I'm sorry," I told her. "No, there was never time during the heat of battle to help and by the time the last bullets had flown the injured would have been medevac'd out. Some I got to visit in the hospital while they recovered. Others I watched as their bodies got loaded on a plane and sent back home."

She witnessed the pain in my eyes as I pulled the Band-Aid off a wound that would not heal. "I'm sorry, Mike."

"Me too." I took another pull of the disgusting concoction while leaning over a moaning BT who was luckily still passed out. How long he was going to remain in that status while I delved into his leg was another story all together. I grabbed some sani-wipes from Tracy and cleaned off my hands as best I could, and then drizzled whiskey over them. If it didn't kill the germs, at least it would get them drunk enough to be cooperative. Then I took a deep breath.

"One for me," I took another swig. "And one for you," I said as I poured a liberal amount of the elixir into the wound.

BT's eyes flared open. Fiery pain seared across his brain bucket. He looked right at the source of this intrusion. "What the fuck are you doing Talbot!?" The gods shook under the assault of those words.

It must have been the warmth of the liquor as it spread throughout my body. I felt no fear, only resolve as I explained to BT what was happening. It was tough to tell which of us was more detached as I clinically laid out my plan. I sounded scholarly as I slurred my way through the procedure. BT nodded at all the right moments. I handed him two Oxycodone and the bottle. He didn't shun either one away or question what they were.

"I'm going to wait until those kick in and then I'm going to start." I reached out to grab the bottle back.

"Think you've had enough." He grinned savagely, the pain distorting his features. "I'd appreciate it if you got started now instead of waiting, not sure how much longer I can keep this macho shit up, and I'll be damned if I'm going to cry in front of a woman. The last time I did that, I was six and my mom had just whopped me upside the head for writing on the walls with peanut butter. Don't ask," he told me, just as I was about to.

Tracy came over with three knives, one still smoldering a dull red from the heat. BT looked at the blade and then back at me. "You know what you're doing right? Wait, don't answer, I don't want to know." He finished the bottle. It clattered loudly to the ground as he threw it over the side. I placed a shirt under his head as I gently pushed his head back down.

"You want something to bite on?" I asked him seriously.

"Why, you think this is going to hurt?" He laughed. He then set his eyes hard on some distant object high above our locale. I hoped for his sake it was God. The call of a lone falcon was the only sound as I plunged the knife into the bullet hole. Tears silently streamed down BT's face as I made the hole big enough so that I would be able to plunge my fingers in.

"You sure you don't want to wait until those pills take effect?" Sweat froze on me as fast as it formed.

A curt shake of his head kept me going. My respite was not to happen. BT went rigid as I submerged first one and then a second finger into his bloody laceration. The sheer size of BT's thighs meant I was going to have to go deep in my attempt to find the foreign body. Lady Luck was going to have to be on my shoulder for this. If the bullet had struck and tumbled away I'd never find it. I had gone in as far as my two fingers were going to allow and not struck home yet. There was a hollow sucking sound as I pulled my fingers out of the wound. Nobody commented, but I could hear more than one disgruntled stomach recoil at the noise.

"I've got to make the hole bigger, BT," I apologized.

"Can't get much worse," he replied. I'm glad he didn't realize then that he was wrong.

My hand was steadier as I made the second lengthening incision. BT didn't flinch at all when I stuck my whole hand in up to the knuckle. A potent combination of Jack Daniel's, Oxycodone, and shock were all taking effect, those plus the mind-numbing cold. I concentrated hard on the fact that I was merely feeling around in some beef. Sure, it was warm bloody steak, but it was steak nonetheless and that was what was going to let me keep going. If I were to dwell on the reality of the situation, BT would end up dying from infection. My hand was relatively warm compared to the rest of my body, encased as it was in the living tissue of my friend. That being the case, my fingers were not numb and were therefore able to detect when I brushed up against something that didn't have a right to be where it was. Relief was my immediate thought. Relief to rid BT of the bullet, and relief to get my hand out of his thigh.

I oriented the foreign material as best I could to not damage anything more on its way out. What I removed was not a bullet, not unless they were white, about an inch long and a quarter inch wide. Tracy was the first to recognize what I had removed, I could tell by the sounds of her retching, although the others weren't far behind. The splintered bone fragment shone brightly in the noonday sun. I hastily tossed it before BT had the chance to see it.

"Wasn't it, was it," BT said resignedly.

I shook my head and dove my hand back in. No sense in stalling at this point. For fifteen minutes I pulled various sized pieces of bone out, most no bigger than a toothpick. Two or maybe three fragments were taken out that were roughly the size of my pinkie. I didn't think there was going to be any bone left to knit together when I was through. Blood coated the bottom of the truck bed. BT was drifting in and out of consciousness. My timeline for success was rapidly diminishing. Either I got the bullet, or the bullet got BT. It was that simple of an equation, but one which I'm sure was never up on any algebra teacher's chalk board.

"Where is the fu...got it!" I could tell by the mushroom shape this wasn't another bone fragment. BT couldn't share in my elation, he had passed out, I think. "Jen?"

Jen had hopped up on the bed of the truck to help. "He's still breathing," she answered. "But it's thready."

"That sounds mighty ER-ish," I said triumphantly as I pulled the bullet free from its human stockade.

"What can I say, I had a crush on the triage nurse Margulies played on that show," she said, a smile spreading across her face as she also saw the bullet. "Now what?"

"Well, I'll sew him up, we'll set and splint his leg as well as possible, and then we'll get out of Dodge."

"I meant what about internal damage."

"From the bullet or my ministrations?"

"Well, probably both," she said honestly.

"Shit, Jen, I'm already five orders of magnitude above my pay grade. I can only sew him up and hope his body will take care of the rest. IF he's lucky he'll only have a pronounced limp when he can walk again."

"Worst case scenario?"

"Are you kidding me? Do you see the blood we're sitting in? Do you see how sterile an environment I'm working in?

Or, better yet, my surgical skill level. The bullet looks fairly whole but I'm not completely sure I didn't leave a piece of it in, plus there's no way I got every bone fragment out, but if I don't close him up soon he'll bleed out. Which may still happen depending on how many blood vessels, veins, and arteries were damaged. That he's alive up to this point is near miraculous. We're going to have to pump him full of antibiotics for the next two weeks and pray."

"Pray?" she looked at me incredulously.

"Figure of speech," I said as I turned away. Seemed like the wrong time to spurn God, but I wasn't feeling very pious at the moment.

Within a half hour I had closed the wound. Jen and Tommy got him cleaned up and put new clothes that weren't blood soaked on him. And then, after getting him placed in the back of Brendon's minivan, I set his leg in a close approximation of the position I felt it should be in. Two ax handles and a roll of duct tape completed my handiwork. It wasn't pretty. He was going to be eating Oxys like Pez for the next month and we had about a week's worth. Great, another stop on the journey. Those always go so well.

Another set of clothes down the drain, so to speak. The only thing salvageable on me was my shirt. The jacket had caught the brunt of arterial spray. I shivered on the side of the road as I stripped out of the stiff clothing.

Tracy had come up to me with the box of baby wipes to clean up with. I couldn't have been more grateful if she had showed up with a cheeseburger right now.

She started laughing at me. There I was, nearly naked in the dead of winter on the side of a highway.

"Hey that's not cool!" I yelled. "It's because of the cold, it causes shrinkage you know. It's like when you go swimming!" I was now yelling to her laughing retreating back. "Not cool," I said angrily to myself as I washed up. I was still muttering angrily when I rejoined the rest of the caravan.

"What do you think, Mike?" Brendon asked.

"Most people don't have the nerve to ask that question, Brendon. At least not open ended like that."

"You really are nuts aren't you?" he smiled

I left the question dangling. There really isn't a way to answer it legitimately anyway. See Catch-22.

"Well, Carol's is still our ultimate goal, for now. But we're going to need more antibiotics and more pain killers, which means another effen stop."

He rolled his eyes.

"My sentiments exactly. I want to pack up the pick-up truck that isn't all bloody because we're taking it, and then I want to completely disable the other. I don't think Redneck number one and his dipshit driver are going to come back and claim it but I see no reason to tempt the fates. And most of all, I want to get the hell out of here."

"What do you think about BT's chances?"

"Well, a normal person would probably be dead already so he's got that going for him. Plus he's too mean for Heaven, and Hell doesn't want the competition." I didn't get the expected laugh from my flippant remark. I guess he wanted an actual answer. Doesn't he know I try to avoid those? "Fifty-fifty. I just don't know how much damage he suffered." I left it at that.

"Mike, one more thing."

Those statements are never good. When someone waits until the very end of a conversation to bring something up, it's usually because it has taken this long to build up the nerve to say it. "If you tell me my daughter is pregnant, I'm going to be pissed."

"What?" His eyebrows knit together. "No, wait? Huh? No, that's not it. It's Justin."

"I know."

"About the fever dreams and Eliza?"

"I know."

"What are you going to do about it?" he asked me.

"No clue." I started to walk away.

"That's it?" he yelled. "Seems to me that Justin has an open line with the enemy and you're not going to do anything?" he said heatedly.

I stopped and turned. "Got any ideas? I'm all ears." I meant what I said, but my words were infused with malice. Brendon could feel the taint of vileness emanate from them...but youth does not always pay heed to wisdom.

"Oh I think you know what needs to be done, Mike! Aren't you always the one that preaches the sacrifice of the one for the many?"

I didn't hesitate one second from his words, though they struck me deep. "Take the other truck then," I said.

He physically stepped back, I'm pretty sure he wasn't expecting that. I had basically told him he was welcome to leave, without Nicole. I had painted him into a corner; for that I felt a measure of guilt. He was as close to family as you can be without being family, a fine distinction, but a distinction nonetheless. I would choose family over others a hundred percent of the time. It was as simple as that. By now, we had drawn a crowd. This was starting to become commonplace. He shook with rage. If he came at me now I would have only one or two chances to take him down before his size, youth, and speed overwhelmed me.

Travis breeched a round into his shotgun, Brendon turned towards him. Fear, hurt, and betrayal flitted across his features in less than the span of a second. His shoulders drooped as he walked towards the bloody Ford. The passenger side tire was blown and Tracy had made sure when she scraped down the side of it that it would never win 'Best in Show,' but other than that, it was mechanically sound.

"We'll wait until you get the tire changed," I told him.

"Dad?" Nicole questioned. "What are you talking about?" I didn't answer her. "Brendon, what are you doing?"

He didn't answer her as he reached into the cab and got the jack and tire iron. She started tugging on his arm as he began to break the lug nuts on the tire.

"Brendon, you can't leave us...me!" she cried. "Dad, fix this."

"He's a big boy," I said with an ice-cold edge.

"Talbot!" Tracy chimed in.

"What!" I yelled right back. I hadn't even got to the 'h' in 'What' when I knew that was the wrong answer.

She didn't even have to say 'Really?' Her arched eyebrow let me know how screwed I was.

Already down for a nickel, might as well increase the Talbot national debt. "You know what, Tracy, if he wants to stay with us fine! But I'm not going over there and begging him to come. He doesn't like the way things are shaking out right now. Why don't you go see what his plans are? I'm sure you'll be just as thrilled as I was. I'm going to pack the truck." And with that I walked away.

Tracy now knew the root of the problem as she looked over to Justin still sitting in the minivan. She shuddered as she saw the ghost of a smile play across his features. I had taken my time moving our stuff from the minivan to the truck in the hope that cooler heads would prevail, mainly Brendon's. But for as slow as I was moving, Brendon was moving that fast, maybe he didn't want to think about what he was doing because he'd realize just how fucking stupid he was being...dumb ass. I almost went over to him to start round two, but I didn't want to burden Travis with the guilt of having to shoot him.

Brendon kissed Nicole and then gently pushed her trembling body away from his as he stepped into the cab of the truck.

"No, Brendon!" she wept. "You can't leave me!"

My heart was breaking for my daughter.

"I'm sorry!" I heard him yell through the closed windows.

I thought Nicole might try to get in the cab and go with him. I would have physically restrained her if it got to that point. I was thankful it didn't. She stood stock-still and sobbed as Brendon started the truck, did an illegal U-turn and drove off. That was it, he left. We watched for a minute until he was a dot on the horizon. Tracy slid an arm across my waist and wept silently on my shoulder.

I put Nicole in the truck with me. She didn't react at all as I put her seat belt on. Her head slumped against the cool glass.

"Jen, you up for driving?" I asked her.

Of us all she looked the most prepared. The Talbots as a whole had just suffered a crushing loss. This wasn't the movies. We weren't going to be all joking around in the next scene, one of our own was gone. Whether literally or figuratively didn't really matter. We weren't ever going to see him again. If he somehow survived on his own, which was doubtful, he would never know how to find us again. I was going to turn around and get him. I had made up my mind. BT changed it back.

His screams pierced the day. I ran over to him, shook out a couple of Oxys and handed them to him. He swallowed them without water, the tears that leaked from his eyes causing enough lubricant to get the large pills down. Within minutes he had passed out again; not from the pills but from the pain.

"Let's go, we've got to find a pharmacy." There was no more milling about. We had a mission to complete now. We would have enough time later to mourn.

Tommy was nearly as catatonic as Nicole. He had really ratcheted up the empathy button. Tommy had a serious crush on Nicole. Everyone knew it, though somehow Tommy didn't know we knew. That was the funny part about it. He would get so flustered around her that he would call her everything but her real name, and Brendon was ALWAYS, 'that other guy' or 'him.' So, of all of us, the big kid had the most to, 'in theory,' gain, though not in a millennium would he have ever conspired for this sort of outcome. He had taken

235

on Nicole's pain…not to ease, but to share.

CHAPTER 21

I don't want to gloss over it. It was what it was, though. We smashed into a pristine Rite-Aid. We startled the zombified pharmacist and two techs even more than ourselves. We dispatched them in the most humane way possible. It was a quick, precise, antiseptic kill. They were of the slow variety and maybe even a little slower since they probably hadn't fed in weeks. That would be something to file and look back on later.

I've always considered myself a glass half full type of guy, but the fact that this store was relatively untouched disturbed me. Don't get me wrong, I was absolutely ecstatic that we were getting the meds BT and Justin were going to need along with everything from toe nail fungus inhibitor to Viagra (I figured if we ever got to the point where Tracy wanted to have sex, I was going to make up for lost time). The problem was that this store being virgin territory to looters meant that there weren't enough people of the living variety around to do any looting. And to top that off, Brendon's leaving had had a crushing effect on us all. He had died to us, pure and simple, no matter what happened to him physically.

Nicole was inconsolable. I picked up every antidepressant known to man. How I was going to administer them was beyond my scope, though; maybe one of each. I knew things were at an all-time low when I actually had to point out the Pop-Tart boxes to Tommy as he walked right by them.

Jen stayed with BT while we ransacked the store. She wasn't nearly as devastated as the Talbots, but it affected her. We were already counting the number of us on two hands. Removing just one finger had a profound impact. As a viable fighting force we were in dire straits. We were down to Travis, Jen, and me. Any opponent bigger and meaner than a Girl Scout troop and we were going to get our asses kicked – and by asses kicked, I meant killed.

I was sick of reflecting. The image coming back was horrible, so when the horn sounded it was a welcome if at the same time ominous sound. If the world ever got back to some semblance of normality, I would never be able to drive again. The mere sound of someone beeping at me would send me into panic attacks. We all looked up like meerkats waiting for the hawk to descend. Travis was first to the door, shotgun at the ready. No matter how many zombies he killed or how long we survived, I was never going to get over the bounce in adrenaline my heart took every time he was exposed to danger. I couldn't get the picture of him as a seven-year-old out of my head. Although I knew he was capable, if not more so, to get us out of any sticky situation. I could almost watch him harden to the world by the hour, whereas I felt I was heading the other way. Stop pondering! I ran to the door.

Jen had stepped out of the car. She didn't seem too particularly out of sorts. She pointed to her left, somewhat out of our view. I walked past the shopping carts and looked. Zombies were coming.

Travis came up beside me. "No speeders, that's good."

He had ascertained a fact that took me another few long moments to realize. "Nope," I drawled out, making it look like I had known all along.

He looked up at me, no, that's not quite right, he slightly lifted his eyes to make them level with my own. *Holy Shit, when did that happen?* I wondered in amazement.

"I'm gonna finish loading the truck," he said as he turned.

A small wall of the living dead were coming our way with what I would imagine was less than grand intentions and he gave less than two shits. Maybe a piss and a squirt, but that was about it.

He had already gone back into the store when I answered him. "Okay, sounds good."

Tommy came up beside me, seemingly more in character as he devoured a Hostess Cupcake. "Wanff onef?"

"You know what, Tommy, I think actually I do." I took the offered cupcake from him and we shared a moment there eating our chocolaty snacks, watching the advancing zombies as if it were the most natural thing in the world, like maybe it was a sunrise. I guess it was more like a sunset and not quite so beautiful.

Tommy had at some time departed. I had somehow eaten a cupcake I couldn't remember chewing and Travis had finished loading the truck bed.

"You coming, Dad?" Travis asked with some concern. I guess I looked like the village idiot standing there. I would imagine I had chocolate on my face and I was gazing off into the distance, dimly aware that a viable threat was approaching.

"Uh...yeah," I answered as I absently dropped the cupcake wrapper clutched in my hand. I bent over and picked it back up, disposing of it in a trash barrel that would never again be emptied. What was the point? I didn't have one and I couldn't see the reason to look for one.

"You alright, Talbot?" my wife asked as I got behind the wheel.

"That noticeable?"

"We've been married a long time, but even if I had just met you I'd be able to tell."

The zombies were still coming and would soon be within bow and arrow range, but still I turned to face and answer

Tracy as if I had all the time in the world.

"Brendon?" she asked, beating me to the punch.

"That's definitely a big part of it. I'm not sure if I did more harm than good to BT. Chances are he'll still die, whether from infection or my ineptitude."

"Mike, you saved him, what happens to him next is in God's hands."

"You still believe, huh?" I asked her. In retrospect it was mean spirited and wasn't going to help my bargaining power when I got to the Pearly Gates, provided that they existed.

Her facial features said it all; how dare I question what she did and did not believe in. I always used to give her a hard time that she didn't believe in extraterrestrials. I would pull out the arguments of how could there NOT be with the billions upon billions of solar systems, and if only a billionth of those could support life, there would still be an infinitesimal amount of probable planets that were capable of harboring life. She'd have nothing to do with it. She also used to scoff at me when I would sometimes let it leak that I was preparing for Armageddon in one of the many different ways it was bound to happen – including zombies. Being right sucked if you couldn't rub the ones you loved noses in it. Maybe we'd luck out and Alpha Centauri would get their shit together and attack us. Then I could have a twofer. I laughed out loud.

"Something funny?" Her arched eyebrow let me know that I was beginning to tread on uneven ground.

Zombies to the front, Tracy to the side, I was weighing my options carefully.

"No, no, I was just thinking about aliens," I answered truthfully.

"What's this got to do with Mexicans, Mike?"

I busted out laughing. If I had waited to start the truck and get out of the Rite-Aid parking lot AFTER I got myself under control, we would have made a wonderful lunch for the zombies. At this point I was thankful for the lack of traffic. My vision was distorted from the tears. Tracy glowered at me.

I had been in a foul mood for the majority of the day. I hadn't completely pulled out from that dank place in my spirit, but I had been granted a momentary reprieve. It was those small candles of light on this unlit path we lived on now that were going to sustain us all.

The drive up the highway was damn near uneventful, which in itself is a good thing. We saw an occasional bloated, frozen cow or sheep. The more disturbing ones were picked to the bone. That could only mean one thing. There were some cars abandoned on the road, most likely from empty gas tanks. I pitied the fools that had gotten out to walk, and then I thought back to the bone frameworks previously mentioned. Nothing like a mass exodus had happened here. Sure, North Dakota wasn't known for its population explosion…but still.

"Here, Mr. T," Tommy said as he handed me a heavy brown paper bag.

Normally I would tell him to wait because I had to concentrate on driving. I was pretty sure some pimply faced teenager wasn't going to be coming in the other direction texting his friend lying about who he had banged the night before.

"Whatcha you got here, Tommy?" I asked as I took the bag. Although from the weight of it and the feel of the glass bottle it couldn't have been anything other than booze.

"I got you some Jeff Daniels," he answered.

I laughed, again thankful for the small release of endorphins. "I think you mean Jack."

"That's what I said," he answered.

"But why, Tommy, you know I can't stand the stuff."

"Oh, it's not for you," he answered with a smile.

Tracy turned to look him in the eye. A mischievous grin spread across his face. He knew something and he wasn't going to spill all his beans at once.

241

"Tommy, I'll hide your Pop-Tarts," Tracy threatened, going right for the jugular. Dancing lightly around the subject had never been at the top of her repertoire. Tommy grabbed his backpack and pushed it behind himself. "I'm serious," she added, making a mock attempt to reach around him.

I watched in the rear view mirror as a sheer look of terror came over his face. It released an even bigger amount of happy juice into my veins. I didn't laugh out loud though. If Tracy couldn't get that bag from him, she might make me try to. I had no desire to be such an abject point of fear for the kid.

She resorted to less than honorable tactics. She started tickling him. Tommy's face turned a bright crimson. His laughter made everything around him shine. The minivan swayed down the highway as his bulk thrashed back and forth in a vain attempt to get away from her ministrations.

"Alright...alright!" he croaked out in between laborious inhalations of breath. When he hesitated for a fraction more of a second longer than Tracy was willing to tolerate, she started up again. I felt for the kid, if he had been older I would have feared his heart wouldn't be able to take much more. "I'll tell!" he squealed.

Snot, tears and chocolate goo coalesced in a pool on his shirt as he fought to regain control. On anyone else that would have been the most disgusting sight I had seen; on Tommy it was merely endearing. "Aw, I messed up my *Star Wars* shirt," Tommy said as he looked down at his belly.

"Tommy!" Tracy shouted as she held her hand up high in a claw like fashion, ready to strike and do more damage.

"Okay, okay, stop, but my shirt." Tracy's hand got higher. "Your mom likes Jeff Daniels."

"Jack," I said.

He looked over towards me. "That's what I said."

Tracy looked over at me, pissed that I was helping Tommy stall. I might be a big bad Marine, but I'm as ticklish as a puppy. If she started that crap with me, this minivan would be cart-wheeling down the roadway in about ten seconds. "We're good," I said, holding up my hands.

She redirected towards Tommy, convinced that I would no longer interfere with her. She was right.

"Ryan said your mom likes Jeff Daniels!" he yelled out before Tracy could descend back on him.

She sat back down hard in her seat, a look of bafflement, relief and wonderment across her face. After long seconds of processing the information she turned back towards Tommy.

"You sure?" she asked querulously.

Tommy beamed. No answer was necessary at that point.

"Ryan said my mom likes Jack Daniels?" Tracy reiterated, nearly sobbing.

"Yep, Jeff Daniels."

"Jack," I said, adding my penny and a half.

"That's what I said," Tommy said, looking at me in the rear view mirror like I had gone daffy. The earnest way that he was looking at me made me wonder if maybe he had said Jack and I was slowly going insane. Okay so 'slowly' would probably be the wrong descriptor, something along the lines of breaking the speed of light might be more apt.

My eyebrows knitted of their own volition. "Tracy, what did Tommy say?" I needed help.

"Oh, Mike, he said my mom was alright." Now she was full on crying.

Now whether Tommy had said Jack or Jeff was open to debate, but not once did he say Carol Yentas was okay. Sure, it was implied. Dead people don't really like anything except maybe staying dead. I'd be damned though if I was going to be the one that pissed on her Cheerios, rained on her parade, took a dump on her tulips, whatever. We had a glimmer of hope in a sea of somberness. The home team needed a win, and right now Tommy was pitching a gem.

Tracy fairly bounced in her seat the remaining hour of our journey. I could tell she was wavering with bouts of happiness and fits of caution. It is a tough thing to open one's self to the prospect of something happening that is beyond the belief of what is expected, and then once you attain that state of inner balance to have what you hoped for ripped from you.

To get the full effect of this analogy, just for a moment consider yourself a huge, NO, HUGE Red Sox fan (like me) and it is the magical year of the Lord nineteen hundred and eighty-six and it is Game Six, the Sox are ONE FUCKING OUT from winning the World Series, something you never expected to see in your lifetime. You suck Babe Ruth! A dribbler, a DRIBBLER is hit up the first base line. I had literally, along with all my friends, popped that bottle of champagne. Cold liquor was bubbling all over my hand as I watched in disbelief as the ball went through BILLY BUCKNER'S legs. I had never known up to that point in life what getting a dream crushed felt like. It was something akin to waking up and realizing you weren't dating the prom queen. Blood, fur and bone bits everywhere, yep it was pretty much like that. So I'm basically saying that I could empathize with her, in a roundabout way.

The rural road that led up to Carol's was, for the minivan, nearly impassable. It had seen some random traffic, and if I kept the speed low enough I could follow in the barely visible grooves some other traveler had made. On two occasions some gentle bumper pushing from Jen got me out of some deeper furrows.

"Maybe we should let Jen go first. She can make a better trail for us, hon."

Tracy's unspoken look of 'Not a fucking chance' shut me up.

When we got to 7 Washburn Road, we were met with a sea of white. An unbroken blanket of snow lay a foot deep. It might as well have been a moat. There was no way this car was getting through it. The old Victorian style house was set a good two hundred yards off the roadway, but even from here it was impossible to not see the blotches of crimson that dotted the yard.

"Talbot, is that blood?" Tracy asked. We both saw the giant dream-crushing boot hovering over us. "Where are the bodies?"

"My guess is under the snow."

My thoughts however traveled a little darker. I figured that they had got what they came for and long since left. Tracy started to fumble with the door lock.

"What're you doing?"

"I'm going up there," she said matter-of-factly. "I've got to see what happened." She gulped.

"Hold on. You can't walk up there. That snow's at least a foot deep. If something or somebody is still here, you'll never be able to run for it. We'll hop in the back of Jen's truck."

Within a minute we had armed ourselves and climbed into the back of the truck. My concern lay in my thoughts of how I was going to pick up Tracy's pieces of broken soul when she discovered her mother was gone. Oh...and gone I hoped she was. If we found her eaten body, or worse yet, her as zombie, I didn't know how the Talbots would be able to muster on.

The cold reddened Tracy's features but even that couldn't compare to the red in her eyes. Tommy was busy wetting his fingertips and smoothing back an invisible cowlick, as if trying to make himself presentable. Well, of all the signs he could be portraying, that was one of the better ones. As we jostled our way up the yard, I wasn't convinced we were still on the driveway as the splashes of blood became more pronounced. But it wasn't just blood, I noticed a boot sticking up in one of the piles. In another was an outstretched hand. It sort of reminded me of a sapling struggling for light. I would have shot it if I really thought it was going to take root.

One thing I could tell was that there hadn't really been a battle here. Some of the bodies had been out for a lot longer than the others. There was one that, apart from a tuft of hair sticking up, I would have never known was there. The blood had been completely covered with subsequent snowfall. A few were fresh, and that could only mean one thing, there was something here worth trying to eat.

My sight was brought to the fore by movement. Someone had risen out of a chair and was standing on the porch. Even from this distance, I could tell that they had one mean mother of a breech-loading shotgun at the ready.

Tracy shocked me as she yelled out, "Mom!?"

I wanted to say something about her giving us away but the roar of the truck engine as it struggled to cut through the snow could probably be heard for miles in this new, quiet world. Come to think of it, I was never ever going to miss the sound of a jackhammer at 7:33 in the morning on a Saturday. The shape of the person on the porch had the general shape of someone's grandmother, but the majority of my focus was on that ten-gauge shotgun. We were close enough that, if that person started to shoot slugs, we'd be able to count ourselves among the other lawn ornaments.

I banged on the roof of the truck for Jen to stop.

She looked out her window. "What's up, Mike?"

"Stop the truck and kill the engine," I told her.

"You sure that's a good idea?" she asked.

"Nope," I answered truthfully. The truck engine simmered to a stop, the pinging of the heated motor the only sound to break up the muffled day.

"Mom?!" Tracy yelled out again.

Nothing…no response. Only the steady unwavering double barrel of a large caliber shotgun. After a few seconds the barrel dipped imperceptibly.

"Tracy?!" came the tremulous reply.

That was it. Tracy was down off the bed of the truck and running at full tilt, which really wasn't all that fast when you're knee deep in snow. I banged on the roof of the truck again.

"Wagons forward!" I yelled and gestured. Don't ask me why, seemed like the right thing to do and say at the time. Tracy was PISSED OFF when we passed her on by, and even more so when Jen nearly blocked off the entire porch entrance. As she caught up to us, her passing glance was so cold it burned my face.

"Mike?" Carol asked.

"Hey, Mom," I said as I jumped down off the bed of the truck.

Tracy had rushed full-tilt into her mother's arms, there was some crying and sobbing and some general tear jerking and I think that Carol and Tracy might have also blubbered. I wasn't sure, couldn't see much through the haze of salty water. Must have sat on my keys again.

I joined in the small huddle, God she smelled like chocolate chip cookies, how do grandmothers do that? "We brought you something," I told her. "It's Jeff Daniels," I said needlessly, the shape of the paper bag gave away the contents. Kind of like trying to gift wrap a bike, why bother.

"Jack Daniels?" Carol asked.

Tommy had come down off the truck and was watching the reunion. "That's what he said," with a tone that implied we all must have gone over the edge.

Carol gasped as she looked at Tommy. "You're the one from my dreams."

Tommy looked perplexed. "I'm not sure I know what you're talking about, Gran Y," he said.

"Sure you do. You're the one that likes those little flavored shingles in the foil packs."

Tommy looked aghast. "Pop-Tarts aren't shingles, Gran Y."

I thought I was going to have to catch Carol from falling when she saw all three kids, safe and sound.

"Oh my God! I prayed for this day! I never thought that you would all make it." She was openly crying. Yeah I was too, so sue me. "Come here! Come here!" she motioned to them all. Our group huddle was ungainly, but it felt so right.

"Oh my God, Mom, we never thought..." Tracy hitched.

"Me?" Carol laughed. "I'm too tough an old bird for them. Not sure if they even got by Big Bertha here," she said, shaking her shotgun, "that they'd even want me." She shook her head. "I've spent damn near my entire life on this farm. I'm as tough as the soil Daddy used to try to cull crops from." She smiled grimly for a moment and then burst into joyous laughter at the sight of her family gathered around her.

I couldn't help myself. I hugged her again. I was having a heavy estrogen flow day.

"You smell just like cookies," I told her out loud.

"That's because I'm making some. Don't look so surprised. Tommy told me you were coming. Of course, I didn't believe him at first. I thought it might be the onset of advanced Alzheimer's or maybe schizophrenia, or maybe even just plain old loneliness, but I figured what the hell, might as well be ready. Oh and by the way, Tommy," she said, stopping to look at him.

Had we told her his name? I didn't think so.

Carol continued, "I didn't have any gummy bears to put in with the chocolate chips."

Tommy handed her a bag of gummy bears from his pocket. Was it coincidence? Now Tommy is usually a walking pantry to begin with, but he didn't even hesitate when he reached into one of his many hidden storage compartments.

Carol took the bag as if she had been expecting this. "Great, I'll put them in with the next batch."

"You still have power out here, Carol?" I asked her.

"Gotta be pretty self-sufficient when you live this far in the outskirts. See any power lines, city boy? The generator is in the barn."

I waited until she went back into the house before I did a complete 360-degree scan of the area. No poles. I did a little happy dance as I realized I was going to take a hot shower tonight.

"What's the matter Talbot?" BT asked as Jen and Travis helped him up the steps. "Gotta pee?"

Except for being a few shades paler than he ought to be, the big man looked pretty good. This was turning out to be a pretty good fucking day and I was about to eat some chocolate chip cookies!

Tommy was already through the door. I could hear mock slapping as Carol was trying to shoo him away from her cookie sheet.

"Wait until I at least get them off the tray, you'll burn yourself!" Carol shouted at him. Tommy hovered over her like a News helicopter at a crash scene.

Seeing her grandmother had reignited a spark within Nicole's eyes. The sadness was still there, but it had been layered over a little with love. And that was how people survived. They moved on. The bleeding, gaping wound slowly became infused with coagulants and then the bleeding would trickle to a stop. The flesh would scab over and slowly begin to knit itself together and eventually the scab would fall off leaving fresh shiny puckered skin that would in time eventually fade to a scar. It would be something you would remember the pain of for your entire life, and you would always have the visible reminder. But it no longer consumed the resources of the body any more to heal it.

The smiles around the kitchen table as we devoured first that sheet –and then another sheet – of cookies with the surprisingly good taste of gummy bears mixed in, renewed my faith. My faith in what? God, humanity, survival, just plain old cookies? I wasn't sure, but I wasn't going to question it. If I didn't have another ultimate destination in mind I could have seen myself spending the rest of my days in this loving household. Then it struck me, why should I drag my family still another fifteen hundred miles across the country. And for what? There was no guarantee that any of my family survived. Carol survived, though, and if she could do it, then so could they. But she's in rural North Dakota, not much happened here when everybody was alive. Yeah, and my family is in rural Maine. If I could Google it, I'd bet the populations were similar.

Not knowing what had happened to my family weighed heavily but the thought of exposing my immediate family into even more danger to satisfy my curiosity was not an option.

I grabbed Tracy's hand and took her in to the living room.

"I think we should just stay here, Trace."

Her look questioned me, but I could see the excitement beyond. "Are you sure, Mike? I know how much you want to get back home."

"I think maybe we are home."

She hugged me fiercely, her leg crushing into my pilfered bottle of Viagra stashed in my pants pocket.

"You happy to see me, Mike?" she asked with a smile.

"I sure as hell could be," I answered her. She smacked me. We headed back into the kitchen. Her first, and then me after some slight man-parts adjusting. At least the momentary estrogen flood hadn't completely emasculated me.

After a bunch more laughing and eating, I went out to the porch. I would like to say that I had to loosen my belt because of the meal. These last few weeks stripped any fat reserves I had stored. I looked down the yard at the minivan wondering how many trips it was going to take to get everything up here. I also wasn't thrilled with the prospect of leaving it down there either. It looked too much like an invitation.

I heard a burst of merriment as Carol opened up the door to join me on the porch.

"I can't tell you what a wonderful thing you've done here, Mike," she said.

"We had to come and see if you were alright, Mom."

"That's not what I'm talking about, and I think you know it." I wanted to protest, it might have rung hollow though. "I mean bringing my daughter and my grandkids to me, alive and safe." I started to speak. "Hush, I know what you're going to say. But most people didn't feel like it was what they *had* to do, Mike. A good number of folks turned their guns on their kin rather than stand and fight." I looked at her in bewilderment. "No, Mike, you didn't HAVE to do anything, but you did. You know…when Tracy first married you, I wondered what the hell she saw in you."

"Don't hold back on my account."

"Oh, I won't. To be fair, you're a looker, but I wasn't sure of your character."

"Holy shit, Carol, is this a pep talk?"

"Hush I'm not done talking yet."

"Can you at least bust open that bottle of Jeff?" I asked her

From somewhere deep inside the house I heard Tommy yell "Jack!"

"You always seemed nuttier than a pecan pie to me."

"Oh, this is just getting better and better." I took a long pull from the Daniels that she handed me.

"But when Nicole was born and I saw how you were with her, I thought I might have made a mistake about you."

"Great." I took another swig.

"Now stop! That's not an easy thing for me to admit. You know Tracy is my only child and I damn near lost her in childbirth. So I only wanted what was best for her and, at the time, I didn't think that was you. But I watched you with Nicole. She stripped away your East Coast sarcasm and your ill temper towards the world. You loved her like no other ever could. The father's pride that beamed in your eyes every time you held her, that alone made me realize my error. I've seen you with all your kids, Mike, and I know that you would do whatever it took to make sure that every one of them was safe. And for that, Mike, I'm sorry that I ever doubted you.

But if you take one more swig off my bottle like the last one, I'm taking it all back."

I handed her the bottle back, I had actually taken a fair hit against the contents. I felt a little bad but it was rapidly becoming covered over with the warm tingly feeling of a buzz.

"What are you two doing out here?" Tracy asked, donning her coat.

"Reminiscing," I told her.

"Reminiscing, huh? How much of that paint thinner have you had, Mike?" my wife asked me.

"More than he should have," Carol said, holding the bottle up.

"We gots to get that minivan off the road."

"*Gots*, huh? I don't think you should be driving anything, Mike," Tracy said.

"Aw, it's not like he's going to get a DUI. Loosen up, girl," my wonderful mother-in-law said between swigs.

"Mom! Don't encourage him."

"You still got that tractor, Carol?"

"Actually had it running about a month or so ago, was going to plow the driveway. Don't really have a desire much now to go out. Though if you hadn't brought this whiskey I might've been changing my mind soon."

CHAPTER 22

Mike's Journal Entry Nineteen

Now the question was, did I want to plow the driveway and let any old schmoe have a direct route up, or did I want to drag the minivan and all its contents up here? If I dragged it up here and something happened where we needed to get out again we were screwed. Plow the driveway it was then. If anybody came a knockin' we'd deal with it at that point. Not like this was I-95 to begin with.

I went back into the house and put on everything and anything that I thought would stave off the frigid cold. Whiskey glow was only going to get me so far. And yes, I know that alcohol doesn't really warm you up. It does the opposite, in fact, by thinning your blood. It just makes you FEEL warmer.

I had bundled up near to the point of becoming a beach ball with appendages and was three steps down the porch before I realized I had forgotten something. Now I know this was the safest I've felt in weeks, but still I marched back in pretending to ignore my wife's questioning gaze and grabbed my nine millimeter.

The barn where the tractor was located was about a hundred yards or so from the house. I encountered six death blotches between the house and the barn. I shook my head in admiration of how Carol had survived. Had she slept? It wasn't like she could post a guard. She didn't have a dog anymore. Bastion had died, I think two summers ago, struck by the tractor. Tracy had cried for near on a week.

Her father had got that coon hound the day he found out he had cancer. He often told people that on his worst days of getting chemo, it was the tail wagging, tongue-licking Bastion that helped him get through the day. Even on his deathbed he had told Carol that the dog had probably given them an extra half of a year together. Carol loved that dog, if only for the fact that it had given her and her beloved husband some extra time.

It was two years after Everett's death that she had hired a handyman to get rid of some trash from the back acreage, something Everett had been promising for close on fifteen years. It was more of an inside joke that Everett had never gotten around to it than a point of contention. When the man had come running up to the household with a broken bloody bundle in his arms, Carol had intrinsically known what he carried. She had wept nearly as many tears for the mangy Bastion as she had for her husband. Another link to him was gone. She buried Bastion alongside her husband in the family cemetery.

So I circled back to the original question. How could she sleep knowing that at that very minute a mindless, hungry predator might be closing in? I shuddered. I had reached the front door to the barn, now not nearly as prepared to enter into the gloomy interior.

"They don't lie in wait, Talbot," I said out loud.

It was a trick nearly everyone uses to steel their resolve. I think it's more to let whatever monster is lurking know that we're coming in, ready or not. I just wish the monster gave the same courtesy. I clicked on the ancient light switch. Two light bulbs lazily lit the room. You could still wear night vision goggles in here and not get any glare through them. The tractor stood dead center in the barn and every deadly implement known to farming kind graced the walls all around me. I was sweating. I felt that it was dignity saving to blame it on the multiple layering I was swathed in.

I had reached the tractor when Justin shouted to me from the door. I realized then my mistake. Not that I was going to shoot Justin or even that he startled me enough to do it accidentally, but if someone of ill intent had come up on me, my multi-layered fingers couldn't fit in through the trigger guard. "You are just all sorts of a hot mess, aren't you, Talbot," I again said out loud to myself.

"I asked if you needed any help, Dad," Justin answered, thinking I hadn't heard his first question, which I hadn't. I had been whistling demons away at that time.

He looked like shit, and five degrees below zero was going to do little to help him. "Sure." I didn't completely understand what the cause of his recent detachment to us was, but if he was going to throw a lifeline it was my duty to reel him in. "Gotta gun?"

"What do you think? I'm your son."

"Smart ass. Okay let's just do a quick search through the stalls and the loft. This place gives me the willies."

"You sure it's not me?" he asked, half of the question was smart ass reply...half was a true question.

I didn't have a fifty-fifty answer. I let it drop. Within minutes we discovered that the only other tenants of the barn were some pigs, chickens, goats, a dairy cow and an extended family of field mice. I decided that if the mice were going to leave us alone, then I would follow suit. Yep you guessed it. Mice scare the crap out of me. Yes, I've been to battle. I've killed my fellow man and monsters of myth. It's just something about that hairless tail that really shoots a spike of fear through me. I don't really want to talk about it. Just add it onto the growing list of Talbotisms.

The tractor cranked after the third time and a good blast of starting fluid into the carburetor. "You up for doing some plowing?" I asked Justin.

He looked at me like I was pulling his leg. "You

serious?"

"Sure, go ahead," I told him.

Those of you that thought I did this only because I didn't want to be out in the North Dakota winter only have it partially correct. Isn't this part of the reason we have kids at all? So they can do the shit jobs that we used to do. Like taking out the trash, mowing the lawn, shoveling walkways. You don't really wonder why farm families used to be so huge, do you? It's not because screwing was the only thing to do. It was because there was so much work to be done. Okay...and screwing was really the only form of entertainment.

I stepped back before Justin had the chance to lurch the tractor into gear. The kid really couldn't so much as drive a nail, if you catch my meaning. He definitely inherited that from his mother. I figured the tractor to be about eight feet wide and the doors to the barn easily double that width and still I wondered if he would hit the frame. Would that kind of strike be enough to take the ancient structure down? And would we survive being buried by eighty-seven tons of sharpened metal objects? Probably not, I walked out to guide him through. *Not bad*, I thought, as he had a good six inches of clearance on his left hand side.

"Alright!" I shouted. "Just make a pathway down to the minivan so we can get it back up here." Justin gave me a thumbs-up.

I turned to walk back to the house and hopefully a steaming mug of cocoa. I was lost in the reverie of melted marshmallows when the warning shout came.

"Look out!" came the distant shout from the house. I looked up towards the porch. Tracy was cupping her hands together for the bullhorn effect. When she realized she had caught my attention she made an over agitated gesture with her arm. I dove to my left and the blade of the plow pushed air past my face. I looked up at Justin and saw he was looking off to his right and had not even noticed that he had almost made me a snow angel. So angel might be a little liberal, but it's more of an analogy. He turned back towards me as he passed. Something between 'I'm sorry' and 'Damn' crossed his face. I stood up and brushed the snow off of me, just staring at him as he passed.

I looked back up at the porch. Tommy had an expression on his face I couldn't remember ever seeing. It was rage. The glare he directed at Justin got to me more than the mice. All of a sudden Carol's house didn't seem quite as accommodating. We were going to bring our problems with us no matter where we went. I had momentarily let myself get swayed into a false sense of security. I wouldn't let that happen again.

Eliza was still out there and apparently we were of great interest to her. Maybe not me as much, however, we were on her short list for people she wanted dead.

The cocoa was good, but I was too distracted to thoroughly enjoy it. Instead of going in and staying in, I sat out on the porch and watched Justin actually do an admirable job of clearing a pathway. He only stopped once as the plow bit into the frozen corpse of a zombie, spreading frozen chunks of meat along a twenty-foot swath of driveway. He hopped down off the tractor, showing the right amount of disgust as he untangled the ensnared carcass. Or was it pity?

I froze twice as much on that porch as I would have if I had stayed on the tractor. I waited until Justin pulled the tractor back into the barn. This time he did take off a chunk of door frame. I shuddered thinking that could have been my skull. I heard the engine rattle to an end and then I began my long ascent out of the deck chair, convinced at this point that the fluid around my knees had completely frozen. My injured knee popped like a firecracker when I got it to full extension. Numbness from the cold kept the pain down to a dull roar. When this thing de-thawed I was going to be whimpering like a kid at Toys 'R' Us that didn't get the Deluxe Batman figurine with a fully stocked utility belt.

"That sounds like it hurt."

I had been too wrapped up in my own misery to hear Tracy come out.

"Not as much as it's going to tonight."

"You going down to get the van?"

It was obvious what I was doing. She was fishing for something. I knew the game. I just rarely – if ever – won.

"Yeah, figured I'd better get it now before either it or me freezes."

"You want me to go with you?"

I turned to look at her. "What's up, hon?"

"What? I can't walk with my husband."

"Hold on. That's not what I said. We both know you like the cold weather about as much as I like ham." (Did I not tell you about that yet? I'll get to it eventually.) "And yes, I appreciate the company but it's got to be closing in on negative ten out here and I think a wonderful cooling northerly breeze has begun to kick up. So what gives?"

"Fine, let's walk."

We were halfway down the driveway before she spoke. But I noticed her turn towards the barn before she said anything.

"What's going on, Mike?" I didn't need any clarification. If I had, just her previous look to the barn would have erased all doubt of what subject we were broaching. "Mike, Justin was looking right at you as he drove that plow."

"Figured as much," I said.

"He tried to kill you, Mike." Tracy said with force and conviction.

"I would imagine."

She grabbed my arm and forcibly spun me towards her. "How can you be so cavalier about this? I saw his face, Mike. He was smiling! Fucking smiling!"

How I could feel any colder was beyond me, but I did. I was freezing from my core outwards. I looked back towards the barn and the source of my unnatural icebox sensation.

Justin stood between the great doors looking at us both. He waved with all the enthusiasm of a dead cheerleader. Tracy saw what I was looking at and wrapped both her arms around herself in a useless tactic to hold in body heat, or keep evil out.

"It's got something to do with that scratch he got when he went to get Paul. He got infected with something...but that's not quite right. It's more like he got possessed."

Tracy gasped at that word. When she was twelve she had slept over her best friend Dawn's house. Dawn's father had the brilliant idea to bring his daughter and Tracy to the drive-in featuring arguably one of the scariest movies of all time, *The Exorcist*. From that point forward, Tracy had always had a higher than ordinary fear of the Devil and his minions. Hey, all of our psychoses need to start somewhere.

"But not completely," I added hastily. It did little to moderate her fear. "Justin's still in there and he knows something is wrong. There are times like earlier today where I felt that his old persona was closer to the surface. Now I don't know if that was an act on his part or not, but I've got to think that when he lets his concentration lapse or when he's focused on something else that whatever is inside of him can gain some measure of control."

Tracy jittered again.

"Come on, let's get down to the van. We stand out here too much longer and we're going to look like we ran into Medusa." She didn't argue.

"Do you think the antibiotics are helping?" she asked as a frozen tear descended her cheek.

"I think it keeps the infection in check. I'm not sure the meds alone can cure it, though. But without them, whatever it is would be able to gain a bigger if not complete foothold."

"Mike, what are we going to do?"

We had reached the van. I fumbled with the keys, partly to stall an answer, but mostly because I couldn't feel my fingers. I struggled with my door which seemed like it had frozen in place. I couldn't really blame it, although I looked like a dork as Tracy's opened up with a minimal effort. The inside of the car was little better than a meat locker. If the car didn't start, I wasn't sure we'd be able to make it back up into the house before we solidified.

Heat and humidity suck as far as I'm concerned. I've voiced that opinion over and over throughout my life. My argument was that you could only get so naked to get cooler whereas you could always put more clothes on in the winter to get warmer. But this was different, I was physically distressed at how cold I had become. My thought pattern felt addled as I nearly snapped the key in half trying to turn it the wrong way in the ignition. Tracy didn't look much better off than me.

"Did you say they have Philly Cheesesteak's in Chicago?" she asked.

I had no clue what the hell she was talking about, but it distracted me enough before I sheared the key off. The engine did the slow 'whirring' sound of a car that has no desire to start and wants to make it abundantly clear on its stance. I held the key in place many long seconds after I should have let it go. Whirrr... whirr... whir... vroom! Glacial air spewed from the heater vents as the engine caught. My breath cascaded down into my lap in frozen droplets of water. The slap of winter-infused air slapped across Tracy's face and she broke out of her fog.

"Holy shit, that's cold!" she said as she placed her hands over the vent.

"If only I could invent an air conditioner to work that well."

She didn't see the humor as I reached to shut the 'heater' off. After some careful thrusts on the gas pedal to flood the engine with some fuel, I placed the car in gear, somewhat certain it wouldn't stall. We both held our breaths as the transmission engaged, drawing some life from the engine and nearly extinguishing it. I held one foot on the brake and one halfway down on the gas as I flooded high explosive fluid through the valves. A minute or two later we were up by the house. Tracy got out before we stopped moving, heading straight inside.

"Don't sweat it, hon." I said to her retreating back. "I'll get the stuff out of here."

I didn't even get the customary wave over her back for that. I shut the car off, grabbed what was immediately close to me and rushed to follow. My damaged knee made forward progress an aggressively slow endeavor. There was an infinitesimally long delay as I got to the door and there was a flood of people heading out to grab stuff out of the van. Courtesy dictated that I move to the side and let them out so they could help. I pushed myself through the throng, courtesy be damned. I was a heartbeat and a half from frostbite and I liked all my digits exactly where they were.

Tracy hovered dangerously close to the roaring fire. I almost pushed her in as I jockeyed for position to gain some heat. Degree by degree we came back to our own. The tingling pain of blood flowing back to extremities was an actual welcome sensation. It meant life, life in all its glorious triumphs and disasters. I kissed Tracy long and hard there, reveling in the fact that we still endured and doubly thankful that one appendage still had the grace to feel the press of blood.

"Get a room," Jen said as she sat down in one of the lounge chairs next to a bookshelf.

We broke our kiss; warmth radiated down from my lips. Tracy even looked a little flushed. I was going to try that Viagra out tonight, guaranteed! I shouted 'Yes' in my head, with the fist pump and all.

"We got all the stuff in. Some of the food is frozen solid, though," Jen finished.

To reiterate her point, Tommy came into the room with a Twinkie clamped in a pair of salad tongs. He pushed me over a little to the side so that his Twinkie could get some heat.

"Am I in your way, Tommy?" I said with good-humored sarcasm.

"A little bit, Mr. T, could you move over a scootch?"

I laughed. "Yeah, I figured it was time to get some of these clothes off anyway."

"Great!" Tommy said, never taking his eyes off his cold prize. "You were kind of in the way."

I moved a step and, like I expected, my knee let it be known about its condition. I wondered how a Percocet would interact with a Viagra. I couldn't see the sense of having a hard on I could slam in a door and not be able to feel. I involuntarily crossed my legs at the errant thought.

"You alright, Mike?" Tracy asked.

"Yeah just my knee." Although it was obvious from my gesture that wasn't the case.

"Maybe you should get that checked out."

Again, obviously she was talking about my knee, but when I answered I was thinking completely about something a little closer to my belt line. "Yeah you're right, I'd definitely like to get that checked out." My lascivious leer almost gave me away as Tracy looked questioningly at me.

I shuffled out of the room like someone double my age and half hopped, half pulled myself up the stairs to the old room Tracy and I used whenever we came to visit. Now that I thought about it, we hadn't been in years. Not since Everett had died to be specific. Sure, Tracy and Carol talked almost daily, but that's not the same as basic human contact. Again I marveled at how she had survived so well in such an inhospitable place all by herself. In point of fact, the reason she had survived was most likely because she was in such a place.

I finally made it to my room, thankful that someone had the presence of mind to bring some of my stuff up here. There wasn't a whole hell of a lot, but I had grabbed a crap load of knee braces and ace bandages when we were in the Rite-Aid and I was going to make good use of them now. I was going to have to peel my layers of clothing off like an onion sheds skin before I could do so.

My knee was a sorry sight when I finally got down to it. It was black and blue and nearly double the size of its brother. I gingerly wrapped it in two ace bandages. The elastic knee brace I had snagged would not stretch large enough to accommodate the swelling. I knew I needed to put ice on it, but after my near death-by-Popsicle-experience today, I couldn't even begin to imagine placing frozen water anywhere on my body.

I took two Tylenol and was immediately thinking about taking something stronger. The pain in my knee was beginning to rage. It was as if the heat from the fire had taken this long to thaw out the half gallon of fluid that surrounded my injured joint. If the pain in my knee was a grizzly bear, the Tylenol was like firing two air soft pellets at it.

I dropped onto the bed with my bag of goodies from the pharmacy as pain lanced through my leg. I greedily downed first one and then another pain killer and...then another. I lay like that for at least ten minutes. The pain never truly went away, it just became muted. When I felt I could get up without crying too much, I used the headboard to prop myself up. I was greeted instantly and not so unpleasantly with the fogged over countenance of one under the influence of drugs, which thankfully I was. The pain in my knee was still sharp. On some level I realized that and still I didn't care.

Unbeknownst to me I had somehow levitated down into the kitchen. Carol looked up from some delicious smelling stew she was preparing.

"Mike, you been in my Jack again?"

I'm pretty sure I answered with the ever witty, "The what now?" More likely it came out as, "Duh?"

"You know you're in your underpants, right?" she said pointing what appeared to be an oversized spoon at me.

"Tightie whities?" I asked, hoping that wasn't the case.

She cocked her head. "Just how much of my booze did you drink Mike?"

"Whitie tighties?" I mumbled, slivers of drool escaping from the corner of my mouth.

"Maybe you should just sit down," she said as she pulled a chair out from the kitchen table.

I obeyed. Not that standing anymore was becoming much of an option. Drool landed on my blue boxer shorts. "Ah, not frightie mighties!"

"Tracy!" her mom yelled.

"Yeah, Mom?" I heard the response from the living room.

"You might want to get in here," her mother answered, turning back to the crock pot.

Tracy came in, looked quickly over to her mom and then to me, the source of the issue at hand. "Oh, Talbot, what are you doing?"

"I'm not wearing nightie bities," I answered gallantly.

"That's a good thing, I guess." What the hell else could she say. "Come on, let's get you into the living room."

"Not so sure I can get back up, hon." I think that came out nearly perfect, though my tongue felt as thick and dry as a plank.

"You don't smell like booze. What's the matter?"

I pointed to my knee. Just since my short jaunt down into the kitchen my knee had grown nearly half again what I had started with, so much so that the ace bandage was nearly stretched to its capacity.

"Talbot!" Tracy said alarmed. "What the fuck?"

I don't remember much about the walk out of the kitchen and onto the most comfortable couch I have ever had the pleasure of laying down on, except for a lot of finger pointing and laughing. Most of that coming from BT and he was more drugged up than I was.

CHAPTER 23

Mike's Journal Entry Twenty

I didn't have a clue how long I slept. When I finally awoke it wasn't to the easy, peaceful, content feeling one arises to after a deep and satisfying sleep. There was no exaggerated stretch as I alit from the bed and casually scratched my nuts. Oh come on, that's the first thing after the body unfolding that every guy does when they get out of bed. Don't ask me why, maybe it's an evolutionary legacy, probably to rid oneself of prehistoric mites.

Anyway, back to the story.

The distinctive sound of a gunshot prohibits one from the normal routine. I stood up as rapidly as my vertigo-addled brain would allow. Who knew we were in the midst of a 7.0 earthquake? I braced myself against the couch until the worst of the shakes had subsided. I took no small pleasure in the fact that the pain in my knee had subsided to something I could live with, if not entirely like.

I still pushed off with my right leg though. No sense in tempting the fates. BT stirred on his resting place but did not awaken. Had I imagined the whole thing? I heard nothing else. The only thing that gave me pause was that a single gunshot these days was rarer than a virgin Catholic schoolgirl. It was approaching dawn. I could tell by the murky light filtering through the windows, but no one was up yet that I could tell. There was no sense of alarm, no commotion, no damn bacon cooking, (*ooh, that sounded good*). I had finally managed to gingerly walk my way up to the hallway that led to the front door, when a fully winter weather bundled Carol came in toting her shotgun.

She didn't seem particularly startled to see me standing there. "You know you're still in your underwear right?" she asked me.

Reflexively, I looked down, slightly more embarrassed this time than the last.

She laughed. "Don't worry about it, want some coffee?" She stooped over and placed her shotgun next to the door, in a holder that seemed perfectly tailored to that specific job. She looked up to see me watching her. "Did I wake you?" she asked.

I had a sarcastic comment all lined up but then I thankfully remembered she was my mother-in-law and wisely thought better of unloosing my dumb-ass comment on the world.

"No, I was ready to get up anyway."

"Hadn't seen one in a couple of days, was kind of hoping that was over."

What she had seen, well, let's just say there isn't much of a bear problem during the late winter season.

"Speaking of that, Carol. How did you know it was out there? I'd been meaning to ask, got a little side tracked last night."

"Oh those first few days were tough. I was too scared to sleep. However, even fear will only go so far. More than once I woke up to one of those things at the door or the window. Damn near sent my ticker into overdrive. I can't tell you how many times I just wanted to shoot through the door or the window. Good thing the practical side of me took over. I don't have the materials to fix what I would have destroyed."

"What the hell did you do?" I asked alarmed.

"I opened the window up and then killed them," she said as naturally as if she had opened a window to let an apple pie cool on the windowsill.

"Fuhhh…" I started. Her watchful gaze made me pull back from my colorful phrasing. "I think I would have shot the glass out."

"Have you felt how cold it is out there?"

I nodded, not only did I get her point but also felt it. "So then what?"

"You mean how did I sleep and still defend the homestead?"

I nodded again, completely enraptured, bacon momentarily forgotten as I followed her and her story into the kitchen.

"Well, I rigged an alarm. I went out about fifty or so feet from the house and set wooden stakes into the ground, every twenty feet or so in a circle around the house. Then I screwed an eye hook in each one, about waist high," she said as she held her hand roughly at her belt line. "Then I threaded rope through all of them. Then finally I brought a rope all the way up to the house and attached it to a bell. Damn thing was worse than an alarm clock. Couldn't hit snooze, if you get my meaning."

My mouth must have been agape.

"You know, Mike, I've been on a farm most of my life. Hard work is nothing new to me."

"Sorry. That's just genius."

"Necessity. You want sugar in your coffee?"

"Please," I said absently as I grabbed the mug from her. "Where is it now, I didn't see it when we came in yesterday?"

"After Tommy's message, I took down the part that led to the house and the barn. I didn't want you to run it over mistakenly. Just because I can do hard work doesn't mean I want to repeat it and a good portion of what is still up is under snow. Last night after our little talk in the kitchen…"

I flushed with embarrassment. "Sorry about that."

"Don't be. I saw your knee after Tracy unwrapped it. I wasn't even sure how you were still standing. I did my best to drain it."

"Oh, so that's why it feels better. Thank you, and you won't mind if I don't ask how you did it?"

She laughed again. "No, I'll get over it. So after you went to sleep," she emphasized 'sleep,' "I restrung the alarm. Didn't expect to get company, but I didn't want to make any unexpected guests feel welcome."

"Was there just the one then?" I asked her.

She looked hard at me. "You must have been sleeping pretty heavily. There were three. Travis and Jen took care of them all. They're still out there making sure no more are coming. I wanted to get my old bones inside and by the fire. Now that I've got help I'm not too proud to use it."

"Three?"

"And by the looks of them they look like they've traveled a ways."

I bet they had! Fucking Eliza, I was going to slit her throat personally. I momentarily thought about heading outside, but garbed like I was, my manhood would shrivel to half its size and that I could not stomach or afford.

"I brought some clothes down for you, figured you'd want to go out as soon as you got up and the less stairs you climb right now the better."

I nodded to her, my terse thoughts elsewhere.

"Mike, your knee hurting again? You look mighty upset all of a sudden."

"I just think we brought a whole lot of heartache down on you, Carol...by coming here, I mean."

She gently caressed my cheek. "You've done no such thing. You want bacon for breakfast?"

"There could be sainthood in this for you, Carol."

"I'll take that as a yes," she said as she turned back around.

I heard Jen and Travis come inside. It would have been hard not to as loud as they were stomping the excess snow off their boots. I had just finished pulling on my third sweater and met them in the hallway. Jen's color was nearly the shade of the material she was liberally shedding in the mudroom.

"Is that bacon?" Travis said happily as he headed into the kitchen.

I noticed that Jen waited patiently until Travis was out of earshot before she spoke.

"I won't swear it, Mike, the damage was just too great, but I'd bet money those people, I mean zombies," she shook her head, "were from Little Turtle."

To think something bad is happening is bad enough, but to get confirmation is downright shitty. "Are you sure?"

We both knew I was hoping for an alternate outcome.

"Like I said, Mike, when you blow someone's head off it's a little difficult to get a positive I.D."

"Well to be fair, you didn't quite say it like that."

"You know what I meant."

"Yeah I know what you meant. I just want to choose not to believe it."

"Are you going out to check?"

"No."

She studied my less than poker face. "You knew they'd be coming?"

"Figured as much. I'd sort of hoped that maybe this was the place where we could finally stop and plant some roots. It feels so right here. Cold, sure, but the energy seems so strong. I guess maybe I thought this might be some sort of hallowed ground. Crazy right?"

"No I don't think so. We all want somewhere that we don't constantly have to feel like it could be our last moments on Earth. I love this place, too, but it's not the most easily defendable."

"Wow, I think you may have been around me too long.

My crazy is starting to rub off."

"Not necessarily a bad thing, Talbot. Now let's get some of that bacon. I'm starving."

Tommy was already sitting at the table, strips of bacon hanging out of both his hands, his broad smile dappled with the fried goodness. "Morfning, Mftr. T!"

There was one way in to the kitchen and I had been standing in the hallway that led in. I would have bet a mountain of Kit-Kats that the boy had not stepped into that hallway to get past me. "How'd you get here, Tommy?"

"I walked," he smiled again.

I was looking for more than the literal explanation. Tommy looked down at his hands, seemingly more concerned from which hand he was going to take his next bite than answering me.

Travis and Carol were not going to be of any help. They were both at the stove. Carol was showing Travis how to make an omelet. Although I could tell from his posture he was more intent on eating said omelet than on learning how to make it. Maybe I would have pressed the issue, most likely not, but the rest of the family chose that time to come in. Tommy's eyes twinkled at mine.

"You got them up. Didn't you, you sly dog," I conspiringly said to him.

"Bacon?" he said, pushing his meat-laden fists under my nose.

"Thanks, I'll get my own." He seemed immensely relieved at that answer.

Breakfast was phenomenal. Farm fresh everything. I knew processed and artificially preserved foods were a necessary evil of our society. Oh, but what we had given up when we had moved off of our family farms and into the dens of depravity (that would be cities, in non-sarcasm speak). Then it all came rushing back to me why we moved away, as I cleaned out the pens and fed the animals that had so graciously allowed us to gain sustenance from them. I enviously eyed the dairy cow. She had seemed completely at ease when I had first entered the animal enclosure, but each subsequent time that I stopped to stare longingly at her, she more and more sensed the predatory nature of my visits.

Milk was grand, especially fresh milk. But a steak! Now that would be special.

"Hope you don't have an accident, Bessie," I said as I patted her snout.

She pulled away and eyed me warily.

"I'm just saying," I told her.

Bessie wasn't appeased much. She didn't go back to chewing her cud until I was well past her stall.

It was close on lunch by the time I had finished my chores. It wasn't steak but there was absolutely nothing wrong with the pork tenderloin chops Carol was dishing up.

"I would have made sandwiches, but I ran out of flour to make bread with a few weeks ago," she said apologetically.

"No," Tracy told me, without a word coming out of my mouth.

"But—" I started.

"No Talbot, you're not going anywhere."

"Fine." I pouted as I sat down to my mounded plate of meat. "Some barbecue sauce, maybe shredded a little. Man it would make a—"

"Talbot!" Tracy said.

"Fine." I dug in. I didn't think that after smelling animal ass for the last four hours I'd be hungry. I was wrong.

I parked my butt in the living room after lunch. The couch was inviting. The fire was warming. About the only thing that could have made this perfect was if ESPN were on. Carol had never had a television as far as I knew. Was that even possible? Wasn't there a law against that or something? I shuddered at the thought. I think the only reason she ever got a phone was to stay in touch with her daughter.

BT was sitting up. "Why you looking all content and shit?" he asked me.

"I almost feel like I've come home," I told him honestly.

"Almost?" he asked. He grimaced as he shifted his position so he could look at me easier. "It's not over then?"

"What! Do I have a playbook on my face?"

"Let's just say, Talbot, you have an uncanny ability to say everything without opening your mouth," Tracy said from the entryway. She came over and kissed my face. "And that's what I love about you."

"When we leaving then?" BT asked.

"I was hoping to give you more time to recover." I was surprised when he nodded in agreement. He must be hurting if he couldn't even manage a small semblance of male macho bravado.

"You tell me when, Talbot. I'll make myself ready."

Justin came in at that point and sat down heavily in the large chair by the fire. "We have a week."

Nobody doubted his source. I just doubted the message.

"We leave in three days, BT," I said never taking my eyes off of Justin.

Justin smiled maliciously, realizing I had just caught him in his lie and absolutely not caring.

"Two days," I hastily amended. Justin's and BT's faces almost mirrored each other exactly in their disappointment.

Tracy's shoulders sagged as the weight of my words weighed on her. "My mom won't leave, you know."

"I know that. You're going to have to convince her it's for the best."

"What's for the best?" Carol asked.

"Is it me?" I asked Tracy. "Or is the timing of people showing up at the right time uncanny."

"Canny," Tommy filled in.

"So what's for the best?" Carol asked again.

"That you come with us when we leave," I said hastily, hoping that maybe the shock value of the words would be lost in their fast delivery. It wasn't.

"I'll do no such thing," Carol answered adamantly.

"Mom."

"Hush, Tracy. This is my home. I'm seventy-nine years old and I have no desire to start somewhere else. I was born in this house. God willing I'll die in it."

"Mom?!" Tracy cried with more volume.

"And what's more, I don't see the point in any of you leaving. There's plenty of chickens and pigs to get us through the winter. Plus there's Bessie."

"Yeah, for hamburger," I added much too quickly.

"For milk," Carol answered while she glared at me.

"Right, that's what I meant." Even though I hadn't.

"Mom, the zombies are coming. We have to leave," Tracy nearly begged.

"Then let them come," Carol answered defiantly.

"Carol, this isn't going to be in ones and twos. There's going to be hundreds," I added.

Her countenance shifted subtly but she recovered quickly. "Then they come," she answered again but with noticeably less vigor.

"At least think about it, Carol. We're leaving in two days." That did shake her. I watched as all those years of hard farm work suddenly caught up with her. She gripped the couch arm much like I had earlier this morning. Tracy helped her to sit.

There was not much said the rest of that afternoon. Mostly idle talk about 'remember whens.' The past had a much glossier shine now that the future was so tarnished. BT plunged himself into sleep, most likely in a desperate bid to accelerate his body's healing capabilities. Tommy stayed on the far end of the room from Justin, but I would occasionally catch him staring raptly at him. If Justin knew or cared that he was sometimes Tommy's center of attention he never let on. Tracy and Carol had left after a while to most likely discuss what they were going to do. I felt it was best not to intervene. Henry was laying by the fire, which coincidentally flared up every few minutes or so. Better that whatever noxious gases were spewing from him were consumed in the fire than disseminated out into the rest of the room.

Jen prowled around the house like a panther, constantly looking out the windows for party crashers. Travis had the air of many a military man I had been exposed to. He was able to pull off the duality of having heightened awareness while looking casually indifferent. I had envied those men and their façade of calm demeanor. Nicole had at some point come down from her room, eyes puffy from crying, and walked straight into my arms. She had almost instantly fallen asleep; mourning can be an essence-draining process. And me? Besides keeping a mental note of where and what everybody else was up to, I stared at the fire. The shifting shapes, patterns and colors helped to ease my troubled mind.

Jen was right. This was not an easily defendable location. Sure, we could see the enemy coming for a quarter of a mile in nearly every direction. Then what? They would have a 360-degree angle of attack. We were vulnerable from all sides. The two largest egresses were the front door off the hallway and the back door in the kitchen. There were at least twelve windows on the lower level that were big enough for an intruder to gain entry. This was a nightmare. I knew without asking that there was no way Carol was going to let me shore up our meager defenses. I'd never be able to pull off cutting her staircase up. Tracy would kill me. The more I thought about it the more I concluded that our best defense was to not have one. We had to get gone.

I now regretted my decision to tell Justin about my amended plans. Whatever Eliza had originally planned she was surely making her own adjustments. I could only hope that she wasn't in a position to move too quickly. I would have left that same evening if BT had been in better shape. I could leave him with Carol. That stray thought came out of left field and was quickly denounced. I shuddered to think of both Eliza and BT hunting us down.

My thoughts alternated constantly that day about the

silence in the house. On one side it felt like the calm before the storm. On the other was the peace and harmony with the world that living on a farm can bring to one's soul, although I knew the falsity of that fantasy. I guess I was in a sort of self-induced trance as I watched that fire, so much so that my eyes began to itch from lack of blinking.

"Miss me?" I heard a male voice say almost as if we were using cans and string and he was about a mile away. It was that indistinct.

I didn't 'speak' these words, but for ease of following the conversation I will make it appear that way.

"Who are you?" I asked. I tried my best to conceal the tide of unease that was rising within me.

"Oh, me and you go way back." And the disembodied voice began to laugh.

I had finally cracked up. I mean, I always knew this was an eventuality. Years of upbringing from a narcissistic mother, the intake of multiple drugs (including every hallucinogen known to man), Marine Corps boot camp and subsequent tours of duty in Afghanistan and Iraq had left me vulnerable. Throw a zombie apocalypse on top of that and what do you have? Aberration Apple Pie. I had finally succumbed. I had slipped over the edge. The question now was how far was I going to fall? Was this to be a free-fall into a bottomless pit, or was it going to be a slow, steady descent into insanity? If it was the slow descent, I could watch and take notes of each agonizingly hideous step down the path into Crazy Town. I was not strong enough to handle a duality within me. Hell, Tracy could barely handle one of me, what was she going to think of this new development?

"You still there, shithead?" my other half asked.

Oh great, not only am I delusional but my other half is a rude prick. Wonderful.

"I'm talking to you!" it shouted. The voice was gaining clarity, as if the person on the other end was getting stronger or closer, or both.

"Dad!"

Oh no! It thinks I'm its father!

"Dad! You're pulling my hair!"

And like that, the hold over me was gone. Now if I could just untangle the grip of Nicole's hair I had in my fist, I'd be all set.

"Sorry, honey, sorry," I said as I inadvertently pulled some of her hair out. "Sorry."

"It's alright, Dad," she said as she sat up and rubbed her head. "Were you dreaming?"

"God, I hope so." I said earnestly.

Tommy was looking over at me.

"Was I dreaming?" I asked him. He shrugged in return.

Justin was no longer in the room. The fire flared a violent purple and then went back to its normal hues of orange and yellow. What the hell could Henry have aired out that would do that? Whatever it was, it must have been rancid. Even he couldn't take it as he stood up and walked a few feet away from the offending zone and plopped back down contentedly.

BT managed to eat some dinner before he returned into his self-induced coma. Jen could barely contain herself at the table, if I hadn't known better I might have thought she had a serious case of crabs. She was more like an animal that could feel the change in the air, way before their 'superior' human masters could. A storm was brewing and not of the atmospheric kind either.

I was feeling loosely detached tonight, whether from my earlier encounter with my bad half or else I was picking up on whatever wavelength Jen was. Carol, however, was whistling in merriment as she placed dish upon dish of good old country cooking on the table.

I was going to say something about last meals and all but that seemed in very poor taste. Even if it was to be, what was the point in pointing it out? Tracy barely picked at her food. Apparently her mother had made it abundantly clear on what she was doing, and that involved not going with us. If we got out of here soon enough, that was the best decision she could have made. Being on the run is hard on the young and the hale, something even I wasn't feeling much of these past few days as I absently rubbed my knee.

"I'm thinking of growing some jalapeno peppers this year," Carol said as she dropped off a tray of what looked like mashed sweet potatoes. "I've never grown those before, they've got so much more flavor than the bell peppers I usually grow."

"Mom, are you sure?" Tracy asked.

"Of course, Tracy, I bought the seeds last year for just that purpose."

"You know what I meant."

Carol smiled and dropped off a plate stacked with sweet half ears of corn. I smiled too as I grabbed an ear and smeared two liberal pats of butter on it. Okay, so Bessie had her pluses besides being a walking T-bone. Two days on a farm on a steady diet of meat and cream and I could already start to feel my body filling out. In three months I'd be one of those monstrosities they used to show on *truTV*; five hundred pounds and expanding.

"Carol, sit down and eat," I told her as I took another bite of wonderful fulfillment.

Henry had fallen asleep under the table waiting for something to find its way onto his domain – the floor. For some reason he had decided to use my feet as a headrest and his drool had soaked through my socks. When he finally picked his head up, I was relieved. When he barked I was concerned. No one moved except for Carol who laid another plate of what looked like cranberries on the table. It was difficult for me to tell though, all the cranberries I had ever bought were of the cylindrically shaped kind and usually had to be sliced with a knife. It went deathly quiet awfully quick. My glass of water, as I put it down and it struck the top of the salt shaker, was the loudest thing in the room. Nothing and nobody else moved. Henry stood up. I could almost feel him bristling as he growled.

"That's the first time I've ever heard him growl," Jen said as she pushed her chair back stood up and took out her .45 Desert Eagle from her shoulder holster, she must have taken Redneck Number One's discarded weapon.

We all stood when the bell rang, but not the zombie alarm, the actual doorbell.

"Well I'll be," Carol said. "Who could that be?" she asked as she began to head out of the kitchen.

I quickly stood and got past her. "I'll check."

I grabbed my AR that was propped against the kitchen wall. Travis stood, grabbed his shotgun, and without any prompting from me, stood watch over the back door. Jen was half an inch from me as I took the safety off my gun.

I slowly approached the door, figuring that at any moment it was about to crash violently inward followed by every unfathomable, unimaginable, inexplicable horror known to man and womankind. I wished I had thought to put my shoes on before I opened the door. Scrambling for my life in traction-less socks on a highly polished wooden floor was not an optimum way of meeting my maker. I would have taken the extra thirty or so seconds to grab my shoes, but the doorbell ringing had progressed to violent door knocking. Alright, so much for the theory of a wayward Robin flying straight into the doorbell mechanism.

"Well hurry up now," Carol called out from the kitchen. "Whoever's out there is probably freezing to death."

"That's just fine with me," I said softly.

Jen agreed.

BT about made me piss my pants as he appeared on my right side at the opening to the living room.

"Why you creeping around ali stealth like?" BT asked. The door shuddered. "Oh."

BT hobbled back into the living room and grabbed his new gun of choice, a semi-automatic Browning .30-06 with a banana clip. I wouldn't have even thought they made such a thing if I hadn't seen it with my own eyes. I couldn't even begin to imagine repeatedly pulling the trigger on such a powerful weapon. In my present state of footwear the recoil would send me shooting across the floor a la *Risky Business*.

BT was all seriousness when he asked me, "What the hell are you smiling about?"

"You're no Rebecca DeMornay."

"Yeah and you don't much look like Halle Berry," he retorted. "If anything happens, Talbot, you and Jen get the hell out of there. I'll cover your retreat."

"Dad!" Travis yelled. "I've got movement back here!"

"Shit." I was stuck in indecision. The opaque glass on the front door rattled under the newest assault. I could barely make out a figure standing on the other side. Would Carol be pissed if I shot first and then opened the door? Jen's Desert Eagle hung precariously over my shoulder, the breach inches from my ear. "Umm, any chance you could move that away a little?"

"Sorry."

The gun went from two inches away to four inches. Somehow I didn't think that was going to make much difference except give the drum splitting noise a little more time to gain momentum as it slammed into my ear canal. Great, maybe the force of the explosion by my head would drive out the evil spirit that lurked within.

"Carol?" The muffled voice said from the other side of the doorway. "You in there?"

"Oh for goodness sake," Carol said exasperatedly as she pushed past Jen's and my wide-eyed expressions. "This isn't very neighborly behavior, you two," she berated us as she went to the front door.

I reached out to stop her but could not gain enough traction to do so. Once the door was open the assault would begin and Carol would be directly in our line of fire. Valuable seconds would be lost getting her out of the way, neutralizing the threat, and getting the door secured again.

The door opened. A purplish faced man stood there dancing around on his toes. His similarly toned companion, probably his wife, was huddled behind him.

CHAPTER 24

Mike's Journal Entry Twenty-One

"Fred, Esther? What are you two doing out here? Come in, come in," Carol motioned.

Fred took one look down the hallway at the arsenal confronting him.

"You sure?" he turned to Carol.

"Oh, that's my son-in-law and his friends," she answered as if this were the most natural thing in the world.

"Carol?" I asked.

"It's fine, Mike. These are my neighbors from up the road, Fred and Esther Spretzens," she answered me. "Where are the kids?" Carol asked with concern.

'Jack and Jill' as I was to later learn their names had gained entry through the back door. Travis had let them in at almost the same time as Carol had opened the front door. His explanation was that zombies didn't seem much phased about the weather and the two kids were huddling together for warmth. As for the Jack and Jill thing, don't ask me. Some parents have a weird sense of humor when it comes to naming their kids. Just ask the poor bastard whose name was Orangejello. He'll tell you it's no bargain being named after your mom's favorite food. Well, at least it wasn't Meatloaf, although that had been done before, too.

Carol ushered Fred and Esther into the living room and as

close to the fire as was humanly possible before becoming a s'more. It was humorous watching Fred's reaction as he tried to give BT as big a berth as was possible in that confined space. Odds were that Fred wasn't much exposed to men of BT's color much less that imposing of a size. Travis brought in the two kids, twins by the look and size of them. They couldn't have been much more than eight years old. I didn't envy them the world they were about to inherit. Henry followed closely behind having learned that children of this age tend to drop more food than they eat.

The vacancy in their eyes was not lost on me as they sat by the fire, finally realizing that they were for the moment at least, safe. Fred was the first to break the silence.

"I...I went out to see what had the horses all in an uproar." He choked on a sob as Esther rubbed his back. "They were kicking and whinnying something fierce. The last time they had been that upset, a pack of coyotes had circled the barn and were digging around the frame looking for a way in."

"No coyotes out in this weather, though," Carol finished for him.

He looked up at her with his red-rimmed eyes. "No, not coyotes. The barn door was broken open. I had my scattergun ready to shoot and when I got to the first stall it was full of *them*. They had dragged my plow horse down and were devouring him. He was still alive!" his voice rising. "The look of terror in his eyes is something I'll never forget. He was frothing blood and kicking. I couldn't do anything but stare at him." He sobbed a bit. Esther kept up her calming ministrations on his back. "And then one of them must have noticed me because it got up. I mean it got up fast. Faster than I'd seen any of them move. If it wasn't for pieces of my horse Hank hanging out of his mouth, I might have thought he was human. Damn, he still might have been, never thought to ask. But he killed my Hank so I figured I had every right to do the same to him. No matter how hungry he was."

"It's alright, Fred," Carol told him calmingly. "You did the right thing."

He looked grateful. "I was gonna run for it, but he was on me so fast that I barely had enough time to pull the trigger. Caught him in the side, I watched as pieces of his midsection blew against the wall. He didn't even care. He kept coming. I must have lowered the gun a bit, 'cause my next shot caught him square in the knee. I don't think he cared much about that shot neither but it brought him to the floor. His friends never even looked up. Hank had finally quit kicking. I was out of bullets and I had three more horses. Even if I got more ammo I'd never be able to load it fast enough to kill them all 'fore they got to me. Now I love them horses like only a farmer can, but after God, my family comes next."

Esther placed her head on Fred's shoulder.

"There was so many of them, I knew I'd never be able to keep them out of the house. So I loaded up the truck and was planning on heading down to my cousin's in Bismarck."

That was the first thing he'd said that I hadn't agreed with. A city even of the relatively small size of Bismarck was the last place you wanted to be.

"We got eight miles from the house when I realized I had drained all the gas out to keep the generator running."

Carol gasped. "You walked for five miles in this cold! Oh heavens!"

"Thirteen miles away and they're your neighbors?" I asked incredulously.

"Exactly how many of them were there, Fred?" Jen asked.

Fred was busy staring vacantly into the fire. Slow seconds passed before he answered. "Must of been seven or eight crammed in there." He shuddered.

BT had at some point slumped back down onto his couch. He looked like he was fighting a losing battle with consciousness. Logistically, the Spretzens had just fucked me. We had no room for four more people no matter how you sliced it. Even if I could somehow convince myself that MY family's survival was more important than theirs, Tracy would never let me.

"Here we stand," I said. "Or here we fall."

Now that Carol's options were reduced to one, she didn't seem so enamored with it.

Jen knew immediately what was going on. "How much time you think we have to get ready?" she asked me.

"I'd say until tomorrow night," I replied, looking at Justin. He nodded sadly in confirmation.

"Any ideas?" she asked.

"One to start with." I pointed my gun at Justin. "Give me your weapon."

"Dad?" Nicole yelled.

"Talbot!" Tracy joined in.

"Heavens to Betsy," came from Esther.

Can't remember the last time I heard that expletive.

"I can help, Dad," Justin said earnestly.

"I wish I could believe that, son, I really do. But for now I don't. Give me the gun or I will shoot you," I said it without malice or menace, but no truer intent to my words had Justin ever encountered. Sure, there were the thousand times I had told him while he was growing up that if he ever did THAT again he would get a whipping. Empty threats those had been, this was not one of them.

I could see the workings of his mind as he tried to play out how this encounter could go down. I wasn't going to give him the chance to reason himself into an early grave.

"You'll lose," I told him matter-of-factly.

"Talbot, what are you doing? What are you talking about?" Tracy said, approaching from the far side of the room.

I didn't take the chance to look over at her. "Do not come any closer, Tracy! If you try to get in the way I will drop him where he stands!"

"Now see here!" Fred said standing up.

"Listen, Fred! I don't know who the fuck you are, and I really don't give a shit. Your showing up here has already put my family in jeopardy. Because I have these stupid fucking qualities called morality and honor. These WORDS are more than likely going to get everything I care about in this shitty little world destroyed. NOW SIT YOUR ASS DOWN before you give me a reason to get rid of you and all the troubles you entail!"

Fred complied. Tracy was inching closer but still not a threat to thwart me yet. Justin's eyes shifted rapidly from my eyes, to the barrel of the AR, to my trigger finger which was beginning to whiten at the knuckle. I think Justin was getting messages of 'Go for it.' He was sweating at the brow and his eye movements were becoming more frenetic.

"Justin, stop," I said calmly. "You'll lose."

"But so will you, Michael Talbot." The sound came from Justin but the words did not. "How long can you live with the guilt of killing your son?" He croaked out a harsh laugh. "What will your honor and morality do to you?" He/she laughed again.

"Dad, help me!" Justin cried, as he struggled to keep his wayward hand from gripping the pistol out of its holster.

"Give me Tommy," Justin's voice said. "And I will give you this back," Justin said as he beat his fist against his chest. "At least for a while." That grating laugh erupted again.

"Give you Tommy, huh? And then what? Will you leave us alone? Can we get some paperwork signed to that effect? I've never been big on verbal agreements."

Justin's smile faded. "How funny will you be when you're de..."

Justin folded in on himself under the assault of BT's ham-sized fist. "God I was sick of listening to her drone on." He fell back on the couch and was almost instantly asleep.

Tracy rushed over to Justin's side. I went over and grabbed his gun. Tracy looked up at me. Hurt and anger were running through her, but she didn't know where to direct it. What I had done was not palatable, but it was a necessary evil.

"Jen, Trav, tie him up and put him in the basement."

Tracy stood up. It looked like Vesuvius was about to erupt all over again. But she had witnessed what we all had witnessed. Justin was a known threat that could not be swept under the rug anymore.

"I just want him out of the way while we set up some sort of defense, Tracy." She nodded in agreement. "He's a direct pipeline to the enemy. What he sees they see."

"He's my baby," she sobbed.

Jen and Travis looked to me for direction. I nodded. "Bring him down some blankets. One more thing." Jen stopped. "I want him blindfolded."

"Why, Mike?" Tracy asked, but the fight was out of her.

"The less he knows, Mom, the less *she* knows." Travis filled in for me. Tracy walked away, face in hands.

"Carol, we need to talk." I waited until Justin was secured in the basement and Jen and Travis returned. I had the beginnings of a plan and it was pretty much a 'do-or-die' scenario. Getting Carol on board was surprisingly easier than I had expected. We all talked there for a few hours, going over the finer points and how we would deal with what could go wrong as opposed to what needed to go right. The list of 'wrong' was growing at a near geometric rate.

"This is suicide, Mike," Jen said after we had gone over the plan for the twenty-third time.

"Not really, I give it a solid five or six percent chance of success." I smiled.

"Bullshit," BT threw in. "It's three or four at best."

Carol, Fred, and Esther's faces drained of all color at our macabre humor.

"There's a major flaw in your plan, Mike," Jen said.

I laughed, what else could I do. "Only one?"

"You know what I mean, ass," she finished.

286

"It is a big one, I'll admit that, not much I can do about it, though."

Jen sighed in agreement.

Finally we had finished formulating our idea – I hate to say "plan", that implies you think it might actually work. "Idea" gives it more of an abstract feel.

Tracy started to speak. "I..."

I cut her off. "Abso-fucking-lutely not." She, as expected, started to protest. "This is not open for discussion." I didn't raise my voice, but the force I laid on those words would have given pause to most Marines. Tracy plowed on.

"Mike," she began again.

"No." I said as I held up my hand. "Listen, for the twenty-three years we've been married I've known all along that I'm more of a figurehead, I know it and the kids know it. Shit, even Henry knows it."

"Yeah he does," Tommy said.

"Thank you," I said to Tommy.

"No problem." He smiled.

"There have only been a handful of times in our long marriage where I have finally exerted an authority that is only implied." Tracy nodded in agreement. "And this is going to be another one of them. We do this my way, Tracy. There are no other options."

"Mike," she said solemnly. "What makes you think that I could ever let you stand alone? All of our married lives we have met every challenge together. No matter the menace. I could no sooner leave you than I could the kids."

"But don't you get it?" I told her as I cupped her face. "You stand with me...you are walking away from the kids." She pulled away.

"You can't make me choose!" she cried.

"I'm not *letting* you choose, Tracy. The decision has been made. Besides, you heard BT, there's a good four or five percent chance this'll work."

"I said three or four," BT chimed in.

287

"Thanks, big man," I said sarcastically.

"Whatever I can do to help. Oh, and by the way, I'm staying."

"Fuck." I turned from Tracy to him. "BT, that's not what we discussed."

"You gonna tell me otherwise?" he asked threateningly.

"Fine, BT, your funeral."

"Mike, you said this could work," Tracy said with desperation in her voice.

"It was just a figure of speech, hon."

"Poor choice of words, Dad," Travis chimed in.

"What is wrong with the peanut gallery tonight?" I asked the heavens. (There was no answer...go figure.)

"Dad, an extra gun could be useful," Travis said.

"NO!" Tracy and I yelled in unison, at least we agreed on this one thing.

CHAPTER 25

Mike's Journal Entry Twenty-Two

The next morning was industrious. Fred was becoming more of a stalwart ally than I would have been willing to give him credit for. His knowledge of how to shore up a house for an incoming storm was invaluable. This wasn't your prototypical storm so to speak but the theory was the same. We wanted to keep the outside elements from coming in.

Travis, Jen, and I prepared more than a few surprises. Nothing that would stop them, alas I didn't have a nuke, this was more of a giving the finger gesture. It was right up my alley. Had I known what surprises Eliza had for me, I might not have been so inclined.

Tracy and Nicole made preparations for our hopefully hasty retreat once the time came. She questioned me once on the room in the cars. "If there's no room now, Mike, then how will there be when we leave?" I just stared at her until she understood and walked away.

To be fair, if this worked, it could be all over for all of us, not just some of us. Carol walked around her house in a daze, crying as she randomly picked up objects and set them carefully back down in the same location. She was mourning a loss she hadn't suffered yet, but I wouldn't begrudge her that.

Esther, Jack, and Jill killed six chickens for lunch. We

had fried chicken fit for a king.

"Reminds me of home," BT said longingly as he rubbed his belly. He had only awakened long enough to consume two of the chickens all by himself.

After lunch Carol and I headed out to the barn that housed the animals.

"Oh, Mike." She buried her head in my shoulder.

"It's for the best, Carol. You heard Fred, apparently they've expanded their diets."

I could feel the revulsion convulse through her.

Earlier, we had taken care of the chickens. I burped quietly, my belly content in the greasy soaking. I opened the pigpen. The giant five hundred pound sow named Charlotte looked expectantly at me like it was feeding time. Her suckling saw daylight and went, I would imagine, wee, wee, wee all the way home.

Charlotte was having none of it. She had spent her entire life in this fifteen by fifteen foot stall while the human caregivers had constantly brought her food and water. Her rudimentary mind had come to the conclusion that she must be some sort of revered being, which in all actuality isn't too far from the truth. Problem being, when her end came it wasn't going to be on a burning Viking ship. More like a burning barbecue pit with some spice rub and a keg of cold beer. Maybe the Super Bowl on TV.

"Mike?" Carol asked. "You alright?"

"Sorry, thinking about something infinitely better."

"Aren't we all," she responded.

I could only nod in agreement.

Bessie saw me coming, her eyes widened in fear. Couldn't say I blamed her. How long would it take to field dress a T-bone out of her? The chicken grumbled in my belly.

"You're lucky, old girl."

"Lucky?" Carol asked. "She's most likely going to freeze to death."

"Oh, that," I answered guiltily.

Carol opened the door to Bessie's pen. Bessie looked around in confusion. Sure she was a cow, but she had to know on some level that when animals left this barn they didn't come back. Had her time finally come? She looked directly at me. I must have had one of those huge cartoon clouds over my head with a hamburger in it because she took off for the door.

"Good luck, girl," I said to Bessie's retreating back. "I wish we could have spent more time together." I rubbed my belly.

"Mike, don't make me take back all those good things I said about you."

I put my arm around her shoulder as her tears flowed freely.

"It's really over isn't it?" she asked as she sniffed.

"Pretty much." I had come to terms with my fate. I'm not saying I enjoyed it or was looking forward to it, but there was a breath of freedom in it all the same.

Carol and I walked up to the old house. The departing cold winter sun was slowly being replaced by an even colder full moon. It looked as large as a plate as it hung low on the horizon.

"At least we'll be able to see them," I said.

"And that's good how?" Jen asked rhetorically as Carol and I approached up the stairs.

I don't think the zombies much cared about the psychological effect of attacking at night. This was going to be more of a timing issue for them. When they got here they would attack; pure, plain and simple. As soon as Jen had helped Carol get back into the house, I reattached the rope alarm. No sense in getting caught with our pants down. Then I thought of Cash, and all of a sudden my analogy didn't seem quite so humorous. The sun setting in the West and the moon rising in the East were near equidistant to the horizon when I implemented the most crucial element of the plan.

There was some resistance and much wailing and gnashing of the teeth, but in the end I stood firm and got nearly all that I demanded. BT smiled at me as if he realized he was the only fly in my ointment. For an hour Jen and I idly pretended to play cards at the kitchen table. BT had long since retired to his couch. I wondered if he would stay awake long enough to see this through. The house was unnaturally quiet; however, that was more me imprinting my feelings on my surroundings. What noises should the house be making? At this point I was even beginning to miss Henry's world-class ass attack.

BT, much to my amazement, was first up when the alarm bell rang...once and only once.

"Any chance that could be Bessie coming home?" Jen asked.

"For her sake, I hope that isn't the case, I'm starving," I told her.

"Me too," BT said.

"Men." Jen said exasperatedly. "Is someone going to answer the call?" she asked.

"Women first," BT said gallantly. "I would, but I can't walk so good."

"I'll get it," I told her. The walk down the hallway was dreamlike. I felt like a condemned man finally going to make atonement for his transgressions. As fucked up as it sounds, I wanted to say 'Dead Man Walking!' But I thought my last words should be something more noble. Like 'Tell my wife I love her.' I kept my stray thoughts to myself, why now though? Why all of a sudden? I might have brought the thought to fruition, but the death bell rang one more grave time.

"Wow, someone's hungry," BT said.

"Ugh," was the loose translation from Jen.

"Not cool, BT," I said without ever turning back around.

I might have ran and hid if I did. He laughed it off. I grabbed the handle to the door and took what I felt was going

Zombie Fallout 2: A Plague Upon Your Family

to be my last breath. I turned the knob, opened the door and stood witness to what can only be described as an 'awake' night terror. Hundreds, maybe thousands of zombies surrounded the house, the front line of them within a hand span of the rope alarm. The only being holding the rope was someone I knew all too well.

"Hi, roomie, did you miss me?"

I was more pissed than anything that I had shown weakness, but I could not stop it. The splash of vomit that issued forth from me was no more preventable than the incessant tide.

Durgan laughed at me as I slammed the door back into place. Jen turned white as a ghost when she saw my face.

"Bad?" she asked.

"You could say that." The words tasted funny through all the bile.

"What would *you* say?" BT asked, looking a lot more serious all of a sudden.

"Um, fucking horrible comes to mind. Maybe really fucking shitty, that's another set of adjectives I'd use, there's—"

"Enough, Mike, what's going on?" BT asked.

"Let's just say that the zombie invasion has made this Ground Zero and they have a leader."

"Eliza's really here?" Jen gulped.

"Why didn't you shoot her, this could already be over!" BT said.

"Sorry, too busy puking," I said as I looked out the storm shutter. "And no, it's not Eliza, she sent one of her lackeys. It's Durgan and he seems pissed."

"Oh, I can't imagine why," Jen said. "First you run him off from his own store. Then you kill all his buddies while simultaneously shooting his leg off at the knee. You cave-in his one remaining good knee with a leg kick and then, to top it off, you leave him locked in a cell surrounded by zombies."

293

"See! You know what I'm saying," I said, pointing to Jen. "He started every one of those encounters. I just ended them. And here he is again, starting more shit. I guess it's up to us to finish it."

"No sense in messin' with tradition," BT stated matter-of-factly.

It started like a whispering wind over a graveyard and turned into a full blown crescendo as thousands of tortured vocal chords tried to chant what I could only surmise was a war cry.

"What the fuck is that?" BT asked. I could tell by his expression that it was as disconcerting to him as it was to me.

The house vibrated under the assault of the low bass range the collective moan put out. Zombies were one thing. This deadly lament was wholly something else. There was a bizarre feel to it as the oscillation passed through my body threatening to liquefy the contents in my bowels. Was this planned? Did they know the effect this would have on us? I peeked through one of the shutters, hoping maybe to get a shot off at Durgan. He must have assumed this too because he was no longer in sight, choosing to lead his troops from the rear instead of the front, I suppose. Well, one good outcome from the moaning was that the zombies weren't moving.

"Seems like we've got a bunch of blonde zombies," I said, pulling my face away from the glass.

"Huh? What are you talking about, Mike?" Jen asked, clearly upset.

"They can't moan and move at the same time," I finished.

Jen rolled her eyes. BT shook his head.

"Hey, they can't ALL be gems," I defended myself.

"Yeah, but at least one or two would be nice!" BT yelled over the cacophony.

And as quickly as it had started, it stopped. How could the moaning have been better? Because when the zombies were moaning they weren't moving. The alarm bell crashed to the floor in a tumble of forewarning.

"This is it!" I yelled, louder than the situation dictated, nerves getting the better of me. "Might as well have a front row seat to the apocalypse."

I opened the front door, pulling the trigger on my rifle as I did, not even waiting to acquire a target – that would have been excessively extravagant. It amazed me that they could even move forward being wedged that tightly together. Maneuverability was out of the question for them. I could only hope that as they closed in around the house they would grind each other into oblivion as the space between them became less than nonexistent. Some would surely die this way, crushed in a sea of zombianity. Good.

I was halfway through my first magazine when Jen stepped out beside me. She had moved on from her original pistol and was now touting her own assault weapon, an HK-17. I've got to admit, even in the crappy predicament we were in I was a little jealous of her gun. It was a bigger caliber than my AR's 5.56 mm round. It toted a much toothier 7.72 round, which had the added benefit of going in and out of one target and sometimes in and out of another. It was a pleasure to watch multiple heads snap back from the impact of her bullet. She was shredding through rows of zombies.

She looked over at me from the corner of her eye and through clenched teeth and a strained voice she said to me, "It might be better if you started shooting and stopped watching me."

"Oh yeah...sorry. It's just that if I had known how cool that gun was going to be I would have grabbed another one."

"Grabbed another what?" BT asked as he shouldered his way onto the porch.

"HK," I told him. "Look what that thing is doing."

"Holy shit," BT said after a few seconds.

"Guys! Come on!" Jen shouted.

"Right."

"Sorry."

Although it didn't really matter, our shots were more of a morale booster on our side. No amount of firepower we could muster was going to stop them. My barrel would melt before I so much as made any sort of noticeable difference. No, this was a show of defiance under insurmountable odds. We would not go like sheep to the slaughter. I scanned the zombies for any sign of Durgan. Just one shot, I just wanted one shot at his ass. Okay, so not really his ass, but you get the point. I wanted to kill him now so that I'd also have the opportunity to kick his ass as we made our ways to our respective resting places. No such luck; he was out of sight.

"Mike," Jen said, pulling up from her sights.

BT was still happily triggering away, his semi-automatic .30-06 making short work of whatever got in its way. "I hope Hell's got some extra people working at the reception desk today!" he yelled.

"Hey, that's pretty good," I told him.

"You liked that?" he yelled, still firing.

"One of your better, I've got to admit."

"GUYS!" Jen yelled. "You two are worse than seven-year-olds."

"I'll take that as a compliment," I told her. BT laughed.

"I figured you would. BT, stop firing, they've stopped."

And they had. The zombies had paid a dear price for the ten feet of real estate they had captured. If lives were money, they were a very rich opponent.

"What are they doing, Mike?" BT asked me.

"Well, seeing as I am the imminent zombie zoologist expert, I would assume that they—"

"Fuck you, I get it, you don't know either," he said plainly. "This plan looked a lot better on paper."

"Yeah, smelled better too," I said, pulling one of my sweaters over my nose. "You tend to forget how much they stink."

Jen added her own refuse to my cooled bile pile. "Eww,

fucking gross," she said as she spit to get out the last remaining bits of ort. "I'll never be able to eat again."

"Might not be a lasting situation," I told her.

She shrugged. We had known the odds were for shit. See, this is exactly why I never liked to gamble.

"Talbot!" came an artificially enhanced voice. "You ready to give up yet?" The bullhorn infused voice shouted again.

Shouting was not necessary over the shuffling zombies, but I was looking more for dramatic effect. "Durgan, come out from whatever hidey-hole you're in and I'll give you my answer face-to-face! Man-to-man, if I thought you were one!" His laughing cut off short.

"I'm going to kill you for that, Talbot!" he shouted, this time without the aid of the bullhorn.

"Just for that?" I questioned Jen. "There's so many other things he could have hung that card up on."

"Come on, big man!" BT yelled disparagingly. "I'll take you on without my gun!"

"What makes you think I would sully my purity by tangling with the likes of you!" Durgan shouted.

"Wow, I honestly didn't think he could become any bigger of an ass than he already is (was) but then he goes and surprises me and adds racism to the mix. He's really almost sort of amazing. That's a lot of hate for one person," I said to Jen and BT, making sure it was loud enough to be heard by all that were willing to listen.

That must have struck a chord in Durgan somewhere. He didn't say anything else, at least not anything we heard, but the zombies started their relentless march up to the house.

Jen took a controlling breath like I had taught her and brought her rifle up. "Fuck, my shoulder's going to hurt tonight," she said before she started pulling the trigger.

"Let's hope so," I mumbled as I brought my rifle to bear.

BT had not taken the opportunity to reload during the break in action and was struggling to catch up now. "Why doesn't he just send them all out, Talbot? Why this fucking game?" BT asked as he nearly shoved his bullets through the bottom of his magazine well.

"He's like a little kid that just got a lollipop and he has no idea when he might get his next one." BT looked over at me trying to figure out my bad analogy. "Savoring, BT, he's savoring this. He wants to be able to replay this whole thing repeatedly in his pathetic twisted little fucking—"

"Racist mind," BT finished.

The snow turned a rusty red as drums of blood were spilled. This ground was going to be the most fertile it had ever been next season and there would be no one here to tend the fallow fields. I shouldered my weapon, careful not to touch the dimly glowing barrel. I reached out and grabbed BT's and Jen's shoulder.

"Stop for a second!" I shouted. "You're going to want to see this." The echoing from BT's last shot had just completed its airwave rippling when the first of my surprises struck. The loud metallic clanking was muffled by the foot of snow it was under, but the effect was not. The lead zombie crumbled face first into the snow, in what I could only imagine was extreme pain, although stoically he didn't show it.

"What the hell happened?" Jen asked as another and then another zombie fell in succession.

"Bear traps," I said triumphantly. With 1,250 pounds per square inch of pressure, the device designed to incapacitate a bear would sheer right through the comparatively fragile leg of a man. This tactic would normally have a demoralizing effect on the enemy, but for that you had to have a conscience... and be conscious. The following rows of zombies merely stepped onto and over their ground-wriggling brethren.

"Well, not exactly what I was looking for, but entertaining nonetheless."

"Good one," BT said with a smile on his face.

"Men! And people wonder why I'm a lesbian," Jen said

as she brought her HK back up.

Fun time was over. I went into the house and grabbed my Dick's sporting Goods pilfered .30-30; the AR was going to need a few minutes to come down to a serviceable temperature. I had a good ten seconds to think, which was nine more than I wanted. I wished that Tracy had left while the opportunity was available. I knew she wouldn't, but still, it would suck to go ahead and sacrifice ourselves for nothing. It would be cramped in the van and the truck with the fourteen of them, but cramped beats dead every time. And we still come back to the original problem. IF Jen, BT, and I somehow survived, how the hell would we all fit? Sure we could sit in the back of the truck for a mile or two before we froze completely solid.

But making this stand was not completely about escape. It was about creating a chance to end this thing once and for all. Eliza not showing had thrown a serious wrench into my plans. I needed to kill the bitch. Without her death, her inexplicable link to Justin would remain and through him she had us. No, there was another way around that problem. I could sever the connection on my side. I banged my head against the wall. No, that was not an option.

"You coming back to the party?" BT shouted from the porch.

"Just getting a sandwich," I told him as I collected my wits – which were nearing their ends – and headed out to join the fray.

Again the zombies stopped; they were no more than twenty-five yards away from us.

"Aw, this shit is getting old, Durgan!" I yelled.

"Any chance our boy is pulling an end around?" BT asked.

"What?"

"You know, while we're all here going to town out front he sends all of his boys in the back."

"Oh shit, that would really not work out to our

advantage."

"I'll check!" Jen yelled, already half way down the hallway.

"She's fast," BT noted.

"Who would have thought a lesbian would have that kind of speed?"

"You get into a lot of trouble with that mouth of yours, don't you." It wasn't a question from BT, it was a statement.

"Now that you say it…more than you'd figure."

"Oh, I doubt it," he said.

"They're about the same distance away back here as they are out there," Jen shouted from the kitchen.

"Do you think lesbians are more spatially aware than your normal female?" I asked BT. "I mean, they have to put their own furniture together and shit. Use a tape measure to hang shelves, that kind of thing."

"Do you ever think before you start spewing from the mouth?" BT asked me.

"What? It's an honest question," I pleaded.

"What are you two children talking about?" Jen asked as she rejoined our small fire team.

"I was just wondering—"

"Nothing," BT said as he thumped my chest with his forearm.

"I don't even want to know. If it came from you two it must have to do with farting or something equally juvenile."

"Hey, don't lump me in with Talbot."

They might have continued on for a few more seconds if I hadn't intervened. "Wait, something's happening."

Zombies were shifting their positions, turning completely sideways when possible.

"What now?" Jen asked.

"It almost looks like they're moving to get out of the way," I answered her.

"Getting out of the way for what?" BT asked. "They can't have cave trolls can they?"

"Holy shit, BT, are you a *Lord of the Rings* fan?" I asked him.

"Must have seen it ten times."

"I didn't figure you for a fantasy movie type," I told him.

"Yeah, that war at Isengard..."

"Oh God, no!" Jen wailed.

I turned from her terrified face to the yard beyond. I wished I had shoved a bayonet into my eyes instead of looking out there. BT added his own pool to the upchuck muck.

"I can't, Talbot! I can't deal with this!" Jen screamed.

Children from the earliest stages of walking to somewhere around ten years of age began to spill out into the front ranks of the invading horde. Jen's gun clattered to the deck as she turned around, placing both hands over her eyes, trying in vain to suppress the image forever burned in her retinas. They were five feet thick before they stopped coming. Some were in pajamas. Some just in diapers and nothing else. Some completely naked and still others that looked as if they had changed into zombies mid-snowball fight.

So many of them! My heart was crushing in on itself. Breathing was becoming more difficult than it was worth. My instinct was to go out and comfort every one of them. Their flat black eyes belied no need for alleviation of their hurts. Never again would any of them need a boo-boo healing kiss on a scraped knee. Never again would they need a kind word after a tough loss in pee-wee baseball. Never again would they need an ice cream cone after Susie called them a doo-doo head. I dropped onto my knees from the pressure of the heartache. I just wanted to roll over and watch the stars travel on by in my last moments on earth. Of all things, Durgan saved me.

Not so much him as his personality, but it was a fine line anyway. And definitely not anything he did on purpose. But the cocksucker took my misery and despair and magically transformed it into rage. Pure unadulterated rage.

"How do you like me now, Talbot?" came his derisive voice.

"How could you do this!?" Jen shouted. "You're crazy, do you hear me, you're crazy!"

Durgan's laugh echoed all around us. "Those small little teeth are going to feel like puppy's teeth when they tear into you."

Jen sobbed even more loudly.

"BT, get her in the house," I said coldly. BT didn't look much better than Jen sounded.

"What are you going to do, Talbot?" he asked as he grabbed at Jen to bring her into the house. He winced as he bent over to grab the discarded weapon.

"I'd like to tell you that I was going to do what I should have done a long time ago, go and kill that bastard. But that's going to have to wait. No, I'm just going to watch your backs while you go in, and then we'll just have to start phase two of our plan, I mean idea, a little earlier than expected, is all."

"We'll meet again, Durgan!" I shouted out into the night. He responded before I had a chance to close the door.

"There's no room for me where you're going, Talbot." And he laughed some more.

Was he that far gone that he didn't even realize what he'd just said? Are there many people that think going to Hell is the epitome of a successful life? I wanted to open the door and get some clarification, but that didn't seem like a great idea. Insanity by definition is not rational and besides there was no sense in refreshing the image of hundreds upon hundreds of hungry zombie children in my head.

BT and Jen were huddled by the fire in the living room. Jen was shivering uncontrollably.

"BT, get her down into the basement, I'll take care of what needs to be done up here."

He nodded at me and scooped her limp but not lifeless body into his arms. She wrapped her arms around his neck and buried her face into his broad chest. The added weight was causing him some serious pain in his injured leg, but besides a small grimace he never voiced concern one over it. The house was bathed in darkness. The small candles and fire in the living room could only chase so many shadows away. The diffused moonlight that filtered through the storm shutters did more to stimulate this effect than diffuse it.

It was in this setting that I splashed gasoline across every treasured belonging that Carol and her family had ever owned. The propellant washed over and around picture frames, bleeding pictures into first something that resembled something from the twisted mind of Salvador Dali and finally into unendurable blotches of indefinable color like so many other things in this life that were now irretrievable. I had covered the house in nearly five gallons of the volatile fluid, upstairs and down. There was more than triple that amount laid out in various containers located strategically throughout the house. This house was going to burn like the fires of hell. My only concern was the hope that it took as many of Eliza's earth-wandering despots with it as possible.

Jen's fits of shivering had nearly stilled by the time I got down there, but she had not let go of BT's neck as he sat in an old chair that had been relegated to the basement before it was to become a permanent fixture at a land fill.

"She going to be alright, when the time comes?" I asked BT.

"I'll carry her if I have to," BT said.

Jen didn't move from her spot. Her words were muffled. Her message was not. "I'll be fine when the time comes, but for now I'm staying where I'm at." That didn't seem to bother BT in the least. He was getting as much comfort from her as she was from him.

The smell of gasoline had begun to settle into the basement; it did wonders to mask the stench of death. Not sure if this was an angle Glade would want to use – 'NEW Gas scented plug-ins for all your zombie stench needs. Is

Grandma's rotting corpse beginning to embarrass you? Do
guests avoid coming to your house because of the
decomposing children? Whisk away those horrible odors
with our new GAS plug-ins, now available in Diesel and Oil
fragrances!' – Yeah, you're probably right, not much of a
market for that.

We didn't have long to wait as the first thump of a
thwarted zombie hit the front door. The sound was not as
loud as it should have been in the quiet house. Mostly
because the zombie that walked into the frame of the door
was probably only a girl of seven. An involuntary tremor of
revulsion coursed through me. It was an instinctual response.
I could no more control it than the weather. The thumping
began to pick up in frequency and intensity as if whoever had
been holding the invisible leashes had let go.

Dust from the floorboards above our heads showered
down upon us as the house began to vibrate under the assault.

"You should get some Prell," BT said. "It might help
with that bad case of dandruff you've got going on, Talbot."

"Prell! Prell? How fucking old are you, BT? They don't
even make Prell anymore."

"Sure they do, I bought some the da—"

"Stop it you two! Don't you realize what is going on?"

I did it, I don't know why, but I did it. "No, what?" That
set her off. She went on and on about being in the midst of
some sort of apocalypse or such. I kind of lost the train of her
rant.

"Stop it, you two, just stop it!" BT roared. Jen looked up
from BT's chest, her face looked like she had gone ten
rounds with Mike Tyson. And not the soft, brain addled Mike
Tyson…this was the lean, mean, ear-biting machine.

The house was shaking on its foundation as the zombies
closed in from all sides. I didn't even want to think about the
children that were pressed up against the walls. An explosion
of glass tinkled to the ground in first one and then two and
then a dozen different locations. This was followed almost

immediately by the crashing open of what sounded like the back door, at least by the location of the many footfalls now above our heads. The front door lasted the longest but ultimately could not withstand the assault. Zombies had breached our meager defenses. The floorboards above us creaked and protested against the strain of so much weight.

Zombies rushed in to fill every void within the house looking for tasty treats. Furniture splintered and knickknacks were ground to dust under so many feet. I waited as long as I could to allow as many as the enemy as I could into the house. It wouldn't be a fraction of the number it needed to be, but my options were rapidly becoming diminished. Someone had smelled our hiding spot and zombies began to bump up against the cellar door. It was reinforced with two-by-fours that I had nailed across it, but they wouldn't hold forever; although I was more concerned at this point with the ceiling over our heads giving out first. There was a noticeable bow to it.

"You two ready?" I asked as I stood up, grabbing the road flare from the cabinet next to me.

Jen extracted herself from BT and did her best to gingerly help BT to stand. I noticed as he shifted his weight around, he was being especially careful not to put any weight on his injured leg. He half hopped over to where I was and leaned against the cabinet. Jen had walked over to the bottom of the staircase, nervously looking up at the basement door as if expecting it to open.

BT leaned in to make sure Jen couldn't hear but unless she had a bionic ear, that wasn't going to be a problem. The general melee free-for-all upstairs made the simple act of thinking a difficult proposition.

"I can't run, Mike."

I knew he was serious. He had called me by my first name. "Figured as much. What's your idea?"

He looked candidly at me.

"Come on, man, you wouldn't have shuffled over here

and tried to be all sneaky if you didn't have some shitty idea."

Jen involuntarily jumped when the door took a particularly savage blow.

BT looked nervously over at Jen before he began to speak. "I was thinking I'd stay behind and watch your backs."

I took my pointer finger and thumb and grabbed my chin like I was really contemplating something deep. "Can't do it, BT."

He looked incredulously at me. "What do you mean, Mike? You gonna carry me? Maybe buck ten Jen over there could heft me on her shoulders?"

Jen looked over. "What's going on?" she asked as she crossed her arms over her chest and rubbed her arms, possibly to wipe the chill of death from herself.

"Oh, BT thinks we should leave him behind when we leave."

"What? Is he fucking nuts?" Jen yelled.

"That's what I thought. So I basically told him no."

"Guys, I'm right here," BT lamented.

"And what did he say when you told him that?" Jen asked.

"Oh, well he got all indignant. And then he was berating me about being able to carry his extra-large ass, and that maybe you'd be able to."

"Mike, I'm right here!" BT shouted.

"So you told him that there was no way in hell that we were leaving him behind?" she asked.

"Well, we hadn't got that far, but those would have been my next words. And then he would have replied with something heroic like 'You guys could save yourselves. If you try to help me then we'll all die.' And I would have come back with something equally heroic like 'Either we all get out of here alive or none of us do.'"

"I get it, guys," BT said. "We knew this was a one way

trip anyway."

Jen gripped herself tighter. "Wow, just got a chill. Someone must have just walked over my grave."

I laughed my ass off. We all did. "That's hilarious because well, because..." And I pointed to the ceiling where the shuffling of hundreds of feet was going on.

"You must be psychic," BT added. And we started laughing all over, like the crazed doomed souls that we were.

Jen's tears of joy, slowly but inevitably turned to real tears. BT went over to comfort her.

"Now seems as good a time as any." I lit the flare and walked over to the far corner of the basement where I had previously drilled a silver dollar sized hole through the kitchen floor and into the basement. I had drilled the hole through a cabinet in the kitchen thus avoiding any chance the hole would be plugged by someone standing on it or by knocking over the large container of gas that was next to it. I looked at the flare for a few seconds more, letting the brilliant fire burn its final images into my memories.

This fire represented the end of so many things, and hopefully the beginning of a new safer life for my family. "I wish you were here to enjoy this with me, Eliza," I muttered as I thrust the flare up and through the hole. The flame flashed brilliantly as it came in contact with the gaseous vapors. I crinkled my nose as the smell of burnt arm hair wafted up. If I found this smell offensive, it was a vale of roses on a warm spring day after a brief rain shower compared to what assaulted my olfactory senses next. The smell of zombies can be topped by only one other smell – that of burning zombies. Roasting on an open pit was preferable to the cloying stink of melting decayed flesh that ran rampant through the farmhouse.

There were no screams of mercy coming from upstairs, no shrieks of terror or pain, only the mindless hunt for food. There was no mass exodus from the premises. We knew this by the unrelenting assailment on the basement door. Would the door give before the floor? Or would we succumb to smoke inhalation, death by breathing in the dead. Oh, just fucking gross.

"You guys ready?" I asked again.

"Let's give this a shot," BT said, making sure his rifle was fully loaded.

Jen didn't say anything, but thankfully she picked up her HK, popped in a new magazine, and nodded to me. We three stood for a moment side by side looking at the door that led to the bulkhead. Long moments passed. Realizing your death is imminent is one thing. Rushing headlong into it is completely another matter. The basement door cracked or it may have been a floor joist.

"Well, that's decided," I said as I opened the basement door that led outside and to freedom, in theory anyway.

The aluminum bulkhead doors were heavily dented from the sheer number of zombies standing on them trying to get into the house.

"I guess the fire didn't scare them away so much," BT noted.

"Yeah, didn't work in Little Turtle. Was expecting sort of the same result here," I said. "Seems like the fire and heat might actually attract them instead of repel them."

"Talbot, I figured we wouldn't get out of this, but why did you volunteer? You have so much more to lose than either of us," BT asked, pointing to himself and Jen.

"I thought this was going to be a chance to give my family a fresh start. I didn't think Eliza was going to pull a no-show on me. I wanted to be there in person when she took her last…whatever she takes."

It was definitely the cellar door that had shown signs of weakness previously. Zombies literally began to tumble down the stairs and onto the basement floor. BT unloaded a clip of .30-06 rounds up and through the aluminum doors. Heavy, congealed, bluish tinted blood ran in rivulets through the holes. I wanted to jump out of my skin as the, what I believed to be caustic liquid ran down my head and neck and pooled in the small of my back as we all pushed up on the doors. A couple of zombies still on the doors had the actual benefit of a small carnival ride as they slid off and into a snowdrift.

Zombies were within touching distance before we opened up a large can of ass whooping. Those unlucky few that were closest to us quickly became nourishment for next year's crops. But this was more futile than trying to bale water out of an already sunken ship. A veritable sea of healthy flesh-challenged people awaited our embrace. Jen ran back down the stairs. I figured she had panicked when in actuality she may have saved a few extra precious seconds of our time remaining.

I heard the basement door slam shut below us. Jen had closed it to protect our backs. Zombies in front, zombies behind, and the crackling heat of the fire to our backs was becoming increasingly difficult to tolerate.

"Any ideas?" BT asked me. "You know, because if you do, now is not the time to keep them to yourself."

"Only one at this point."

BT didn't look at me as I spoke, too intent on firing his rifle. "Yeah, what is it?"

"Keep firing until you have one round left." The implied meaning in that sentence was clear.

He looked over briefly at me and lifted his eyebrows and shrugged his shoulders. "Makes sense to me." And he kept on firing.

Jen had shut the bulkhead doors and was standing on them looking out over the Dead Sea. "I can see them!" she said excitedly.

"Why haven't they left yet?" I yelled back to her.

"I don't know, but at least they're safe."

That was a heavy burden I could release from myself. At least they were safe. That part of the plan had worked perfectly. Carol's homestead had two tornado shelters which were used more for pickling and canning jam than anything else. One was located near the animal barn. The other was out in the field at least a good half-mile from the house, put there so that if someone was caught unawares of an impending storm they would still be able to seek shelter. It was a well-known family secret that, during Prohibition, that shelter had served as a lucrative still.

The plan was that, with Justin knocked unconscious, we would move him to the shelter and blindfold him so that he would not have any idea that he was anywhere but where he thought he was: the basement. Eliza and her horde of smelly citizens would then converge on the house where we would allow them to come in, en masse, and then lay waste to Carol's house. Once the zombies had passed the shelter on by, Tracy was supposed to get them all out of here, and we would (theoretically) meet up a mile or so down the road. That way if Eliza somehow survived this holocaust she would not know that we had also survived.

The problems with the plan were numerous. First off, Eliza hadn't come to the dance. Secondly, we had way more party crashers than we had intended. And thirdly, Tracy hadn't fuckin' left before we died!!

"She sees us! She's waving!" Jen yelled.

"If she tries to rescue us, I'm going to shoot her myself!" I cursed under my breath.

Jen jumped down off the doors as the heat from the melting house began to blister us all.

We couldn't see anything except the nearest wave of zombies, which thankfully weren't children. Most of them had become roasted fare in the house behind us. But we all heard what came next.

BT looked up from his sights. "Is that a horn?"

CHAPTER 26

Mike's Journal Entry Twenty-Three

"Oh, fucking Tracy! What are you doing, woman?" I moaned. "Don't make me die for nothing."

We were all down to the dregs of our ammo, and I had been completely serious about holding one bullet for myself when the cannon fire erupted and I saw the familiar front grill of the white Ford pickup bracketed by two military vehicles. Trailing was your standard-issue Marine Corps Humvee, in front was a six-wheeled lightly armored troop transport. There were waves of joy and waves of despair, was the violence of existence worth it? Joy because help was coming, despair because it was too far away. The .50 caliber machinegun mounted on the turret of the troop transport was shredding through zombies, head shots weren't warranted when bodies were literally being torn in two. There's a reason why the Geneva Convention had expressly forbidden the act of shooting personnel with this type of gun. It made identifying the deceased a nearly impossible task.

I was gauging the number of rounds I had with how long it was going to take the trucks to get here. It was looking like a typical Vegas wager, the house was the favorite and we were the mark.

Maybe the sight of us, or my thoughts actually held sway over the caravan, because they began to speed up.

"That's not Tracy," BT said from his higher vantage point.

"Nicole? Travis? Please tell me no," I begged.

"Brendon."

"Are you fucking kidding me, BT?"

"Does now really seem like the time, Talbot?"

As I was pondering this new information, my AR dry-fired. My Glock was up next, I had five hundred rounds, but only five magazines. Once those fifty rounds were gone, it was over; unless of course I could call 'time-out' and the zombies would allow it. Then I'd be able to reload and have a fighting chance.

The house behind us began to crumble; we had been able to push forward fifteen feet or so away, close enough to the flame that zombies couldn't circle behind but not far enough to be safe from an imminent collapse and probable barbequing.

"I sure wish they'd hurry," BT said with no more expression than if he was waiting for a pizza.

"I'm out!" Jen yelled on adrenaline fueled lungs.

I was two mags down, and now I would have to pick up the pace with Jen's sector of containment now flooding through. Zombies were close enough that I could see individual gore-stained teeth and black cracked fingernails clawing through the air attempting to seek purchase. Foul breath escaped through decayed airways. Zombies lit by flame began to spill out of the house behind us, somehow still able to hone in. Three magazines down, and the Marines and Brendon were still fifty yards away.

"So fucking close." We might have all said it. I can't credit it to any one of us.

The trucks slowed minimally as the .50 cal shots had to be aimed more precisely lest they take us out too. The troop transport was in danger of high centering over the sheer number of zombies becoming so much road kill. The snail-paced crawl may be saving the truck from getting stuck but at the cost of our lives.

I saw exactly when the driver of the transport weighed those two factors on the scale and said 'Fuck it.' The bluster of the truck's engine hitting full throttle cut through the dull roar of the burning cinder block behind us. Zombies were flung in the air like a giant spoiled baby was done playing with his GI Joes and Barbie dolls and was throwing them around in the fits of a tantrum.

The armor was beginning to fold in on itself under the pressure of so many collisions. As the lead vehicle pushed past, Brendon pulled up broadside just as I had expended the last bullet.

"All aboard!" Brendon yelled in his best train conductor voice.

Jen almost cleared the other side of the truck bed as BT hurled her up and in. BT's leg might not be working well, but his arms were fine as he followed her immediately. BT's ass had no sooner made contact with the bed and I was in his lap.

"Didn't know you cared," BT said as he put me in a more respectable position.

"Where's everyone else?" Brendon asked.

"Safe," I shouted back.

He smiled. "Okay then, please have your tickets ready to be punched!" Brendon yelled through the rear facing windows as he crushed down on the accelerator.

Zombies pressed in from all sides. I grabbed a shovel and did my best to keep them at bay as the truck swayed violently from side to side. BT had found a tire iron and was making anything within striking distance rue the day it had gone over to the dark side. Jen had found an axe handle that looked like it had already been used for nefarious purposes as the end of it was deeply stained a suspicious brownish red color.

Jen was swinging the handle violently. When she made contact, the vibrations shot up her arms.

"Be careful!" I yelled to her.

Whether she would have heeded me or not, the warning

was a beat too late. The zombie she had been lining up to strike had fallen when Brendon ran over its leg. Jen pitched forward, precariously balanced between relative safety and death. Death won out. I watched the resignation in her face as she fell out of the truck bed.

"JEN!" I screamed. I jumped to the other side of the truck bed. My hand brushed hers as she slid away from my touch. Her other hand shot out even as the first of the zombies sunk his teeth into her back. I was able to make a tenuous grasp on her hand, dragging her along behind the truck.

"Don't let me go, Mike!" she screamed. "PLEASE!" she begged as another zombie took hold of her thigh, teeth first. He tore a ragged piece of flesh away from her as I continually pulled her behind the truck.

She was dead. We both knew it. But I was not going to let go. The blood vessels in her eyes burst as a zombie ripped through her calf muscle, long strips of meat hanging between its greedy lips. I turned to gain as much momentum as I could before I began to pull her back into the truck.

Her hand went slack. The weight I dragged increased as zombies jumped on her, feasting as we went. I let go of her hand and sat back up, the sharp pain in my shoulder a reminder of what had just happened. BT was looking at me in what I could only describe as shock. He moved faster than any man his size had a right too. He grabbed me and slammed me to the floor of the truck bed. I was beginning to feel light headed. He must have really knocked my head against the floor.

"It wasn't my fault, BT," I said through fogged vision.

"I know that, you damned fool, you've been shot."

"Shot? Zombies don't shoot guns. You're crazy, man. It sure is getting dark quick."

"Not a gun, a crossbow."

A crossbow! A fucking crossbow? Who shoots somebody with a crossbow? What am I, an elk? What's next? Someone gonna whip out a mace? Maybe a scimitar?

My shoulder, for lack of a better term, unraveled. Muscle, tendon, sinew, whatever, just literally began to curl like wet parchment. My biceps bulged, rivaling the Hulk, as my ripped tendons rolled up into them. I noticed with a note of envy how large my muscles looked even as my vision began to blur. (Guys can be vain! Just because I was dying of blood loss and shock didn't mean I couldn't appreciate how large my damaged muscles looked.) Searing pain immediately made me wish I would just pass out and die and be over with this. As bone separated from tissue, I'm pretty sure I involuntarily blackened my eye as my arm flung up. That was the least of my problems and I wouldn't have even registered the fact had not my right eye dimmed and then blacked out before my left one.

"Talbot!" someone screamed. Sounded like someone I knew. Well, I must know them if they knew my name, right? Who gives a shit. "Talbot!" Again with the screaming, but it sounded further away, even as I felt arms around me.

From somewhere very distant I heard my wife. "Talbot, don't you di...."

I accelerated along a black tube as light emanated from every direction. Its source I could not discern. My speed seemed to be accelerating, although I think it was all relative. It wasn't me that seemed to be moving so much as the tunnel was streaming past. I wanted to reach out and touch the wall to see if that was the case but I was afraid of doing more damage to my injured wing. Aw what the hell, my arm was barely attached anyway, what more could I do. I moved my right arm around, unbelievably happy with how pain free the movement was.

"Holy crap," I muttered. "He must have missed. Maybe it's the wrong arm."

Having been ambidextrous my entire life I often confused my left from my right. When I moved my left arm and again felt no pain, the light of recognition dawned. *Holy Shit! I'm dead!* That thought wasn't nearly as dreadful as I would have

315

imagined. Oh I was scared to a point, maybe more concerned. Alright I was a little freaked out. My thoughts obviously revolving around what is at the end of this tunnel. Do I pull a Wile E. Coyote and smash face first into a faux hole in the wall? Do I come out to a huge drop and fall eternally? (Oh that would suck.) IS there a Heaven? Or worse, a Hell? My actions thus far in my life could probably gain my entry into either. Was my eternity going to come down to a "rock, paper, scissor" game between God and Satan? Wow, blasphemy on my final journey cannot be good in the ledger books.

Maybe it would be possible to hang out in this tunnel a little longer and weigh my options. Wind buffeted me back as I tried in vain to approach the walls. The speed was picking up, I knew I was nearing my final destination, no stops, no layovers. I had a momentary pang for my wife and kids. I did feel remorse that I was dying, but only because I wouldn't be there for them. I had ultimately accepted my fate, for what other choice was there?

When I felt another presence nearby, it wasn't nearly as comforting as I would have expected from the Almighty. There was a great sense of anger, of sadness, of a life truly unfulfilled. It took me long moments to pull these vaporous thoughts away from my own, the intermingling almost made me believe these errant thoughts were mine. Out of the corner of my awareness I caught movement as it at first trailed behind me by some lengths and then hastened to catch up and pass me by.

"Brendon?" I shouted.

So lost was he in his mortality he took no notice of me as he shot on by. I watched in the distance as a light infinitely brighter than what I was experiencing now blazed in acceptance, in love, in its warm embrace. These euphoric feelings washed over and around me. My pang of regret paled, faded, and was washed away. Those feelings lasted long after the walls of my tunnel slowed and then began to shift direction, back into the blight, the pain, the hurt, the uncertainty, the love.

"He's back," someone familiar sobbed from a hundred million miles away.

EPILOGUE

Cops vs. Talbot

TALBOTSODE #1

So I started early dealing with the po-po. I was sixteen years old when my high school thought it would be a good idea to deter drunk driving by placing a wrecked car on the front lawn of the school. For some reason that completely eluded me at that moment in life, I thought that was the most inconsiderate act possible. So of course, that night, my friends and I went and bashed in any remaining glass on that car.

By the time the cops got there we were out of sight in the woods across the street. We watched them as they shone their lights across the wreckage of the wreck. We also saw them park inconspicuously across the street hoping that said vandals would return.

You know I went back. It's in my nature. This time it wasn't with a tire iron. I had made a Molotov cocktail out of some gas and shampoo poured into a Coke bottle. My friends had told me 'I was crazy' and 'You're not going to do it.' So, you know of course, all that really does is incite somebody above and beyond normal stupidity into super stupidity. I was a fast kid, I played halfback for the freshman team. How fast was about to be tested.

I went a little further in the woods, away from the cops, and emerged from a spot where they could not see my egress.

As I walked back up the road towards the school I tried my best to act as innocent as possible. I knew they were watching me. I could feel it. They wanted me to do something wrong just as bad as I wanted to.

My first step off the relative safety of the sidewalk and onto the lawn of the school had the police on high alert. My time was short. I pulled out my trusty Bic. The first flick of flame ignited the gas soaked rag immediately. I was momentarily stunned by the flash of fire. The cops, however, were not. Their car popped into drive and the engine revved followed almost instantaneously by their headlights turning on. I was bathed in headlights. The iridescent blues and reds sent me hauling ass.

I ran as close to the wreck as I dared. Reaching back for all I was worth I hurled the bottle at the car, hoping that I hadn't missed and have it hit anticlimactically on a tire, or sail harmlessly overhead landing on the soft grass. Neither of those things happened as the bottle smashed throat first into the rear quarter panel. The ensuing fireball probably saved my ass as the cops sheared off from their intercept course.

I'll give them this, though, they recovered quickly and were again in hot pursuit. At one point, the bumper of the cop car actually touched my ass. If I had stumbled there wouldn't have been a thing in the world he could have done to avoid running me down, like some common criminal, which I guess I was now. When I got to the end of the school grounds I was met with an eight foot high chain link fence. Now remember, I was 16 and in great shape, one jump had me three quarters up and my body was half over the top when the cop car fishtailed to a stop directly underneath me.

The cop actually had the nuts to yell at me to stop. I told him to fuck off as I retreated into the woods. I was semi-surprised he hadn't shot me. The car was towed off the grounds the very next day.

Talbot – 1, Cops – 0

TALBOTSODE #2

At the ripe old age of seventeen, having not learned a damn thing from the smashed up car in the previous story, I decided to leave a party I was at. Bad idea. I was closer to four sheets to the wind when I decided that I needed to go to my house and grab my marijuana paraphernalia. Must have been ten different bowls at that party to smoke out of, but NO, I had to have mine. So I got behind the wheel of my car and luckily, not one hundred yards from where I started, I smashed into a curb. It blew out my right front tire. I grabbed the keys out of the car, opened the trunk and then drunkenly scattered everything I had in there on the ground around the car.

I couldn't find the jack to save my life. Although looking back, not finding the jack probably did save my life and someone else's. I must have been making a hell of a racket because someone yelled out their window that I should just leave because they had called the cops. I might have mumbled something incoherently back to them, but in my befuddled brain all I could think was that I'd better change this tire quick before they got here.

Now I don't know if it was a slow night at the old police station or I blacked out somewhere along the line, but the Boys were at the scene in what seemed like a heartbeat.

"Son, you need to stop what you're doing right now," the cop said to my back. How I missed the glaring lights on the top of his car is not really all that much of a mystery.

I stood up, smacking my head on the trunk lid as I did so. 'Stuff' was littered in a semi-circle around my position, there was an empty cooler, a lawn chair, a blanket or two, a bunch of clothes, most were not mine (no clue), and the jack. I stared down at it like it had just materialized.

"Son, why don't you put that stuff back in the car," the cop said to me. By now his partner had rolled up in another squad car.

I've got to admit I was pretty impressed with myself that I hadn't said anything stupid up to this point. I just kind of bent at the waist, wobbled a bit and put all the stuff back. 'Stupid jack,' I mumbled as if that were the root of all my ills.

Another squad car rolled up. "Why don't you come over here, son, so we can do a field sobriety check?"

"Sounds good," I answered him. At least those were the words I intended. I think "Smoods gound," came out.

"Okay, son, I want you to walk heel to toe for ten steps." And then he proceeded to show me the technique to perform this magic routine. It's kind of like when you go to a carnival and the carnie working the booth where you have to stand the Coke bottle up with the ring attached to a rope on the end of a stick demonstrates the proper techniques. He does it like five times in a row. So you figure when you hand him over your five bucks you've got this thing in the bag and your girlfriend is going to be so happy. Maybe just maybe, you'll get second base under the shirt instead of over. What you don't realize is that the ring on the end of your rope is slicked with Vaseline and you have absolutely no chance of ever winning that teddy bear or of feeling Suzy's tits.

So that was the same perspective I had when I went into the sobriety test. The moment I placed the heel of my left foot onto the toe of my right I lost all sense of equilibrium. The cop had to literally catch me as the ground rose up to meet me.

"That's far enough, son." His statement was followed immediately by handcuffs.

I was being fingerprinted when my mother came to the station to bail me out.

"What the hell is wrong with you?" were her first words to me.

Mine to her: "Who are you?"

I was that gone, that's no exaggeration. I didn't recognize

my own mother. How far down the rabbit hole do you have to be for that to happen? I had dodged a bullet by having to take the keys out of the ignition to open the trunk. In a newer model of car, had I had a switch to open the trunk, my charge would have gone from public intoxication to DUI.

Talbot – 1, Cops – 1

TALBOTSODE #3

The next story isn't earth shattering, more of another slice in the pie. I was somewhere in the eighteen-year-old range and a gaggle of us had gone up to New Hampshire to go camping. It was one of those lost weekends you spend with friends, laughing, partying, having a great time, kids being kids. So now it's Sunday afternoon and we're heading back down I-95 to Massachusetts and of course we're drinking. That's what you do as stupid kids. At least this time I wasn't driving or attempting to do so.

The driver of the van I was in needed to stop and do what any beer drinker does, pee. So we pull into this rest stop for a break and someone pulls out a Frisbee. We spread out in the parking lot of this rest area and just start playing some catch. Nothing that so far was going to get me on the FBI's Most Wanted list.

So my buddy Kevin throws me this wicked long pass. I chase it down and snag it one handed. The other hand was wrapped firmly around a Budweiser. I turn back around smiling, only to witness the six people I was playing with whipping what I could only imagine were full bottles of beer into the woods. I was like 'WTF' is going on as I took a long pull from mine.

"How old are you, son?"

I turned, bottle still to mouth; a cop in a cruiser was inches from me.

"Twenty-one." I gulped down what I had just drank.

"Got any ID to that effect?"

Five minutes later I was handcuffed and in the cruiser: Minor in possession.

Talbot – 1, Cops – 2

TALBOTSODE #4

Alright, so you are starting to get a recurring theme: Talbot plus alcohol equals bad. It was freshman year at college. My buddy Paul and I were hanging out in the common grounds of our new school just partying it up with some other people. We were having a good time playing Frisbee. Holy shit, now that I'm writing this down, maybe it's the Frisbee that attracts the trouble, food for thought.

Eventually Campus 5-0 shows up. They're about as intimidating as mall cops. They tell us we need to get rid of our beer. My friends all start pouring their beers on the ground, like we had done so many times before with local cops. But see, that's not what I heard. I took the literal translation. I started pounding my beers down. I was two beers down and going for my third before the shocked cop could even begin to react. I just think he was so amazed that somebody wasn't complying with him, but in my defense I feel that I was. He said, 'Get rid of those beers.' He never once said how and that's what I told him.

He was effen pissed as he slapped the bottle out of my hand and maybe a little amused. He chewed me a new one for a minute or two but didn't give me a ticket. So I figure that's a win for me because until the day the zombies came that was still a source of amusement among me and my friends.

"Oh dude, you remember that time that cop told us to get rid of our beers and you just started drinking all of yours?"

Of course I do, that shit's hilarious!

Talbot – 2, Cops – 2

This next story again does involve alcohol. It was my first foray into a more serious realm of difficulty and more importantly I now had a record. It started off innocently enough as most things like this do. It was the summer after freshman year and I had gone to one of my high school buddy's house for a party. He used to live in an awesome house right next to a lake. You could literally walk off his backyard and into the water.

The party went as you would expect most parties to go, there was beer drinking, much raucous noise, loud music and the occasional couple necking in discreet corners. Chris Walsh changed all this when he committed the most heinous of party fouls. He passed out first. I'm not much into what happened to him next, but if you pass out first, it's pretty much an unwritten rule you're going to get fucked with. He got the typical sharpie treatment to the face, you know 'Insert Penis Here' and then someone drew a pretty good replica of a penis next to the message. I came back later to find out that someone had busted open some make-up and applied liberal amounts of eye shadow and rouge. He was the ugliest hooker I had ever seen.

When it became evident that these small time measures were not going to awaken Sleeping Beauty, the ringleaders upped the ante. They wrapped him up in a blanket, walked him through a cheering crowd in the backyard (I might have been one of them), to the end of the pier and then unceremoniously threw him and the blanket into the water. At the end of the pier the water is somewhere in the three foot range, entirely too shallow to drown in, under normal circumstances. But when you are passed out drunk and wrapped tightly in a blanket the equation changes a bit.

The trio that had carried Chris and then dropped him in the water had walked off the pier and were busy high-fiving themselves. A few party goers, myself included, were beginning to become concerned when Chris didn't immediately surface spitting out lake water. This girl Maureen was the first into the water. Her friend Sandra was next, followed almost immediately by myself. By the time I got in the water the party was quiet. Someone had even lowered the music to a dull whisper. Maureen had grabbed the soaked blanket and was dragging it ashore, Sandra and myself quickly aided her.

Within a few seconds, we had the frantically thrashing about Chris on the shore. He looked like a butterfly trying to shake its cocoon. He wasn't having much luck. He had been moving so violently to get free that he cracked Maureen in the side of the head with his fist as she helped him. She fell to the ground with a solid thump. Chris was enraged as he stood, screaming at the now cowering Maureen.

Everything seemed to slow down as he picked up a fist-sized rock. He raised it high over his head and was threatening Maureen. Terror showed in the whites of her eyes. If he brought that rock down, it would be all over for her. Nobody moved. It seemed like the moment was frozen in time.

I didn't think, I reacted.

In the four steps it took me to get to him I was going full speed. It's amazing what adrenaline can do for you. I didn't punch him, I didn't tackle him, I didn't try to swat the rock out of his hand, I just full on slammed into him, right into his back. Maureen scrambled out of the way as the two of us toppled like cut trees in a forest. Chris had brought his hands in to brace for the fall, unfortunately one of them was still clutching the rock. The force of me landing on him drove his face and chin into the stone. The horrifying crack that resounded from the rock shattering his teeth and jaw was ear splitting.

When I got off of Chris and he rolled over, I thought he was wearing a mask. What remained of his jaw line was two inches left of center. Seven teeth had been shattered and blood poured profusely through his nose and mouth. More than one person came up to help only to walk away retching. I stumbled away stunned. I hadn't made it more than three steps before Chris' mournful wailing began. If I thought the bones breaking was bad, this was horrible. An ambulance showed up within minutes, the cops a minute or two after that. They found me sitting in the living room...drinking a beer. They let me finish it before they arrested me. I was charged with attempted manslaughter. It was dropped down to assault after the police figured out that I had nothing to do with the initial near drowning.

Talbot 2 – Cops 3

TALBOTSODE #6

This final encounter with the police is what saved me and my family's life. When I was a kid, nineteen, I used to work for a small paving company. We were working in downtown Boston and if you work on any street in Boston you have to have a police detail for traffic. So it's high summer, it had to have been ninety degrees and ninety percent humidity. Crappy combination to begin with. Then you throw on top of that the 375 degrees of the material we are working with and you have a recipe, not so much for disaster but definitely for flaring tempers. My job that day was to operate the ten ton street roller. As the paving spreader machine lays down roadway it is my job to follow behind and compact the material down.

Before the asphalt is rolled it is a very soft and pliable material, so much so that a man walking across it can mar the new surface up to two inches deep, not to mention what a car can do to this new surface. Well, our traffic detail cop decided that he was going to let crossing traffic go across the new hot top. I asked him for just two minutes so that I could get the roadway rolled and at least reasonably ready to withstand traffic. He didn't listen. What happens to cops that they get such an arrogant attitude about them? I know they deal daily with some of the scummiest people on the planet but to become so jaded to the rest of us doesn't make any sense. You would think that they would want to cling to those people that are the reason they do the job in the first place. Somewhere along the way they must have lost their people GPS.

In a nutshell he basically tells me to 'Go fuck myself.' No matter that this cop is the dick that lets the traffic cross over, I'm going to be the one blamed for letting the pavement get ruined. So I gunned the engine on the roller and was now traveling somewhere in the whopping four mph range. I was going to try to get at least one roll through before the cars started across. All the cop could see was this giant machine bearing down on him. So even though he could have made himself a sandwich and had it half finished before I got to him, I was charged with intent to commit harm with a deadly weapon. Are you kidding me? A toddler could have outdistanced me, but this fat, doughnut eating, cynical prick was just pissed off that I held up the traffic and went against his direct orders. The life I was living came to an abrupt halt as I stood in that court room.

The judge had my record in front of him and he wasn't impressed.

"Mr. Talbot, I have thought long and hard about what I should do with you." I kept silent, it seemed the better part of valor. "You have a decent high school record. You are in college. You work, which a lot of kids your age choose not to do. But you have this streak that runs through you, Mr. Talbot. Something which I feel if it is not reigned in will lead to an untimely demise for you. I am going to give you an option, Mr. Talbot, it might not be the easy route, in fact, I'm hoping that it isn't. But it might be just what you need. The court recommends twenty-four months of jail at the Dedham Correctional Facility followed by thirty-six months of probation."

My heart dropped. Jail? That was my option?

"Or..."

I seized 'Or' like a drowning man seizes a life jacket.

"Five years active duty in the United States Marine Corps. Which is it, Mr. Talbot?"

"*Semper fi*, your honor."

"I had hoped so. Good luck, young man." The gavel crashed. "Court is adjourned." The judge actually came down and shook my hand. I was in a mild state of shock, but it wasn't jail.

Talbot – 2, Cops – 4, Marine Corps – 1

About The Author

Visit Mark at www.marktufo.com

Zombie Fallout trailer

https://youtu.be/FUQEUWy-v5o

For the most current updates join Mark Tufo's newsletter

http://www.marktufo.com/contact.html

Also By Mark Tufo

Zombie Fallout Series book 1 currently free

Lycan Fallout Series

Indian Hill Series

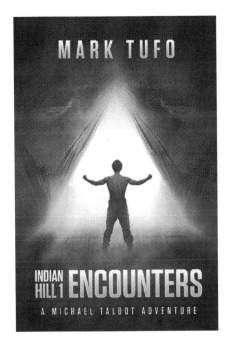

The Book Of Riley Series

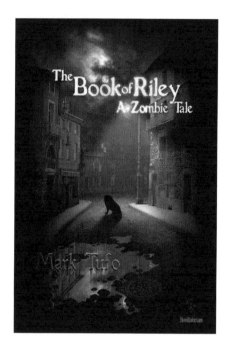

Also By Devil Dog Press

www.devildogpress.com

Burkheart Witch Saga By Christine Sutton

The Hollowing By Travis Tufo

Chelsea Avenue By Armand Rosamilia

Thank you for reading Zombie Fallout 2: A Plague Upon Your Family. Gaining exposure as an independent author relies mostly on word-of-mouth; please consider leaving a review wherever you purchased this story.

43184095R00191

Made in the USA
San Bernardino, CA
15 December 2016